BODYGUARD UNDER THE MISTLETOE

BY
CASSIE MILES

AND

CAVANAUGH JUDGEMENT

BY
MARIE FERRARELLA

MILLS &
BOON

"I'll keep you and your daughter safe."

Fiona wasn't too proud to accept charity, especially when her daughter's safety was involved. And his calm tone and steady gaze bolstered her confidence. Her fear began to recede. "You'll stay with me and Abby until this is over?"

"Your guest room looks comfortable."

Gratitude urged her toward him. Avoiding his sling, she hugged the right side of his body. "Thank you."

His right arm encircled her. For a long moment, they held each other in a clumsy embrace. Fiona had touched plenty of men since her husband's death; she was an unrepentant hugger. But being this close to Jesse was different. His nearness awakened the memory of what it was like to be a woman.

BODYGUARD UNDER THE MISTLETOE

BY
CASSIE MILES

All the characters in this book have no existence outside the imagination of the author, and have no relation whatsoever to anyone bearing the same name or names. They are not even distantly inspired by any individual known or unknown to the author, and all the incidents are pure invention.

First published in Great Britain 2010
Harlequin Mills & Boon Limited,
Eton House, 18-24 Paradise Road, Richmond, Surrey TW9 1SR

© Kay Bergstrom 2009

ISBN: 978 0 263 88271 1

46-1110

Harlequin Mills & Boon policy is to use papers that are natural, renewable and recyclable products and made from wood grown in sustainable forests. The logging and manufacturing processes conform to the legal environmental regulations of the country of origin.

Printed and bound in Spain
by Litografia Rosés S.A., Barcelona

Though born in Chicago and raised in L.A., **Cassie Miles** has lived in Colorado long enough to be considered a semi-native. The first home she owned was a log cabin in the mountains overlooking Elk Creek with a thirty-mile commute to her work at the *Denver Post*.

After raising two daughters and cooking tons of macaroni and cheese for her family, Cassie is trying to be more adventurous in her culinary efforts. Ceviche, anyone? She's discovered that almost anything tastes better with wine. A lot of wine. When she's not plotting Intrigue books, Cassie likes to hang out at the Denver Botanical Gardens near her high-rise home.

To Rick. I thought about you a lot when
I was writing this book.

Chapter One

He wasn't dead yet.

The darkness behind his eyelids thinned. Sensation prickled the hairs on his arm. Inside his head, he heard the beat of his heart—as loud and steady as the Ghost Dance drum. That sacred rhythm called him back to life.

His ears picked up other sounds. The *beep-beep-beep* of a monitor. The shuffle of quiet footsteps. The creaking of a chair. A cough. Someone else was in the room with him.

The drumming accelerated.

His eyelids opened—just a slit. Sunlight through the window blinds reflected off the white sheet that covered his prone body. Hospital equipment surrounded the bed. Oxygen. An IV drip on a metal pole. A heart monitor that beeped. Faster. Faster. Faster.

"Jesse?" A deep voice called to him. "Jesse, are you awake?"

Jesse Longbridge tried to move, tried to respond. Pain radiated from his left shoulder. He remembered being shot, falling from his saddle to the cold earth and lying there, helpless. He remembered a gush of blood. He remembered...

"Come on, Jesse. Open your eyes."

He recognized the voice of Bill Wentworth. A friend. A coworker. *Good old Wentworth.* He'd been a paramedic in Iraq, but that wasn't the main reason Jesse had hired him. This lean, mean former marine—like Jesse himself— always got the job done.

They had a mission, he and Wentworth. No time to waste. They needed to get into the field, needed to protect…

Jesse bolted upright on the bed and gripped Wentworth's arm. "Is she safe?"

"You're awake." Wentworth grinned without showing his teeth. "It's about time."

One of the monitor wires detached, and the beeping became a high-pitched whine. "Is Nicole safe?"

"She's all right. Arrests have been made."

Wentworth was one of Jesse's best employees—a credit to Longbridge Security, an outstanding bodyguard. But he wasn't much of a liar.

The pain in his shoulder spiked again, threatening to drag Jesse back into peaceful unconsciousness. He licked his lips. His mouth was parched. He needed water. More than that, he needed the truth. He knew that Nicole had been kidnapped. He'd seen it happen. He'd been shot trying to protect her.

He tightened his grip on Wentworth's arm. "Has Nicole Carlisle been safely returned to her husband?"

"No."

Dylan Carlisle had hired Longbridge Security to protect his family and to keep his cattle ranch safe. If his wife was missing, they'd failed. Jesse had failed.

He released Wentworth. Using his right hand, he detached the nasal cannula that had been feeding oxygen to his lungs. Rubbing the bridge of his nose, he felt the bump where it had been broken a long time ago in a school-yard fight. He hadn't given up then. Wouldn't give up now. "I'm out of here."

Two nurses rushed into the room. While one of them turned off the screeching monitor, the other shoved Wentworth aside and stood by the bed. "You're wide-awake. That's wonderful."

"Ready to leave," Jesse said.

"Oh, I don't think so. You've been pretty much unconscious for three days and—"

"What's the date?"

"It's Tuesday morning. December ninth," she said.

Nicole had been kidnapped on the prior Friday, near dusk. "Was I in a coma?"

"After surgery, your brain activity stabilized. You've been consistently responsive to external stimuli."

"I'll say," Wentworth muttered. "When a lab tech tried to draw blood, you woke up long enough to grab him by the throat and shove him down on his butt."

"I didn't hurt him, did I?"

"He's fine," the nurse said, "but you're not his favorite patient."

He didn't belong in a hospital. Three days was long enough for recuperation. "I want my clothes."

The nurse scowled. "I know you're in pain."

Nothing he couldn't handle. "Are you going to take these needles out of my arms or should I pull them myself?"

She glanced toward Wentworth. "Is he always this difficult?"

"Always."

FIONA GRANT PLACED a polished, rectangular oak box on her kitchen table and lifted the lid. Inside, nestled in red velvet, was a pearl-handled, antique Colt .45 revolver.

In her husband's will, he'd left this heirloom to Jesse Longbridge, and Fiona didn't begrudge his legacy. She'd tried to arrange a meeting with Jesse to present this gift, but their schedules had gotten in the way. After her husband's death, she hadn't been efficient in handling the myriad details, and she hoped Jesse would understand. She was eternally grateful to the bodyguard who had saved her husband's life. Because of Jesse's quick actions, she'd gained a few more precious years with her darling Wyatt before he died from a heart attack at age forty-eight.

People always said she was too young to be a widow. Not even thirty when Wyatt died. Now thirty-two. Too young? As if there was an acceptable age for widowhood? As if her daughter—now four years old—would have been better off losing her dad when she was ten? Or fifteen? Or twenty?

Age made no difference. Fiona hadn't been bothered by the age disparity between Wyatt and herself when they married. All she knew was that she had loved her husband with all her heart. And so she was thankful to Jesse Longbridge. She fully intended to hand over the gun to him when he got out of the hospital. In the meantime, she didn't think he'd mind if she used it.

Her fingertips tentatively touched the cold metal barrel and recoiled. She didn't like guns, but owning one was prudent—almost mandatory for ranchers in western Colorado. Not that Fiona considered herself a rancher. Her hundred-acre property was tiny compared to the neighboring Carlisle empire that had over two thousand head of Black Angus. She had no livestock, even though her daughter, Abby, kept telling her that she really, really, really wanted a pony.

Fiona frowned at the gun. *Who am I kidding? I'm not someone who can handle a Colt .45.* She turned, paced and paused. Stared through the window above the sink. The view of distant snow-covered peaks, pine forests and the faded yellow grasses of winter pastures failed to calm her jangled nerves.

For the past three days, a terrible kidnapping drama had been playing out at the Carlisle Ranch. Their usually pastoral valley had been invaded by posses, FBI agents, search helicopters and bloodhounds that sniffed their way right up to her front doorstep.

Last night, people were taken into custody. The danger should have been over. But just after two o'clock last night, Fiona had heard voices outside her house. She hadn't been able to tell how close they were and hadn't seen the men. But they were loud and angry, then suddenly silent.

The quiet that followed their argument had frightened her more than the shouts. What if they came to her door? Could she stop them if they tried to break in? The sheriff was twenty miles away. If she'd called the Carlisle Ranch, someone would come running. But would they arrive in time?

The truth had dawned with awful clarity. She and Abby had no one to protect them. Their safety was her responsibility.

Hence, the gun.

Returning to the kitchen table, she stared at it. She never expected to be alone, never expected to be living in this rustic log house on a full-time basis. This was a vacation home—a place where she and Abby and Wyatt spent time in the summer so her husband could unwind from his high-stress job as Denver's district attorney.

Water under the bridge. She was here now. This was her home, and she needed to be able to defend it.

She lifted the Colt from the case, surprised by how heavy it felt when she supported it with one hand. The lethal weapon seemed foreign in her cheerful kitchen with its tangerine walls and Abby's crayon artwork decorating the refrigerator.

It was a good thing that her daughter was with the baby-sitter in town. She didn't want to frighten the child. Or, more likely, send her into gales of laughter at the sight of her mousy, pottery-making mother acting tough.

Peering down the long barrel, Fiona aimed at the toaster on the counter. She snarled, "Go ahead. Make my day."

The toaster didn't back down.

Through the kitchen window, she saw a figure on horse-back approaching the rear of the house. Carolyn Carlisle.

Quickly, Fiona tucked the antique gun back into its case and placed it on top of the refrigerator. She grabbed a green corduroy jacket from a peg by the back door. Thrusting her arms into the sleeves, she pulled her long brown braid out from the collar and went down the steps into the yard.

After a skillful dismount, Carolyn met her with a quick hug. A tall woman with her black hair pulled back in a ponytail under her cowboy hat, Carolyn looked comfortable in boots, jeans and a black shearling vest.

Though Fiona had grown up near San Francisco, she loved Western outfits, except for the boots. They squeezed her toes. She preferred sandals. Or the sneakers she was wearing today.

"Good news," Carolyn said. "Jesse Longbridge is awake. He's expected to make a full recovery."

"That's a relief."

"I don't know if my brother ever thanked you for rec-ommending Longbridge Security. Jesse and his men have been more than competent."

Fiona wasn't surprised. Her husband always said Longbridge Security was the best. "What about Nicole?"

"We've heard from her. She says she's okay, and we shouldn't worry."

"But she's still not home?"

"Things didn't work out the way they should have."

Fiona's heart went out to her neighbor. "I'm sorry."

"I have no intention of leaving things this way. My brother's sulking around like a whipped puppy. We lost a million-dollar ransom. And I won't believe Nicole's all right until I hear the words from her own lips." Her hand fisted. "I'm not done yet. Not by a long shot."

Fiona wished she had one-tenth of Carolyn's determination. When she wasn't at the ranch, Carolyn was a hard-driving businesswoman, the CEO of Carlisle Certified Organic Beef—an international, multimillion-dollar business.

"Would you like to come inside?" Fiona asked. "Have a cup of coffee?"

"Not necessary."

Fiona moved closer to Carolyn's horse. Elvis was a big handsome mahogany brown stallion with a black mane and a white blaze on his forehead. She glided her hand along his bristly coat. Gently, she encouraged her friend to open up. "I heard that the kidnappers were arrested."

"The FBI closed down that survivalist group that was staying at the Circle M Ranch. Nicole wasn't there."

"You said she called last night."

"It's crazy. I don't even know where to start."

While Fiona waited for Carolyn to sort out her thoughts, she continued to pet the horse. Elvis ducked his head and bared his teeth in a horsey grin. "Is he flirting with me?"

"Elvis is shameless, but don't give him anything to eat. The last thing I need is a fat Elvis."

Fiona chuckled, but Carolyn didn't crack a smile. She was so tightly wound that Fiona thought she might start spinning like a top. Apparently, she wasn't ready to continue with her story because she changed the topic. "I haven't even asked about you, Fiona. How's Abby?"

"She's fine. Right now she's with the babysitter in Riverton."

"You're not usually at your cabin in December."

Not wanting to launch into a dissertation about her own problems, Fiona looked up at the cloudless blue sky. "The weather's been amazing. Almost as warm as Denver. Do you think we'll have a white Christmas?"

"Christmas is Nicole's favorite time of year." Her voice cracked. "She decorates like mad. I don't know how to do any of that stuff."

"I'll help," Fiona offered. "Let's walk while we talk."

With Elvis following behind them, they made their way across the dry winter grass, skirting the edge of the lodge-pole and ponderosa pines that formed a natural barrier around Fiona's house. Her rocky, forested land had never been intended for farming or grazing.

"Before Nicole was abducted," Carolyn said, "she and my brother had an argument. Last night, when they met face-to-face, she told him that the kidnapping gave her time to think, and she decided not to come home. She never wants to see Dylan again."

"She wants a divorce?"

"Apparently." Carolyn kicked a pinecone from her path. "Dylan won't talk to me. Or anybody else. Whatever Nicole said, it was enough to convince him. He called off the search."

"Can he do that?" No matter what the victim said, kidnapping was still a crime. "Isn't the FBI involved?"

"The FBI profilers and search teams were willing to back off. They blame Nicole's behavior on Stockholm syndrome."

"They think Nicole fell in love with her captor?"

"I don't believe it. Nicole and my brother are soul mates. Damn it, she wouldn't leave him. Not like that." Carolyn's determination flared. "I'm not letting this investigation die. I convinced one of the FBI agents to stay. Even if my brother doesn't like it."

She stopped walking. They stood at a high point on a ridge, looking down at the barbed-wire fence that separated their property. In a pasture near the trees, a large herd of cattle were grazing. A field of improbably green winter wheat, planted in late September, stretched out to the road.

Fiona loved this view—a patchwork of subtle winter colors punctuated by the green of the wheat and the heavy black shapes of cattle.

Elvis stepped up beside her and nudged her shoulder like an oversize dog who wanted to be petted. She stroked his neck. "If Nicole is with her kidnapper, that means he's still at large. Right?"

"There are two of them. One of them has a criminal record as long as your arm. The other is Butch Thurgood— supposedly the guy Nicole likes. He's won top prizes in rodeos for bronc busting, and he has a reputation for being a horse whisperer."

"Last night," Fiona said, "I heard two men arguing. I didn't see them, but they were close to my house."

"Did you search?"

Fiona shook her head. It had never occurred to her to go poking around in the dark. "Do you think it was them?"

"It's worth investigating. I'll tell Burke, and we'll come back over here."

"Burke?"

"The FBI agent who stayed behind." When she said his name, her features relaxed. "Can I ask you something? Woman to woman."

"Okay."

"How did you know? When you met Wyatt, how did you know he was the man you wanted to spend the rest of your life with?"

"It's not something I planned for. My heart told me."

"Lucky you." Carolyn gave a wry grin. "My heart isn't so direct. I'd know what to do about Burke if I could refer to a balance sheet or see a prospectus."

Though Fiona respected her neighbor's keen business sense and focus, she didn't believe these denials. "It's obvious that you care about him. Even if it doesn't make rational sense, you might even love him."

"I've been in love before, and it hasn't worked."

"You'll never know what's going to happen with Burke unless you give it a try."

"Oh, hell. I couldn't possibly pick a more inconvenient time for this to happen." She stuck the toe of her boot into the stirrup and mounted Elvis. "I'll be back with Burke to investigate your mysterious voices in the night."

"I can't wait to meet him."

Fiona watched as Carolyn rode down the ridge to the road where she wouldn't encounter any barbed wire. Though they were the same age, Fiona felt much older. She'd already been through her own cycle of life— marriage, childbirth and the death of her husband.

Now she was alone again. Starting over. She envied the

glow of first love that flushed Carolyn's face when she spoke of the FBI agent. Someday, she hoped to feel that way again. She remembered the sudden rush of emotion that came with love. The shivers. The heat. Hot and cold at the same time.

Instead of walking directly back to the house, she climbed the ridge. From a vantage point behind a boulder, she looked down at her property.

A cool December wind shook the branches of the pines. In spite of the bright sunlight pouring down, she shivered. The voices she had heard last night could have been coming from the barn. Or the toolshed. Or the unfinished pottery studio Wyatt had been constructing for her.

She glimpsed something moving at the back of the house. A shadow that resembled the silhouette of a man. She squinted hard, trying to be sure of the vague shape she thought she'd seen. Was someone creeping around her house?

Her back door slammed. The noise jolted through her like a shot. She hadn't locked up when she'd gone to greet Carolyn. That shadowy figure could have gone inside her house.

Chapter Two

Riding in the passenger seat of a black SUV with the Long-bridge Security logo on the side, Jesse stared through the windshield at the blue Colorado sky. He was on his way to the Carlisle Ranch to put things right.

Behind the steering wheel, Wentworth sat tight-lipped and disapproving. He hadn't said a word on the drive from Delta to the small town of Riverton.

Red and green Christmas decorations were plentiful on the storefronts. An inflatable snowman stood outside the drugstore. No chance for making the real thing; the weather had been mild for December.

Wentworth pulled up at a stop sign. To their left was the only gas station in town. In front of the auto repair bay, a cowboy slammed the door on his truck and cursed.

"For the record," Wentworth muttered, "I think you should have stayed in the hospital."

"Duly noted." Jesse looked toward the gas station where the cowboy's ranting got louder. "What's going on over there?"

"That guy sounds like he's unhappy about the repair job on his truck. Not exactly in keeping with the spirit of good-will to all."

As Jesse watched, the cowboy grabbed a tire iron and stormed toward the office. "Pull over."

"Aw, hell. I don't want to get involved in this."

Still, Wentworth swung the SUV into the gas station and parked by the pump. Longbridge Security wasn't connected with law enforcement, but Jesse felt a personal obligation to uphold public order.

A white-haired man in coveralls shuffled out of the gas station office. In his grease-stained hands, he aimed a double-barrel shotgun at the cowboy. "Take your business elsewhere," he growled. "Your truck ain't worth the rubber you leave behind on the road."

"I got no problem with you, Silas." The cowboy backed off. "Where the hell's your grandson?"

"I'm not the boy's keeper. Or his parole officer. Get off my property."

"I'm going."

As the cowboy made his prudent retreat, the old man lowered his shotgun and glared at Wentworth. "You boys got a problem?"

"No, sir."

Wentworth backed up and made a speedy exit.

"Quaint little town," Jesse said.

"The old man's a real character. Silas O'Toole. He opens the gas station when he feels like it and charges what he thinks is right. I got a fill-up for less than twenty the other day."

"Colorful."

"I notice you didn't jump right out of the car to help. Are you feeling a little pain?"

"I'm fine."

That wasn't entirely true. He'd taken three bullets, and the left side of his body was hurting. His upper left thigh had been shot clean through. His left arm was nicked. The worst damage had been in his upper chest near the shoulder where the bullet burrowed deep through muscle and flesh, requiring surgery to remove it. He wore a sling to keep his left arm and shoulder immobilized.

He'd signed half a dozen forms releasing the Delta hospital and the doctors from liability if he croaked because of his insistence on leaving before they recommended.

"You lost a lot of blood," Wentworth said.

"Just flesh wounds. No bones broken. No internal organs harmed."

"When you were in surgery," Wentworth said, "the doc thought he lost you. You were dead for four minutes."

"I remember."

Jesse hadn't experienced his death as a white light. Instead, he saw himself as a youth on the reservation where he went to visit his grandparents. His mom—a blue-eyed woman of Irish descent—always encouraged him to stay in touch with his deceased father's Navajo heritage.

In his vision, he climbed up a crude wood ladder from the ceremonial kiva. His chest heaved as he inhaled a breath redolent with the richness of the earth and the scent of burning sage. His black hair hung past his shoulders, much longer than he wore it now.

Across the plain, he saw his grandfather, a white-haired shaman wearing a turquoise belt and holding an eagle feather.

His grandfather beckoned. But Jesse's feet were rooted to the soil. He couldn't go. Not yet. There was still something he needed to do on this earth.

"You remember dying?" Wentworth asked.

"Something like that." He adjusted the sling to fit more comfortably around the bandage and dressing near his shoulder. If his grandfather had still been alive, the old man would have given him herbs to use for healing. "Tell me what happened to Nicole."

"How much do you remember?"

Jesse thought back to the morning before she was grabbed. Her husband, Dylan, had hired Longbridge Security for surveillance and protection. There had been several incidents of sabotage on his ranch, including a fire that burned down one of the stables.

Jesse and three of his men, including Wentworth, had only been on the job a few hours when Nicole stormed out of the ranch house. Though she'd been warned not to take off by herself, she saddled up and rode across the field into the pine trees near a creek. Jesse followed on horseback.

He'd gotten close enough to see the two men who abducted her. He'd heard them say, "Dylan will pay a lot of money to get her back." And then…disaster.

If he'd moved faster, if his horse hadn't stepped on a twig, if he'd had a clean shot, he could have protected Nicole. Instead, he'd been shot.

"I remember getting back on my horse. But I didn't make it far before I fell out of the saddle. I talked to a woman."

"Carolyn Carlisle," Wentworth said. "Dylan's sister."

"Then I went unconscious. Tell me what happened next."

"The first thing? I saved your sorry ass."

"And I thank you for that."

"Wasn't easy," Wentworth said. "I slowed the bleeding, threw you in the back of a truck. One of the ranch hands—a kid named MacKenzie—drove like a NASCAR racer to get you to the hospital. Might have been the best triage I ever did as a paramedic."

"Is this your way of asking for a raise?"

Finally, Wentworth laughed. The level of tension between them dropped. "I guess you've done okay by me."

"That's good because I'm not sure who's going to hire Longbridge Security after word gets out that I let our client get kidnapped. What happened next?"

"The FBI was called in. There was a ransom demand for a million bucks. The FBI tracked down the kidnappers—a bunch of survivalists who were also smuggling. Case closed. Right?"

"Was it?"

"Hell, no."

Jesse shifted uncomfortably in his seat. With his right hand, he felt in his jacket pocket for the amber vial of prescription painkillers. "Go on."

"They couldn't find Nicole. Last night, she called her husband, met with him and told him that she wasn't coming home. She wants a divorce."

Jesse wasn't sure he understood. "I thought you said the kidnappers were arrested."

"Two are still at large."

"And the ransom?"

"Gone."

The Carlisle ranch house came into view in the distance. The property was bordered by a white slat fence. A gently curving road led to a big, two-story, whitewashed house with a veranda that stretched all the way across the front. Pine-covered foothills framed the area. Hard to believe so much turmoil had taken place in such an idyllic setting.

The drumbeat inside Jesse's head started up again. A low, hollow throb. "What else do you know?"

"That's about it," Wentworth said. "I haven't been to the ranch house. The client instructed me to stay at the hospital.

To protect you. You're the only eyewitness, and it seemed likely that the kidnappers might want you out of the way."

Jesse hadn't seen their faces well. They were wearing cowboy hats that shadowed their features. When he closed his eyes to get a mental picture, his pain intensified. He opened a vial of painkillers, tapped one out and gulped it down.

He didn't know what he'd say to Dylan. The word *sorry* sprang to mind. *Sorry I messed up and let Nicole get kidnapped. Sorry you lost a million-dollar ransom. Sorry your wife left you.*

He winced. All of a sudden, leaving the hospital seemed like a really bad idea. He wasn't ready for a confrontation. "Don't go through the gate. Take a left."

Wentworth followed his instruction. "Are we headed any place in particular?"

"I need a few minutes to think before I face Dylan."

It went without saying that Jesse wouldn't quit this job until it had reached a conclusion that satisfied both him and his client. Even if Dylan was ready to take his wife at her word, Jesse wanted confirmation from Nicole.

He turned his head and looked out the window. On the other side of a barbed-wire fence was a field of winter wheat. Still green. Even in December. "Slow down."

"What are you looking for?"

"Not sure."

He was hoping for clarity—a flash of insight that would point him in the right direction. In the skies above the field, a hawk circled. His grandfather would have called the bird an omen, a sign that Jesse should be like the hawk. He should be the hunter. Find Nicole. *Find the money.*

Wentworth stepped on the brake.

A woman was running toward the SUV. Her green jacket matched the low grasses growing in the field. Her long brown braid flipped back and forth behind her.

She yanked open the passenger door. She was thin, delicate. Her cheeks flushed with the effort of running. Her gray eyes shone with a feverish light that made him want to look deeper.

"Your logo." She gasped. "You're Longbridge Security."

"Yes, ma'am," he said. "I'm Jesse Longbridge."

"I have your gun."

His gun? As she bent at the waist to catch her breath, he climbed down from his seat. His muscles were stiff from lying in a bed for three days, and his bandaged left leg trembled with the effort of supporting his weight as he stood in the road beside her. "What's your name?"

"Fiona Grant."

Wyatt Grant's widow. He never would have recognized this waiflike creature from the photograph her late husband kept on his desk. Wyatt had been proud of his young bride. In that picture, Fiona was as serene as the Mona Lisa. Her long hair fell around her shoulders in shining curls. A diamond necklace glistened against her smooth olive skin. He'd been hired to protect Wyatt Grant a little over four years ago. If he recalled correctly, Fiona had been pregnant at the time and on bed rest.

When she caught her breath and looked up at him, he said, "I was sorry to hear about your husband's death. Wyatt was a good man."

"You have to come with me right away," she said with a sense of urgency. "I think the kidnappers are at my house."

"Did you see them?"

"Last night, I heard voices. And just a little while ago,

I left the house and didn't lock the door. As I was coming back, it slammed."

"But you didn't actually see or hear them?"

"I saw something. A man."

"Describe him."

"It was only a fleeting glimpse. A shadow." She shuddered. Whatever she'd seen had scared her. "I'm not even sure I saw anything. And the wind could have slammed the door. I might be overreacting."

He reassured her. "You're right not to take any chances."

"Do you believe me?"

Much of what she'd said was jumbled, especially the part about having his gun. But she was obviously distressed, and she didn't strike him as being crazy. "We'll make sure your house is safe."

After losing Nicole to the kidnappers, he wouldn't take any more risks. Fiona needed his protection.

Chapter Three

Jesse shifted his thinking from speculation to action. If there really was an intruder at Fiona's house, they needed to act fast to make sure he didn't escape.

"Wentworth, call the Carlisle ranch for backup. Tell them we're heading to the Grant house." He opened the back door of the SUV for Fiona. "Climb in."

In the few moments it took to reach the turnoff to her ranch, Jesse formulated a simple plan. He and Wentworth would cover the front and back of the house, keeping the intruder trapped until backup arrived. With more manpower, they could search the house, then spread out and search the entire property.

Wentworth got off the phone. "Agent Burke and some men from the ranch are on the way."

"How long until they get here?"

"Five or ten minutes."

They drove up the packed dirt road leading to the house. Unlike the other ranches in the area, there was no fence circling Fiona's property. Her long one-story log cabin nested in a stand of aspen that would be beautiful in the fall when the leaves turned to gold. Behind the cabin, he saw a barn and a couple of outbuildings.

"Fiona, how many entrances does your house have?"

"Only front and back." Her voice was soft but not breathy. The tone reminded him of gentle notes played by a wooden flute. "But there are windows. If somebody wanted to escape, they could go out a window."

"Stay in the car, Fiona." Jesse glanced at Wentworth. "I'll take the front. You go around back. Don't enter until backup arrives."

As soon as Wentworth parked outside the detached garage, Jesse got out of the car. The adrenaline rush masked his pain. His gun felt natural in his hand. He could handle this. No problem.

Moving as quickly as he could with a bum leg, he took a position at the corner of the house beside a long, one-step, wood-plank porch covered by a shingled roof. From this position, he could see the entire front of the house and another side in case the intruder decided to exit through a window.

Leaning against the logs of the cabin, he felt his heartbeat drumming inside his head. His blood pumped hard. He was sweating. In his peripheral vision, darkness began to close in. *Not a good sign.* He shook himself. *Stay awake. Stay alert.*

If Fiona's intruder was, in fact, one of the kidnappers, they were armed and dangerous. They hadn't hesitated before opening fire on him when he tried to rescue Nicole.

His knees began to weaken. Wentworth had been right. He needed more time to recuperate. *Too late to turn back now.* No way in hell would he allow himself to collapse. This was his job. His life.

When he glanced toward the car, he was surprised to see Fiona dart across the yard toward him. What the hell was she doing? Didn't she know it was dangerous? She flattened her back against the log wall beside him.

"What can I do to help?" she asked.

"You could have stayed in the car," he said dryly.

"This is my home. I need to be ready to defend it."

In different circumstances, he would have read her the riot act about why she ought to leave the business of security to professionals. But he wasn't exactly a shining example of rational behavior. Not today. Not when he'd left the hospital only an hour ago. Not when he was taking prescription painkillers. He wasn't fit for duty.

Later, he'd reprimand himself. For now, the best he could hope for was to avoid getting himself or Fiona shot.

"Stay close," he said to her.

"Are you all right?"

"Fine." *Damn it, I'm fine.*

"I've thought about you often, Jesse. I never got to thank you in person for saving my husband's life."

"You sent me flowers in a handmade vase." A strange gift for a man like him whose job meant he was seldom home. "And a note."

"Which wasn't enough. That was such a crazy time. I was pregnant, and the doctor told me I had to stay in bed. Then I had the baby."

"Boy or girl?"

"My daughter's name is Abigail. Abby." As she spoke her child's name, her voice turned musical again. "She's with the babysitter."

As he focused on Fiona's delicate face, the dark edge of unconsciousness receded. Conversation might be what his brain needed to stay alert. "You said this cabin was your home. I thought you lived in Denver."

"Not anymore." She peeked around him to see the front door. "Shouldn't we be rushing inside or something?"

"We're waiting for backup." He didn't tell her that the idea that he could rush anywhere was just about as likely as sprouting wings and flying. "Why did you move up here?"

"Not by choice," she said. "I lost the house in Denver. And the Mercedes. And the boat. Pretty much everything, actually."

Her problems distracted him. He couldn't imagine that Wyatt Grant, a savvy attorney, would have left his widow in such bad shape. "Everything?"

"Forget it. I shouldn't have said anything." Her gaze turned downward. "I haven't told anybody."

"You can tell me," he said. "It won't go any further."

"Are bodyguards confidential? Like lawyers."

"Not in a legal sense. But I wouldn't have many clients if I started telling them their business."

"I'm not your client," she pointed out.

"As of this minute, I'm working for you. No charge. Pro bono."

"Deal." She held out her hand for him to shake before realizing that he was holding a gun in his right, and his left was in a sling. Her confusion ended with a fist bump against his left elbow.

"Now you can tell me anything," he said.

"There's not much to say, really. Wyatt had an ex-wife, and two adult children from that marriage. They weren't happy with the terms of his will. Their attorneys froze everything that was jointly owned, including our checking and savings accounts. When I couldn't pay the bills, they swooped in. The only reason I have this cabin is that Wyatt signed the deed over to me on our first anniversary. It's in my name only."

"You must have contested the family's actions."

"Not as much as I should have. Obviously." There was an edge of bitterness in her voice. "I didn't have a taste for arguing. Nothing seemed to matter, except for my daughter. It took all my energy to crawl out of bed and take care of her."

"You let everything go." Probably even that diamond necklace she'd been wearing in the photograph.

"Didn't seem worth the effort to hold on. Not when I'd already lost the most important thing in my life."

A caravan of vehicles from the Carlisle Ranch made the turn off the main road and poured toward them. Jesse would have liked to be the man in control; leadership was natural to him. But he was in no shape to be calling the shots.

He looked down at the slender, delicate woman who stood beside him. "I'm sorry, Fiona."

"Don't be." A mysterious Mona Lisa smile lifted the corner of her mouth. "Starting over isn't the worst thing that could happen."

Two trucks and a Jeep parked beside the Longbridge SUV. Nine or ten armed men disembarked. Through a blurry haze, Jesse watched the guy who seemed to be in charge disperse the other men to surround the house. Then he ran across the yard toward Jesse and Fiona.

"Special Agent J. D. Burke," he introduced himself. "You must be Jesse Longbridge."

"Must be." Burke was a big guy, as broad-shouldered as a linebacker. Standing next to Fiona, he looked like a giant—a competent, intelligent giant. "You got here fast."

"We were already planning to come over here when Wentworth called. Carolyn mentioned that Fiona heard voices last night."

"But I haven't actually seen anyone," she piped up.

"Agent Burke, you're not going to break my front door down, are you?"

"I'd rather not."

"The back is unlocked."

He gave a brisk nod. "We'll enter through the back. You both stay here and keep an eye on the front. Does that sound all right to you, Jesse?"

"It does."

He appreciated the way Burke had consulted him before taking action. Jesse wanted to think he was still capable. Like all marines, he was a sharpshooter. Even with blurred vision, he trusted his aim. "Stay behind me, Fiona. If I need to open fire, you should run to the back of the house."

"I've never done anything like this," she whispered.

"You shouldn't have to. You're a mom."

"That's exactly why I should know how to protect myself and my daughter."

From the rear of the house, he heard Burke making his entrance. Jesse's muscles tensed. He raised his handgun and stood ready to shoot.

No one came out.

After a long couple of moments, he heard Wentworth call to him, "All clear, Jesse. There's nobody in the house."

Staying focused had been a strain. His gun hand dropped to his side. He sagged against the wall. As soon as his eyes closed, darkness welled up around him. Sweet and silent. For three days, he had rested in the embrace of darkness, peaceful as a tomb.

He felt a hand against his cheek. Her touch was cool, soothing. He blinked and focused on her wide gray eyes.

"Jesse? Are you all right?"

"Fine," he mumbled.

As she studied him, her face filled with concern. Though her lips didn't move, he heard an echo of her soft voice inside his head. *Starting over isn't so bad.*

After his failure to protect Nicole, he wouldn't mind having a fresh start. A new direction for his life.

He'd been looking for a sign, a reason he had come back from death. And he sensed that Fiona might hold the answer to his deepest questions. She might provide him with a reason to go on living.

Chapter Four

Standing in her front room, Fiona wasn't sure whether she should be scared or embarrassed that she'd reported an intruder who didn't exist.

She couldn't turn to Jesse for guidance; he'd disappeared into the kitchen, moving slowly. When they were outside and he leaned against the wall with his eyes closed, she'd thought he was going to keel over, which wasn't surprising considering his injuries. Carolyn had told her that he was unconscious for three days. Jesse was still weak and ought to be in bed. Not that he'd ever admit it. Typical man! When men got sick, they either put on a macho attitude or curled up in bed and whined like babies.

Agent Burke was giving the orders. "Everybody out," he said. "We need to spread out and search."

It went against her instincts as a hostess to have these men troop through her house without offering hospitality. "I should make coffee."

"Later," Burke said.

Turning away from her, he spoke to the man who had been in the car with Jesse. Wentworth? Burke rattled off instructions about how the outbuildings should be searched and reminded him that they should proceed with caution.

Fiona could see why Carolyn had fallen for this big, rugged FBI agent. Not only was Burke a fine-looking man, but he seemed strong-willed enough to stand up to Carolyn's dynamic personality. These two would strike sparks off each other for sure.

While the searchers dispersed, she asked, "Is there something you'd like me to do, Agent Burke?"

"I'll get the sheriff over here to dust for prints, but I doubt we'll find anything. You keep a tidy house, Fiona."

"Except for the enclosed porch off the kitchen. I'm using that as my pottery studio."

"Let's take a look around and see if anything's missing."

Dutifully, she scanned the living-room furniture and the shelves near the door where she stored some of her finished pottery. The TV was still there. And the computer. Nothing seemed out of place.

Burke followed her down the hall to her bedroom where she checked the contents of her jewelry box that rested on the knotty pine dresser. "Nothing appears to be missing, but the door to my walk-in closet is open. I didn't leave it that way."

"It might have been opened when we searched," he said. "Take a look inside."

Against the back wall was a neat row of dressy clothing, still in plastic dry cleaner's bags. Matching shoes were stored in their original boxes. She never wore those clothes anymore. They were part of her old life.

Jesse joined them. Though still pale, he seemed to have regained some of his strength. "I'll take over in here," he said to Burke. "You might want to keep an eye on the search."

"Thanks. Except for your man Wentworth, these guys

aren't trained in forensics. They wouldn't know a clue if it jumped up and bit them on the ass." He gave Fiona a wave. "I'll be back."

Jesse came toward her. In spite of his slight limp and the black sling on his left arm, he moved with confidence.

"You seem better," she said.

"I'm getting a handle on these pain pills. Just a little foggy around the edges." He peeked around her into the closet. "Tidy."

"I haven't touched most of those things since I unpacked." She looked up into his eyes. His pupils were so dilated from the medication that she could barely see the dark cognac brown of his irises. "Maybe you should rest."

"When I need a nap, I'll let you know." He flashed that killer grin. "In the meantime, I'm your protector."

In spite of his light tone, she took him seriously. Her instincts told her this was a man she could trust with her life. In a way, she already had. Within moments of meeting Jesse, she'd told him the secret behind her move to the mountains. None of her friends in Denver knew how much she'd lost. Fiona's story was that she and Abby were going to live at the cabin and seek a more peaceful life. Peaceful? Not today!

She cleared her throat and said, "Burke told me to look for signs that someone had been in my house."

"Keep at it."

She closed her closet door and led him into Abby's room, which was more cluttered than the rest of the house but didn't seem to have been ransacked.

"I can't imagine why anybody would want to rob me," she said. "I don't keep valuables here."

"From what you told me, you don't keep valuables at all."

"Things aren't important to me. I care about people. People matter."

He mattered. She'd only just met Jesse, but he mattered to her. Why was she so drawn to him? Very likely, because he was an incredibly good-looking man. His straight black hair was combed back from his forehead. He had high cheekbones, deep-set eyes and a firm jaw. But his features weren't perfect. His nose looked as if it had been broken more than once. And he had a scar on his chin. An interesting face.

"Let's go to the next room," he said.

The guest room with the colorful handmade quilt was neat as a pin. Again, the closet door stood open. It was the same in the den.

The only rooms left to search were the kitchen and her studio. She backtracked through the living room, passing the dining table where she and Abby had begun their Christmas decorating with a centerpiece of handmade clay elves and reindeer.

In the kitchen, her gaze went to the top of the fridge where she'd left the antique Colt .45. The rectangular box appeared to be unmoved. She should take it down and make sure the gun was still inside. But something else caught her attention.

"The apples." She pointed to a bowl on the table. "There are only three, and I'm sure I had four. I remember because I was going to run in here and grab an apple for Elvis."

"Elvis?"

"Carolyn's horse. She dropped by earlier." It seemed crazy that someone would break into her house for a healthy snack. "I could be wrong. Nothing else is out of place."

That left only her pottery studio. She went through the

laundry room attached to the kitchen and stopped outside a closed door. "I always keep this door locked so Abby can't come in here unsupervised. Too many sharp implements. And a kiln."

She reached up for the key that hung from a hook near the top of the door frame. It was gone. Had she misplaced it?

Jesse reached past her and turned the doorknob. "It's open."

She stepped inside. Her potter's wheel was in one corner. The kiln in the other. The long table between them was cluttered with sketchbooks and current projects. On the opposite side of the room, tall storage cabinets against the wall were opened. The larger boxes had been dragged out to the center of the room and opened. "Someone was in here."

"Don't touch. There might be fingerprints." Using one of the sketching pencils, he opened the lid on one of the boxes and peered inside at an assortment of small kitchen appliances that she didn't use anymore. "Anything missing?"

"Hard to tell. That's just clutter."

"Your intruder didn't come here to rob you. He didn't take the flat-screen TV or the computer. I'd say he was looking for something specific."

But her house hadn't been torn apart. The drawers and cabinets in the kitchen were untouched. "He was searching for something big enough to fit into one of these boxes."

"Something that's about the size of a suitcase." With the fingers of his right hand, he raked his black hair off his forehead. "Something that's gone missing."

Fiona realized that she should have been frightened. The unlocked door and the boxes were evidence. *An intruder had been inside her house.* Instead, she felt angry and confused as she imagined a stranger wandering through her house, poking into her things. "I'm not in the mood for guessing games. What was he looking for?"

"The ransom," he said. "A million dollars in cash. That much money in small bills would fill a suitcase."

"Why would anyone think the ransom was in my house?"

"That's a million-dollar question."

"How about an answer?"

"Your property is close to the Carlisle's. If the kidnappers were on the run and had to stash the money, they might have stopped here."

"If so, they wouldn't have to search," she said. "They'd remember where they stashed it."

"There are two of them." He rested one hip on a high stool beside her worktable. "One of them might have decided he didn't want to share with his buddy. So he hid the money in your house. Now his buddy is looking for it."

She remembered the voices she'd heard last night. It has been late, after two o'clock. She couldn't make out the words but they sounded angry.

Her awareness of fear became reality. The danger—real danger—had come too close.

She stared through the window of her studio and saw the searchers approaching the barn. If anything was hidden here, they'd surely find it. But if they didn't, what should she do?

"Fiona." He spoke her name softly. "It's all right. Nothing bad is going to happen."

"How can you say that? Those men could have come into my house last night. How would I have protected Abby?"

"I'm here now. I'll keep you and your daughter safe."

Panic shivered through her. She wanted to run, to get as far away from here as possible. But where could she go? She didn't have a house in Denver anymore, didn't have enough money to stay in a hotel. "I can't afford to hire you, Jesse."

"You already did. Remember? Pro bono."

She wasn't too proud to accept charity, especially when her daughter's safety was involved. Still, she asked, "Why?"

"I owe you," he said simply. "Your husband took a chance on hiring Longbridge Security when I was first starting out. Because I proved myself capable of protecting Wyatt Grant—the district attorney of Denver—my reputation was established. I've been busy ever since."

His calm tone and steady gaze bolstered her confidence. Her fear began to recede. "You'll stay with me and Abby until this is over?"

"Your guest room looks comfortable."

Gratitude urged her toward him. Avoiding his sling, she hugged the right side of his body. "Thank you."

His right arm encircled her. For a long moment, they held each other in a clumsy embrace. Fiona had touched plenty of other men since her husband's death; she was an unrepentant hugger. But being this close to Jesse was different. His nearness awakened long-suppressed feelings of sensual warmth, the memory of what it was like to be a woman.

She stepped away from him. "There's something I need to give you."

She saw a subtle change in the way he looked at her. Had he felt it, too? The tiny sparks of passion that might ignite into a wildfire?

"You don't need to give me anything, Fiona."

"It's a bequest. Something Wyatt wanted you to have."

She turned on her heel and went back to the kitchen. Reaching up, she removed the polished oak box from the top of the refrigerator. It didn't seem right to just plop the box into his hands. This occasion required some kind of ceremony. "Are you well enough to walk?"

"Not for a twenty-mile trek," he said. "But I'm mobile."

"I'd like to take you to the place where I scattered Wyatt's ashes. That way I'll feel like he's with us."

Jesse nodded. "Lead on."

She took him out the front door and followed a single-file path that led through the white trunks of aspens surrounding the south side of the house. Over her shoulder, she said, "This property has been in Wyatt's family for generations. His great-grandfather built the cabin."

"But they weren't ranchers."

"Definitely not. The Grants were always professionals. Lawyers and doctors. They used the cabin as a hunting lodge, a vacation place where they could get away and relax."

Wyatt had loved coming up here. Every time they made this trip from Denver, he told her it felt as if he'd shoved his daily hassles and responsibilities in a bottom drawer and locked it tight. At the cabin, he was free.

When he died, she knew this was where he would want to be laid to rest—eternally a part of the mountain landscape that fed his soul.

She turned to watch Jesse making his way along the path. There was a slight hitch in his stride, not even a full-fledged limp. His strength was returning, but she didn't want to push him too far.

At the edge of the aspen grove, she stood on a rise overlooking a knee-high fence that surrounded a small plot of land. Four weathered wooden crosses marked the graves of past generations. The hand-carved cross she'd made for Wyatt still looked new. "In the summer," she said, "I plant flowers here. It's a nice view, don't you think?"

"Beautiful."

"Wyatt never forgot what you did for him, Jesse. In his will, he specifically requested that this gun be given to you."

She opened the case. Afternoon sunlight glistened on the silver barrel of the pearl-handled, antique Colt .45.

Jesse lifted the gun from the case, balancing it easily in his right hand. "I'll treasure this gift as much as I appreciate the memory of the good man who wanted me to have it."

A gust of wind kicked up, and she imagined Wyatt's spirit watching over them, approving of this moment between her and Jesse Longbridge.

He made his way closer to the small graveyard, circling a boulder that stood in the path. Abruptly, he came to a halt. His body tensed.

"What is it?" she asked.

He returned to her and placed the gun back in the case. "Go back to the house, Fiona. Get Burke and tell him to meet me here."

Though she trusted Jesse's judgment, she wouldn't allow herself to be brushed aside like a child. "You saw something."

"Let me save you from this nightmare." He positioned his body to block her view and held her arm, keeping her from going any farther on the path.

"I need to know."

"There is a dead man on the other side of this boulder. He's been murdered, and the coyotes have gotten to him."

She froze. Her blood ran cold. A dead, mutilated body. Here. Only a few steps away from her front door.

Chapter Five

Jesse clearly remembered the interior of the Carlisle ranch house from when he'd been here before. Generous-size rooms. Rustic but not old-fashioned. He sank into a chair on the far side of the dining-room table, mindful of the need to protect his injured shoulder from being accidentally bumped. Under the dressings that covered his wound, his skin felt damp, and he hoped it was only sweat, not blood oozing from the stitches. The pain had subsided to a dull throb. Though tempted to take another painkiller, he kept the amber vial in his pocket. He needed to be alert.

His job as a bodyguard was mainly reactive. He saw a threat and took action to stop it. His preparation consisted of briefings on possible enemies and memorizing dozens of photographs so he could scan a crowd and pick out those individuals who might pose a risk. His powers of observation were pretty good; he could tell the difference between a man reaching for a gun and a casual gesture.

When it came to his work, he was confident. In any situation—from a black-tie diplomatic reception to a ski slope in Aspen—he could assess the possible points of attack and take steps to avoid them. He and the men who worked for him at his Denver headquarters were expert marksmen, capable with a handgun or a sniper rifle. They were skilled drivers, knew hand-to-hand combat maneuvers and crowd control techniques.

But Jesse wasn't a detective. He left the crime solving to others…until now. This situation would tax a different section of his brain.

Burke had brought him to the Carlisle ranch house to look at mug shots. Hopefully, Jesse could identify the men who had shot him and grabbed Nicole. As for the dead man on Fiona's property, he couldn't tell if he'd seen that person before. Half of his face had been gnawed off by indigenous scavengers, like coyotes and mountain lions.

Fiona fidgeted behind the chair at the head of the table, too agitated to sit. She'd asked to come along, preferring not to be at her house while it was being processed by the Delta County Sheriff's Department. Her voice was low and worried. "What if Abby had found the body? What if she'd run down the hill, playing a game with her imaginary pony, and stumbled over a dead man?"

"It didn't happen that way," he said.

"You're right. No need to borrow trouble when I've got plenty of my own problems." She rested her palms on the tabletop leaned toward him, staring intently. "How are you doing?"

What the hell was she up to? "Is there a reason you're right up in my face?"

"I'm checking your eyeballs for dilation."

"Don't." He wasn't her patient. "I'm fine."

Looking down, he glided his fingers on the surface of the table. Someone had recently dusted and cleaned. Underlying the lemony scent of furniture polish was another fragrance. *Coffee!* Though he hadn't eaten solid food in three days, he wasn't really hungry. But he deeply craved a rich dose of caffeine.

A tall, slim woman with black hair charged into the room. She held out her hand to him. "I'm Carolyn Carlisle."

"I know." He shook her hand, remembering that she was the first person who had gotten to him after he was shot. "You tried to stop my bleeding. Thank you."

"You're the one who deserves thanks," she said. "You risked your life to help my family. You're a hero, Jesse. If there's anything I can do for you, just ask."

"A cup of coffee," he said. "Black."

"I'll get it," Fiona said. She darted toward the kitchen.

Burke strode into the dining room and placed a laptop computer on the table. Though he only briefly glanced toward Carolyn, Jesse recognized the look of love in his eyes.

"Just a few hours ago," Burke said, "this dining room was command central for the kidnapping. There were banks of computers and dozens of agents."

"Why was the search called off?" Jesse asked.

"We had accomplished our secondary objective," Agent Burke explained. "The survivalist group, known as the Sons of Freedom or SOF, rented the Circle M. Computer forensics showed they were linked to a smuggling operation. Guns and drugs. Additionally, their leader is suspected of murder. We've arrested the perpetrators, and relocated the witnesses into protective custody."

"What about the primary objective? The kidnapping."

"My brother wanted the FBI gone," Carolyn said. "After

Dylan talked to Nicole, he was convinced that she's all right and doesn't want to come home."

No victim meant no crime. Jesse understood that part of the equation, but a million dollars had gone missing. "What about the ransom? That money is as much Carolyn's as Dylan's."

"True," she said through gritted teeth. "And I want the ransom back. But Dylan called off the investigation. He's saying that the million dollars is a divorce settlement."

"Assuming that it went to Nicole," Jesse said. "That she ran off with one of her abductors."

"Finding the body at Fiona's house sheds a new light on the situation," Burke said. "We'll have to wait for DNA to be certain of his identity. Based on his height, hair color and the custom-made belt buckle, I'm pretty sure the dead man is Butch Thurgood."

Jesse had never heard the name before. "Was he one of the kidnappers?"

"You tell me." Burke placed the computer in front of him. "Scroll down and tell me if you recognize the men who shot you."

Concentrating, Jesse stared at the computer screen. Though he didn't have a clear view of Nicole's abductors, he'd been close enough, and he was good at remembering faces. The line of a jaw. The curve of a nose.

The first three images were unfamiliar. Then came the fourth. "This man," he said. "He's the one who shot me."

"Are you sure?"

Jesse studied the weak chin and narrow lines of the face. In the computer image, his eyes were visible. His cruelty, apparent. "He didn't have as much facial hair as in this photo, but this is him."

"Pete Richter," Carolyn said.

Tapping the computer key, Jesse looked at other faces. Most of them were average—the kind of men who didn't stand out in a crowd. One of them looked like a cowboy from the Old West with a thick mustache and lantern jaw. "This might be the victim we found at Fiona's place."

"Is he the other kidnapper?"

Jesse shook his head. "The guy who grabbed Nicole was fair-haired. No mustache."

He stopped on another image. "This is the second kidnapper. He's the one who said that Dylan would pay a lot of money to get his wife back."

Carolyn gasped. "It's Sam Logan. Damn him. I should have known."

"Logan was the leader of the SOF," Burke explained. "We suspected he was behind the kidnapping but didn't think he was also the primary kidnapper."

"He's been taken into custody?"

"Correct."

Jesse had a lot more questions about the delivery of the ransom and the evidence that had been gathered in the prior investigation. "I'd like to review your files on the case."

"It's all on this laptop," Burke said.

"If you print it out, I can take a copy with me. I'll be staying at Fiona's until we're sure there's no danger to her or her daughter."

"Good plan," Carolyn said with obvious relief. "I was going to suggest that she and Abby move over here, but I'm sure the little girl would feel better in her own house."

Fiona marched back into the dining room with a tray that she placed in front of Jesse. "Milk and oatmeal," she said.

"No coffee?"

"Not until you have something else in your stomach. You probably haven't eaten solid food for days."

He glared into the bowl of mushy oatmeal. "I want coffee."

"After you're finished with this," she said.

Being treated like an invalid wasn't his thing. Even though he'd been injured. Even though he'd technically died for a couple of minutes.

But Fiona stood firm. She was so determined to nurture him that she just might pick up the spoon and start feeding him herself.

Reluctantly, he shoveled in a mouthful of oatmeal. Sweetened with brown sugar, it didn't taste half bad. But it was heavy, thick. When he forced himself to swallow, it felt as if he could trace the lump through his digestive system.

He looked up at Burke. "How about it? Can I look at your files?"

"This is official FBI business. Technically, I shouldn't share." He looked toward Carolyn. "But I've already broken too many rules to count, and I'd like your input."

"I appreciate your trust." Jesse washed down another bite of oatmeal with a swig of milk.

Fiona turned to Burke and asked, "When do you think the sheriff will be done with my house? I need to pick up my daughter from the babysitter."

"A couple more hours," Burke said. "They're looking for prints and other forensic evidence. And they have to process the body."

"Have dinner with us," Carolyn said. "I know Abby loves to be around the horses."

"Wonderful." Fiona beamed. "Maybe we can get started with those Christmas decorations."

While the two women chatted about Christmas trees and

family ornaments, Jesse worked on his food. His gut roiled, but he knew Fiona was right. He needed solid food. He needed to recover his full strength.

When he looked up from the nearly empty bowl, he saw Dylan Carlisle standing in the dining-room entryway. A few days ago, when he'd first met Dylan, Jesse had the impression that he was dealing with a strong, reliable man who was capable of running a cattle ranching empire. The tall, lean cowboy who stood so silently was a pale reflection of his former self.

Dylan's shoulders were stooped. His clothes, rumpled. The circles around his green eyes made him look as though he'd been punched in the face. His cheeks were hollow. Losing his wife had nearly destroyed him.

"I'm glad to see you've recovered, Jesse." Dylan's voice was as cold as a January blizzard. "As of now, your services are no longer required."

Apparently, Dylan didn't share Carolyn's opinion about Jesse being a hero. As he rose from the table to face the devastated man, Jesse felt the bitter ache of failure. There was truth in Dylan's accusation. He'd been hired to protect the Carlisle family, and he had failed.

"I want to see this through," Jesse said.

"There's nothing more to do."

"Don't be ridiculous," Carolyn snapped at her brother. "We still need security. They just found a dead body at Fiona's place."

Dylan looked at Fiona as if seeing her for the first time. "Is Abby okay?"

"She wasn't home, thank God."

"It was one of the kidnappers," Carolyn said. "Butch Thurgood."

Dylan's eyes narrowed. "Thurgood? The horse whisperer?"

"We need to keep investigating," she said. "That's why Burke is here, and I want to keep Longbridge Security."

"Damn it, Carolyn. It's over. Can't you get it through your head? Nicole isn't coming back. She doesn't want to be with me anymore."

"I want to offer my services," Jesse said. "No charge."

"Haven't you done enough?" Dylan lurched forward and braced his hands on the table. "You were supposed to keep us safe."

"That's not fair," Carolyn protested. "Nicole didn't follow protocol. She went riding off by herself without telling Jesse."

"She's never coming back to me." Dylan straightened. "She's gone."

"Listen to me." Fiona's gentle voice cut through the tension. "Dylan, you might be giving up on Nicole too soon."

When he turned to look at her, pain twisted his features. "She turned her back. She walked away."

"I've lost someone I loved," Fiona said. "I understand your sorrow. But I'll tell you this. If I could have one more minute with my husband, I'd go through hell to get it."

"What if he didn't want you?"

With her long brown braid and her quiet manner, Fiona seemed delicate—so fragile that a gust of wind could blow her away. But she had an unshakeable inner strength. "I'd still fight for him."

Her words resonated. The relationship she'd had with her husband was deep and true. Special. Jesse hoped that, someday, he could find a connection like that—a love that went beyond the grave.

Dylan turned away. "I want no part of this."

He left the room quickly.

From down the hallway, Jesse heard a door slam. He turned to Carolyn. "I'm leaving two men here at the house. Wentworth and Neville. I'll be staying at Fiona's."

"You're welcome to stay for dinner," she said.

"It's better for me to leave."

He didn't want to face Dylan again. Not until he had something to report.

PETE RICHTER LIKED being up high, above it all. In the nest he'd made in a pine tree, twenty feet off the ground, he was damn near invisible. Not many people looked up when they were searching. They were too stupid. They kept their eyes on the dirt.

He looked down at the Carlisle ranch house, peering through small binoculars for a better view. He was close enough to hear them talking but couldn't make out the words.

All the feds, except that one guy who was having sex with the high and mighty Carolyn Carlisle, had left early this morning, taking their chopper and sniffer dogs along with them. They'd arrested Logan and everybody else in the SOF. Fine with him. As far as he was concerned, they could all go to hell.

He leaned back against the rough pine bark. Years ago, when he worked as a lumberjack in Oregon, he had stayed in the treetops all day. Except for the cold, he was comfortable. Earlier, he'd used a hand ax—a tool he carried on his belt—to chop away the small branches that poked into his back. This was a good perch for a watcher, even better for a sniper. If he'd wanted, he could have taken aim from here and picked off ten men before they noticed him.

But that wasn't his plan.

As soon as he found his share of the ransom, his five-hundred-thousand-dollar share, he intended to leave the West to the cowboys and their stinking cattle. He'd move to Baja. Live on the beach. Climb the palm trees and get coconuts for food. He'd never work again.

If damn Butch Thurgood hadn't double-crossed him, he could have been in Mexico right now. He should have known better than to trust Butch. That cowboy had been coasting on his rodeo reputation for years, but he was weak.

Richter hadn't meant to kill him. When he started hitting Butch, he only wanted to punish him, to make him talk. But things got out of hand. Butch made him mad. Real mad.

He remembered using his gloved fist, punching again and again. Then he'd picked up a rock. Butch died with his eyes wide open, staring up in surprise.

Hearing voices from the ranch house, Richter peered down. He saw the security guard he'd shot leaving the house with the fed. They got into a truck and drove south, toward the widow Grant's property where the sheriff and his deputies were digging around and searching.

The worst thing that could happen was for one of those lamebrain deputies to find the ransom. But they weren't that smart. He'd already gone through the outbuildings on the widow's land. And he hadn't found a damn thing.

Still, he knew the money was there. Butch didn't have time to move it. But where? The way Richter figured, the widow had to know. Maybe she'd been working with Butch. Or maybe she found the money and stashed it herself.

Either way, Pete needed to get his hands on Fiona Grant. He'd make her talk.

Chapter Six

Sunset painted the December skies in streaks of pink and gold above distant, snowy peaks. For a moment, Jesse watched and marveled. He'd almost died. This might count as the first sunset of the rest of his life. Inborn wisdom told him to take a moment to appreciate this miracle of light.

He sat on the one-step covered porch outside Fiona's front door. Beside him was Sheriff Trainer from Delta. His deputies had removed the body and dusted for prints. They were still combing the area—looking for evidence and finding nothing of importance.

The sheriff took a drag on his cigarette. "I've been around a long time. Never been tangled up in anything this complicated, but I've dealt with my share of lawbreakers. And it seems to me that when people get in trouble, they're usually asking for it."

"Not in my line of work," Jesse said. "Most of the people I'm hired to protect are victims of circumstance. Like the Carlisles. Like Nicole."

"Miss Nicole was in the wrong place at the wrong time," the sheriff conceded. "Those boys from the SOF didn't set out to kidnap anybody. But you've got to admit that they wouldn't have kept Nicole if she hadn't been Dylan's wife. They knew he'd pay any price to get her back."

"Are you saying that it's Nicole's fault that she got kidnapped?"

"Hell, no. I'm not blaming her." His long, narrow face grew even longer when he frowned. "I might be a rural county sheriff, but I'm not an idiot."

"Didn't say you were."

But he'd thought it. Before the kidnapping and murder, Sheriff Trainer might have been a good-natured, easy-going guy. Now he was as nervous as a squirrel guarding his winter cache of pinecones.

"I'm trying to make a point," Trainer said. "There's got to be a reason why the kidnappers are searching here."

Jesse knew where the sheriff's logic was headed. They'd all been asking the same question: why here? Logic pointed toward Fiona. She must have done something to bring trouble upon herself.

He also knew that those assumptions were dead wrong. His instincts told him that Fiona was completely, entirely innocent.

The sheriff looked down at the growing ash on his cigarette and asked, "How well do you know Fiona Grant?"

"I met her for the first time today," he said. "But I knew her husband. A good man who died too young."

The sheriff shot a glance toward Jesse. "Do you think she's got something to hide?"

"Hell, no."

Not Fiona. Not that sweet, gentle woman with the appealing gray eyes. When they found the opened boxes in her pottery studio, she was genuinely surprised. Until he mentioned the ransom, the thought hadn't occurred to her.

When they discovered the body of Butch Thurgood, he'd seen her terror.

"It doesn't make sense, Sheriff. If she knew where the ransom was stashed, why wouldn't she grab it and run?"

"Could be that Butch hid the ransom before she got her hands on it."

"Think again," Jesse said. "If she knew the ransom was here, she'd want to keep it a secret. She wouldn't call in a search party."

"Unless she was scared. Pete Richter is still at large," the sheriff reminded him. "Maybe she decided it was better to hand over the cash than to face Richter's vengeance."

Though he had a counterargument for everything Jesse said, it was all speculation. "You seem to be drawing a hell of a lot of assumptions based on zero evidence."

He stubbed out his cigarette. "If the ransom is hidden here, it seems like Fiona would know something about it."

"You're wasting your time suspecting her," Jesse said. "In my line of work, I need to read people. And I'm good at my job. I can look at a crowd and know from their faces and body language if they're dangerous. Believe me when I tell you this—Fiona Grant isn't a liar or a criminal."

"You have to say that." The sheriff rose slowly and stretched. "She hired you as a bodyguard. You're her employee, and I'll bet she's paying you a pretty penny. She must have inherited a ton of money when her husband died."

"If that's true…" Which it wasn't, but Jesse didn't have the right to tell the sheriff or anyone else about her distressed financial situation. "Why would she be interested in the ransom money?"

"Don't know. But I'm making it my business to find out."

Jesse stood as Wentworth came out on the porch and announced, "I've done the best I can to make sure the house is secure for the night. Windows are all locked. I installed braces on the front and back doors."

"Good work," Jesse said.

"I'd feel a lot better about Fiona's safety if we called down to the Denver office and got Max up here to install a real security system."

Max Milton was one of Jesse's most valued employees. He couldn't shoot, wasn't in top physical condition, and wore glasses an inch thick. But his ability with computers and electronics was first-rate.

Jesse had already checked in with his office manager, who told him the other five bodyguards who worked for him were all on the job, as was Max, who was on-site in Cheyenne, Wyoming, setting up security at an auto parts warehouse. "I arranged for Max to come here when he's finished with his current project."

"How's everything in the office?"

Jesse knew that Wentworth really wanted to know about their office manager, who happened to be his sister. "Elena is just fine. She likes being in charge. And she's better at coordinating things than I am."

With a sheepish grin, Wentworth said, "Someday, we're all going to be working for Elena."

"Don't tell her that. She already thinks she's the boss."

The sheriff took another cigarette out of his pack. "I think we're done here. My boys are just about packed up and ready to leave."

Good riddance as far as Jesse was concerned. The sheriff's suspicions regarding Fiona were way off base. Why the hell was he so anxious to put the blame on her? Because he had secrets of his own?

His chain-smoking and nervousness could be signs of a guilty conscience. Perhaps Sheriff Trainer had something to hide.

WHILE THEY HAD BEEN EATING dinner at the Carlisle Ranch, Fiona tried to find a way to explain to Abby that bad things had been happening. But how could she tell a four-year-old about a dead man on their doorstep? How could she explain that Nicole had been kidnapped? In an ideal world, children didn't need to know about such things.

As she drove home with Abby buckled into her car seat in the back of the station wagon, Fiona tried again. "Do you remember in preschool when Officer Crowley came to talk to your class?"

"Stranger danger," Abby said. "Don't talk to people you don't know. Don't take candy. Run away fast."

"You need to remember those lessons. Even at our house."

"Okay."

"We have someone who will help us. A man who's going to stay with us for a few days. His name is Jesse Longbridge."

"Does he have a horse?"

"I don't think so." But he did own a gun. Should she talk to Abby about gun safety? "He was a friend of your daddy."

"Then he's my friend, too."

A child's view of life was so wonderfully simple. "If you have any questions about anything, talk to me about it. Okay?"

"Okay, Mommy."

Their short ride was over. Fiona parked outside the garage, not wanting to pull inside where it was dark. She'd always been afraid of shadows, and now she had a tangible reason to avoid the dark corners.

After she unbuckled Abby from her car seat, she held her daughter's hand and walked toward the front door. Sheriff Trainer had been considerate enough not to festoon her house in yellow crime scene tape. Though some of the low-lying shrubs had been trampled, her log cabin looked pretty much the same. The curtains were drawn, but the porch lamp glowed cheerfully.

Jesse opened the front door before they got there. The porch light shone on his thick black hair. Standing above them on the porch, he appeared taller than his six-foot height. Though he was lean, his shoulders were wide. He looked strong and capable, even with his left arm in a sling. She was incredibly glad that he was staying with them.

He ushered them inside quickly and closed the door. When she introduced him to Abby, he squatted down to the child's level and extended his good hand. "Pleased to meet you," he said.

Abby's blue eyes brightened as she shook his large hand and studied him. With her blond curls and dimples, she looked like a little pixie. "Jesse, are you an Indian?"

"Navajo," he said. "Half Navajo."

"Navajo," she repeated. "Thank you for the maize and turkey you gave the pilgrims."

Fiona wasn't surprised that Abby remembered the Thanksgiving stories she'd learned in preschool. This year, when she and her daughter were celebrating, Abby insisted on doing her own version of the Thanksgiving story, complete with dancing turkeys and a singing yam.

"That wasn't my tribe," Jesse said. "But you're welcome."

"How come you don't wear a feather?"

Though Fiona winced at the stereotyping, Jesse grinned.

"Different tribes wear different clothes, but we all believe in hospitality and sharing. I have a gift for you."

"You do?"

Jesse stood and went to the hooks by the front door where his denim jacket with the Longbridge Security patch was hanging. From an inner pocket, he took out a small leather bag and opened the drawstring. "My grandfather was a wise man, and he gave me many totems."

"What's a totem?" Abby asked.

"It can protect you. Or it can remind you of your heritage or your dreams. A totem can be anything. A necklace or a coin or a picture."

"I have a locket with a note inside from my daddy. It says, 'I love you, Abigail.'"

Fiona's heart clenched. Though she tried to shield her daughter, life happened. Her father was dead, and Abby understood the importance of cherishing the past while looking toward the future. Quite possibly, she'd learned that lesson better than her mother.

Though the limited use of his left hand made him slightly clumsy, Jesse opened the bag and took out a small blue stone. In an open palm, he held it toward Abby. "It's turquoise. This stone will bring you luck."

"Thank you." Solemnly, she took it from him. "When I get my pony, I'm going to name him Turquoise."

"That's a wonderful idea," Fiona said, "and we'll talk about it tomorrow."

"My pony will have a blue tail."

"I'm sure he will." She smiled. "Now, it's late. You need to get ready for bed. Don't forget to—"

"Brush my teeth." Abby twirled once and scampered off toward her room.

Jesse rose stiffly and stretched his shoulders. "She's bright."

Of course, Fiona agreed. "Smart, pretty and healthy. Everything a child should be."

"You've been a good mother."

She wasn't so sure about that part of the equation. After Wyatt died, she'd been depressed and not as responsive to Abby as she should have been. And she hadn't handled the disbursement of her husband's inheritance well. Thank goodness, she'd hung on to Abby's trust fund. When her daughter turned eighteen, there would be sufficient money for her to go to college and get a decent start on her life.

But that was a long time away, and Fiona had more immediate concerns. She looked toward Jesse. "Did the sheriff figure out who was snooping around my house?"

"No proof, but plenty of fingerprints," he said. "Let me show you the security we've installed."

At the front door, he showed her how to use a brace that held the door shut even if the lock was unlatched. Additional dead bolts had been added on front and back doors. She was familiar with security systems. "Our home in Denver had an electronic burglar alarm with a keypad."

"Wyatt knew how to take precautions. I'm kind of surprised that he didn't have more up here. From what you've told me, this house is vacant for weeks at a time."

"Months," she said. "We hardly ever came up here in winter. Wyatt used to pay a caretaker. After he died, I hired someone to stay here full-time."

"A local?"

"The same woman who babysits Abby," she said. "She has a little boy who's the same age as Abby, and sometimes I take care of him. When she separated from her husband, having her stay at my house was a good solution for both of us. She had a place to live. And I had somebody who could handle the upkeep. Her name is Belinda Miller."

"Sounds familiar."

"She's Nate Miller's ex-wife." She frowned. Though Belinda always swore that Nate hadn't abused her, he was that type—mean-spirited and angry at the world. "He owns the Circle M Ranch. But he wasn't part of the survivalist group. He was only leasing his property to them."

"Nate Miller." Jesse repeated the name. She had the sense that he was storing that bit of information away in the back of his head. She knew he'd been reading Burke's case files while she and Abby were at dinner. Jesse probably had a great deal of information on the locals.

He asked, "Was Belinda living here when you decided to move back?"

"A few months ago, she moved in with her boyfriend in Riverton. He's a decent man. Works at the meatpacking plant in Delta."

"Did Belinda continue her duties as caretaker?"

"Absolutely. She came up here two or three times a week to make sure everything was okay."

"Did she know people from the survivalist group?"

Fiona was taken aback. If he was hinting that Belinda might have something to do with the missing ransom, he could forget it. "She's my friend. A good friend. Abby and Mickey are nearly inseparable."

"I'm glad Abby has someone to play with."

Living here at the cabin with no nearby neighbors was far too isolated for her gregarious daughter. Abby needed to be around other kids. "After the first of the year, Belinda and I are hoping to organize a cooperative preschool for the local toddlers. Maybe a kindergarten, too. The regular grade school is all the way in Delta. That's a forty-minute ride on a school bus for Abby."

"Like I said, Fiona, you're a good mom."

His gaze came to rest upon her, and she suddenly felt self-conscious. Messy strands of hair had escaped her long braid. She hadn't bothered with makeup this morning, and her clothes felt clammy against her skin. It would have been nice to present herself in a better light to Jesse. She wanted him to appreciate her, maybe even to think she was attractive.

She hadn't dated since Wyatt's death, hadn't cared what anybody thought of her appearance. *Now I care. I definitely care.*

Warmth flooded her cheeks. She stood a little straighter, aware that the waistband on her jeans was too loose. She'd lost too much weight. All her shirts drooped straight down from her shoulders. *I want to be pretty again.*

Turning away from him, she peeled off her green corduroy jacket and draped it on a peg by the door. "Have you eaten?"

"No more oatmeal," he said. "How are you at solving puzzles?"

"I can usually make things fit together." Her fingers laced together. "Working with clay gives me a good sense of space and balance."

"This isn't about spatial relationships. It's logic."

She winced. "Not my best thing."

"I can use your help, anyway. I've been going over the crime files on the computer Burke gave me. There's a rational sequence of events, but I'm missing something."

She glanced down the hall toward her daughter's bedroom. "After Abby goes to sleep, we can go over the files."

Suddenly alert, he pivoted on his heel and strode toward the window. "Someone's coming."

"What?"

"Don't you hear the approaching vehicle?"

She listened hard, vaguely hearing the sound of a car engine. "I'm not expecting anyone."

Jesse moved to the edge of the window and peeked through the drapes. "A silver SUV. Cadillac."

She never paid attention to cars, but she knew one family who drove only Cadillacs. It couldn't be them! Fate wouldn't be so cruel. She had enough to worry about.

The car door slammed with a solid thunk. She came close to Jesse and looked through the window. When she saw the driver emerge, she gasped. He looked like her late husband—a younger version. He had Wyatt's walk. His blond hair was curly, like Wyatt's. For a moment, she thrilled to a deeply embedded memory—seeing Wyatt come home from work, come home to her waiting arms.

But this young man despised her.

"It's Wyatt's son from his first marriage. Clinton Grant."

Chapter Seven

Years ago, Fiona met her stepson for the first time at a Grant
family dinner that took place a few weeks before her wedding.

Clinton had been a sullen teenager who resented her and
blamed her for the failure of his parents' marriage even
though Wyatt and his first wife were divorced for over a
year before Fiona met him. The first words young Clinton
had spoken to her were "You're too young for my father.
And you aren't even pretty."

His mother had laughed at his unsubtle inference to Fiona
as a trophy wife. Clinton's younger sister had merely glared.

Fiona's pride had ruled the day. She refused to be drawn
into a bitching match. Without hurling a single insult, she
lifted her chin and walked away.

That brief exchange set the tone for all future confron-
tations. Even now, when Clinton was all grown up, a
graduate of law school who had already started work in the
family firm, his attitude toward Fiona had not mellowed.

He hammered on the front door. With each heavy thud
of his fist, her anger ratcheted higher, but she refused to let
Clinton know how much he affected her. Over the years,
she'd always faced him with ice, not fire.

She stiffened her spine and opened the door. "Clinton, I'm so surprised to see you. Unfortunately, this isn't a convenient time."

He peered past her shoulder and saw Jesse. "Am I interrupting a booty call?"

"May I introduce Jesse Longbridge? He's my bodyguard."

"Whatever." He stepped forward, but she didn't move. "Let me in, Fiona."

"Not convenient," she repeated.

"I'd advise you to step aside. Otherwise, I'll be back with the sheriff and a warrant. You have several items that belong to me."

Clinton and his mother had already taken more than their fair share. After Wyatt's death, they swooped in like vultures. Now he was back to pick the bones. "I have no idea what you're talking about."

"Heirlooms," he said. "Valuable objects that have been in my family for generations."

Before she could slam the door in his face, Abby flew into the room and wedged her way in front of her mother. Wearing her pink flannel pajamas, she beamed at Clinton and held up her little hand. "High five."

Not even a greedy creep like Clinton could resist Abby's charm. His mouth loosened in a grin as he slapped hands with her. "High five."

She tugged on his trouser leg, pulling him into the house. "I'm going to get a pony," she said. "And his name is going to be Turquoise, and he'll have a long, curly blue tail."

Clenching her jaw to keep from screaming, Fiona stepped aside. Abby was at that curious age when everything interested her: bugs, snakes and obnoxious stepbrothers.

Her daughter pushed Clinton to the dining-room table

and ordered him to sit. When he was seated, she cocked her head to one side, then the other. Clinton played along, matching her movements. The physical resemblance between them was obvious. And somewhat depressing.

Playing hostess, Abby said, "Me and Mommy will bring you a healthy snack."

"No snacks," Fiona said. "It's past your bedtime."

"But, Mommy, it's polite."

Her daughter had picked a lousy time to remember proper behavior. Fiona couldn't bear the thought of sitting down at the table with Clinton.

Jesse stepped forward. "Let's go, Abby. I want you to show me your room. We'll leave your mom and Clinton alone for a while. They have something important to talk about."

"More important than a pony?"

He chuckled as he led her from the room. "I don't suppose there's anything more important than a blue-tail pony."

As soon as they left, Fiona confronted Clinton. Her icy veneer was beginning to melt under the heat of her anger. "Don't ever use my daughter to get to me. Leave Abby out of this."

"But my little stepsister loves me."

"Just tell me what you want."

He reached into the inner pocket of his Harris tweed sports coat and took out an inventory sheet, which he placed on the table so she could see it. "This is it."

Over twenty items were listed, ranging from a Tiffany lamp to a pink crystal tiara. Fiona pushed the list back toward him with one finger. "I don't have any of this stuff. Nor would I want it. Out here in cattle country, there isn't much call for tiaras."

"Then you shouldn't mind if I take a look around." A

purely evil sneer distorted his handsome face. "Abby can help me search. We'll make it a treasure hunt."

The fact that he wanted to recruit her daughter to help in his scheme almost blinded her to the more obvious truth. "You want to search my property."

"If you were more cooperative—"

"Were you here before? Did you enter my house without my permission?"

"Of course not."

She didn't believe him. It wasn't a stretch to imagine Clinton sneaking into her house and searching. He could have pulled out the large box in her studio while looking for a Tiffany lamp she never owned. This scenario made a hundred times more sense than kidnappers searching for a ransom.

"It was you," she said. "You saw me leave with Carolyn, and you took advantage of my absence to search."

"I don't know what you're talking about."

Grasping at shreds of her composure, she said, "Please leave."

"You're crazy, Fiona."

He was dangerously close to being right. She was mad, mad, mad. "Please. Leave us alone."

"Or else? What are you going to do? Sic your bodyguard on me?"

Right on cue, Jesse appeared behind him. "You heard the lady. It's time for you to go."

Clinton stood to confront him. In his tweed jacket and cashmere sweater, he resembled an old-fashioned gentleman, the lord of the manor. Fiona wouldn't be surprised if he took a formal pugilistic stance with his fists raised.

But he didn't dare.

Even with his arm in a sling, Jesse exuded masculine

confidence. If it came to a physical fight, he could handle Clinton without breaking a sweat. Jesse's dark eyes shone with a hard, cold strength. He meant business.

And Clinton didn't challenge him. Her stepson might be pushy and underhanded, but he wasn't stupid.

He stalked toward the door, yanked it open and turned back toward her. "You need to pull yourself together, Fiona. This isn't a fit environment for raising a child. If you're not careful, you might lose Abby, too."

His threat went way over the top. There was no way in hell he could dispute her custody of Abby. The idea was not only absurd but infuriating. How dare he even suggest that she wasn't a fit mother! Her self-control shattered. She was beyond mad.

She thrust her hand toward Jesse. "Give me your gun."

Clinton gaped. "What are you doing?"

"Something I should have done a long time ago. Teaching you some manners."

"You can't—"

"I'm within my rights. Around here, we shoot trespassers."

He slammed the door as he left.

Rage swirled around her like a red tornado, but she was calm in the eye of the storm. *This is what it feels like to defend your home.*

It felt damned good.

JESSE WAITED AT THE dining-room table for Fiona to finish reading Abby a bedtime story. Her attack on Clinton had surprised him. Who knew she was such a firecracker?

He'd overheard enough of her earlier conversation with her stepson to know that she suspected him of breaking into her house and going through her things. In a way, he hoped her accusation was true. Clinton was a mean son of a bitch who took pleasure in harassing a widow, but he presented less of a threat than Pete Richter.

Unfortunately, Jesse didn't believe that Clinton was the culprit. Sure, he had a motive to search for his supposedly valuable things. But no reason to murder Butch Thurgood. Nor could Jesse imagine the polished young lawyer creeping around in the forest, waiting for his opportunity to sneak inside and search.

Fiona's stepson was another piece of a big puzzle where nothing fit together right. Too many details about the kidnapping and the kidnappers—from the haphazard way Nicole was abducted to her refusal to come home—were skewed.

The only part that made sense was the way Burke and the FBI had closed down the survivalist smuggling operation. Using high-tech precision, they took all the men into custody and protected the women and children from harm. They'd even rescued a pregnant woman in the throes of childbirth who was still at the Delta hospital, accompanied by one of the FBI profilers, Mike Silverman, who seemed to have formed an attachment to the new mother and child. According to Burke's notes, Silverman was taking a leave of absence so he could escort the mother and child home to her parents.

Fiona came to the table and sank into the chair to his right. She folded her arms on the tabletop and rested her forehead upon them. While she'd been putting Abby to sleep, she'd unfastened her long braid. Her long brown hair tumbled around her shoulders in shiny waves.

He reached over and stroked her hair. His intention was to comfort her, but another urge rose up within him. He wanted to caress her, to pull her toward him and feel her slender body pressed against him. From the first moment he saw her, he'd been drawn to her quiet beauty. He liked her spirit, her warmth, even the anger that hinted at a deeper passion.

Only one thing held him back. He couldn't help thinking of her as another man's wife. She'd never stopped loving her husband.

She lifted her head and looked at him with tired gray eyes. "It's been a long day."

Reluctantly, he withdrew his hand from her shoulder. "Very long."

"You must be exhausted."

"Hell, no. I slept for three days in the hospital. I'm fine." Not exactly true. He'd been taking pain meds, and his body was sore. He was worried about how he'd stay awake tonight to keep watch. "Tell me something. If I'd given you my gun, would you have shot him?"

She grinned and pushed the curtain of hair away from her face. "I wanted to. But I don't think I could have pulled the trigger. It would probably upset Abby if I killed her stepbrother."

"Probably."

"By the way, thank you for giving her that turquoise stone. She loves it. And now you're on her Christmas list."

"I don't need a present."

"Making Christmas presents is as much fun for her as giving them. She's sculpting little clay figures that we fire in the kiln. A lot of them are ponies."

Her mention of Christmas reminded him of a possibility that would ensure her safety more effectively than having him here as a bodyguard. She could go home. "Do you have family nearby?"

"My parents are archeologists. A couple of months ago,

they rented out their house in California and went to a dig site in Peru."

"You have no one you could stay with until the threat of danger passes?"

"There's Wyatt's family. They all adore Abby, and most of them aren't as obnoxious as Clinton. But I wouldn't be a welcome guest." She tossed her head. "I'd rather stay here. We're safe. Aren't we?"

He wished that he could reassure her, but he wouldn't soon forget the ravaged corpse in her front yard. "I can't guarantee it. Not while Richter is still at large."

A series of emotions played across her face. A frightened twitch. A worried frown. Her gaze flicked upward as if searching for an answer. She was one of the most open people he'd ever known, utterly without guile.

Her jaw set. She showed determination. "We'd better figure out this puzzle and get Richter arrested."

He turned the computer screen toward her. "You can read Burke's case file."

With a gesture that managed to convey exhaustion and disgust, she waved the laptop away. Her hands were nearly as expressive as her face. "I'm too tired to read. You can tell me the important points."

With a nod, he started at the beginning. "Nicole was kidnapped by Richter and Logan and taken to the Circle M. When Burke interviewed Logan, he learned that Logan—the leader of the SOF survivalists—sent Nicole away with Richter and Thurgood for safekeeping."

"He told Burke that?"

"Logan is in custody and talking his head off, hoping to make a deal. He says that after Richter and Thurgood took Nicole, he never saw her again."

"Does Burke believe him?"

"There's no evidence that shows Richter and Thurgood returned to the Circle M. But Nicole herself gave them the clue that she was there."

"How?"

"Proof of life," Jesse said. "Standard operating procedure in kidnap cases is to demand proof that the victim is still alive. Here's the first photo of Nicole."

On the computer screen, he pulled up a still picture of Nicole with a newspaper showing the day's headline. "Look at the way she's holding the paper. Her fingers form a circle and an M."

"She doesn't look scared at all." Fiona leaned closer to the screen. "I wouldn't have been that brave."

"Sure you would. I saw how you stood up to Clinton."

"Dealing with a jerk isn't comparable to being held captive."

"Keep in mind," Jesse reminded her, "that Nicole might have been falling in love with one of the kidnappers, probably Butch Thurgood. He was a former rodeo star and an accomplished horseman."

"And she's a large-animal veterinarian. I guess they have a lot in common."

Because Fiona was so sensitive, he was interested in her interpretation of Nicole's actions. "Do you think she's the kind of woman who'd run off with a kidnapper?"

"It sounds kind of romantic. Some women are attracted to bad boys. But I thought Dylan and Nicole were truly, deeply in love." She shook her head. "I could be wrong. It's hard to know what goes on inside a marriage."

Jesse tapped a few computer keys and played a video. Nicole looked into the camera and said she'd be fine if they paid the ransom. "Again, watch her hands. She made a circle when she tucked her hair behind her ears. The way she touched her lips is a sideways M."

"The way she's dressed," Fiona said. "It isn't right. She wears practical ranching clothes. Not a worn-out cotton shirt with a flower print."

In Burke's notes, others had come to the same conclusion. "Here's the third proof of life. Another video."

He and Fiona watched and listened as Nicole apologized for causing so much trouble and said everything might have worked out for the best.

"No clue this time," Fiona said. "And her attitude is different. More resigned. In the other pictures, she has more spark."

"And this one?"

"Her eyes are empty and hollow." Fiona turned her head, averting her gaze from the screen. "I saw that same expression on my own face every time I looked in the mirror after Wyatt's death."

"What does it mean?"

"Loss of hope." Slowly, she rose from the table. Her voice dropped to a whisper. "Knowing that you've lost something precious, and you might never find it again."

He came up behind her and gently turned her toward him. "You don't have to hide your tears from me. I understand. I know how much you cared for your husband."

But when she looked, her eyes were dry. "Tennyson said it's better to have loved and lost than never to have loved at all."

She stood so close to him that he could feel the radiant warmth of her body. He sensed the beating of her pulse, the rhythm of her heartbeat. "That's what Tennyson says. But what do *you* say?"

"I'm not a poet."

"But you're an artist."

"Which means I'm *not* good with words. I could draw you a picture."

He didn't need for her to pull out her sketch pad. He could see that she was aware of the chemistry between them. Her lips had parted. Her breathing was shallow.

The fire was there.

The question was: would she fan the flames?

If she wanted him to back off, now would be the time to tell him. "I know you have an opinion about love and passion."

Her eyes invited him to come closer. A gradual smile spread across her face. "I haven't given up on love."

Chapter Eight

While Fiona had been sitting beside him, the dining-room table provided a natural barrier. Now there was nothing but air between her and Jesse. That air was charged with tension and promise.

"You're not wearing the sling anymore," she said.

"I'm feeling a lot stronger."

She could see that was true. He didn't seem like the same man who'd nearly collapsed. "The oatmeal cured you."

"No doubt."

She reached toward his shoulder and lightly touched the bulge of bandages under his blue flannel shirt. "Do you need help changing the dressings?"

Too easily, she imagined peeling away his shirt and gliding her fingers across his bare chest. A rising tide of sudden warmth elevated her temperature. Her skin prickled with sensual awareness that penetrated deeper, causing her blood to race. It had been a very long time since she'd felt this kind of arousal, and she didn't know what to do about it.

"You're blushing," he said.

"Am I?" She pulled her hand back. Fantasizing about him wasn't appropriate. He'd only agreed to stay with her because of an imagined debt to her late husband. She needed to be careful not to misinterpret his kindness as something else.

Jesse glided the back of his hand along her cheek. "I like the color in your face."

Oh, good. Because she felt as if she was turning bright red from the roots of her hair to her toenails. She was glad to realize that it definitely wasn't kindness that emanated from him. "Your eyes."

"What about them?"

"The color is like a glaze I use in pottery. Rich, dark, coffee-brown."

"I'd like to see some of your work."

That should be a cue to take him into her studio. To put some distance between them. But she didn't want to separate. Instead, she leaned closer. The tips of her breasts were mere inches away from his chest. She tilted her chin up.

When their lips met, the teasing warmth became a powerful torrent. She actually felt as if she were being transported, swept away by one gentle kiss. Never before had she experienced anything like this. Excitement rushed through her, leaving her breathless.

Gasping, she stepped backward, out of his embrace. Looking into his face, she saw her desire reflected. She knew, without a doubt, that this attraction could only end one way. Soon, they would be in each other's arms. Soon, they would be making love. *Am I ready? Is it time?*

Her longing was tempered with panic. She'd never imagined that she'd be able to feel this way. She was a widow with a small child, resigned to a life of responsibility without passion. How could this be happening? "Jesse, I—"

He laid his finger across her lips, stopping her words. "No need to speak."

He was right. These churning emotions required no explanation. She could trust the way she felt and know that he'd felt it, too. For now, that was enough.

"Fiona." His voice caressed her name.

"Yes?"

"I appreciate your offer to change my dressings, but Wentworth will be here soon. He's a medic. He likes messing around with surgical stuff."

She might enjoy messing around, too. *Tell him.* She wanted another kiss. If she let this moment pass, it might not come again. Which was a good reason *not* to tell him. *But it's too soon. And I'm afraid.*

She cleared her throat and took another step back. "I have an ointment that might be soothing. When I'm sculpting, it seems like I'm always getting cuts and burns on my hands."

"Some kind of nontraditional medicine?" he asked.

"I didn't make it myself, but all the ingredients are from nature."

"My grandfather had a remedy for healing, made from creosote bush, prickly pear and some mysterious herb with a Navajo name I can't pronounce." His smile turned nostalgic. "He believed the strongest medicine came from within. Trusting your body to heal itself."

"You've mentioned your grandfather before." She wanted to know more about Jesse. "Tell me about him."

"He lived on the reservation."

She returned to her seat at the table, and he did the same. Though she regretted the distance between them, she was also relieved. With her long-suppressed hormones raging, she wasn't able to think straight. "Did you live there, too?"

"I'm a city kid. We lived in Denver. My mom isn't Navajo, but she wanted me and my sister to know and appreciate our heritage. She sent us to live with our grandparents every summer."

"And was she right? Did you learn to appreciate that life?"

"Probably more than the kids who grew up on the rez. Our time there was limited and special. We were hungry for knowledge, fascinated by the old ways and rituals. And we knew we could always return to our urban life. My sister said we had the best of both worlds."

"Are you close to her?"

"Elena is the office manager for Longbridge Security."

He seemed to be devoted to his family. That was a check mark on the plus side. "You haven't mentioned your father."

"He was in the marines. He died when I was seven. I hardly remember him."

"I'm sorry," Fiona said.

"My mother remarried a couple of years after he died. My stepfather is a good man, a good provider."

His mother—a widow like her—managed to find love again. Not an unusual situation. Lots of people had second chances. There wasn't a rule that said Fiona had to live the rest of her life alone, draped in widow's weeds. She just wasn't accustomed to thinking that way.

"My grandfather," Jesse said quietly, "passed away a few years ago. Sometimes, he seems to be with me."

"I understand. His memory lives through you."

"It's something more," he said. "When I was in the hospital, they said that I died on the operating table for a few minutes. I saw him. My grandfather."

Many people talked about seeing a white light and being

reacquainted with others who had passed away. "Did he say anything?"

"He was there to welcome me," Jesse said. "But I wasn't ready to go with him. Not yet. There's something more I need to do with my life."

Had he come back from death to be with her? Were they both being given a second chance? "What is it, Jesse? What do you need to do?"

"I'll wait and see. And trust that I'll recognize the true path when it appears before me."

She wanted to walk beside him on that trail. No matter where it led. Their brief kiss had been the first step. She could hardly wait to see what came next.

PETE RICHTER WATCHED as the lights inside the widow Grant's house were turned off one by one. From where he was standing in the forest, he couldn't actually see inside because the curtains were pulled. But the glow at the edges of the windows went out until only one lamp in the living room was still lit.

Richter figured the bodyguard would station himself there, near the fireplace. Even though no smoke rose from the chimney, the thought of a warm blaze made him feel even colder. It was below freezing out here. He needed to act soon before he turned into a damn icicle.

The widow's bedroom was at the end of the cabin, far away from the front room. He could break through her window and grab her, but he wouldn't be able to haul her away before her security man responded. It might be smart to kill him first.

But the curtains were drawn. Richter couldn't see to get a clear shot at the son of a bitch who, by all rights, should already have been dead.

Walking carefully so he wouldn't make any noise, he tried to come up with a plan. There had to be a way for him to get to the widow—another way into her house.

He'd find it soon enough. Then he'd make her tell him where she'd hidden his money.

WITH FIONA SAFELY TUCKED into bed, Jesse sat in a wooden rocking chair beside the fireplace with his gun resting on the table beside him. Though he would have been a hell of a lot more comfortable on the sofa, he couldn't allow himself to take off his shoes and relax. If he did that, he'd be asleep in minutes.

Leaning forward with his elbows resting on his thighs, he listened. Both doors to the bedrooms were ajar, and he could hear Abby and Fiona shifting in their beds. He thought of Fiona's long hair spread across the pillows, and her graceful body stretched out across the sheets. Her face in repose. Her lips.

He hadn't planned to kiss her, but he didn't regret that moment. It tasted right. And the sensual jolt to his system had gotten his heart pumping and his blood circulating. He felt better now than he had since he woke in the hospital. If he made love to her, he'd probably be completely cured.

A sound outside the window interrupted his reverie. The wind rattling the bare branches of the aspens near the front door? He wouldn't take any chances. Gun in hand, he went to the curtains and peered around the edge. From this limited vantage point, he saw nothing suspicious.

One-man guard duty was difficult. If Wentworth had been here, one of them could have gone outside to check while the other stayed here. Alone, he couldn't risk leaving the house unprotected.

He checked his wristwatch. Wentworth was supposed to be here any minute.

He sank into the rocking chair again. Waiting. Listening.

The next sound seemed to come from overhead. A tree squirrel running across the roof? He looked up.

It was quiet again.

Then he heard the tires from Wentworth's vehicle pulling up the gravel drive. He stood at the front door, watching as Wentworth got out of the car, and motioned him inside.

With the door bolted, Jesse said, "I heard something on the roof."

"How big?"

"Don't know. It was a scraping noise."

Wentworth exhaled a weary sigh. It had been a long day for him, too. "What should we do about it?"

"You stay here. I'll go out and take a look around."

Though Jesse would have preferred using a rifle, his left arm wasn't steady enough to be trusted. He took his handgun and stepped outside. Earlier today, he'd had an opportunity to check out her house from various angles, figuring out which direction an intruder might take. But he hadn't considered the roof.

The cold night air was bracing. After taking a moment to allow his eyes get accustomed to the moonlight, he circled around to the rear of the house. None of the aspens at the front of the house were good for climbing; the branches started too far from the ground. At the back, there was one tall pine tree.

He stared into the depths of its branches. Nothing there.

The roof of Fiona's one-story house formed a shallow peak—just enough of an angle to encourage the snow to slide off. He saw nothing in the back or the front. But he sensed a threat.

When he returned to the inside of the house, Wentworth escorted him into the kitchen. "Here's the deal, Jesse. I'll change those dressings. Then you go to bed. I'll wake you in three hours to relieve me."

"You should go back to the Carlisle Ranch."

"They don't need me. Our man, Neville, is there. And Burke. And a whole mob of cowboys with rifles."

Though Jesse didn't like to admit that he needed help, he wasn't a fool. "I won't lie. I could use some rest."

He had the feeling that the next couple of days weren't going to get any easier.

Chapter Nine

By dawn of the following day, Jesse felt damn good. The aching lessened. His drumming headache was gone. He'd recovered a decent range of movement in his arm and shoulder but continued to wear the sling as a reminder to be careful.

Best of all, his appetite had returned. He sat at the table in Fiona's cheery tangerine kitchen, scarfing down the excellent pancakes she'd whipped up. On the other side of the table, Wentworth polished off the last morsel of food on his plate. Fork in hand, he eyed a sausage link on Jesse's plate.

"Don't even think about it," Jesse growled.

"As a medical professional," Wentworth said, "I'd advise you to turn over the meat."

"Based on what diagnosis?"

"Anatomy charts. There's a link-size space in my belly."

"To match the hole in your head," Jesse said. "You're crazy if you think I'm not eating this."

Abby was between them, kneeling on her chair because she was, as she had informed them, too grown-up for a booster seat. Her eating process was complicated. Each bite she took was followed by a bite for her plastic palomino pony. "What are we going to do today?" she asked.

"Mickey is coming over," Fiona said as she slid another pancake from the frying pan onto Wentworth's plate.

"Mickey?" Jesse glanced up at her.

"Abby's friend."

"My best friend," Abby clarified.

Jesse couldn't believe what he was hearing. Fiona had scheduled a playdate? "You'll have to cancel."

"Or not." She was pretty in the morning with her long brown hair pulled back in a ponytail and her cheeks flushed pink from the heat of the stovetop. "Mickey's mom should be dropping him off any minute."

"So early? It's barely light outside."

"Yee-haw," Abby cheered. "I gotta get dressed."

Fiona looked down at her daughter's plate, gave a satisfied nod and said, "You're excused."

Abby hopped off her chair and bolted from the room with her pony tucked under her arm.

Jesse had the distinct feeling that he was losing control of the situation. "This is wrong, Fiona. Wentworth and I are here as bodyguards. Not babysitters."

"Mickey always comes over on Wednesdays while Belinda works the morning shift at the café. I couldn't ask her to reschedule on such short notice."

He reminded her, "Richter is still at large."

"He's not going to attack while you're here," she said. "Besides, it'll be easier for everyone if Abby's occupied with her friend. Otherwise, she'll be underfoot."

After she shoveled the last pancake onto his plate, Fiona excused herself and went to oversee her daughter.

Jesse cut his sausage in half, looked at Wentworth and shook his head. "A playdate."

"I used to date a single mom," Wentworth said. "There's nothing more sacred than their babysitting schedules."

"Even when you find a dead body in the front yard? Fiona ought to have the good sense to be more cautious."

"That's why she's got you, buddy."

"And you." Jesse shoved the sausage into his mouth. "I need you here today, instead of at the Carlisle Ranch."

Wentworth carried his plate to the sink. "Have you got a plan?"

"Searching." He envisioned a widening circle. "We'll start here at Fiona's house."

"But we already searched," Wentworth said.

"I need to see for myself. And I want Fiona with me. She might notice something that others missed. Then I want to take a look around at the Circle M where Nicole was held prisoner. After that, I'll check the site where the ransom was dropped. Maybe I can pick up the kidnappers' trail."

"After two days?" Wentworth scoffed. "You're a genius tracker, Jesse. But that's nearly impossible."

"It's a long shot," he agreed. "But we haven't got much to go on."

He heard Abby racing through the house and shouting, "Mickey's here. Mickey's here."

Jesse went to the front door, where Abby tugged at the brace that was holding it shut. She looked up at him. "The door's broke."

"This is a special lock." *A childproof lock.* Though the brace was supposed to keep intruders out, it also ensured that Abby couldn't go racing outside whenever she wanted. An unexpected benefit. "Whenever you want it moved, ask me or your mom or Wentworth."

"Open," she said.

Fiona stood beside them. "Did you hear what Jesse said? For the next few days, you aren't to go outside without permission."

"Yes." Her blond curls flounced as she nodded. "Open."

Fiona opened the door and welcomed her guests. Mickey was a skinny, three-and-a-half-foot tall bundle of energy with a buzz haircut and freckles. He threw off his jacket and ran down the hallway behind Abby.

His mother had a nicely rounded figure. Her full hips were packed into black slacks. The fringe on her leather jacket jiggled when she moved.

"Belinda Miller," Fiona said, "this is Jesse Longbridge and Tom Wentworth."

Though her smile was dimpled and friendly when she shook hands, he saw caution in her brown eyes. Belinda couldn't have been more than twenty-five years old, but she'd already learned to be wary of men. From what Jesse had read in Burke's reports, her ex-husband had a nasty temper.

"Tell me the truth," she said. "Is there any real danger?"

As Jesse said, "Yes," Fiona said, "Not really."

Belinda planted her fists on her hips. "Which is it?"

"Even if there is somebody after us," Fiona said, "these two men are professional bodyguards."

Belinda's gaze assessed him and Wentworth; then she gave a satisfied nod. "Nobody is going to mess with you guys."

Fiona gave her a hug. "See you after lunch."

"Thanks, hon. I really need this shift. It's almost Christmas, and I'm dead broke."

He watched Belinda return to her car and drive away. The morning skies grew brighter. It was a new day. When he returned to the house and locked the door, he was warm. Comfortable. His belly full of good food.

At the far end of the hallway, he heard the kids playing. Fiona smiled at him, and he fought the urge to give her a little peck on the forehead. *This must be what it's like to have a family.*

He seldom considered the idea of having a family of his own. Bodyguards needed to look on the dark side, to recognize potential threats before they became lethal. If he had his own family, there was also the possibility that he might lose them.

But when he looked around this comfortable cabin, he felt content. He wouldn't have minded starting a fire in the hearth and spending the whole day playing with the kids and gazing into Fiona's soft gray eyes. Maybe read a book. He remembered a December, long ago, when he had whittled kachina dolls for Christmas presents. Whittling was a good hobby. He should take it up again.

Yeah, right. Then he could have some hot chocolate with marshmallows. Coming back from death might have mellowed him, but he wasn't about to turn into a lazy, domesticated tomcat. Clearing his throat, Jesse took command and issued orders. "We need to get started. Wentworth, you stay here with the kids. Fiona, come with me to search."

Someday, there might be time for whittling and reveries in front of the fireplace. But not today.

FIONA ZIPPED HER WINTER parka all the way to her chin as she led Jesse to the structure nearest the house. "This was going to be my art studio. Wyatt never had a chance to finish it."

They went up two steps and entered through the un-locked double-wide door. The single room was two stories high at the front with large windows to admit natural light. The ceiling slanted down to a single story at the rear. Except for a couple of sawhorses and a stack of two-by-fours, the room was empty.

Jesse strode across the wood floor. His footsteps echoed. He stopped at the rear where there was a section of concrete. "You'd put the kiln here."

"Right. This whole building rests on a concrete slab. You wouldn't believe how much Wyatt enjoyed that part of the construction. He got to use a backhoe."

"Heavy equipment," Jesse said with obvious relish. "Yeah, that's fun stuff."

"A lot of the men in the Grant family seem to think so. Most of them are professionals who sit at a desk all day. But when they come up here—supposedly to relax—they take on building projects."

"It's satisfying to create something solid." Jesse rested his hand against an exposed stud on the framed wall. "Wouldn't take much to finish this. Add the insulation and the drywall."

"And the electric," she reminded him. "And minimal plumbing. I don't need a toilet, but I'd like a sink. And a tile floor so it would be easy to clean up."

He removed his hand. "A bigger job than I thought."

"I've had Belinda's ex-husband out here to give me an estimate on finishing. Nate's a handyman, and he's pretty good."

"I saw in Burke's investigation notes that he was a suspect in Nicole's kidnapping."

Fiona wasn't surprised. Nate was an efficient worker,

but she didn't have a high opinion of his character. "He hates the Carlisles and blames them for losing his ranch."

"Any truth to his opinion?"

"It's an old grudge. Years ago, when Carolyn's father changed his ranching procedures to all-organic with grass-fed cattle and no antibiotics, everybody thought he was nuts. Organic beef is more expensive to raise, and involves a lot more effort. But old Sterling Carlisle knew what he was doing. Carlisle Certified Organic Beef grew into a multimillion-dollar international success story."

"And Nate lost almost everything."

"I think it was his father who told Sterling Carlisle to go to hell when he offered to buy Circle M cattle if they made the required changes in ranching procedures. The Circle M became less and less profitable. Nate finally closed down the cattle ranch and sold off some of his land. He was lucky when the Sons of Freedom rented his property."

Jesse scowled. "Given that he's not a particularly charming individual, why did you hire him?"

"Indirectly, I was helping Belinda. If her ex-husband has money, he can pay his child support."

"Anything else?"

"I guess, in a way, I feel sorry for Nate. He was terrible to Belinda. When they were first separated, he pestered her until she took out a restraining order. But he adores Mickey. When he's with his son, he lights up."

"You like to find the good in people. Even when you have to look deep."

"It's my greatest flaw."

Her positive attitude had certainly betrayed her. Instead of seeing how Wyatt's first wife and grown children would greedily gobble up every asset they could get their sticky fingers on, she believed they were—like her—grieving his death and wishing her the best. Had she made a similar mistake with Nate Miller?

Jesse stamped his foot on the floor again and listened to the echo. "Is there a basement under here?"

"Just a crawl space. It's probably only three feet high."

"Big enough to hide the ransom," he said. "We'll need a flashlight."

"There's one in the barn. I'll get it."

"Fiona, wait. You shouldn't be alone."

"Don't worry. I know exactly where the flashlight is. I'll be right back."

She darted out the door and jogged across the yard toward the old barn with a stable in back. She hadn't been in here recently. Since they weren't keeping livestock, there wasn't a need to visit the barn.

She opened the small door on the side and slipped inside. It smelled stale and stuffy. This old, empty building reminded her of how much she'd lost. It'd take a miracle for her to get Abby the pony she wanted so much.

She flicked the light switch. None of the lights came on. The bulbs must be burned out.

It didn't matter. The light from the door and the two high windows was enough for her to see. She carefully picked her way through the junk stored in the central area below the loft: a space heater that didn't work, camping supplies, an ancient tractor, a Jeep with a snowplow attached to the front.

Near the tool bench were several metal boxes where Wyatt had stored his tools when he wasn't using them. Some of the lids stood open. When Burke and the deputies searched last night, they must have dug through here. She was glad that others had been the first to search. They probably knocked away most of the cobwebs.

She reached toward the dusty shelf above the workbench and found a heavy-duty silver flashlight. She'd purchased it herself because it had a specially designed reflection system and a fancy battery that was supposed to last for years and years. True to that guarantee, a strong, steady beam shot through the musty air as soon as she touched the switch. She moved the flashlight back and forth; the light scanned across the discarded equipment and the muddy footprints on the wood floor. The old wood creaked beneath her sneakers.

She sensed that she wasn't alone.

Shadows seemed to take solid form. From the loft overhead, she heard a scuffling noise. She aimed the beam at the rough wooden staircase leading to the loft. What if Richter came charging down those stairs?

She'd be a fool to stand here and wait for him. Gathering her courage, she ran for the door and burst outside into the fresh sunlight.

Jesse was walking toward her. He immediately picked up on her mood. "What's wrong?"

"It's nothing." Only an overactive imagination. She held up the flashlight. "Found it."

"If you saw something, Fiona, you need to tell me. Anything out of the ordinary might be a threat. Or a clue."

"I got spooked." She shrugged. "The barn is kind of creepy with all that old discarded equipment. I should just get rid of it all."

"You could sell it."

The thought hadn't occurred to her, but it was a good idea. "You're absolutely right. There might be someone who'd pay for a broken-down snowplow."

"That's a project for another day." He took the flashlight from her. "Let's see what's under the studio."

Inside, he'd found an access point—a trapdoor that he'd already opened. Jesse took off his cowboy hat and slipped his arm out of the sling.

She watched as he climbed down into the crawl space and disappeared. Peeking down, she saw the flashlight beam slashing through the darkness. She asked, "Do you see anything?"

"Boards and braces. Nice solid construction."

She stroked the brim of his hat. The dark brown felt was weathered but not worn-out. Tied around the crown was a leather thong with two turquoise beads at the end. Another totem? She recalled the small pouch he carried in his pocket and smiled. Even a bodyguard like Jesse felt the need for reassurance and protection.

He emerged from the hole. "Nothing down there. Not even a raccoon's nest."

"Too bad. I was hoping for a quick solution."

Instead, they could cross this building off their list of places to search. Jesse raked his hair off his forehead and slapped his hat back onto his head. "Next, the barn."

Halfway across the backyard, he paused and looked past the house toward the driveway. Following his gaze, Fiona saw a truck approaching her house. "It's Nate Miller."

"Any reason for him to be here?"

"None at all."

Chapter Ten

Jesse hustled toward the front of the house, coming around the corner in time to confront Nate Miller as he left his truck. "Can I help you?"

Nate squinted under his battered flat-brim hat. The skin on his pointed jaw was red and nicked as if he'd shaved with a dull razor. His clothes were clean, and his jeans were ironed with a crease down the front. It appeared that he was trying to make a good impression. For Fiona? Did the handyman have a crush on her?

Unsmiling, he stuck out his hand. "Don't believe we've met. I'm Nate Miller."

Jesse accepted the handshake. "Jesse Longbridge."

"You're the fella who got shot. The security man. Glad to see you up and around."

Though Nate had offered proper condolence, his tone was offhand and insincere. He had something else on his mind, which didn't matter to Jesse because he had an agenda of his own. He wanted to take a look around at the Circle M, and that property belonged to Nate.

Fiona joined them. "Hi, Nate. Jesse is staying with us until this trouble is over."

"I suppose that's a good thing. A young woman like you shouldn't be alone when there are dangerous men on the loose."

His comment might have implied an interest in her, but Jesse didn't get that sense. Nate's gaze darted nervously; he barely noticed Fiona.

"Thanks for your concern," she said. "Did we have an appointment?"

"Nope. I was just thinking that maybe I could take Mickey off your hands. For an hour or so."

As soon as he mentioned his son's name, Jesse understood why Nate had cleaned himself up and shaved. He was on his best behavior—anxious to show Fiona that he was trustworthy, capable of taking care of his son.

Nate continued. "Since Logan and his people got arrested, the Circle M belongs to me again. I got eight horses that belonged to Logan. I'm paying to board those animals, and I figure they might belong to me pretty soon. I bet Mickey would like to see those ponies. And Abby, too."

"That's very thoughtful," Fiona said. "Have you okayed this plan with Belinda?"

"She won't mind." A note of anger tainted his voice. "We don't need to bother telling her."

"No bother." Fiona pulled her cell phone from her jacket pocket. "I'll just call the café and make sure that—"

"Don't bother."

As Nate's hand shot out to stop Fiona from punching in the phone number, Jesse reacted. He caught Nate's wrist midair and gave a sharp twist, spinning him around.

Nate recovered his balance. A sneer curled his lower lip. Underneath his veneer of polite behavior, he was angry. "I didn't mean any harm."

"I know." Jesse had positioned himself in front of Fiona, protecting her from Nate's hostility while she called his ex-wife. "If I thought you'd meant to hurt her, you wouldn't be standing."

"You're pretty damn sure of yourself."

"With good reason." Jesse wasn't bragging, just stating the truth. He was a trained protector. Even with a bum shoulder, he could handle Nate Miller. "You share custody with your ex-wife?"

"That's right. I usually have Mickey on weekends. But not this last one. Belinda took him into Grand Junction to stay with her parents overnight." He hooked his thumbs in his belt. "The way I figure, I should have some extra time today. Belinda owes me."

"It must be hard. Being separated from your son."

"Damn right. Mickey needs to be with me. A growing boy needs his father's influence. Know what I mean? I should be showing him how to do chores, how to fish, how to hunt."

"Hunting? He's only four."

"You can't start too soon. I was helping my pappy brand steer when I was only six. It's my God-given right to show my son these things. My right, damn it."

He was bitter, anxious and a little bit obsessive. Though Fiona thought Nate was a good parent, Jesse saw a darker side to this possessiveness. He wondered how far Nate would go to be with his son.

He tucked that concern into the ever-expanding puzzle surrounding Nicole's kidnapping. "I suppose you've heard about the missing ransom."

"You bet I have. That's one of the reasons I moved back to the Circle M as soon as the sheriff's men gave the okay."

"Have you been searching?"

He gave a sly nod. "A million dollars would change my life."

"You'd have to return the money," Jesse said.

"Finders, keepers. The Carlisles already have too much damn cash. Dylan wouldn't miss a million. That's chump change to him."

That wasn't the way the law saw it, but Jesse didn't bother pointing that out. He wanted Nate's cooperation. "I'd like to take a look around at the Circle M."

Nate's jaw tightened. Offering hospitality didn't come naturally to him. "I suppose it would be all right. Just don't bring any of those damn Carlisles with you."

Fiona rejoined them. "Belinda says thanks but no, thanks. She's a little concerned that Mickey might be getting an ear infection so she wanted him to stay inside."

"She's coddling the boy. Turning him into a sissy."

"Hold on, Nate." When Fiona touched his arm, he barely kept himself from flinching. "Belinda said she'd stop by the Circle M with Mickey when her shift is over."

"Fine. I'll be waiting."

He turned on his boot heel and went back to his truck. Jesse watched as he drove away. "That's one angry man."

"But you see what I mean? He's crazy about his son."

Crazy *being the relevent word,* thought Jesse.

AFTER NATE'S SURPRISE VISIT, Fiona wanted to check in with Wentworth and the kids before they did any further searching. If Mickey had noticed his father's truck, he might have questions.

On the phone, Belinda had been adamant about refusing to let Nate take the kids. She'd argued with her ex-husband about the weekend visit to her parents, which had actually been a chance for her mom and dad to meet her new boy-friend. He and Belinda had been living together for six months, and marriage was in their future. Another bone of contention with Nate.

Wentworth opened the door, wearing a tinfoil crown.

"Nice hat," Jesse commented as he entered.

"I'm the king," Wentworth said. "King of the Wild Prairie. And these are my two ponies."

Abby and Mickey trotted toward them, bobbing their heads and making whinnying noises.

Fiona chuckled. "What wonderful steeds!"

Mickey bared his teeth and snapped at her fingers. Apparently, he was a carnivorous breed of horse.

"Here's the magic part," Wentworth said. "I pat them on the head. Poof. They turn into kids."

Playing the game, Abby immediately dropped the horse act and gave Fiona a hug. "Where were you, Mommy?"

"Jesse and I were out back, looking around."

"Looking for what?"

Fiona squatted so she was eye level with her daughter. No way would she frighten Abby with stories of kidnap-ping and ransom. Neither would she lie. Picking her words carefully, she said, "There might be something hidden on our property. It's about as big as that coffee table."

A frown puckered Abby's forehead. "Is it in a secret hiding place?"

Fiona realized that she might be encouraging her daughter to go on a treasure hunt. That was the last thing she wanted. "This is a grown-up problem. Jesse and I will take care of it."

Abby glanced toward Jesse, then back at her mother. She seemed unconvinced. "What if you can't find it? What if you need me and Mickey to find the secret place?"

Did she know about the ransom? A chill crept up Fiona's spine. She hated to think of her daughter being connected in any way to these horrible crimes. "Is there something you want to tell me?"

Mickey whinnied and pawed the air with his hands.

"Got to run," Abby said. "Run like the wind."

As her daughter galloped down the hall with Mickey at her side, Fiona rose slowly. "She knows something."

"She does," Jesse agreed. "Mickey, too."

Abby had immediately mentioned a secret hiding place. Usually, she and Mickey were outside, racing around. It was entirely possible that they'd discovered many things that Fiona knew nothing about, including some kind of hidey-hole.

Convincing her daughter to open up wouldn't be easy. Abby could be intensely stubborn.

"I'll talk to her," Jesse offered.

She raised a skeptical eyebrow. "Why would she tell you if she won't talk to me?"

"You're her mother. Abby's secret might get her in trouble with you, and she doesn't want that. On the other hand, I'm just some guy who gave her a turquoise stone. No threat."

Fiona certainly didn't see him as nonthreatening. The way he'd manhandled Nate in the front yard had been quick, efficient and a little bit scary.

And there was an even greater threat. Jesse knew how to shatter the wall she'd built around her heart to protect herself. When he looked at her with those deep-set eyes, she had the urge to unburden all the thoughts and emotions she usually held back. Within an hour of meeting him, she'd confided details about her financial situation that she hadn't told anyone else. Last night, they were even more intimate. After knowing him for less than a day, she'd been kissing him. Oh, yes, he was dangerous. A huge threat to her self-control.

But she was certain that he didn't mean to hurt her or her daughter.

"Go ahead and talk to Abby." She turned to Wentworth. "So, Your Royal Highness, how about a cup of coffee?"

"If you're buying, I'm drinking."

He followed her into the kitchen, removed his crown and sat in the same chair he'd used for breakfast. He rested his elbows on the tabletop as she poured two cups. Remembering that he took his with milk and sugar, she placed both on the table within easy reach.

"Have the kids been driving you crazy?" she asked.

"Playing king is a whole lot more fun than hanging around in the hospital waiting for Jesse to wake up."

"He seems to be recovering quickly."

Wentworth stirred the milk into his coffee. "It takes more than dying to keep Jesse down."

She didn't like to think of Jesse dying, being summoned to the hereafter by his grandfather. After one sip of coffee, she set her mug down on the table. "If you don't mind, I should get these dishes done before it's time to make lunch."

They'd never installed a dishwasher at the cabin. Though they had a good well, water was a precious commodity in the Colorado mountains, and she tried to practice conservation, teaching Abby about the three *R*s. Reduce. Reuse. Recycle.

One half of the double sink filled with sudsy water. The other half was for rinsing.

"How long have you been working for Jesse?" she asked.

"Almost five years. And I've known him since high

school in Denver. He was a couple of years older and didn't pay much attention to me back then. I was friends with his younger sister, Elena."

"The office manager for Longbridge Security," she recalled. "Is she like Jesse?"

"Oh, yeah. She's tough, and she's smart. Went to law school and passed the bar exam on her first try."

"I know a lot of attorneys in Denver."

"Elena's more than a lawyer. She's an excellent marks-woman. And she can kick my ass in hand-to-hand combat."

"Tough and smart." Fiona was intrigued by the idea of a female version of Jesse. "How else is she like her brother?"

"They both like to be the boss. It makes things real interesting when they're together."

His grin made her think that he cared about Elena. "Is she your girlfriend?"

The smile wilted. "Just friends."

"Don't give up on her." Fiona turned back to the dishes. "It takes some women a while to get warmed up. Relation-ships happen in all kinds of surprising ways."

Like the feelings she had for Jesse. The electricity that raced through her when they touched. Her fascination with his chiseled features. If anyone had told her that she'd move to an isolated mountain home and find a man who attracted her, she wouldn't have believed them.

She glanced toward the kitchen door. "Why do you think it's taking Jesse so long?"

"Interrogations take time."

"Interrogation? He's not going to pressure my daughter, is he?"

"Don't worry. Abby will be fine. She's a persuasive kid. Hell, she got me to wear a crown and play king."

Jesse strode into the kitchen and came up close beside her. In a low voice, he said, "You have to promise that you won't be mad at Abby."

Was her daughter in danger? A tremor raced through her, and she placed the last dish in the rack on the counter to dry. "What has Abby done?"

"She broke one of your rules, and she's scared that you'll be angry."

She turned to face him. "Which rule?"

"First, you have to promise."

Her imagination ran through all the potentially dangerous situations her daughter could have gotten into. "I promise."

"When you first moved up here, Abby and Mickey were playing outside. They went exploring in the barn."

"She knows better than that. I've told her a hundred times not to go into any of the outbuildings. It's not safe. There are—"

"You promised," he reminded her.

"Fine." Her lips pinched together. "What did the kids find?"

"A secret playhouse under the floorboards. They only went in there a couple of times. They accidentally left the lights on in the barn and the bulbs must have burned out."

"A playhouse?" She rested her hand on her chest. Her heart fluttered as she thought of all the terrible things that might have happened.

"You've never heard of this before?"

She shook her head. "Never. But it's entirely possible that one of the Grant men built something like that as a weekend project. Maybe a root cellar?"

But why would anyone put a root cellar in the barn? She needed to see this secret playhouse.

After giving Abby a hug and assuring her that she was a much-loved child who should never, under any circumstance, go exploring without telling her mother first, Fiona followed Jesse to the barn.

Though they had the flashlight, Jesse opened the two wide doors at the front. Sunlight flooded into the barn, banishing the ominous dark. He picked his way through the discarded junk that had taken up residence.

Fiona saw every bit of this stuff—the tractor, the Jeep and the beat-up boxes of junk—as potential hazards. Abby and Mickey could have seriously injured themselves while playing in here.

"Wouldn't Burke or the sheriff have found this playhouse?" she asked. "They searched all over the barn."

"You'd think so," he said. "According to Abby's directions the playhouse is in this corner. On the other side of the barn from the workbench."

Tucked into that corner was a stack of logs covered by a tarp. Jesse shone the flashlight on the floorboards. "You can see footprints here. They searched in this area."

"I don't see a trapdoor."

"It's hidden under the wood," he said. "Abby said that when she and Mickey found it, the door was already open."

"Somebody was in here. They hid the entrance."

He removed the chunks of firewood, revealing a spot on the floor that was swept clean. Even though they knew what to look for, the latch wasn't noticeable. Jesse pulled up the trapdoor.

He shone the flashlight into a dark space. "Maybe you should stay up here."

"Not a chance." She needed to know what was down there, what had been hidden on her property.

Jesse climbed down a short ladder, and she followed.

After a moment of fumbling around, he turned on a lamp.

She stood in a small room, less than ten feet square. The floor was packed earth covered by two threadbare carpets. The ceiling was only six feet high—too low for Jesse to stand upright. The ceiling was insulated, as were the walls, and it was warm.

There was a single bed, a table and a lamp.

Jesse's eyes were grim. "I think we've found the place where Nicole was held prisoner."

Chapter Eleven

Richter lay flat on the floor of the hay loft in the barn, peeking down through a crack between the boards, watching the widow and her bodyguard as they opened the trapdoor hidden under a pile of wood.

His gun was cocked and ready. If they climbed out of that secret hiding place toting the ransom, he'd kill them both.

How the hell had he missed that trapdoor? He'd been all over this damn barn. He'd even pulled logs off the woodpile, thinking the ransom could have been tucked underneath.

She'd known. Fiona must have known.

The more Richter thought about it, the more he was convinced that she and Butch had a thing going on. She must have shown him the hiding spot.

He licked his lips, anticipating the moment when she'd shove a big, fat bundle of cash out of that hole onto the floor of the barn. He'd wait until they both climbed out and were patting each other on the back, congratulating themselves for getting their mitts on that money.

Richter figured he'd shoot the bodyguard first. He should've made sure he killed that guy before. Three bullets weren't enough to stop him. This time, he'd go for a clean head shot. At this range, he couldn't miss.

Fiona climbed out first. Her long hair wasn't braided today, and her ponytail tangled around her shoulders. She stood below him, brushing the dust off her hands.

The bodyguard climbed up beside her.

Richter's trigger finger twitched.

But the bodyguard's hands were empty. He didn't have the ransom.

"I never knew that little room was there," Fiona said. "Do you think it was meant to be a playhouse?"

The bodyguard slapped his hat back onto his head. "I think someone was living there. An adult."

"Why?"

"It's set up nice and cozy with a bed and a lamp. The furniture has been there long enough to make marks on the floor. There's even electricity."

"But why would anyone want to live there?"

He shrugged. "We need to call the sheriff. There might be fingerprints."

As they walked toward the open door of the barn, Fiona shook her head. "Too bad the ransom wasn't stashed in there."

Richter eased up on the trigger. It was too bad *for him* that they hadn't found the ransom, but lucky for *them*. The widow and her bodyguard would live to see another day.

FIONA STAYED IN THE house with the kids while Jesse and a herd of law enforcement people inspected the small room under the floorboards in the barn. Though unaccustomed to having so many visitors at her mountain home, she'd been a political wife long enough to know the rules of proper hospitality. *Offer them something to eat and make a fresh pot of coffee.* She whipped up a chocolate cake from a mix.

Drawn by the sweet aroma of baking, Abby and Mickey appeared in the kitchen door. Abby's little face crinkled with worry. "Mommy, are you mad at me?"

"Not mad. Just worried." She pulled her daughter into a hug. "You know I always love you."

"Love you back."

"You did the right thing by telling Jesse about the secret place. You can always tell me anything. You know that, don't you?"

Abby nodded. "Can we go out to the barn and say hi to everybody?"

"No," Fiona said, firm and final. The sheriff and his deputies would be annoyed by kids underfoot. But more important, she wanted to shield the children from all the fearful events surrounding Nicole's kidnapping.

Abby tilted her head to one side. "Can we have cake for lunch?"

"If you finish your fruit and sandwich, you get chocolate cake for dessert."

"I'm hungry," Mickey said in plaintive tone. "Now."

"Fifteen minutes until lunch." She'd set up drawing projects on the dining-room table. "First, I want you both to make me a picture of Christmas."

They dashed off. She barely had time to swirl frosting across the sheet cake when there was a knock on the back door. Since she'd been told in no uncertain terms to use the dead bolt at all times, Fiona had to flip the lock before opening the door.

Carolyn charged inside, talking as she came. "She was

there, right there under your barn. Can you believe it? We had helicopters searching and bloodhounds and—"

"I want to hear everything," Fiona said, "but quietly. I don't want to scare the kids."

"Right." Carolyn lowered her voice to a whisper. "They've found several blond hairs that surely belong to Nicole. And she scratched her initials into the wood near the door. So close. She was so close."

Jesse came into the house and shut the door. "Fiona, they need you at the barn. To take a closer look and see if you can identify any of the furniture or bed linens."

"Sure, no problem." She turned to Carolyn. "I feel terrible that Nicole was held here. Like you said, she was so close. If I'd gone out to the barn, I would have heard her. I could have helped her."

"You're not the only one who feels like she should have done more." Carolyn's fist clenched as if grabbing a missed opportunity. "At the very beginning of all this, I could have stopped Nicole from riding off by herself."

There was plenty of reproach to be spread around. "You're not to blame."

"I know you're right. But why do I feel so guilty?"

Intuitively, she knew the answer. But it was difficult to put into words.

When her husband died from a heart attack, she had tried her hardest to figure out why it happened. She needed a reason, needed to make sense of the tragedy. It had to be somebody's fault. She'd blamed his doctors for not catching the warning signs, blamed his coworkers for not responding quickly enough, but mostly she'd blamed herself for not taking care of him properly.

"Much of what happens in life is beyond our control,"

she said. "We can regret what happened to Nicole. Or be angry about it. But the kidnapping wasn't our fault."

"I'm not in control?" Carolyn frowned. "I don't much like that idea."

Of course not. She was a CEO who took her responsibilities seriously. "Do you feel guilty about the bad weather when it snows?"

"No."

"Or when the Broncos lost last weekend?"

"Definitely not my fault," Carolyn said. "I used to think if I wore orange underwear, they'd win. Not true."

"So you regret the loss. But don't feel guilty."

Abby and Mickey raced into the kitchen, waving crayon drawings of Santa and reindeer. In unison, they shouted, "Lunch, lunch. Munch, munch."

"I'll take care of these two," Carolyn said. "What should I feed them?"

"Sandwiches. The fixings are in the fridge."

"Dijon? Maybe Brie?"

"They're children, Carolyn. Mayo and cold cuts are fine."

Fiona grabbed her coat from the peg by the door and walked with Jesse toward the barn.

"I liked what you said about guilt. Wise words."

Never before had anyone accused her of wisdom. It felt a bit uncomfortable. "Life's too short to waste time feeling guilty. I just go with the flow."

"Do you?"

"Like the California girl I am." She pantomimed surfing. "Wherever the waves take me, I go."

And the current of her emotions was sweeping her inexorably toward him. Ahead of them—in the barn—several law enforcement officers were working hard to find clues.

Behind them—in the house—her daughter demanded attention and reassurance. But when she was with Jesse, everything else faded into the background. His presence commanded her full concentration. She liked that feeling, liked how she felt when she was near him.

"There was a time," he said, "when I had a situation that turned out wrong. It was bad, real bad. I blamed myself. The guilt nearly did me in."

"It helps to talk about things that hurt," she said.

"Maybe later." He forced a smile. "The sheriff is waiting."

When she looked toward the barn, she saw Sheriff Trainer with his arms folded across his chest and a cigarette dangling from the corner of his mouth. "I'm not a fan of tobacco, but that man looks like he needs a smoke."

"He's ticked off at himself. His trained forensic people haven't found much, and it took a lead from a couple of four-year-olds to locate the secret room."

As she approached, Fiona smiled, hoping that an offer of cake and coffee would make the sheriff feel better. "Good afternoon, Sheriff. If you'd like a snack—"

"Not now." He stubbed out his cigarette. "Why didn't you tell me about this secret room?"

Taken aback, she said, "Because I didn't know."

"This is your property. Your barn. How is it possible that you didn't know?"

She had several logical reasons: she never went into the barn, wasn't here when it was constructed, had no reason to suspect a hideout. But she refused to dignify his question with an explanation. It was absurd to think that she'd been concealing evidence from the police. "Is there a reason you wanted me to come out here?"

His mouth puckered as if sucking through a thin straw.

"Nicole Carlisle was held captive in your barn. The dead body of Butch Thurman was found in your front yard. Hell, you found him."

No cake for you. "It almost sounds like you're accusing me."

"I don't believe in coincidence, Fiona. You're in the center of this mess. And I want to know why."

In the past, she might have politely demurred, hoping that someone else, like Jesse, would step up and fight her battles. But she needed to stand up for herself. "Don't blame me."

"Why shouldn't I?"

"Your men searched in the barn. They couldn't find the trapdoor."

"What's your point?"

Aggression didn't come naturally to her, but she pushed back at him with an accusation of her own. "Maybe your own men missed finding the secret room on purpose. They might be the ones with something to hide."

Agent Burke emerged from the barn and waved to her. "In here, Fiona."

Grateful for Burke's timely summons, she brushed past the sheriff.

Jesse leaned close to her ear and whispered, "Nice job, surfer girl."

"I was rude," she said.

"He deserved it."

For the second time that day, she climbed down into the secret room. Burke and Jesse followed. Both men had to duck to keep from hitting their heads on the low plywood ceiling.

The extra-large Agent Burke looked especially cramped in the small space. "Take a careful look around, Fiona. Tell me if any of the furnishings look familiar."

"Why?"

"This stuff came from somewhere. If we find the original owner, we might figure out who built this room."

She reached up and touched the ceiling. "This looks like plywood that was being used to build my studio. I can't really tell if it's part of that load or not, but we had plenty of wood and insulation lying around. I have invoices somewhere."

"When was that construction taking place?"

"Three years ago."

Only three years ago? She swallowed hard, uncomfortable with the idea that some unknown person had built a secret hideout in her barn so recently. They'd had plenty of opportunity. Before she moved up here, the property had been vacant, except for when Belinda lived here.

"What about the furniture?" Burke asked.

The single bed had a painted metal frame with rails—unlike anything in the house. There was a bedside table with a drawer and a shelf made of particleboard covered with a wood veneer. "I'm pretty sure that the Grant family never owned such inexpensive furniture."

On the edge of the frame at the foot of the bed was a ragged scar where the paint had been scratched away. She touched the mark.

"We think a chain was fastened there," Burke said.

Fiona shivered. "She was chained to the bed?"

"A long chain. It gave her a fair amount of mobility." He pointed to Nicole's initials carved into the wall near the ladder. "She could reach this far. I think he was trying to make her comfortable."

Fiona shuddered. "By confining her?"

"As prisons go, this is a Hilton." Jesse pointed to the

lamp on the table. "There was light. The bed isn't bad. And this whole place is insulated so it's warm."

"He gave her clean clothes," Burke added.

"In the proof-of-life videos," Jesse said, "Nicole didn't appear to be suffering."

Fiona knew better. She knew Nicole was putting on an act to keep others from worrying. For someone like her neighbor, a woman who loved the outdoors, not being able to see the sun and feel the wind would be torture. Fiona had only been in here for a few minutes, and it already felt as if the walls were closing in on her.

"There's nothing I can tell you about these furnishings."

"Here's what I don't understand," Jesse said. "In those proof-of-life tapes, Nicole made signals that pointed toward the Circle M Ranch. Did she think she was there?"

Burke shifted his shoulders. His huge body seemed to take up all the space in the room. "Here's the sequence of events as we know them—she was kidnapped at the creek and taken to the Circle M. Then Butch and Richter took her. They went to a cave on the Indian Trail. Then she was here."

"Not the Circle M," Jesse repeated. "Why would she point you in that direction?"

"She could have been drugged when she was brought here. If all she'd seen was the Circle M, she'd assume she was there."

Fiona's gaze fixed on the rough wooden ladder leading out of the room. Imagined echoes of Nicole's suffering rang in her ears. It was hot in here; a light sweat coated her forehead.

"We need to figure out who built this little cubbyhole," Jesse said. "If it wasn't Butch or Richter, someone else might be involved in the kidnapping."

"Sam Logan," Burke said. "You identified him from the mug shots."

"You think he built this place?"

Burke considered for a long moment before shaking his head. "Secret hideouts aren't Logan's style. He likes attention."

"Who else?"

"Me," Fiona said. She couldn't stay here for one more minute. She reached for the wooden ladder. "Sheriff Trainer seems to think so."

She climbed out of the hole into the cluttered barn. Ridding herself of suspicion was going to take more than going with the flow. Her laissez-faire attitude needed to change.

Jesse came up behind her, rested his hand on her shoulder. "I don't suspect you."

"But others do." She gulped down the musty air of the barn, which tasted wonderful compared to the closed room. "How am I going to prove them wrong? I'm not an investigator. Or a hunter."

"I am." His dark eyes were steady and confident. "Trust me."

She had no other choice.

Chapter Twelve

Sitting on a porch bench at the Circle M ranch house, Jesse waved goodbye to Fiona, Belinda and the kids, who were being escorted across the grounds toward the horse barn by a proprietary Nate Miller. Still dressed in his clean, pressed blue jeans, Nate lectured them about how the Circle M had once been the finest cattle ranch in the valley—a boast that was wide open to debate. From what Jesse understood, the Carlisles always had more land, more cattle and more influence.

Nate had reclaimed the Circle M with a vengeance. The yellow crime scene tape that marked the violence of two days ago had been torn down and stuffed into a bin beside the porch.

According to Burke, Nate had arrived at the Circle M shortly after the Sons of Freedom were taken into custody and wasted no time in stating his claim. It was his legal right to move back to the Circle M when the premises were vacated. Burke said there had been some concern about the ownership of the SOF horses, but the FBI was willing to leave that issue for the local authorities to settle.

Nate glanced over his shoulder at Jesse, who remained

seated. He wanted a chance to search the premises without Nate hanging over his shoulder, so he'd told them he was tired, still recovering from his wounds.

Much to his surprise, Fiona had backed up his claim with a vivid description of his injuries, even though she hadn't seen a single scar. She talked about "oozing pus" and "too many stitches to count." Her willingness to lie worried him. Though he didn't believe Sheriff Trainer's suspicions, his only proof to the contrary was his belief in her honesty. He knew he wasn't making a mistake by trusting her. Still…

As soon as they all disappeared into the barn, Jesse left the porch. Though it was a long shot, he hoped to find evidence that Nicole had been here. In the proof-of-life videos, she signaled clues that pointed to the Circle M. He wanted to find an indication of where she'd gone.

Jesse circled behind the ranch house. Across the open yard were a couple of sheds and a smokehouse for curing beef and venison. He took a quick look inside these smaller structures on his way to the main bunkhouse—a long, low building with several windows covered over with heavy plastic to protect against the winter cold. The door was unlocked.

He stepped inside, turned on the light and entered an open room with two long tables. Near the entrance, there was a wood-burning stove and a podium. This must have been where Sam Logan preached to his survivalist congregation. Twelve men, eleven women and four children. There was nothing spiritual about this organization. The women had been picked up from the street, promised shelter and drugged into submission. The men had been getting rich from a smuggling scheme.

When the FBI raided the place, it must have been just

after dinner. Dirty plates still littered the tables along with half-filled water glasses and mugs filled with congealed coffee. A scrawny Christmas tree stood in the corner, half draped with tinsel. Other decorations were scattered about.

Jesse noticed a doll on the bench by the table. A toy truck overturned over on the floor. A couple of aprons tossed carelessly aside.

Life, interrupted.

He went through a door at the back of the room, entering a hallway with four closed doors on either side. He opened the first door and found a small room with a bed and dresser. Two simple dresses hung from an open rack. On the dresser was a cheap wristwatch, a hairbrush and an economy-size bottle of moisturizer beside a stack of fashion magazines. This woman might have been living the simple life, but she dreamed of sequins.

Immediately, Jesse noted that the metal frame on the bed matched the bed found in the secret room under Fiona's barn. If Richter or Butch had constructed that room, it seemed likely that they'd use furnishings from the Circle M.

This connection needed further investigation. He quickly checked the rest of the rooms, searching for clues. Where was Nicole now? He didn't think she'd run off with Richter, a man with a criminal record and a mean streak. Had she simply collected the ransom and ridden off into the sunset?

His gut instinct told him otherwise. Even though Dylan was convinced that his wife was gone, Jesse worried that she might still be in danger.

When he stepped outside, Nate was coming toward him, fists clenched and angry as a wet badger. He called out, "Hey! Looking for something?"

Jesse said nothing. He didn't feel the need to apologize or explain.

"If you find that ransom," Nate growled, "you'd best remember that it's on my property. That makes it mine. Possession is nine-tenths of the law."

"I assume you've already searched all these outbuildings."

"You bet I have. But if you want to poke around, go right ahead."

"When the SOF rented your property, did you provide furnishings? Like the beds?"

"My pappy bought those metal frames a long time ago when we had a full crew, and I've never seen a need to replace them. Good, sturdy frames."

"Are any of the beds missing?"

His thin shoulders stiffened. "What the hell are you saying? Did somebody steal one of my beds?"

Jesse wasn't about to tell him about the hiding place at Fiona's house. Sharing information could only lead to trouble. "Let's head back to the horse barn."

"Fine with me." He lurched forward. His earlier swagger was gone, replaced by tension. "Maybe you can convince my ex-wife that it's okay for my son to get up on horseback. All I want to do is put him in front of me on the saddle and pace around the corral. No harm in that."

"No harm at all."

"She's turning my boy into a scaredy-cat."

He suspected that Belinda's hesitation had less to do with Mickey's safety and more about his father's demeanor. Nate's bitterness was toxic and pervasive. And mostly aimed at his neighbors, the Carlisles. "How did your feud with the Carlisles get started?"

"You really want to know?"

"That's why I asked."

"I'll tell you." Nate came to a halt, stared at the dirt beneath his boots. "Sterling Carlisle killed my pappy."

Though surprised by this allegation, Jesse kept his reaction to himself. He merely nodded.

"Happened six years ago." Nate's lips barely moved when he talked. "The sheriff called it an accident, but I know better."

"How did he die?"

"We only had about fifty head of cattle. They were in the feeding pen, getting fat before slaughter. Pappy collapsed inside the pen. He got trampled."

An ironic death for a man who swore by the procedure of confining cattle in tight pens and force-feeding. "Where does Sterling Carlisle come in?"

Nate squinted as if looking back at the past. "I heard Pappy talking to him. Arguing, real loud. Telling him that his organic methods were a bunch of baloney. He was right."

"Yeah?"

"Beef cattle don't need to roam free and eat grass. They're meat. Nothing but damn meat."

"Did you see anything?"

"Hell, no. I had my chores. After Mama died, I took care of the cooking and housework. It was only Pappy and me at the ranch."

Though Jesse guessed that Nate was in his mid-thirties, he sounded like a kid. Under his pappy's thumb, he hadn't fully matured. "Did you hear Sterling Carlisle make a threat?"

"Not exactly. I didn't have time to stop and eavesdrop." He jabbed the air with a gnarled finger, making his point with an invisible jury. "But I know what happened. Sterling came over here and provoked my pappy into a heart attack. Then he left without summoning help. Left him to die."

Jesse made no comment, offered no judgment. He could tell that Nate believed this unlikely scenario. His eyes shone with a fanatical fervor. His breathing was shallow and strained as if hate had squeezed the air from his lungs.

Jesse's grandfather would have said that Nate was like a man bitten by a rattler. Either the venom would work through his system or he would die a poisonous death.

Nate continued. "The Carlisles ruined us. They're so righteous. So rich. They can all go straight to hell."

Jesse wondered if Nicole was included in his hatred. She hadn't been around six years ago when his father died. "The Carlisles are suffering now. With the kidnapping."

"Nicole isn't kidnapped anymore." But a cruel smirk twisted his mouth. "The way I heard it, she told Dylan she wanted a divorce and wasn't ever coming back to him."

"You believe that? You believe she ran off with Pete Richter?"

"I never would have thought it. Richter isn't a handsome man. Handy with an ax, though. He was a logger up in Oregon."

Jesse doubted that lumberjack skills would be enough to cause Nicole to leave her husband. "What else can you tell me about Richter?"

"He didn't strike me as somebody who was going to be a cowboy for the rest of his life. He kept talking about tropical beaches and hula skirts." Nate scoffed. "Butch Thurgood is a different story. Tall and good-looking. A regular ladies' man. Nicole might have been taken with him."

But Butch was dead.

As Jesse watched Nate stalk toward the horse barn, he wished that he had more training as an interrogator. His gut instincts told him that Nate was withholding vital information, but he didn't have the key to make him open up. Nor the authority to compel him to answer questions.

Inside the horse barn, Mickey ran to his father. "Mommy says I can ride on the saddle with you."

In the blink of an eye, Nate transformed from bitter to better. He'd never be Father-of-the-Year material, but his grin appeared to be sincere. Like a king, he gestured to the horses that he didn't really own. "Take your pick, son."

Nate hadn't thought to include Abby, and the disappointment written on her face was tragic. Jesse could see Fiona holding back, trying not to be rude and demanding. She was a strange and intriguing mixture of passionate emotion and strict politeness.

Jesse was far more simple. "Nate, you forgot about Abby. We'll saddle up two horses, and I'll give her a ride, too."

"Fine with me."

Fiona beamed as if he'd done something incredibly heroic, then leaned down to her daughter's level. "What do you say, Abby?"

"Thank you, Mr. Miller."

"Sure thing, kid. Pick your horse."

Unlike Mickey, Abby knew exactly what she wanted. She marched up to the stall and pointed to a black mare with a calm manner and intelligent eyes. "I like her."

"You've got good taste," Nate said. "She's one of the best riding mounts. But she threw a shoe the other day, and I want to let her rest."

If the choice had been up to Jesse, he'd pick one of the two Arabians—beautiful, proud animals. But he was sure that Nate didn't want to use such prized horseflesh to train kids for riding. He directed Abby toward a dappled mare.

"I'll call her Chip," Abby said, "because she looks like chocolate chip ice cream."

"She probably already has a name," Fiona said.

"It's Chip," Abby insisted.

"That's a take-charge attitude," Jesse said. "You need that when you're riding. The horse needs to know who's boss."

"Don't we all?" Fiona murmured softly. "Did you find anything?"

"Not much."

As he bridled and saddled the newly christened Chip, Jesse regretted the time he'd wasted with this trip to the Circle M. Finding the metal bed frame might confirm that someone from the Circle M—either Richter or Butch—had constructed the secret room under Fiona's barn. But that wasn't earth-shaking news.

When he lifted the saddle, his injured shoulder ached, and he was glad to step back and let Fiona take over. From the way she handled the gear, he could tell that she knew about horses.

"Like mother, like daughter," he said. "Abby must have gotten her love of ponies from you."

"I'm nowhere near as devoted," she replied with an open smile. "Before we started coming up here, I'd never been interested in horses."

"California girl," he said, remembering.

"Hurry up," Abby demanded.

Fiona rested her palm on Chip's flank. "We're ready."

"Mount up," Jesse said. "You ride. I'll lift Abby up to you."

That hadn't been the plan sanctioned by Nate Miller, but Jesse didn't see a problem. As soon as Fiona and Abby were settled on horseback, he took the bridle and led the horse into the corral.

Nate followed with Mickey, who was making wild whoops and waving his arms. Not so for Abby. She took her time on horseback seriously, paying careful attention to everything her mother said.

Belinda stepped up beside him, her fists jammed into the pockets of her black slacks. Her eyes, half hidden by shaggy brown bangs, looked worried. "Do you think Nate will be able to keep these horses?"

He shrugged. "Don't know."

"He thinks he's come into a windfall. He plans to sell his little house in town, move back here and turn this place into a horse farm." She shook her head. "I have a nasty feeling that my alimony checks are about to stop coming."

As Mickey rode by, he waved with both hands. "Look at me, Mommy. I'm riding."

"I see." She waved back.

Jesse watched Fiona and Abby. They looked good on horseback. Fiona's long brown hair in the loose ponytail tousled in the breeze as she urged Chip into a trot, then slowed to a walk, then reined to a stop. The mare responded to her directions. It had been Butch Thurgood's job to train these animals, and he'd done his job well.

"It takes work to run a horse ranch," Jesse said.

"And money." Belinda leaned her shapely hip against the corral fence. "I know Nate means well, but I worry about having Mickey visit him unsupervised. A ranch like the Circle M can be a dangerous place if you don't keep a careful eye on a child."

"It's not the ranch you're worried about."

"You're right," she said. "It's Nate. There are times when he's so angry I think his eyes are going to pop right out of his head. And he doesn't understand that Mickey's a little boy who cries when he falls down and doesn't always pay attention."

"But he cares about his son."

"His one saving grace," she conceded. "I'm not sure how Nate is going to react when I get married again."

In his opinion, she was right to be concerned. Nate had a great capacity for hate. At any given moment, he could erupt. "Is he abusive?"

"He never hit me. Or Mickey." Belinda waved to her son, who was wriggling on the saddle, impatient with his father's instructions. "But he made me feel like dirt."

Verbal abuse could be more painful than physical wounds. Belinda was a strong-looking woman with broad shoulders, but she seemed to shrink when she looked at her ex-husband.

"Breaking up with him must have been hell," he said quietly.

"You have no idea. I had no money. If Fiona hadn't given me a job, letting me move into her vacant house as a caretaker, I wouldn't have had a place to live."

He remembered something Fiona had told him. "You took out a restraining order."

"Nate wouldn't leave me alone. He wanted Mickey. Wanted his son." She shuddered. "Thank God, that part of my life is over."

Jesse hoped she was right. That Nate wouldn't cause her any more trouble.

After they finished their ride and brought the horses back into the barn, Fiona got a call on her cell. Her exhilaration about her ride with Abby dissipated as she talked.

When she disconnected, she came to him. "That was the sheriff. I need to get back to the house. Right away."

Chapter Thirteen

Fiona slammed the door to her station wagon and stormed toward her front porch. She'd arranged for Abby to go home with Belinda and Mickey because she didn't want her daughter to see what was about to happen.

Clinton had called the sheriff, demanding that he be allowed to search her house for his precious belongings. Both of them stood waiting for her. If Burke hadn't been at her house, they probably would have broken a window and entered on their own authority.

As she approached, she couldn't decide which of the two men was more hateful. Sheriff Trainer with his unfounded suspicions? Or her stepson with his unfounded demands?

Jesse strode past her, inserting himself as mediator. "Good afternoon, gentlemen. What the hell do you want?"

Clinton straightened the lapel on his tailored Harris tweed jacket and stuck his nose in the air. "We have a warrant to search this house for stolen property."

"Stolen?" She choked on the word. "In what twisted universe would you think I stole anything from you?"

"My father's property," he said smugly, "belongs to me and my sister."

"Do you think your father would be proud, Clinton?" If she'd had Jesse's gun in her hand, she wouldn't have hesitated to drill a neat little hole in the middle of his handsome forehead. "Do you think he'd applaud your greed?"

"You're stalling," he said. "Like when you accused me of breaking into your house."

"I'm not so sure you didn't."

"Don't push me, Fiona."

When Clinton took a threatening step toward her, she noticed that Agent Burke made a corresponding move. If this confrontation turned physical, she knew that Burke and Jesse would be on her side. A reassuring thought.

But this wasn't their battle, and she refused to hide behind them. The time had come for her to fight. Not for the objects Clinton had listed on his inventory but for her reputation. "I'm not a thief."

Clinton scoffed.

Jesse slipped his arm out of the sling and flexed his fingers into a fist in a not-so-subtle threat. "I suggest you show some respect to the widow."

"Settle down," the sheriff said. "We're here with a legal warrant."

"Show it to me," she said.

The sheriff placed the faxed warrant in her hand. Attached was Clinton's inventory. Blinded by anger, she needed a moment for her eyes to focus. "It's signed by a Denver judge. Does he have jurisdiction in this district?"

"That's a valid question," Jesse said. "I'm sure Special Agent Burke can clear this up with a couple of phone calls to his bosses in the FBI. What is it that you're looking to seize? A Tiffany lamp?"

"And a pink tiara," she said, glancing at Clinton's list.

"A tiara, huh?" Jesse shot a glare in the direction of the sheriff. "That sounds like a threat to national security. Maybe we should call the NSA."

Burke juggled his cell phone. "I can start with the state attorney's office. Or the governor. He's a personal friend of Carolyn's."

"I'm just doing my job," Sheriff Trainer muttered.

He looked so cowed and miserable that Fiona might have felt sorry for him if he hadn't been so hostile toward her. She stated, "I want this issue settled. Immediately. We have much more important things to worry about than Clinton's petty claims."

"Like what?" Clinton said.

She focused on the sheriff. "Making sure Nicole is all right. Finding the missing ransom."

"Not my problem," Clinton said. "I'm not backing down."

"I wouldn't expect you to." Her anger solidified into a hard mass in her chest, blocking her lungs. She had to speak her piece or explode. "Ever since your father died, you and your mother have made your demands exceedingly clear. With the help of your lawyers, you grabbed my house, my car and my bank accounts. But you can never take my most important possession."

"What's that?"

"Memories." If all she had left was the remembrance of her years with Wyatt, their love and their happiness, she'd be a wealthy woman.

She paused to inhale a breath. Now that she'd spoken of her pathetic financial condition in front of both the sheriff and Burke, her secret would be common knowledge. Humiliating, but probably for the best. She couldn't hide the fact that she was running out of money for much longer; soon she needed to look for a job.

She handed her house keys to Burke. "Would you please accompany Clinton while he searches? I'd appreciate if he makes as little mess as possible."

"I understand," Burke said. "This won't take long."

She watched Clinton stalk toward her house. Any hope of reconciliation with that side of Wyatt's family was gone. It pained her to realize that Abby would never know many of her blood relatives.

Jesse stood close beside her, and she was glad for his presence. She'd handled Clinton on her own, but it didn't hurt to have a strong shoulder to lean against for comfort after he was gone.

Sheriff Trainer cleared his throat. "Was all that true? You lost everything after your husband died?"

"Pretty much," she said. "I have a clear deed to this house, but that's about all."

"That explains why you moved here." He took out his cigarettes and tapped the top of the pack. "I didn't understand why a city gal like you would want to live in this cabin. Now I know the truth. You're broke."

"That's enough," Jesse said.

"I haven't even gotten started." He gestured with his unlit cigarette. "There was one thing I couldn't figure out about Fiona and her connection to the kidnapping. I didn't know why a rich woman would get involved. But you aren't rich, are you? You have a motive."

"So do you," Jesse said coldly.

"What?" His voice was a squawk.

"That million-dollar ransom is a big motivator. I've got to ask myself, how were the kidnappers always able to keep one step ahead of the investigation? They must have somebody on the inside. You?"

"That's just plain—"

"The way I figure, you've got a lot on your plate— Butch's unsolved murder, locating Nicole and finding the missing ransom. Yet you made time to personally serve Clinton Grant's warrant. It looks like you're trying to point us in the wrong direction."

"I've got no leads."

"Why not?" Jesse asked. "Richter is no genius. He must have left clues. Unless you're covering up for him."

The sheriff fired up his cigarette. "I don't have to stand here and take this."

Fiona spoke up. "Then leave. Get off my property."

Without another word, he went to his vehicle and got behind the wheel.

Her heart was beating faster as she watched him drive away. She clasped Jesse's hand. "Thanks for backing me up."

"You could have thrown that weasel off your land without my help." He gave her hand a squeeze. "You're a lot stronger than you realize."

With adrenaline surging through her veins, she felt strong and capable, felt as if she could take on the world...as long as Jesse was there to encourage her. "Those things you said to the sheriff. Did you mean them?"

"I've got no evidence that points to him, but I'm pretty good at reading people. Sheriff Trainer has a larcenous streak. I wouldn't be surprised to find out that Clinton paid him a little something to come here and enforce that warrant."

That thought hadn't occurred to her, but it made sense. "And if he took a bribe from Clinton, he might be susceptible to a really big payoff from the kidnappers."

"Like I said, a million in cash is a big temptation."

And so was he. His gleaming white smile drew her toward him. If Clinton hadn't been nearby, she would have gone up on tiptoe and kissed the smile off Jesse's face, capturing it for herself.

Worried that she couldn't resist him, she quickly looked away. "If we can't count on the sheriff, we have to investigate on our own."

"We?"

"You said it yourself. I'm stronger than I look."

She stretched to her full height—five feet three inches of unmitigated self-confidence. She had no intention of living under a cloud of suspicion. If the sheriff thought she was guilty of working with kidnappers, others might think so, too. And Clinton had been quick to call her a thief.

There was no shame in being broke, but she wouldn't stand for attacks on her character. She was a good person. If it meant tracking down a kidnapper to prove her integrity, she stood ready for the challenge.

Jesse was a professional bodyguard, and he knew his business. When the people who hired him wanted to carry their own weapon or show him how they knew enough karate to defeat an attacker, trouble ensued. The client got arrogant and took risks.

As he stood beside Fiona, waiting for Burke and Clinton to emerge from her house, he launched into his standard lecture to clients regarding their safety.

"The reason I'm here," he said, "is to protect you."

"And I appreciate that more than you know."

Her soft gray eyes reminded him of the skies before dawn when the light thinned and the world paused in restful silence before the new day. Though he acknowledged her inner strength, she was gentleness personified. An artist. A doting mother.

"I don't want you to be physically involved in investigating," he said. "Your job is to stay safe."

"But I've already been helping you," she said. "We searched my property together."

Apparently, she hadn't noticed his precautions. He'd been armed and alert. Wentworth had been within shouting distance. If he had sensed a threat, he would have stepped forward.

Or would he? Remembering the moment when they entered the barn, he'd been apprehensive. The shadows in that old structure seemed to have form and menace. Instinctively, his hand had gone to his gun. But he hadn't turned back, hadn't returned her to the safety of her house.

A serious lapse in judgment. It worried him. While focusing on the investigation, he hadn't been an efficient bodyguard. That had to change. Though they hadn't yet encountered a direct threat to Fiona's safety, Richter was still at large. Still dangerous.

Burke held open the door to her house, and Clinton marched through, scowling and imperious at the same time. Jesse guessed that he hadn't found what he was looking for.

"No tiara," Burke announced gleefully. "We didn't find a single item on the inventory list."

"Because I don't have them," Fiona said clearly.

A more honorable man than Clinton would have offered an apology. He gave a sniff and looked away. "My business here is concluded."

"Fine with me," she said. "If I *never* see you again, I'll

have no regrets. But don't forget Abby, your half sister. She deserves a chance to know her family."

Unsmiling, he said, "I suppose."

"You and your sister are welcome to see her. Any time."

"Maybe," he said grudgingly. "Someday."

As Clinton drove away, Jesse looked up to the sky. There were only a few hours of daylight left. Time seemed to be slipping through his fingers. Today's investigation had filled in a few blanks, but they hadn't made much forward progress.

Jesse wasn't playing to his strengths. He didn't have the logical skills of a detective or the glib cleverness of an interrogator. He was a hunter. If he hoped to find the ransom and learn what had really happened to Nicole, he needed to trust his instincts.

Fiona looked at him expectantly. "What do we do next?"

There was that word again. *We.* "I want you to hook up with Wentworth at the Carlisle place. He'll drive you into town to pick up Abby. Then back here."

"I don't want to hide," she said. "I need to be involved. There must be something I can do. Some way I can help with the investigation."

Everything about her—from the glow in her eyes to the way her expressive hands held out a plea—was an invitation. Dealing with Clinton brought out the feistiness in her; she was ready for action.

"You don't have any experience in hunting," he said.

"None."

"And you can't handle a firearm."

"But I'm a really good observer," she said. "I have an artist's eye for detail."

"That's one point in your favor."

"And I'm good at following orders. I'll do whatever you tell me. Except for stay home."

He frankly thought the risk was minimal. And he didn't want to disappoint her. He turned to Burke. "We're going to need two horses."

Chapter Fourteen

Jesse preferred hunting alone. When he was a boy, his grandfather showed him the value of quiet observation. He learned when to wait and how to pursue his quarry, not only by following the tracks but also by listening and sensing. It was his nature to hunt. He never killed for sport, only for food. His grandfather taught him to respect all living things—the wapiti, the hare, the quail—that provided nourishment.

This hunting expedition was different. His prey was a criminal, who he held in low regard. And he was most definitely not alone.

According to Burke's notes, the ransom was delivered at the same time the FBI operation was under way and while Dylan was meeting with his wife for the last time.

The ransom was delivered by Carolyn to a field west of the Carlisle ranch house. That would be their starting place. He and Fiona rode with Burke and Carolyn. As was her habit, Carolyn took the lead.

The terrain beyond the Carlisle ranch house spread from a vast, open valley covered with dry winter grasses and sagebrush to forested foothills. As the sun dipped lower, the shadows grew longer.

He rode close to Fiona. Her long brown hair streamed down her back under her fawn-colored cowboy hat. Though small and wiry, she handled her gray horse with skill. In spite of her sneakers, the former California girl looked as though she belonged in the saddle.

They slowed as they approached the barbed-wire fence surrounding a pasture. She gazed toward him with sparkling eyes. "Thanks for letting me come."

He liked having her here. Wherever she went, Fiona had a calming effect. "I want you to use your powers of observation. Your artist's eye might notice a detail that escapes the rest of us."

Her eyes narrowed as she scanned the surrounding forest. "What kind of detail?"

"What do you see?"

"The big picture," she said. "Vast and wide open. Faraway peaks covered with snow. This landscape is spectacular but subtle as well, with a monochromatic palette ranging from sandstone pink to khaki grasses to deep, rich mahogany shadows." She breathed a reverent sigh. "I love being here."

"Wait until it snows," he warned.

"I'm looking forward to it. A white Christmas."

Carolyn stopped at the gate in the barbed-wire fence. With a flick of her reins, her horse, Elvis, wheeled around to face them. "The kidnapper told me to bring the ransom here. I had the money in one of those huge mountaineering backpacks. He told me to leave it by La Rana."

"What's that?" Fiona asked.

Carolyn pointed to a fat rock formation in the middle of the field. It resembled a giant toad. "La Rana, the frog."

Inside the barbed wire were water troughs and feeding stations. The earth had been trampled to a mix of dirt and hay.

"When she delivered the ransom," Burke said, "there were three hundred head of Black Angus in this field. We moved them to get a better look at the crime scene."

A man had been shot and killed at this site. The ranch foreman. He was a traitor, had been feeding information to the kidnappers. But his last act on this earth had been one of loyalty—trying to protect Carolyn.

Jesse dismounted, went to the gate and unlatched it. "Show me what you did, Carolyn."

She rode through the gate, swung down from Elvis and joined him. "I went through here, dodging around the cattle."

Fiona followed in Carolyn's footsteps, leaving her horse behind. "That must have been terrifying. Those cattle are huge."

"Over a thousand pounds each. This field is the last stop before the slaughterhouse, so these cattle were fully grown."

"She wasn't scared," Burke said. "Carolyn loves her cows."

"They're beautiful creatures," she said. "But when the gunfire started and the herd got spooked, I was plenty worried."

"How did you get out of here alive?"

"Burke." She glanced over her shoulder and gave him a grin. "He rode in here and saved me. My hero."

"Aw, shucks," he said. "Any decent cowboy would have done the same."

Carolyn laughed. "As if you're a cowboy? What kind of cowboy wears a Cubs cap?"

"A cowboy from Chicago."

Jesse strode across the dirt toward the boulder, La Rana. "Where was the kidnapper?"

"I never actually saw him. But he was near the rocks.

That's where the gunshots came from. And the ransom was gone almost as quickly as I left it."

Burke, still on horseback, rode up beside him. "We tried to gather evidence, but there was nothing. The cattle obliterated everything. Didn't even find a footprint."

The kidnapper had come up with a simple and effective plan for grabbing the money. He lured Carolyn into the pen, fired his weapon and spooked the cattle. She was too busy trying to make it to the fence to go after him. "How fast did Burke get here?"

"Five to ten minutes."

"In the confusion," Burke said, "the kidnapper made his getaway."

Jesse leaned his back against the rocks and surveyed the area. Hundreds of cattle and dozens of horses trod this patch of earth. Picking out the track of the kidnapper inside the enclosure would be impossible.

Beyond the fence, a couple of dirt truck paths crossed back and forth, providing access for delivering feed to the pasture. The forest reached almost to the edge of the fence on the north side of the barbed wire.

If Jesse had been planning a getaway, he would have preferred the mobility of being on horseback to using a vehicle. "Did you see his horse?"

"Afraid not," Carolyn said. "I was dancing as fast as I could, trying not to get squashed."

Jesse returned to his horse, stuck his boot into the stirrup and braced himself for the jab of pain that came from using his shoulder. The stress on his body was taking a toll, but he couldn't take the time to sit back and recuperate. The fastest route to full recovery would be to find the ransom.

"Where are we going?" Fiona asked.

"We'll search along the perimeter of the barbed wire on the north side," he said. "The kidnapper had to get out of this enclosure, carrying a ransom. His horse must have been tethered in the trees."

"We already searched," Burke said. "None of the fencing was cut."

Still, there might be a sign where the kidnapper slipped through. They left the enclosure and rode slowly along the fence line. Five horizontal strands of barbed wire stretched from weathered posts. The lower two feet were reinforced with chicken wire that would act as a break against snowdrifts.

Jesse knew from experience that climbing through a barbed wire fence was a lot harder than it looked. All it took was one snag to get hopelessly entangled. But these fences weren't impermeable.

Hoofprints at the edge of the fence showed the efforts of a search team, and also obscured any prints from the kidnapper. He wished he could have searched immediately after the ransom had been delivered. The ground was too dry and hard to take neat, perfect footprints. But there would have been broken twigs and shrubs.

He swung his horse around and started back again. "Who were your searchers, Burke?"

"The FBI team had their hands full, rounding up the survivalist gun smugglers. As soon as they were free, we sent the chopper over this area with a spotlight."

That method was akin to using a monkey wrench when you needed a pair of tweezers. Tracking was about noticing the tiny details.

"And the sheriff," Burke said. "He and his deputies looked over here."

"Sheriff Trainer seems to be establishing a regular pattern of searching and not finding."

He paused at a spot where the top strand of wire had been pulled loose from the staple attaching it to the post. In the packed earth outside the fence, he saw rectangular marks about eighteen inches apart.

"Over here." He pointed to the sharp-edged tracks in the dried grass about ten feet away from the fence.

Carolyn dismounted and measured the distance between the two marks with her hands. "A ladder. He rested a ladder on the top wire and climbed over."

"Consistent with his m.o.," Burke said. "Low-tech."

"But effective," Carolyn said. "No wonder he got out of here so fast."

Burke scowled. "How did we miss this?"

"Good question," Jesse said. Once again, he was thinking of Sheriff Trainer. He'd been quick to point the finger of suspicion at Fiona. To divert it from himself?

"I don't get it," Fiona said. "Did the kidnapper make a getaway on horseback while he was carrying the backpack with the ransom and a ladder, too?"

"He must have disposed of the ladder." Jesse peered into the thick forest. "If they'd made a full search with one man posted every three feet, they would have found it."

"And what would that prove?" she asked.

"Not a damn thing. We don't need the ladder. Finding this track is enough."

"Enough for what?" She cocked her head, curious about his process. "We already know the kidnapper was here and took the ransom. So what are we looking for?"

"We want to pick up his trail, which probably starts

somewhere in those trees. Then we can track him, figure out where he went from here."

She gave a quick nod. "Got it."

"Spread out," Jesse said. "Let's move into the trees."

They dismounted and led their horses into the forest. Daylight was fading, and he hoped they could pick up the trail before dusk settled. Tracking at night presented a whole other set of problems.

It was Fiona who called out, "I found something."

He hadn't expected her to be able to notice a track. She wasn't a hunter. "What is it?"

"Well, I stepped in it. There was a horse here, and he left behind a nasty little present." She stood with her foot in the air above a dried pile of manure. "Can I wipe off my sneaker?"

"No way." Jesse turned to Burke. "Those road apples are evidence, right?"

He stifled a chuckle. "Absolutely."

Jesse took out his cell phone. "Stand right there, Fiona. I need a photo of this. Lift that foot up a little higher."

Aware that she was being teased, she pointed her toe and posed. "How's this?"

He took the shot. Even with dried manure on her shoe, she was damned cute. "Okay, now let's zoom in for a close-up."

"I'll zoom you." Laughing, she dragged the sole of her shoe across the trunk of a tree. "Okay, smart guy. I found where the horse was. Let's see you do your tracking thing."

His "tracking thing" turned out to be easier than he expected. He hunkered down and studied the hoof marks. Immediately, he noticed, "This horse was missing a right front shoe."

"Like the horse at the Circle M," Fiona said.

"The black mare that Abby wanted to ride." That minor

irregularity meant this track would stand out from the many others. "Finally. We caught a break."

"What break?" Carolyn demanded. "What are you two talking about?"

Fiona explained, "We were over at the Circle M earlier today. One of the horses owned by the SOF had thrown a shoe. The kidnapper must have been riding that horse when he picked up the ransom."

"Which means," Jesse said, "that we now have a trail."

His instincts were leading them in the right direction. Though he wasn't a detective, he had found the key to this investigation by being true to himself. He should have done that from the start, followed the course of less thinking and more action.

THOUGH FIONA WOULD have enjoyed staying with Jesse and Burke while they tracked, the trail got really complicated: uphill into the forest, then across a rocky area and down to a dirt path. It was obvious that they'd be tracking for hours, and she needed to pick up her daughter from Belinda's.

She and Carolyn returned to the Carlisle ranch house.

Inside, they were greeted by Carolyn's mother, Andrea. A tall, slim woman in denim and cashmere, Andrea greeted them with a warm smile. She didn't hug. Andrea was reserved.

She'd divorced Sterling Carlisle and left the ranch when Carolyn and Dylan were children. Fiona couldn't imagine ever leaving Abby, no matter what the circumstance. But she was sympathetic to Andrea, who—according to Carolyn—had wanted the children to move with her to New York City. Both Carolyn and Dylan had chosen the ranch.

As an adult, Carolyn had spent some time with her

mother, who was remarried and had a twelve-year-old daughter. Their relationship seemed okay. When Carolyn called her mother and told her that Nicole had been kidnapped, Andrea hopped on a plane and came to the ranch to offer her support in this time of family crisis.

Dylan hadn't been happy to see his mother.

"Good news," Carolyn told her. "We found a track from the kidnapper's horse. Burke and Jesse are following the trail."

A frown pinched Andrea's brow. "I wish there was more I could do. I feel so helpless."

"We all do," Fiona said.

"You must stay for dinner," Andrea said to her. "You and your adorable daughter."

"It's been a long day," she said. "Especially for Abby. I think it's best if I take her home and get her to bed early."

Until that moment, she hadn't realized how anxious she was to get home. She was looking forward to tonight when she would spend time alone with Jesse. He'd promised to return to her house after he and Burke reached the end of their trail.

She had a fleeting thought of sitting close beside him on the sofa, their thighs touching. He'd caress her cheek. She'd trace the line of that tiny scar on his chin. She dragged herself out of her reverie. "But thank you, Andrea."

"Maybe tomorrow I could come to your house for a visit," she said. "Carolyn tells me that you're an artist. I'd like to see your work."

Fiona sensed something more than polite interest in her comment. "I don't have many pieces here. I left several sculptures in storage with an artist friend in Denver, and there's a shop in Cherry Creek that takes my pottery on consignment."

"You might want to dig out your portfolio," Carolyn said as she patted her mother on the shoulder. "Mom runs an art gallery in Manhattan."

With another smile, Andrea said, "I'm always looking for new talent."

Fiona blinked as if a flashbulb had exploded in her face. Opportunities appeared in mysterious ways. "A gallery?"

"I try to showcase artists from across the country. What's your focus?"

"Right now I'm working on pottery that's a variation on the Navajo wedding vase with a drinking spout on each side."

"I'd love to see it," Andrea said. "Tomorrow morning?"

"It's a date."

This timing couldn't be better. She'd been working on a Web site to sell her handiwork. If Fiona could get her worked placed in a Manhattan gallery, her reputation would increase by leaps and bounds. It might even be possible for her to make a living selling her art.

As she hurried out the door with Wentworth, a shiver went through her. Earlier today, her outlook had been pretty gloomy. But now things seemed to be going well. *Maybe too well.*

For one thing, Jesse and Burke had found a tangible trail that might lead to the ransom.

For another, Carolyn's mother had opened the door to possible career opportunity.

And then, there was Jesse. The attraction she felt toward him was growing deeper with every shared glance, every smile, every laugh. An electricity arced between them whenever they touched. She couldn't deny that their friendship was poised on the verge of becoming something more.

And wouldn't that be…amazing? To make love again? To spend the night in his sheltering embrace? It was too much to hope for.

Another shiver creased her spine. Being too happy was dangerous.

Chapter Fifteen

The kidnapper had taken an erratic escape route, dodging into the cover of the trees, up toward a ridge, down to the fence, then back to the forest. Jesse read the tracks and the mind-set of the man who made them—a man who was running scared.

At the time of the ransom pickup, all hell had been breaking loose. Burke described three hundred cattle in the pen, bawling and jostling. A dozen ranch hands poured into the area near La Rana. Two other FBI operations were under way. There had been helicopters, bullhorns and armed assault teams.

No wonder the kidnapper had been clashing back and forth. He was a villain and a criminal but also a mouse peeking out of his hole and hoping to get away.

Finally, he'd settled on a route, eventually leaving the Carlisle Ranch and riding parallel to the main road. Since his horse had lost a shoe, he avoided the hard surface of the pavement. *A lucky break for Jesse.* He had a trail to follow, and it led into Riverton.

By the time he and Burke reached the edge of town, dusk had turned to darkness.

Jesse dismounted and shone his flashlight on a hoofprint at the shoulder of the road. There was no corresponding print on the opposite side. He walked to the corner of the street and back again, finding plenty of other footprints and the track of a mountain bike. No hoofprints. "This is it. End of the trail."

He surveyed the area. There were mailboxes on posts and long driveways. Lights shone through the windows of small frame houses, set back from the road. A single street-light cast dim illumination on the rural neighborhood.

"There could be witnesses," Burke said.

"In a town like Riverton, seeing a man on horseback wouldn't be unusual."

"You never know. I'll contact the sheriff and have his men canvass the area."

"Sheriff Trainer." Jesse spoke the name with undisguised disgust. "He's already missed too many clues. His men should have found these tracks."

"Doubtful." Burke adjusted his baseball cap. "I've done my fair share of hunting, and I've never seen anybody follow a trail the way you just did, especially in the dark. Admit it, Jesse. You're half bloodhound."

Jesse grinned. "Are you calling me a dog?"

"Where the hell did you learn how to track like this?"

"When I was a kid, I spent summers on the reservation with my grandfather, a wise man. He taught me a lot."

"Ute?"

"Navajo." Jesse turned toward the lights of the main street in town. He hated to think they'd come this far to reach a dead end. "Why was he headed into town?"

"He must have planned to meet up with his buddy,"

Burke said. "I can't think of anybody else he'd want to see in Riverton. Most of the townsfolk thought the Sons of Freedom were troublemakers."

"The track we've been following," Jesse said, "do you think it was Butch or Richter?"

"My gut tells me it was Richter. When the ransom was being delivered, he was quick on the trigger. Just like he was when he shot you."

"My gut agrees with yours." Obviously, Richter was the more dangerous of the two. "But if Richter had the ransom, why did he kill his partner?"

"Greed." One of the most common and deadly of motives.

"Carrying a million dollars in a backpack, he sure as hell wouldn't want to be seen. There had to be a damn good reason why he risked coming into town. More than that, why did he cross the road here? At this particular street?"

Burke concluded, "His destination in Riverton—wherever it was—must be nearby."

A block away was the main commercial strip. They mounted and rode at a walk on the edge of the pavement toward the stop sign. Riverton was too small to merit a stoplight or a grocery store. The people who lived here shopped in Delta where Jesse had been in the hospital.

Though it was only seven o'clock, most of the storefronts were dark, except for their twinkling Christmas decorations. The only activity seemed to be at the far end of the block-long business district where the tavern and the diner were located. A number of cars and trucks were parked at the curb outside those two establishments.

They approached the gas station, a shabby-looking place. The office windows were streaked with grime, as were the three garage doors on the repair bays.

"I've never seen this gas station open," Burke said. "The old guy who runs it keeps his own schedule."

"Silas O'Toole." Jesse remembered the incident that took place when he and Wentworth had driven through town. "I saw him in action with a double-barrel shotgun in his hands, warning some cowboy to get off his property."

"What was the argument about? A flat tire?"

"O'Toole has a grandson who works with him. A mechanic, I guess. Silas mentioned his parole officer. The grandson took off before he had finished some work for the cowboy."

"He left town," Burke said. "When?"

"Right after I got out of the hospital. The day after the ransom was delivered." Jesse paused. The significance of this episode was beginning to sink in. "Damn it, I should have paid more attention."

The timing was right. O'Toole's grandson could have been working with Richter and Butch, could have gotten a payoff from them and blown town. *Why didn't I make this connection sooner?* There wasn't time for mistakes.

Jesse dismounted. His boots hit the pavement of the parking lot outside the gas station and jolted him into a state of alertness. There was one light over the pumps and one over the door. He needed his flashlight to peer into corners.

Around the back of the station, four cars—all in varying states of disrepair—were parked. The stink of oil, gas and grit hung in the air. He and Burke prowled, looking for hoofprints in the mud. He needed a sign, an indication that the kidnapper had been here.

"I should have paid more attention," he said. "A grizzled old guy in overalls waving a shotgun is a pretty big clue."

"Or just local color," Burke muttered. "I'll tell you what.

I've had enough of ranches and cattle and cowboys. Can't wait to get back to my office in Denver."

"What about Carolyn?"

"She works in Denver, too. Don't let her cowgirl persona fool you. She's a high-powered businesswoman who likes sushi for lunch and Gucci for shoes. It's a damn good thing. I love Carolyn, but I don't think I could live out here."

"I could."

Though he hadn't been thinking about settling down here, or anywhere else for that matter, Jesse enjoyed mountain living. Every view was as pretty as a postcard. The air was fresh. He liked being here, especially because Fiona was here.

The minute he thought of her, his heart beat a little faster. A vision of her gentle smile filled his mind. He saw her long hair flowing behind her as she rode beside him. Tonight, they'd have some quiet time together. He'd make sure of that.

At the front of the gas station, he twisted the handle on the door to the office, hoping that O'Toole's lax business practices extended to leaving the place wide open. No such luck. The door was locked.

He went to the repair bays and yanked on the first garage door. Also locked.

The second door slid up with a loud screech that made their horses jump. He turned to Burke and grinned. "Ready for a little breaking and entering?"

"No problem. I'm an FBI special agent."

"Which doesn't put you above the law."

"But gives me a lot of experience in coming up with plausible, semilegal excuses."

Jesse entered the garage and turned on the bare-bulb

lights. The inside of the auto repair area gave new meaning to the concept of neglect. Tools scattered across a grime-encrusted counter. Grease-stained rags overflowed a metal barrel. A worn calendar from 2002 showed a sexy redhead in black leather chaps leaning against a motorcycle. These concrete floors didn't look as though they'd been swept since the day that calendar was new.

It didn't take long to find a hoofprint on the floor, clearly outlined in a combination of mud and grease. "There was a horse in here, but this hoof has a shoe. There's no way of knowing if it was the kidnapper's mount."

"It was him." Burke rose from the floor where he'd been picking through a pile of trash. "I might not be a bloodhound, but when it comes to finding money, I'm top dog."

In his gloved hand, he held a grease-stained one-hundred-dollar bill. Part of the ransom.

AFTER FIONA GOT ABBY to bed and made sure Wentworth was comfortable, she got busy in her studio at the rear of the house. Tomorrow, Carolyn's mother would be coming to see her work, and Fiona wanted to show her best pieces.

She still needed to finish the glaze on her interpretation of a Navajo wedding vase. Her intention had never been to create a replica; she didn't presume to understand the rituals of the wedding ceremony. Instead, she'd taken inspiration from the idea of two spouts rising from one vessel: one for the bride, the other for the groom. She liked the idea of both drinking from the same source while maintaining a separate identity.

Though she'd started with the traditional coiled pot method, her creation was more fanciful. The long spouts rose from delicate vines that curled around the pot with overlapping leaves—an effect that was both modern and organic.

She carefully painted a pearly white glaze on the once-fired bisque-ware. The design was elaborate enough without painted embellishment.

Since it didn't make sense to fire up the kiln for only one piece, she found herself adding glazes to a couple of other chalices and cups. The theme of her current work seemed to be drinking. Was she thirsting for something?

"Jesse," she murmured.

These designs had been completed before she met him. But since the moment when she first recognized the man who saved her husband's life, Jesse had never been far from her mind. She'd been ready for him to come into her life.

After placing the pottery in the kiln, she carefully put away the glazing chemicals that she kept in a locked cabinet far out of Abby's reach. She set the timer on the kiln.

What else could she show to Andrea? She pulled open the cabinet doors and started opening boxes that she hadn't touched since she moved into the cabin. Going through these pots and sculptures was like reading a diary.

Before Abby was born, her work had been bigger. The largest piece was two feet tall—an eruption of roses that she'd saved because the coppery glaze was so vivid. She'd been thinking of her marriage when she sculpted this bouquet. Though it was bright and happy, the technique lacked maturity and depth.

After her daughter was born and her time for work was more limited, she made several whimsical little houses. Dwellings for fairies. Her plan had been to build an elfin city, a magical place. Many of these houses had sold, but she still had a few left.

After her husband's death, her work turned predictably dark. Charred vases. Jagged abstract shapes. She opened a box and took out an eight-inch-tall sculpture. A tree struck by lightning with clawlike branches and a glaze that reflected dark, bloodred in the crevices.

The tree appeared to be screaming and dying. When she'd carved these lines, she'd been driven by sorrow and rage. Now she could turn it around in her hands and calmly admire the emotion without being affected by it. "Not bad."

Definitely, she'd show this one to Andrea.

Though her kiln was properly vented, the small studio always got extrahot when she was firing her work. She stripped down to her black sports bra.

Even if Andrea didn't want any of her work for her gallery in Manhattan, this was a useful project. She could photograph these pieces for her Web site. She dug deeper into the cabinets, looking for a photo portfolio of some pieces she had on consignment in Denver.

Andrea had asked for her focus, but Fiona hadn't really settled on a particular style. Her pottery reflected her emotional state, which ranged from happy as a cloud to miserable as a lump of coal.

She wanted to sculpt Jesse. His handsome face showed depth of character. His hands were gentle but strong. Creative energy raced through her veins. Where was her sketchbook? She hadn't felt so dynamic in a very long time.

In a burst, she sketched him. Wearing a flat-brim cowboy hat. Clenching a fist. His dark eyes were fierce. His smile was predatory and, at the same time, sexy as hell. Oh, yes, she'd like to be devoured by him.

A rivulet of sweat trickled between her breasts. Her ponytail was damp on her neck. The intense heat came partly from her kiln, but mostly from an internal fire. She needed to take a break before she erupted.

Leaving her studio, she went through the kitchen to the back door, unfastened the locks and stepped outside. The chill of the night air rippled around her. She lifted her hair off her neck.

When she inhaled a gulp of air, her lungs cooled. She exhaled a contented sigh. She'd been utterly consumed by artistic inspiration, and it felt amazing.

The world settled slowly around her, and she became aware of night rustlings. The wind rattled the bare branches of the aspens at the front of the house.

She noticed movement among the pine trees near the barn. Then she saw him clearly. A man separated from the shadows. He was moving fast, coming right at her. He had a gun in his hand.

Chapter Sixteen

At the ramshackle home of Silas O'Toole, Jesse followed while Burke took the lead. He liked the big FBI agent and thought they made good partners.

Burke was particularly adept at logistics. With a couple of phone calls, he'd found O'Toole's address and arranged for a few ranch hands to drive into town, take their horses back to the stable and provide them with an SUV.

Burke hammered on the door. "Open up. FBI."

Remembering O'Toole's double-barrel shotgun, Jesse had drawn his weapon. He held it down at his side in his right hand. His left shoulder had begun to ache. If he hadn't been running on adrenaline, he would have been tired.

"Silas O'Toole." Burke pounded on the door again. "FBI."

The frame house was midsize, set back from the street on a large front lot covered with dead weeds. An old beat-up sofa sat on the porch. A light shone through a curtained window, and Jesse could hear the television from inside.

The door creaked open. Silhouetted by the dim light inside the house was an old man with wild hair. He wore faded red long johns under baggy jeans that hung from his hips.

Silas growled, "What do you want, Mr. FBI man?"

"We're looking for Zeke O'Toole. Is your grandson here?"

"Nope."

When he started to close the door, Burke blocked it with his foot. "We need to talk."

The old man's eyes were tired. His scrawny shoulders slumped. "What the hell has Zeke done this time?"

"Can we come in?"

O'Toole stepped back. "Suit yourself."

The interior was dingy. A half-eaten sandwich and a can of beer sat on a littered coffee table in front of the television. Using the remote, O'Toole turned off the TV. He flopped into an armchair.

Jesse stood behind Burke, allowing him to ask the questions. "Do you know where Zeke is?"

"Grand Junction, most likely. A couple of days ago, he sold a car. Got cash for it. That money was burning a hole in his pocket. The boy went into Grand Junction to have himself a good time. Ain't nothing wrong with that."

"When did he sell the car?" Burke asked.

"I don't know. Maybe the day before yesterday. Zeke don't tell me everything."

"But he lives here," Burke said.

"When he's between girlfriends, he comes back here. It ain't much, but it's home."

Jesse figured that the cash payment came from the ransom. After the pickup, Richter rode into town to the gas station, where he took the car from Zeke.

As Burke questioned the old man about his grandson's friends and possible association with Richter and Butch, Jesse felt his cell phone vibrate in his pocket. He took it out. Wentworth was calling.

Turning his head, he answered, "What's up?"

"Somebody came after Fiona."

A shock jolted Jesse's system. His fingers tightened on the phone. "Is she all right?"

"She's fine." Though Wentworth's voice was steady, a note of urgency tinged his words. "I didn't see the guy. She said he was running toward her, coming from the barn. He had a gun."

"Was she outside?"

"She went out the back door. It was only for a second."

Long enough for her to be shot or abducted or scared to death. What the hell had she been thinking? He'd told her a dozen times that she wasn't to leave the house. He should have been there to protect her.

"On my way," he said. "I'll be there in less than ten minutes."

FIONA STOOD AT THE foot of her daughter's bed and watched her child sleep. The light from the hallway shone on Abby's round, cherubic face and her blond curls. So sweet. So completely innocent.

More than anything, Fiona wanted to grab Abby out of the bed and carry her away to somewhere safe. How could they possibly stay here? The armed man who came running at her through the shadows was a tangible threat—different than hearing voices in the night or assuming there might be danger. He was real.

The instant she'd seen him, she'd dodged back into the house, called for Wentworth and locked the door. Was it Richter? The kidnapper? What did he want?

Her arms yearned to hold Abby, but she didn't want to pass her terror on to her child. It was far better if Abby stayed asleep and unaware. Facing the threat was her mother's job. Fiona's job.

Leaving the bedroom door open, she went down the hall to the front room. Her gaze fastened on the closed curtains at the window, and she shuddered. He could be out there, hiding in the shadows, peering inside. She pulled her sweater more tightly around herself.

"Jesse is on the way," Wentworth said.

"He's not going to be happy. I went outside. I broke his rules."

"He'll get over it." Wentworth leaned against the door leading into the kitchen with his gun in his hand. "Jesse never stays mad for long."

Though she shouldn't have gone out the door, her action had provoked a response. At least, she knew that her suspicions had a basis in fact. Someone was watching her.

From outside, she heard a vehicle approaching.

Wentworth moved to the window and peeked before unlocking the front door.

A car door slammed. In seconds, Jesse charged through the door. So much energy exploded around him that the air seemed to ripple. His eyes were fierce. Without breaking stride, he came toward her. His strong arms encircled her and held her close.

She clung to him for all she was worth. Her tears came quickly. Tears of relief. He was here. Her protector. She was safe. She literally trusted Jesse with her life. He'd never let anything bad happen to her or Abby.

He murmured, "Are you okay?"

"A little scared."

He stroked her hair. "Do you want to tell me why you went outside?"

"Not really." She wiped the dampness from her cheeks and looked up at him. "But I will."

"Okay."

She owed him an explanation. His instructions about staying in the house had been explicit. "I fired up the kiln in my studio. The room was really hot, and I thought I'd step out for a minute to cool off."

He glanced over his shoulder at Wentworth. "Where were you?"

"Front room, sitting on my butt and thinking everything was fine."

"It's okay. Not your fault," Jesse said.

"By the time I heard Fiona call for help," Wentworth said, "she was already back inside and locking the door. We both went down the hall to Abby's bedroom."

With his arm still around her, Jesse escorted her to the sofa in the front room. After he seated her, he spoke to Wentworth. "Agent Burke and two other ranch hands are waiting outside. I'll stay with Fiona. You take charge. See if you can find this creep."

"And be careful," she piped up. "He has a gun."

The door closed behind Wentworth, and Jesse sat close beside her. She snuggled under his arm and rested her head on his chest. His jacket still held the cold from the night, but his body heat warmed his shirt. For a long moment, she listened to the steady beating of his heart.

"Jesse, what am I going to do? I can't stay here. Not with some crazy person running around."

"You're worried about Abby," he said.

"Tell me what to do." She looked up into the depths of his dark eyes. "I trust you."

Though they were nestled together, his kiss surprised

her. This wasn't a gentle, reassuring kiss. It was hard and demanding. Hot.

Unaware of her movements, she shifted position on the sofa until she was facing him. Her body pressed hard against his chest. There were too damn many clothes in the way. She wanted to be part of him, wanted him to make love to her.

His tongue forced her lips apart, and she welcomed him into her mouth. He exhaled a groan and the sound excited her even more.

When they broke apart, she was breathless and eager for more. She ducked her head and dove toward him, seeking another intense kiss.

"Wait," he said.

"Why?"

"Think about it," he said.

She'd been through a long dry spell when it came to sex, and she was thirsty, parched. She licked her lips.

Of course, they couldn't make love right now. The timing was all wrong. Burke and Wentworth were outside but could return at any moment. Abby was sleeping down the hall. And a madman had threatened her with a gun.

"All right," she said. "Not right now. But soon."

"I never should have left you here alone."

"You didn't. Wentworth was here." She caressed the plane of his cheek. "You've done everything right."

He lifted her off his lap, returning her to a position beside him on the sofa cushions. "I'm glad you trust me."

"Why wouldn't I? Longbridge Security is the best in the West."

"My reputation is no guarantee. You saw what happened to Nicole."

With a quick peck on her forehead, he rose from the sofa and went toward the kitchen. She followed behind him. "You know how I feel about guilt. There's no point to it. You can't blame yourself for what's happening to Nicole. My God, you almost died trying to rescue her."

He opened her refrigerator door and took out a bottled water. "I'm mad. At myself. I failed to protect my client."

And she knew that he wouldn't rest until he found the ransom and Nicole. "Where did the trail lead?"

"To another suspect. Nothing definite."

He took a long taste of the water, and she watched his Adam's apple bob up and down. He'd been on horseback for hours and had to be exhausted. Only a few days ago, he'd been in a coma and near death. "Are you in pain?"

"Hey, I'm the one worrying about you. Trying to figure out what we should do to keep you safe."

"I could pack up and move to a motel." Though she didn't like to spend the money, she wouldn't hesitate if it meant keeping Abby safe. "I hate to tell Abby what's going on. I don't want her to have nightmares."

"I'll keep two men posted outside your house tonight, and I'll stay inside. We ought to be fine." He reached toward her. His fingers combed through her hair. "I wish I could promise you that I'd keep you and Abby safe. Wish that I could say I've never lost a client. But it's not true. I've made mistakes."

"You saved my husband's life."

In a way, he was saving her, too. Bringing her back to life. Reminding her of what it meant to be a woman.

"Three years ago, I was hired as a bodyguard for the family of the CEO of an oil company. They were vacationing at a private lodge in Telluride. I had two other men with me, expert skiers."

"Do you ski?" she asked.

"And snowboard. Why does that surprise you? I grew up in Colorado."

"So, you ski, ride, hunt and are an expert marksman. What about rock climbing and canoeing?"

He nodded. "It's part of the package for Longbridge Security. We protect people who are active in outdoor activities."

"Is there anything you don't do?"

"I get seasick," he admitted. "I'm fine on rivers with a canoe or kayak, but put me on the open sea and I turn green and puke my guts out."

It was nice to know that he wasn't expert at everything. "Sorry for interrupting. Go ahead with your story."

Before he could continue, there was a rap on the front door. They returned to the front room, and Jesse unlocked the dead bolt to admit Wentworth, Burke and two cowboys from the Carlisle Ranch.

Burke sank down onto the sofa and groaned loudly. "I don't know how you guys ride all day. My butt is killing me."

Fiona glanced down the hall toward her daughter's bedroom. "Sorry about your butt, but would you all mind moving to the kitchen? Abby's sleeping."

The men tromped across the floor. Loud as a herd of Angus. Burke groaned again as he sat in a kitchen chair and stretched his long legs out in front of him.

"We didn't find him," he said. "But there were plenty of signs that somebody has been lurking around here."

"Did he leave a trail?" Jesse asked.

"After spending the day with you," Burke said, "I was able to follow his tracks. He went to the driveway, then down to the road. Then nothing."

Fiona busied herself making coffee. Her supply of healthy snacks had dwindled to a couple of packages of granola bars, which she placed on the table while Jesse outlined the bodyguard schedule for the night.

She stood by the counter, watching the coffee drip into the glass pot, trying to make sense of the situation. She looked toward the five men gathered at her table. An FBI agent. Two cowboys. Wentworth. And Jesse.

"I have a question," she said.

Their heads turned toward her. In their overwhelmingly masculine presence, she felt small and feminine. But she wasn't helpless, couldn't allow herself to be a shy little violet. The safety of her child was at stake.

"This afternoon," she said, "we were following the track of the kidnapper who picked up the ransom. Which one was it?"

"We don't know for sure," Burke said. "But we're figuring it was Richter."

"So he had the money," she reasoned.

"Then he killed his partner," Burke said.

"Why?" Her voice was louder than she intended. "He has the money. His partner is dead. Why is he still hanging around?"

"He *had* the money," Jesse said. "But he must have lost it. Butch might have gotten it away from him. Or even Nicole."

Burke added, "When the ransom was being delivered, there were dozens of FBI swarming the area. SWAT teams. Helicopters. They might have figured they should hide the cash and lie low."

"And there's a fine hiding place in your barn."

She pieced together the logic. "So, one of them brought the money here and hid it."

"It's possible," Burke said.

"Then what? The ransom just disappeared?"

No one had an answer.

Without further evidence, they were playing a guessing game. All she knew for certain was that Pete Richter had come after her. And he didn't seem like the kind of man who gave up easily.

Chapter Seventeen

A few hours later, Fiona lay on her bed—too tense to sleep or even to close her eyes. In those brief, terrifying seconds when she saw Richter running at her, he had a gun in his hand. If he'd wanted to kill her, he could have taken a shot. But he didn't fire his weapon. Instead, he charged from the shadows in a desperate attempt to do…what?

She knew well enough that bad things sometimes happen for no discernible reason, but that adage generally applied to natural disasters or car accidents or illnesses. People had motives. What did Richter want from her?

She rolled over to her side. For tonight, she felt safe. Jesse had deployed a team of bodyguards outside her house, and he was inside, wide awake. Through her partially opened bedroom door—a safety precaution in case Richter crashed through her window—she could hear him pacing in the front room.

Only a few hours ago, she'd been in his arms, kissing him and wanting him to make love to her. Her body still yearned for his touch.

She flipped onto her belly. Even if they didn't make love, she wanted to be with him. The way she felt about

Jesse was more than hormones and passion. She trusted him. Within moments after they met, she'd told him her secrets. She truly believed that he'd keep her safe no matter what the threat. Damn it, what did Richter want from her?

The answer came to her in a flash. Simple. Obvious. Why hadn't she thought of it before? She threw off the covers, grabbed her plaid flannel bathrobe, cinched the tie around the waist and went down the hall to tell Jesse.

He was waiting for her. He leaned against the sofa facing the hallway. His right hand rested on the butt of his sidearm, ready for action. His lean, muscular frame radiated strength. No bad guy in his right mind would mess with Jesse Longbridge.

He grinned at her. "What took you so long?"

"Do you think I can't stay away from you?"

"I think you want to talk. I could see it when you went off to bed. Actually, I was counting on it."

Because he wanted to make love to her? The hormonal urges that she'd put aside when alone in her bedroom rushed to the forefront of her mind. She totally forgot her brilliant yet obvious insight. "You were counting on me? To do what?"

"I need some practical help."

"P-p-practical?" If he was talking about lovemaking, that was a really odd description. "Isn't that kind of clinical?"

"It is." He unfastened the first button on his shirt. Then the second. His chest was smooth. His skin, vibrant. The color of a mocha latte. "I need some help changing the bandage on my shoulder."

He pivoted and strode into the kitchen, leaving her gaping. Mentally, she shook herself. He wanted her as his nurse not his lover. She trailed behind him, her wool socks shuffling on the hardwood floor.

On the kitchen counter, he'd laid out the necessary anti-septics, soap, bandages and towels. "I thought we should do it in here," he said. "The bathroom is right next to Abby's room, and I don't want to wake her."

"Are you planning on making a lot of noise?"

"That depends." He arched a suggestive eyebrow. "Will you be gentle?"

He was most definitely leading her on, and she didn't mind being led. But she did have something important to say. "I figured out why Richter is after me."

"I thought you might come up with something." He un-buttoned the rest of his shirt. "You have the mind of an in-vestigator. You're smart and creative. You can look at a problem and see all the possibilities."

He slipped off his shirt.

She struggled to maintain an air of detachment, to look at him as if he were one of the models she sculpted in art classes. His shoulders were wide, slightly out of propor-tion to his narrow hips. His torso wasn't overly muscled like a bodybuilder's, but his abs were nicely defined. There wasn't an ounce of flab on his torso. He was, in her opinion, a perfect male subject, worthy of Michelangelo.

She froze, unable to speak or think or do anything but stand and stare as he peeled off the adhesive and removed the gauze bandage. Black sutures closed the jagged wound, leaving an angry red scar.

She stammered. "D-d-does it hurt?"

"Not the stitches. The wound is healing, but the muscles are still sore, especially when I lift my arm above my shoulder." He illustrated and winced. "Like that."

The muscles in his upper arm flexed as he raised his hand above his head and gave a new perspective to his body. She wished she had a camera to record his pose. Not that she'd ever forget this moment.

She thought of the various sculptures in her studio, each representing the way she'd been feeling at the time. The happy little houses. The angry trees. The empty vessels.

Jesse represented a new phase in her life. Sensual and strong.

"Fiona? Are you going to tell me what you figured out?"

She tore her gaze away from his torso and got busy, grabbing a washcloth from the counter. "Let me get this cleaned up. Is this some kind of special soap?"

"I don't know. Wentworth said to use it."

She turned the water in the kitchen sink to hot, held the washcloth under it and worked the soap into a light lather. When she touched his chest, his flesh quivered. A corresponding shiver went through her. "When I came into the front room, you said you knew I wanted to talk. Why?"

"You had that look. When there's something going on inside your head, your eyebrows tilt up. And I was right, wasn't I?"

"How did you get to know me so well?" She carefully washed the area around his wound, holding her other hand at a clumsy angle to keep from touching his chest.

"The same way you know me. We have a connection."

"We do." And it was more than the link that came when he saved her husband's life so many years ago. "It feels like we were meant to meet at this particular time and place."

"And walk the same path through life."

She wasn't so sure about that. "Your path is a lot more dangerous than mine."

"Not at the moment," he reminded her.

"Okay, here's what I figured out. You and Burke assumed that Richter was the one who rode into town and exchanged his horse for a car he bought from Silas O'Toole's grandson."

He nodded.

"What if it was Butch? Butch grabbed the ransom and stashed it someplace before he met up with his partner. That's why Richter killed him." She rinsed the washcloth in the sink and wiped away the soap on his shoulder. "Richter is coming after me because he thinks I know where Butch hid the money. Because of the secret room in my barn where Nicole was held, he thinks Butch and I were working together."

"Maybe he thought you and Butch were lovers."

"Eww."

"You saw those photos of Butch Thurgood. He was a rodeo star. A good-looking cowboy."

"Not my type." Her type was the man standing bare-chested in front of her. "Richter's suspicions are completely unfounded. They don't really have anything to do with me."

"It has everything to do with who you are," he said softly. "You're so pretty and sexy that even a snake like Richter assumes you have a lover."

"Oh, pul-eeze." With the towel, she patted his shoulder dry. "You make it sound like I'm some kind of sultry siren, luring cowboys to my ranch."

He stroked his fingers through her long hair and spread the tresses on either side of her face. "The new woman in town. The mysterious, desirable Widow Grant."

With a flip of his wrist, he unfastened the sash that held her robe together. His right hand slipped inside, circled her waist and yanked her toward him. The thin material of her jersey nightshirt pressed against his bare chest. Her body molded to his. She arched her neck, ready for his kiss.

Instead, he dipped his head and nuzzled her ear. His teeth caught her lobe and tugged, causing an electric spark.

Her hands glided across his bare back. Her fingertips savored the texture of his skin and the hard muscles beneath.

He held her firmly. One hand stroked her back. The other cupped her bottom and fitted her tightly against his hard erection. She ground her hips, pushing hard, pinning him against the kitchen counter.

His mouth was hot, demanding, passionate. As he kissed her, the spark ignited and fire surged through her veins. She clawed at his back, wanting him, needing him.

In a seemingly effortless move, he scooped her off the floor and lifted her onto the countertop. Her thighs spread. Her bare legs wrapped around him as he peeled off her bathrobe.

She heard a sound outside the sphere of their passion.

Jesse reacted immediately. He separated from her, grabbed his gun and crept toward the back door.

She heard Wentworth's voice. "Open up. I'm freezing my tail off."

"Bad timing," Jesse muttered.

While he answered the door, she pulled herself together, fastening her robe and straightening her hair. There was nothing she could do about the heat pulsing through her. She knew her face was flushed and her eyes alit with passion.

Wentworth tromped into the kitchen, bringing the cold with him. His gaze focused on the floor, and he kept moving as he mumbled something about going to the bathroom.

She looked at Jesse—shirtless with a heavy bulge in his crotch. It was ridiculously obvious what they'd been doing.

She grinned. "I think we embarrassed Wentworth."

"He'll get over it."

But their passion—no matter how urgent—would have

to wait. Having guards on rotating shifts patrolling her house wasn't exactly conducive to intimacy.

"I'd like to finish what we started," she said. "And I'm not talking about your bandage."

He embraced her lightly and whispered, "I want to do this right, Fiona. To make love on satin sheets and spend the night holding you. I want your face to be my first sight in the morning."

She sighed and leaned her cheek against his bare chest. "Sounds perfect."

"I want to give you every luxury. All the special little things."

"Been there," she said.

"I know you have."

"Having a lot of things doesn't make you happy. I'm just as warm in faux fur as in a mink coat. And a whole lot more politically correct."

He stepped back and held her at arm's length. "Wyatt was a good man, a good provider, the father of your child."

She hadn't been thinking of Wyatt. His memory was just that: a precious memory. "I'll never forget him."

"He was the love of your life."

He turned away from her, went to the counter and started sorting through the surgical supplies. Though he had moved only a few paces away, it seemed that a gulf had opened between them. Did he resent her love for Wyatt? Was this going to be an issue?

Her feelings for Jesse were too new to understand or explain. She wouldn't call it love. Not yet, anyway. But when she was with him, she felt joy and hope and an indescribable glow.

"When Wyatt died," she said, "my life didn't end. For

a while, I wished that it had. It would have been easier for me to jump into the grave with him."

He turned toward her. "The grave that's right outside your front door."

She hadn't realized how omnipresent Wyatt was in her life, especially in this cabin. There was a photo of him on her bedside table. Abby's room was full of stuffed animals he'd bought for her. The radio was tuned to his favorite oldies station.

"My life is moving forward," she said.

Avoiding her gaze, he glanced down at the scar on his shoulder. "The stitches are almost healed. I don't think I need the big bandage."

He was changing the subject, avoiding an emotional land mine. Usually, Fiona insisted on expressing her feelings, but she was confused. It was better to get back to business. "Let me put on the antiseptic, and we'll finish with a couple of these extra-large patches."

As she tended to his shoulder, he looked away.

She did the same.

They'd gone from blazing hot to icy. Back to business. Tersely, she asked, "What do you think of my theory about Richter?"

"Makes sense, but it doesn't explain the most important thing. What happened to Nicole?"

"According to Dylan, she's gone. She left him."

"Do you believe that?"

"Carolyn said they'd been arguing. Their marriage was already in trouble, but every couple has times like that." She and Wyatt had their share of spats. Good grief, was she thinking about him again? She placed the bandage on Jesse's shoulder and stepped back. "Whatever Nicole said to him was enough to convince Dylan. He believes that she wants a divorce."

He slipped back into his shirt. "When I hear those words from her lips, I'll believe it, too. For now, she's still my client. I need to know that she's safe."

"Do you think Richter is still holding her?"

"Don't know." He took the bottled water and sat at the kitchen table. His long legs stretched out in front of him.

He looked tired, as if the exertions of the day had finally caught up with him. And she wanted to help, to make him feel better. "Are there other leads to follow?"

"Tomorrow morning, I'll start tracking again. This time, I'll start at the place where Nicole and Dylan met."

"At the same time as the ransom was being delivered," she said. "Can I come with you?"

"No." The merest hint of a smile flickered at the corner of his lips. "You're my client, too. I intend to keep you and Abby under guard."

"Richter wouldn't dare come after me if I was with you."

"No? The last time I tangled with Pete Richter, he nearly killed me. He shot first. And I failed at my job."

"You didn't fail." A frustrated sigh pushed through her lips. "This is the last time I'm going to say this—the kidnapping wasn't your fault."

"Tell that to Nicole."

She thought of the tiny secret room where Nicole had been held prisoner, tethered to the bed with a chain, unable to see the daylight. In the proof-of-life videos, she looked strong and upbeat. But she must have been scared.

The natural empathy she felt for Nicole extended to Jesse. He, too, was suffering. He'd taken on the entire responsibility for what had happened, called himself a failure.

She knew that he had ghosts of his own. She asked, "What happened in Telluride?"

His jaw tensed. She knew it was difficult for him to speak of the incident he'd referred to as a mistake. "I never should have brought that up."

"But you did." She sat at the table. "You told me because you feel like you can trust me. I want that, Jesse. I want to understand you."

"I'm not complicated."

"The hell you aren't." She took his hand. "Tell me."

He exhaled in a whoosh. "Private lodge in Telluride. A CEO, his two teenaged daughters and his wife."

"Were they all skiing?"

"Not the wife. She preferred staying home, reading a book or knitting. A nice woman. I'll never forget the look in her eyes when I told her that her husband had been shot."

Fiona suppressed a gasp. "What happened?"

"The daughters weren't hurt. And their father survived. Barely." He squeezed her hand. "I didn't see the sniper in the trees. Not until it was too late."

She wanted to reassure him, to tell him that he must have done the best he could. But she knew the stark, haunted expression in his dark eyes would not be easily assuaged. His pain was too deep. "You're in a rough business."

"And failure has deadly results. I won't rest until I find Nicole."

Chapter Eighteen

The next morning, Jesse planned to leave Fiona's house early and drive to the Carlisle Ranch, where he'd meet up with Burke and follow the second kidnapper's tracks, much as they'd done yesterday.

He finished brushing his teeth and left the bathroom. In the back of his mind, he was kind of hoping to skate out the door without saying too much to Fiona. He wouldn't purposely avoid her; that would be cowardly. But their talk last night raked up bad memories of a time when he'd almost lost a client. Painful, but he could cope. He'd had years to deal with that failure.

What he couldn't handle was their intimacy—the taste of her kiss, the pressure of her slender body against his, the silky texture of her long hair, her scent and her sighs. His desire for her opened a whole new arena of regret. He connected with her. From the moment they met, he had a sense that she was the woman he wanted at his side as he walked through life. But she'd already found her one true love in Wyatt Grant, and Jesse could never replace him. Falling in love with Fiona would only break his heart.

Steeling himself to face her, he strode into the kitchen.

Abby was at the kitchen table, chatting happily with one of the ranch hands who had spent the night on patrol. Jesse gave the young man a nod. "MacKenzie."

He nodded back. "Morning, Jesse."

Abby bounced down from her chair, took his hand and led him toward the counter. "Come here. Right now. You need coffee."

He followed the bossy, little blonde pixie. "And why are you so sure of that?"

She rolled her baby-blue eyes. "Everybody is sooo tired today."

"I suppose you're right." After a night of rotating shifts with the other men guarding her house, he'd gotten barely enough sleep. And his dreams had been troubled.

"You have to pour it yourself," Abby said as she went to the refrigerator. "I'm not allowed to touch hot stuff, but I can get the milk."

She held the nearly empty container up to him. Though he usually took his coffee black, he added a dollop of milk. "Thank you, Abby."

"I'm a very good hostess."

"You took good care of me."

"I know," she said. "And I would take very good care of a pony."

"Would you give him coffee?"

"Silly." She laughed. "Ponies eat oatmeal."

As she flounced back to the table, he helped himself to a blueberry muffin. No fruit this morning. Food supplies were running low. Later today, somebody would need to make a run to the market.

He gulped down the coffee and ate the muffin over the sink. If he moved fast, he could make his escape without running into Fiona. To MacKenzie, he said, "I'm heading out. Tell Wentworth that I'll be back by noon."

He was unlocking the back door when he heard Fiona's voice behind his shoulder. "Were you going to leave without saying goodbye?"

He turned. Caught. "Goodbye."

She looked rested and alert with a touch of makeup on her wide gray eyes and a glossy pink lipstick. Her shiny brown hair hung in a neat braid down her back.

"Not so fast," she said. "I'd like your opinion on one of the pieces I fired in the kiln last night."

"Can't help you." He gazed longingly at the door. "I don't know much about art."

Much like Abby, she took his hand and pulled him down the hallway to her studio. The females in this family had a definite bossy streak. "My inspiration for this piece was the Navajo wedding vase."

The interior of her studio was transformed. The last time he was in here, sketch pads and tools were piled on the worktable. Now that space held a neat display of finished artworks—small sculptures of bright-colored houses, exotic plants, strange-looking creatures and a variety of pots and vases.

"I liked the idea of the wedding vase," she said. "With two spouts rising from the same vessel. Separate but joined together."

A pearly glaze shimmered on a pot that seemed to be made of leaves. Wintery but not cold. Her talent impressed him, but her words sank deep. *Separate but joined together.* A marriage didn't have to be all-consuming. He touched the pearly ceramic. "It's like living ice."

She beamed. "You like it."

"I like all of it." Some of the odd little animals made him smile. The shapes on the pots were fascinating. "You're good."

"Andrea—Carolyn and Dylan's mother—is coming over this morning. She owns a gallery in Manhattan. If I can convince her to show my work, I gain instant credibility."

With the way she wore her heart on her sleeve, he should have expected this creative side to her personality. She was one of the most expressive people he'd ever known. Every minute he spent in her company fascinated him and drew him closer. "Andrea would be a fool not to show your work."

She went up on tiptoe and gave him a quick peck on the cheek. "That's what I needed to hear. Now you can go."

Now he wanted to stay. He picked up one of the pots— a simple, functional shape with a geometric design of orange and deep blue. "This reminds me of some of the Navajo artists. My grandfather would have liked it."

"That's a terrific compliment. I know how important he was to you."

Jesse remembered. "I dreamed about him last night. I saw him walking across a high mesa. There was a woman with him. A blonde woman."

"Nicole," she said.

"I called her name, and I raced toward them, leaping from one rock to another. But I didn't get any closer. You know how that is? Running in a dream?"

"I know."

"My grandfather came to the edge of the cliff and raised both arms to a glaring sun. The light flared. Nicole was gone."

He feared for her, feared that Richter had killed her and left her body in a shallow grave. Searching these mountains would take months, even years. They might never find her body.

"What does it mean?" she asked.

He wouldn't voice that fear, wouldn't give it substance by saying it aloud. "When my grandfather turned around, I was next to him. Close enough to touch the leather medicine pouch that hung from his neck, but I didn't reach toward him."

Though he didn't believe the lore about ghost-walkers and shape-shifters, he respected the dead. "He spoke to me in Navajo. I don't understand the language very well, but I knew what he was saying. 'Follow your path.'"

"Like the trail you followed into town," she said. "Maybe he was telling you that you're on the right track."

Jesse frowned. He didn't know what the hell his dream meant. He was tired of riddles and pieces of clues. He wanted to know exactly what to do next. "I should go."

"I'll be here waiting."

Whether he liked it or not, he knew that his path would always lead back to Fiona.

AT THE CARLISLE RANCH, Jesse didn't bother going inside. He went directly to the stables. The bay horse he'd been riding yesterday nickered when he came close to his stall. He was a good mount, even-tempered and sensitive to direction. Within a few minutes, Jesse was saddled up and ready to go.

Outside the stable, another rider was waiting. "Need some help?"

It was Dylan. A mantle of anger and grief still draped around him, but there was a different energy as well—a sense of determination.

"How are you at tracking?" Jesse asked.

"Pretty good. I'm a hunter." He nodded back toward the house. "Burke won't be joining us. He got a lead on the whereabouts of Zeke O'Toole."

Jesse flicked his reins. "Let's see what we can find."

Together, they set out across the south pasture. Jesse didn't need directions to the creek where Nicole had met with her husband. It was near the same place Jesse had witnessed the actual kidnapping—the place where he'd been shot.

To their east, a panorama of ranch land, valley and rolling hills stretched toward distant snowcapped peaks. Wispy clouds streaked the blue skies, and sunlight brightened the khaki winter fields. Though he couldn't help but marvel at the vast beauty of this land bordering the edge of the forest, Jesse had a sense of foreboding. Dylan must have been feeling much the same way. At this quiet glen in the forest, his wife had told him their marriage was over.

He glanced toward the man riding beside him. In his shearling jacket and fawn-colored Stetson, Dylan Carlisle was one-hundred-percent cowboy. He'd lived on this land all his life; the acreage and cattle belonged to his family. A heavy responsibility.

When Dylan first hired Longbridge Security—only hours before the kidnapping—he'd been tense. His ranch was under assault from vandals who had burned down an old stable. Though he didn't like the idea that he needed bodyguards for protection, he wasn't rude or arrogant.

The last time they met, Dylan had lashed out at him. *Justifiably,* Jesse thought. Still, it hadn't been Dylan's finest hour.

They slowed as they reached the winding path that led to a stream. In springtime, this trail would have been green and beautiful. Now the white branches of aspens were skeletal and bare. The shrubs were brown, spiky clumps.

Jesse ignored his memory of being shot. They were here to find out what had happened after Dylan met Nicole. Earlier, the cowboy accepted her at her word; he had refused to search for his wife.

"What changed your mind?" Jesse asked.

"Burke told me about what you'd found yesterday. The trail that went into Riverton. Buying a car from Zeke." He shook his head. "This kidnapping plot is more complicated than I thought. Butch is dead. And why is Richter still hanging around?"

"Got to be the money," Jesse said. "Are you thinking we might be able to get the ransom back?"

"I don't give a damn about the ransom." He reined his horse beside the trickling stream. "Here's where she met me."

He stared hard at an empty space in front of a tall spruce. His jaw tightened. Though Jesse could tell that Dylan wasn't a man given to emotional display, he saw a tear spill down his cheek.

He continued. "It wasn't the first time Nicole told me off. We're going through a rough patch in our marriage. Trying to get pregnant. When she said she wanted a divorce, I believed her. And now…" He cleared his throat. "Now I'm thinking I might have been wrong. That she's still out there being held prisoner."

Or worse. Not a thought Jesse wanted to dwell on. "Let's see what we can find."

"A couple of my men were already out here," Dylan said. "They picked up a trail that led toward Fiona's house."

"One rider?"

Dylan nodded.

Jesse was pretty sure that wasn't right. There should have been two sets of tracks. His assumption was that Nicole had been accompanied by one of the kidnappers. Why else would they split up?

One of them grabbed the ransom and rode into town. The other stayed with Nicole. He sat up in his saddle and scanned the surrounding forest. "I'm guessing that she didn't come to this meeting alone. One of the kidnappers was with her, maybe holding a gun on her."

"You think she was coerced? That they threatened to shoot her if she didn't say what they wanted?"

Dylan drew that conclusion quickly. He must have already been considering the possibility that Nicole was acting under duress.

"You're a hunter," Jesse said. "If you wanted a clear shot at this spot, where would you hide?"

"Uphill. It was just after dark when I met her. There are plenty of places he could have been hiding in the trees."

"Leave the horses here." Jesse dismounted. "I'll go left. You go right."

He climbed slowly, taking note of every broken twig, every mark on the ground. The stream attracted more than kidnappers and victims. There were hoofprints from elk. At the base of a pine tree, he found a squirrel's cache stuffed with pinecones.

"Found a boot print," Dylan called out.

The vantage point where Dylan stood was uphill. A sniper in that position would have had a clear shot at Nicole, unless she made a sudden break and raced toward the ranch. She was a good rider, experienced enough to know that she could have escaped, especially since the kidnapper wasn't on horseback.

The beginning of an idea began to take shape in his mind. "Be there in a minute."

He found what he was looking for. A neat set of boot prints behind a tree. His horse had been only a couple of yards away, hidden behind a boulder.

There were two kidnappers watching Nicole, holding a gun on her. Two at this spot. Another at La Rana to pick up the ransom.

Butch and Richter had help.

Chapter Nineteen

When Fiona welcomed Andrea into her house, she was fully aware that this meeting could change her career.

The sophisticated Manhattanite greeted her and Abby with warm hugs. Gazing around the front room, Andrea said, "I haven't been in this house for years. Over twenty years, in fact. Sterling and I used to play cards with the Grants."

"Wyatt's parents," Fiona said. She found it hard to believe that Andrea was part of a prior generation. She didn't look older than forty. And a fabulous forty, at that.

"We used to laugh all night. Drink gallons of wine and ride home singing at the top of our lungs." Her voice was tinged with nostalgia. "Not many people knew that side of Sterling Carlisle. Everyone saw him as the patriarch, the founder of Carlisle Certified Organic Beef."

"And now your children are carrying on his legacy. You must be proud of them."

"Proud? Yes. Also worried."

How could she not be worried? She'd returned to a ranch in the midst of trauma. Fiona placed a sympathetic hand on her shoulder. "Would you like a cup of tea?"

The only coffee Fiona had left was instant. Her food

supplies were running low after feeding all the bodyguards and search teams that had descended upon her house.

"Nothing for me," Andrea said. "With the way Polly has been feeding me, I'll never fit into my clothes when I get back to New York."

"She's an amazing cook," Fiona agreed.

Abby piped up, "Polly gives me cookies."

There had been a time when Fiona would have been gushing with apologies and embarrassed about the lack of fresh ground coffee and the less than pristine condition of her home. During her marriage, she'd taken her duties as a hostess seriously, knowing that Wyatt would be judged on her performance. If Fiona's hemline had been too short or if she'd served the wrong wine with dinner or if she laughed too loudly, people would talk.

Now she was free to be herself, and she liked the feeling. *A fresh start.* Jesse had mentioned walking together on a new path, discovering new adventures. That was the route she wanted to take.

Abby rushed to the dining room and climbed onto a chair. She pointed to the colorfully painted Santa Claus ceramic centerpiece. "I made this."

"It's lovely," Andrea said.

"Mommy says we're going to get a Christmas tree pretty soon and decorate."

"And what do you want from Santa?"

"A pony," Abby said quickly.

Fiona lifted her daughter off her perch and settled the child onto her hip. Though Abby was almost too heavy to carried, she couldn't be allowed to run free in the studio—not while there were so many pieces on display, tempting Abby to touch.

Fiona unlocked the studio door, ushered Andrea inside and got out of the way. Her artwork needed to speak for itself. There was nothing Fiona could say to convince an experienced dealer like Andrea to give her a chance.

Abby, on the other hand, was bursting with comments about the fairy houses and animals and big pots.

While Andrea viewed the many objects on display, her eyes were hard and analytical. "You have talent, Fiona. And imagination. I've seldom seen such a wide range of pottery and sculpture."

Fiona listened for the "but." *Talented, but... Skillful, but...*

Andrea continued. "You're an emotional artist. I can see your happiness. Your anger. And your fear."

But...

"I'd like to show your work. In late spring, I've arranged for a couple of other sculptors." She mentioned an impressive list of artists. "Your pottery would fit in quite well."

She gave Abby a squeeze. Their financial situation was about to take a turn for the better. She couldn't wait to tell Jesse. "Thanks so much."

"We'll work out the details," Andrea said. "Why don't you and Abby come home with me? I'm sure it'll be easier for all of us to be guarded at the same time. We have plenty of food. And coffee."

"And horses," Abby said.

Fiona whipped out her cell phone. "I need to check with Jesse first, but I'm sure it'll be okay."

She wanted to believe that everything would turn out well. It felt as though the tide had turned, and luck was on her side.

At the Carlisle ranch house, Fiona and Abby were well protected. All the ranch hands who weren't actually working the cattle were armed and assigned to guard duty.

After lunch, she and Abby took a walk toward the stable with Carolyn. Fiona said, "It looks like the Old West around here. All these cowboys with rifles."

"The amazing thing," Carolyn said, "is that most of these guys are even less enlightened than their 1800s counterparts."

"Yeah, yeah, yeah. I know you love this ranch."

"But my home is in Denver." She tipped her cowboy hat back on her forehead. "I can't wait to get back to my high-rise condo with the Jacuzzi bathtub and the walk-in closet. I have a pair of designer stilettos in acrylic and silver that I've never worn."

"Not to mention the extra benefit," Fiona said. "Burke lives in the city. Is he more enlightened than a cowboy?"

"I have tickets for *The Nutcracker* next week, and he agreed to go with me."

"To the ballet?" Fiona had a hard time imagining the big, rugged FBI agent sitting still for an evening of Tchaikovsky and tutus.

"He promised. And the ballet is where I'm going to wear those stilettos for the first time."

Fiona appreciated the irony of discussing ballet and designer shoes on her way to the stable with a woman who was dressed like the archetypal cowgirl in jeans and dusty boots.

They reached the corral where Carolyn's horse, Elvis, greeted them with a toss of his head. She lifted Abby onto the second from the top rail on the fence so she could reach across and pet the horse.

"I love Elvis," Abby said. "What are stilettos?"

"Shoes with pointy heels. You've seen the ones I have."

"You don't wear them anymore."

And she didn't miss them. The realization hit her that she was happy living here, running around in sneakers, climbing the hills and breathing the mountain air. Even if she became a successful potter with a display in Manhattan, she'd choose to live here.

Looking out across the south pasture, she saw two men riding toward them. Jesse was in front, leaning forward in a gallop. The unexpected sight of him took her breath away. On horseback, he looked powerful and incredibly masculine. No matter what Carolyn said, cowboys were sexy.

Carolyn nudged her shoulder. "Is there something going on with you and Jesse?"

"I hope so."

She should probably be guarded about what she said around Abby, but Fiona had never been able to hide her feelings. She was drawn to Jesse as a friend, a protector and—please, God!—a lover.

Abby waved with both hands. "Jesse! I'm over here."

He rode up beside the corral fence. "I see you, Abby."

"Did you catch the bad guys?"

"Not yet." He leaned down and lifted the little girl off the fence onto the saddle in front of him. "But I caught you."

Fiona liked the way he swooped in and took charge, walking his horse in a wide arc while Abby held the reins and chatted at a million miles an hour.

Dylan, who had been riding with Jesse, dismounted beside them. He turned toward his sister. "I might have been mistaken about Nicole."

"You? Wrong?" Carolyn looked up toward the sky and squinted. "What's that I see? A pig flying?"

"We don't have time for jokes," he said. "Where's Burke?"

"In the house."

"Take care of my horse." He tossed the reins toward her and stalked toward the ranch house.

As Carolyn watched him, the grin faded from her face. "He's so much like our father. Stubborn. It'd serve him right if Nicole never came back to him."

"You don't mean that," Fiona said.

"Of course I don't."

But the ongoing stress showed in her eyes. Everyone at the ranch was trying to maintain calm, but an undercurrent of dread tinted every conversation. They couldn't help worrying about Nicole, couldn't help fearing the worst.

Fiona's cell phone rang, and she answered. It was Belinda with a request. She had the chance to take another shift at the café and hoped Fiona could take of Mickey for a few hours. "I wouldn't ask, but I really need the money."

Fiona checked with Carolyn, who nodded and said, "I think we can make room for one little boy."

"Here's the deal," Fiona said into the phone. "Abby and I are staying at the Carlisle Ranch, and Carolyn says it's okay for Mickey to come here."

"The Carlisle Ranch? Wow." Belinda paused. "If Nate ever found out that his son visited the Carlisles, he'd explode."

"Is that a problem?" Fiona asked.

"Not for me."

She could hear the smile in Belinda's voice. "See you at four."

Jesse dismounted with Abby tucked under his arm and placed her on the ground. When he stood, his gaze linked with Fiona's. A burst of excitement surged inside her. She hadn't told him about Andrea yet, about new possibilities.

"You two can talk," Carolyn said as she took Abby's hand. "We cowgirls need to go into the stable and tend to the horses."

"Really?" Abby skipped beside her. "Can I help?"

"Only if you do exactly as I say. Got it?"

Jesse leaned against the corral fence. His boot heel hooked on the lowest rung. He took off his hat, smoothed his black hair and put it back on. "We found evidence that there was a third person involved in the kidnapping."

Her news about Andrea would have to wait. This was big. "Tell me."

"At the place by the stream where Dylan met Nicole, we found two sets of prints. Two men. They were positioned in such a way that they had a clear shot at both Nicole and Dylan."

Fiona understood immediately. "They threatened her. If she hadn't told Dylan those things, they would have killed both her and Dylan."

The kidnappers' threat had produced the effect they wanted. Dylan had been convinced by Nicole's performance, and he called off the search for her.

"After she talked to Dylan, Nicole rode south. Near your house, she was joined by both men. They rode to a graded dirt road. We couldn't find tire marks, but a car must have been parked there."

"Zeke O'Toole's car," she said.

He nodded. "I'm assuming that one of them drove into town to hook up with the third man. He's the one who was holding the ransom."

"And where was Nicole?"

"She had to be in the car. Tracks showed that the kidnapper who had been left behind rode to the Circle M to return the three horses. Two horses were riderless."

She hung on every word of his explanation. It amazed her that he'd discovered so much from tracking. "Then what happened?"

"The trail stops there. We don't know what happened next, but I'm assuming two of the men—probable Butch and Richter—came back here, and you heard them arguing."

Once again, the clues had led to her house. "Why here? What were they looking for?"

He shrugged. "I've been asking myself the same question. And I don't have an answer."

"If the sheriff was here, he'd probably tell you that they rode back toward my house because I'm the mastermind of the whole kidnapping scheme."

"Sheriff Trainer has some explaining to do," he said. "Dylan and I found these tracks. Why didn't he?"

"Maybe he didn't know where to look."

"That's what Dylan said. None of the other trackers thought to look up higher on the hillside, to check possible sniper positions."

"You're a better tracker than they are."

"I'm not a genius," he protested.

She reached toward him, and pointed her forefinger, counting each of the buttons on his shirt. "But you're good. Very good. Better than average."

"And how do you know that?"

"Intuition."

A slow grin spread across his face. God, he was handsome. His voice was low and sexy as he asked, "What else does your intuition tell you?"

That we're meant to be together. That you're the man I'm meant to spend the rest of my life with. It'd be crazy to blurt out that kind of declaration. They'd only known each other for a matter of days—not long enough make a life-changing decision. She'd only just decided that she might be interested in sex. Making plans for the future? She wasn't ready to take that giant step.

"My intuition says..." she dropped her voice "...that we should make love as soon as possible."

"I'll put it on my schedule," he said. "Right after I protect you from a deranged killer, rescue Nicole, and find the ransom."

"If we wait too long, you'll be gone."

"Maybe not."

She couldn't guess what that meant. That he intended to spend a little more time here? How long? Where would he stay?

It was all too complicated.

She changed the subject. "Andrea liked my sculptures and pots. I'm going to display in her gallery."

"Good news." He gave her a huge hug, lifting her off her feet and spinning her around. "You're the genius."

She laughed. "I'll settle for good enough to start selling."

"Does that mean you're packing up your kiln and moving to New York?"

"No way." The sky behind him was a pure, deep blue. The winter air felt crisp. "This is home."

When he kissed her, it felt good and right.

How long would she have to wait before they finally made love?

How many days should it take for her to tell him that she'd fallen in love with him at first sight?

Chapter Twenty

After a couple of hours in the dining room with the high-powered threesome of Burke, Dylan and Carolyn, Jesse needed a break. He went outside and stood on the veranda. Afternoon shadows spread across the landscape. Sunset was only a couple of hours away. It would be another night with Nicole missing.

The discovery of a third person working with Butch and Richter put a different spin on their investigation. He'd listened to the different strategies, theories and plans from Burke and the two Carlisles. He'd looked at the maps they laid out, reviewed the prior case notes. Nothing in particular resonated.

Thus far, he'd had success as a tracker. Now his instincts told him that it was time to hunt, time for battle. His wounds had healed enough to take on a fight. Damn it, he was ready to kick ass. But whose ass needed kicking? Who was the third man working with Richter and Butch?

Fiona came out of the house and joined him. She rested her forearms on the railing, arched her back like a cat and stretched. Her round bottom presented an enticing target.

She said, "Abby's busy in the kitchen, making cookies with Polly. I thought I'd catch up on the investigation."

"You're asking the wrong guy," he said, still studying her rear end. "I tuned out."

"Come on, Jesse. I want to know."

"And I want to…"

When he playfully squeezed her bottom, she stood up straight and flashed him a grin. "I can't believe you did that."

"No apology. You were asking for it, waving a red flag in front of a bull."

"Okay, Mr. Bull." She twitched her hips. "You've been in the dining room for hours. You must have come up with something."

"Burke's working his cell phone. Carolyn and Dylan are mostly growling at each other."

"They argue a lot," she said. "Strong opinions on both sides."

And not many answers. With a dearth of tangible leads and Richter disappearing into the forest like a jackrabbit, they had to go back to the beginning, starting with the question: who would want to kidnap Nicole? The wealthy, powerful Carlisle family had offended a lot of people over the years. There was a long list of enemies to consider.

"Dylan wants Burke to call in the FBI again." Which Jesse considered a desperate move. "He's not thinking straight. Going door to door and asking questions isn't going to find his wife."

She cocked her head and looked up at him. "Do you have a better idea?"

"Patience."

As he watched, a cowboy on horseback came from the stables at the rear of the house and rode to the front gate.

He wore a gun at his hip and carried a rifle. At the main road, he relieved the guard on duty. Neat. Efficient.

Under Wentworth's supervision, the security at the Carlisle Ranch—using a combination of ranch hands and Longbridge Security employees—was excellent. Not quite military precision but close enough. Jesse owed his old friend a raise in pay. Or maybe a few weeks' paid vacation. *As if that pays him back for saving my life?*

Beside him, she fidgeted. "I have to ask. Patience? What does that mean?"

"The hardest part of hunting is waiting. We've gathered information. Now we wait for the pieces to fall into place. We need one last clue that will make sense of everything."

"Everything?" Her voice was skeptical.

"It's not that complicated."

"Then how do you explain the secret room in my barn?" She held up her index finger. "That's my first question. Number two, who killed Butch Thurgood? Three, who bought Zeke O'Toole's car and why? Four, who's the third man?"

She waved her four fingers in front of his eyes, and he caught hold of her hand. "The only important questions are, Where's Nicole? Where's the ransom?"

Her fingers laced with his and she leaned closer. "How long? How long before all these questions are answered?"

"One explanation will lead to another. Our best lead is Zeke O'Toole. Burke put out a BOLO with the state police."

"BOLO?"

"Be On the Look-Out," he explained. "When we find Zeke and find out who he sold his car to, we'll have answers."

She glanced down. When she looked up again, her eyes gleamed like silver. "I've never been good at waiting."

"It's all part of the hunt." He raised her hand and brushed his lips across her knuckles. It was becoming increasingly difficult to keep his hands off her. "You have to know when to take action. And when to hold back."

Her voice lowered to a sultry whisper. "We're not talking about the investigation anymore, are we?"

"You know what I'm talking about."

"I want you, too."

Everything about her excited him. The curve of her full lips. The way her chin lifted when she smiled. He wanted to make love to her right now. She was sexy and sassy and had made it damn clear that she was ready.

But he wanted more from Fiona than a one-night stand. He wanted a commitment. They were meant to be together; he'd sensed their connection the first time he saw her.

Thinking back to that time, he smiled. Was it only three days ago? Her appearance was so different from when they met. Before, she was waiflike and fragile. "You've changed in the past few days."

"How so?"

He stepped back and framed her with his hands, as if taking her picture. "You've always shown your emotions. Now you own them. You're confident."

Her eyes widened in surprise. "How did you get to be so perceptive?"

"I think I've told you—about a hundred times—that I need to be able to read people in my line of work."

She moved closer again. Her hand rested against his chest. "What am I thinking right now?"

Her body language was clear. This was a woman who wanted kissing. She was filled with sensual longing. Ripe.

"If we were alone," he murmured, "I could tell you

what I see. And what I want. But those words are going to have to wait."

"Why?"

He pointed toward the front gate. Belinda's aged station wagon turned toward the house. She waved to the guard and drove forward.

Fiona straightened her jacket. "I'm glad Mickey's here. Abby has been driving Polly crazy in the kitchen."

Belinda pulled into the parking area and got out of the car. Mickey dashed ahead of her and jumped up the steps to the veranda. "My daddy has a ranch."

"Yes, he does," Fiona said.

"And horses." Mickey puffed out his chest.

Belinda came up behind him. "I really appreciate this, Fiona. Do you think I could run inside and thank Carolyn?"

"Sure."

Jesse held the door and followed them inside. Mickey disappeared into the kitchen, where he and Abby greeted each other loudly. Belinda and Fiona went to the dining room.

Carolyn sat at the head of the dining-room table while her brother paced behind her. Dylan paused when they entered the room and looked toward them. Both Carlisles were striking—tall with black hair and pale green eyes.

As the shapely Belinda, wearing her fringed jacket, black slacks and waitress shoes, approached them, Jesse was reminded of a maidservant approaching royalty. In a way, that's what Carolyn and Dylan were—the inheritors of an empire, a multimillion-dollar, international business.

Intimidated, Belinda almost bowed as she came closer.

Fiona pulled her friend forward. "Carolyn and Dylan, I'd like to introduce Belinda Miller."

"Nate's wife?" Dylan barked.

"Not anymore," Fiona said smoothly.

"Divorced," he said. "I remember something about a restraining order."

"That's enough," Carolyn snapped at him as she rose from the chair and shook Belinda's hand. "Please excuse my brother. He's has the social graces of a jackass."

"Thanks so much for letting my son come over." Belinda's voice was hesitant. "Like I said to Fiona, I need all the work I can get with Christmas right around the corner."

"Belinda works at the café in Riverton," Fiona said. "And that gives me an idea. Everybody in town comes through the café. Belinda could keep an eye out for us. You know, a BOLO."

"I'd like to help out," Belinda said. "I feel terrible about Nicole. She helped me and Mickey rescue a stray dog that got hit by a car. Nicole's got a big heart."

When she mentioned Nicole, Dylan scowled and folded his arms across his chest. He looked angry and imperious, but Jesse saw deeper. Dylan was coming to realize how little he knew about his wife. Nicole had taken the time to be friends with this woman, and Dylan didn't even know her name.

"First thing," Fiona said. "Do you know Zeke O'Toole?"

"Silas O'Toole's grandson? Sure, I know him. A cheapskate, just like his grandpa. Why on earth do you care about him?"

"He might have sold his car to the kidnappers," Fiona said.

Jesse liked the idea of using Belinda's natural contacts. He asked the next question. "How about Pete Richter? Have you ever met him?"

Belinda's chewed her lower lip. "I'm not sure. The Sons of Freedom guys didn't come to the café often. More likely, they were at the tavern."

"There's a photo of Richter on the computer," Fiona said.

Carolyn flipped the laptop with the case file around so Belinda could see. She tapped a few keys. "The mug shots should be in one of the photo files."

But the image that appeared on the screen was Nicole in a proof-of-life photo. In the background was a pale yellow sheet they now knew had been hung on the wall in the secret room under Fiona's barn. Nicole held the newspaper for the day following her kidnapping. The collar of her flowered cotton shirt seemed to emphasize the paleness of her skin. But her jaw was set, and her eyes showed fierce determination.

Belinda gasped. Her hand flew to cover her mouth. "That's after she was kidnapped."

"Sorry," Carolyn said. "Wrong file."

She flipped to the mug shots, zeroed in on the photo of Richter and made it full screen. "This is Richter."

Nervously, Belinda shook her head. "I don't recognize him. But I'll watch for him."

Burke charged into the room, holding his cell phone aloft like the Olympic torch. "They found the car. Sheriff Trainer found it abandoned outside town."

Inside, there would be a wealthy of forensic evidence. Fingerprints. Hairs. Traces.

This investigation was drawing to a close.

AFTER A SHOWER in Silas O'Toole's bathroom, Pete Richter got dressed fast. The clothes he found in Zeke's room fit him just fine. Zeke had a fine collection of Western-style shirts with pearl snaps. Richter chose one with a black yoke. He was glad to get rid of the clothes he'd been wearing for days. Even the squirrels could smell him coming.

After he fastened his holster on his hip and his hand ax on the other side, he put on fresh socks and his boots. Soon, he'd be able to afford everything new. Soon, the ransom would be his. After all he'd gone through, he damn well deserved that money.

He sauntered out of the bedroom and walked through Silas O'Toole's filthy house. The old man had money; he should have hired a woman to clean up this dump and cook some decent food. The only thing in the fridge was baloney and white bread.

He stood in the kitchen doorway and stared hard at his captive. Richter had grabbed Zeke as soon as the punk walked through the front door a half hour ago. His plan had been to make the kid talk right away and get the hell out of there. But he'd been a little too aggressive with his questions, and Zeke passed out. He'd been sitting here, tied to the kitchen chair with duct tape over his mouth, while Richter changed his clothes and got ready to start his new life.

"You're awake," Richter growled.

Zeke's eyes were scared. Blood matted the dirty blond hair on the side of his head.

"If you tell me what I want to know," Richter said, "I won't have to kill you. Understand?"

Zeke nodded.

This was going to be easy. Richter had wasted days trying to nab Fiona Grant. When he overheard one of those bodyguards talking about the getaway car, he almost kicked himself. He hadn't known the car was newly purchased from Zeke O'Toole when he stuffed Nicole into the trunk and drove to the meeting place. All Richter had been thinking about was following the plan he and Butch had been told over the phone.

He'd been stupid to trust the guy who gave them those orders. At first, he'd thought it was one of the guys from the SOF, maybe even Logan himself. He was wrong. All those boys had been rounded up by the FBI.

Then he figured it might be one of the ranch hands at the Carlisle place. One of them had been working with Logan.

Or it could have been somebody from town.

Or one of the sheriff's men, even Sheriff Trainer himself.

When he couldn't figure it out, he settled on Fiona as his best source of information.

Zeke was better. He knew something for sure.

Richter ripped the duct tape off his mouth. The kid took a giant gulp of air.

"About a week ago," Richter said, "you sold one of your piece-of-crap cars for cash. Who bought it?"

"If I tell you, he'll kill me."

Richter took the hand ax from his belt. "I'll do worse than kill you, Zeke."

The kid was almost crying. "I didn't do nothing."

Richter held the sharp edge of his ax under his nose and pushed his head back. "Maybe I'll break all your teeth. You won't look good to the ladies without a smile."

Richter took a step back and buried the ax blade in the kitchen table. "And you are going to tell me."

"I'll talk. Don't hurt me."

And when he did, Richter wasn't too surprised.

Chapter Twenty-One

While Burke and Dylan headed off to meet with Sheriff Trainer at the site where they'd found the car, Fiona and Carolyn roamed around the dining-room table, picking through bits of shifting evidence.

Fiona scanned a map where the routes of the three kidnappers were drawn with dotted lines. *Patience.* Jesse had counseled patience. How long before these lines converged into a pattern? How much time did Nicole have left?

From the kitchen, she heard Jesse talking to the kids, who were both trying to convince him and Polly that one cookie wouldn't spoil their dinner.

Andrea slipped into the dining room and greeted them both. Her manicured hand trembled as she touched her daughter's shoulder. "Do you have any news about Nicole?"

"The sheriff found the car that belonged to Zeke O'Toole," Carolyn said. "There were a couple of blond hairs in the trunk."

"The trunk? Dear Lord." Andrea sank into a chair at the table. "Anything else?"

"Dylan and Burke went to check out the car while they look for fingerprints and trace evidence."

The argument in the kitchen reached a crescendo with both children shouting "please" at the top of their lungs. Andrea glanced toward the racket, then smiled at Fiona. "I'm assuming one of those voices is Abby. Is there another child with her?"

"Mickey Miller," Fiona said.

"Miller? As in Nate Miller's son?"

"That's right," Carolyn said. "And you don't need to remind me of the feud between the Carlisles and the Millers that's been going on forever. Mickey's mother has nothing to do with Nate. She seems like a nice woman."

"You'll get no argument from me. I never understood why your father and Nate's father hated each other so much—other than the obvious fact that Miller was a truly unpleasant individual."

"Nate's the same way," Carolyn said. "Cranky and foul-tempered. He's on our list of suspects. In fact, his little house in Riverton was one of the first places the sheriff searched. He didn't find a thing. Not a hair. Not a fingerprint. Nothing."

Because Nicole had been held in the secret room under Fiona's barn. Trapped without sunlight. Then stuffed in the trunk of a car. Fiona suppressed a shudder. "I want to thank you again, Carolyn, for letting Belinda drop Mickey off here."

"It's what Nicole would have done."

The two children burst into the dining room with Jesse following.

"Mommy," Abby said, "may we please, please, please have a cookie before dinner?"

"Pleeeeeeze," Mickey said.

"Do you promise to eat all your veggies at dinner?"

"Yes, yes, yes."

"One cookie apiece." She lifted her gaze to Jesse's face. "And you can have one, too."

"Last time I checked," he said, "you weren't my mother."

A good thing. Because the thoughts she had whenever he came near to her were anything but motherly. The cell phone in her pocket rang, and she answered.

It was Belinda. Her voice was tense. "Fiona, I need to talk to you. I didn't want to say anything in front of Dylan and Carolyn. But I can tell you."

Leaving the Carlisle house right now was inconvenient to say the least. And Fiona didn't feel right about dumping the kids with Carolyn. "Can it wait until you come to pick up Mickey?"

"I don't know. I suppose so." Her tone was diffident. "I'm probably making too much of this."

"Wait." Fiona had a sense of urgency. As a rule, Belinda was down-to-earth, steady and stable. She wouldn't have called if it wasn't important. "What's wrong? What is it?"

"Nothing. Forget I called."

"I'll be there in twenty minutes."

When she disconnected the call, Jesse was watching her, patiently waiting for the piece of information that would make sense of everything else. "I need to run into town," she said.

"No problem," Carolyn said. "I'll go with you."

Belinda had specifically mentioned that she didn't want to talk in front of Dylan and Carolyn. "Actually—"

"I'll take her," Jesse said.

"Whoa, there." Fists on hips, Carolyn confronted them both. "Something's going on here, and I refuse to be left out of the loop."

"As soon as I know anything," Fiona said, "I'll call on your cell."

"I want to be there."

Her mother gave Carolyn a hug. "Of course, you want to be there. As soon as you learned how to walk, you insisted on leading the pack. That's why you're a terrific CEO."

"Thanks, Mom."

"But Fiona can handle this. She's quite capable. And she has Jesse to protect her." She pointed them toward the door. "Go."

MINUTES LATER, Jesse was behind the wheel of the Longbridge Security SUV, driving toward Riverton. "Did Belinda tell you what was bothering her?"

"She didn't want to talk in front of Carolyn or Dylan."

He remembered how Mickey's mother had quailed in the presence of the Carlisles. "Making a good impression on them is important to her."

"Understandable. Her boyfriend works at the meatpacking plant in Delta, and his livelihood pretty much depends on the Carlisle Ranch." Though her seat belt was fastened, she reached toward him. Her fingers traced the Longbridge Security patch on his jacket. "She sounded scared."

He was already on high alert with adrenaline pumping through his veins. The end of their investigation was near. Like any good hunter, he sensed the nearness of his prey.

And he didn't like the idea of having Fiona with him at this moment, would have felt better if she'd stayed behind at the house where half a dozen guards could be watching. "We need to be careful. Stay close to me. Do as I say."

"I can't imagine that Richter is going to attack me in town. Not with all these witnesses."

He parked on Riverton's main street in front of the café. Though it was only a few minutes after four o'clock—too early for the dinner rush—several other cars were pulled up at the curb. It was the edge of sunset, beginning to get dark.

Inside, the café was decorated for Christmas with red and green ribbons and plastic Santas. Jesse scanned from the booths along the wall to the countertop, counting a total of twelve customers—cowboys, teenagers and a young couple, holding hands across the tabletop.

As soon as Belinda saw them, she led them through the kitchen into the area behind the café. The alley was bordered by a weathered fence that separated the restaurant from a two-story brick building that looked as though it had been built a hundred years ago. A row of metal garbage cans lined the wall behind the kitchen. In summer, there would have been flies and a stink. At this time of year, it was only an eyesore.

Belinda pulled Fiona into a hug. "Thank you for coming. I didn't know what to do."

Fiona comforted her, patting her shoulder and murmuring about how there was nothing to be afraid of. As Jesse watched, he marveled at Fiona's patience with her friend's nervous chatter. Though he was capable of waiting for hours as a hunter, he was already irritated by Belinda's tears.

With a visible effort, she pulled herself together. Using a napkin from the café, she swabbed at the smeared mascara under her eyes. "I heard you talking about a car that somebody had bought recently and how it had something to do with the kidnapping."

"That's right," Fiona said encouragingly.

"Nate bought a car." Her lips tightened. "He told me about it when we were at the Circle M. He said if I needed a car this winter, he had one for me."

Jesse wasn't too impressed with this vague bit of information. "Did he mention Zeke O'Toole?"

She shook her head. "Definitely not. I would have remembered. I just thought Nate was bragging, pumping himself up now that he's left his little house in town and moved back to the Circle M."

Jesse recalled his brief search at Nate's ranch. He should have gone deeper, but the place had been thoroughly scrutinized the day before by both the sheriff and the FBI. Those searches had taken place before Nate moved back. *Before.*

"Thanks for the information," he said to Belinda. "We'll be sure to have somebody check it out."

"I'm so ashamed that I married him." Her lip quivered. "I was young, only nineteen. But that's no excuse."

Fiona patted her shoulder. "You have your own life, your own identity. Nobody judges you because of Nate."

"Did you see the way Dylan looked at me? Like I was dirt under his feet."

"He's upset," Fiona said.

Jesse added, "His family has been feuding with the Millers for years."

"It's not personal," Fiona said. "He doesn't hate you."

"Not yet." Belinda sighed. "There's something else I have to tell you. It's about that photo on the computer. The picture of Nicole after she'd been kidnapped."

"What about it?" he asked.

"She was wearing my blouse. I threw it away a couple of years ago when I left Nate, but I recognized the print. The cardigan, too. They both were mine. And that sheet hanging behind her? I had sheets that same color when I was living with Nate."

A surge went through Jesse. This was the information he'd been waiting for. Everything would now make sense.

He clarified, "You threw those clothes away."

"I never liked the shirt. Nate bought it for me, and he must have pulled it out of the trash." Belinda shuddered. "When I left him, he took it hard. He was watching me and Mickey all the time. Like a stalker."

"That's when you moved into Fiona's place."

"Living there saved my life." She took Fiona's hand and squeezed. "It gave me some physical distance from Nate. He stopped bothering me."

And Jesse knew why. With his handyman skills, Nate had constructed that secret room under the barn where he could hide out and keep an eye on Belinda and his son, watching them every minute. Like a classic stalker, he'd saved her clothing.

And when the time came, he had a ready hiding place for Nicole.

Though Nicole had been initially kidnapped by Richter, Nate had taken her from him. He was the third man. The man who picked up the ransom.

While keeping a watchful eye on the two women, Jesse took a step back. "I need to make a phone call."

He reached Burke, who was with the sheriff, inspecting Zeke O'Toole's car. Jesse was succinct. "Nate Miller is the kidnapper. He's the third man."

Chapter Twenty-Two

Fiona heard the urgency in Jesse's voice as he talked on the phone. Strategies were being planned. The kidnapping was on the verge of wrapping up.

She turned to Belinda. "You should take off work. Go to the ranch and pick up Mickey."

"What's happening?"

"You need to be with your son."

Belinda chewed her lower lip. "Are we in danger?"

It was entirely possible. No telling what Nate would do when confronted. He might go after his ex-wife and child. "It might be best if you stay at the ranch until we get there."

"I never should have said anything."

"Don't think that. Not for a minute." As Fiona stared into her friend's eyes, she saw a reflection of her former self when she was timid and frightened by voices in the night. "You did the right thing, and you should be proud of yourself. Now go take care of your son."

As Belinda retreated into the kitchen of the café, Jesse motioned to Fiona. He closed his cell. "Burke, Dylan and the sheriff are on their way to the Circle M to arrest Nate."

"Do you need to be there?"

"They've got it covered. They aren't far from the Circle M. Burke is trying to set up some kind of strategy, but Dylan is dead set on charging straight ahead. Can't say as I blame him."

They walked through the alley behind the café to the sidewalk. The sun dipped behind the mountains; daylight faded to a murky gray. "You were right about being patient, Jesse. All we needed was the right bit of information. Now everything makes sense."

"Nate called the shots. He told Richter and Butch what to do and where to go." He frowned. "I'm still not sure why he set up such elaborate plans to arrange the meeting between Nicole and Dylan."

"I understand why." The emotional component to the kidnapping was the most obvious to her. "Nate despises Dylan. He wanted his enemy to suffer the same way he suffered when Belinda left him. He's obsessed with his hatred for the Carlisles."

When they rounded the corner onto Main Street, she noticed Jesse glancing left and right, still on the lookout for danger. She knew that he wouldn't take her hand while they were walking because he needed to be ready in case of an attack.

"I saw how crazy Nate was when we were at the Circle M," he said. "I should have—"

"Don't say it."

"What?"

"Don't blame yourself," she said firmly. "Nate has been suspicious from the start. But he's crafty, and he knows how to fly under the radar. The man built a secret room in my barn, and I didn't even know about it."

"The main thing is that we've got him," Jesse said. "This will be over soon."

Then what? After the danger passed, she would have no more need for a bodyguard. "Will you be moving on to another assignment?"

The question hung between them—a question that should have been asked the first moment she felt herself being attracted to him. Would he leave her?

Instead of answering, he hurried her toward the SUV.

A crisp mountain wind tossed the ribbons on Christmas garlands wrapped around the light poles. Pedestrians in jackets and cowboy hats hurried along the sidewalk. A handful of cars and trucks with headlights lit pulled up to the four-way stop in Riverton's version of rush hour.

This little town hadn't changed too much over the years, and the easygoing pace suited her just fine. She didn't need to go faster. At this moment, she wished time would slow down or stop entirely. She didn't want to start counting the minutes until they had to say goodbye.

He held the passenger door open for her. She paused before slipping inside. "I don't want you to leave."

"Until Richter is in custody, I won't—"

"This isn't about Richter. Or Nate." She lifted her chin and looked up at him. "It's about you and me."

Now would be the perfect time for him to take her in his arms and kiss her and tell her that he wanted to be with her. Instead, he nudged her toward the seat. "We need to get going. I told Burke that while we were in town, we'd look in at Nate's old house. It's possible that he stashed the ransom there."

She slid onto her seat, and he closed the door. In her more timid and depressed days, Fiona would have thought that he was rejecting her. She would have given up without a fight.

But she knew that he cared for her. Damn it, their chemistry was undeniable. Hadn't he told her that he wanted to make love to her? Hadn't he said that he wanted their first night together to be special?

As she recalled, that conversation had ended badly, with Jesse talking about her lifestyle when she'd been the wife of Denver's district attorney. A lifestyle when she had everything she wanted. A lifestyle that no longer suited her.

When he slid behind the steering wheel, she said, "At least stay with me for tonight. I'll arrange for a babysitter. It'll be just you and me. I deserve that much. One night with you."

He fired up the engine. "That's not good enough."

Anger clenched around her heart. As he looked over his shoulder to back up, she yanked at the steering wheel. "We're not going anywhere until you explain yourself."

His mouth formed a hard, straight line, but he wasn't angry. Regret and pain registered in his eyes. "I want more than one night with you, Fiona. I want a lifetime. I want to be the love of your life. Your *only* love."

"Is this about Wyatt? About the fact that I was happily married before?"

"I can never be as right for you as he was. I can't compete with a ghost."

"Oh, Jesse." She wasn't sure whether to cry or laugh or knock him over the head. "Wyatt is a memory. You're real. Flesh and blood and one-hundred-percent real. You're the man I want beside me in bed."

"But you'll never stop thinking about Wyatt."

"I won't forget him." He had been a vital part of her life, the father of her child. "But that was a different time. A different place. I guess, I'm different now."

"Yes, you are."

"You saw it," she reminded him. "The way I'm changing."

"And I liked what I saw." Finally, he grinned. "I'm an ass."

"But a very, very sexy one."

"Promise me more than one night."

"As long as you want. I love you."

"I love you, Fiona." His voice was a smoky whisper. "We were meant to walk together through life. It's our path."

"A different path than either of us has ever walked before. Every step of the way is brand-new."

He kissed her, sealing their understanding, underlining the promise. "About tonight."

"We will be together," she promised. "Let's finish up here in town. Then we can get started on the rest of our life."

JESSE COULDN'T BELIEVE how neatly everything seemed to be falling into place. The kidnapping was almost solved. And, more important, he understood his relationship with Fiona. All it took was one simple word: *love.*

He hadn't been this happy in a long time. Maybe never. This was why he'd come back from death. To find her. To discover the possibility of a new life.

"I think you missed the turn," she said. "Again."

Riverton wasn't a big town, but he'd managed to get lost twice on the way to Nate's house. "I must be distracted."

"In a good way?"

"Very good."

He doubled back and found the right road at the edge of town. Along this dead-end street, the small houses were set wide apart. Three in a row appeared to be vacant.

"This one." She pointed.

The one-story cottage had a peaked roof, but the square footage was hardly bigger than a trailer. There was a small barn and empty corral beside it. Lights shone from the house on the opposite side of the street where a truck was parked at the curb, but Nate's house was dark.

Jesse's cell phone rang. It was Burke.

He answered quickly. "What happened?"

"We found her." Burke's voice was jubilant. "We've got her. Nicole's okay."

"The ransom?"

"Not located yet."

"What about Nate?"

"We're still looking for him. Got to go. See you back at the ranch."

Jesse clicked his phone closed and gave Fiona the good news.

With a joyful whoop, she threw off her seat belt and climbed onto his lap. In the space of one minute, she must have kissed him sixty times. She was crazy-happy. Impulsive. Intuitive. Beautiful. Damn, he loved this woman.

"But no ransom," he said.

She jumped off his lap and opened her car door. "Maybe we'll find it inside."

In her excitement, she'd forgotten the standard security procedures he'd lectured her about. As he watched her dash toward the dark, little house, a sense of foreboding rose up inside him. He drew his weapon. "Fiona, wait!"

She halted and turned. The dim glow of a streetlight on the corner illuminated her features. Her beautiful face.

He strode toward her. "You need to do what I say."

Instead of arguing, she nodded. "I got a little carried away."

He was tempted to bundle her into the car and drive away. *Let somebody else search Nate's house.* But the ransom hadn't yet been found. It was his job to follow every lead.

He walked beside her on the packed-earth driveway.

"How are we going to get inside?" she asked.

It'd be easy enough to break a window or pick the door lock. When he prowled around to the rear of the house, he discovered that neither procedure was necessary. The back door had been kicked open. "Somebody got here before us."

"Richter," she said.

And he could be inside the house. Time to call for backup.

Before Jesse could pull his cell phone from his pocket, he heard a sound. It came from overhead.

He looked up. Saw the glint of a weapon. A man crouched on the slanted roof.

He grabbed Fiona and threw her toward the house. She'd be hidden under the eaves.

Gunfire exploded. Four shots.

It seemed impossible that the gunman had missed. They were less than twenty yards apart. *It's not my time to die. I have too much to live for.*

Without taking aim, he returned fire. He dodged to the left, tried to get a better angle.

Heavy shadows hid the shooter as he scrambled up the incline toward the peak of the roof. His outline seemed misshapen, like a hunchbacked gargoyle.

Jesse fired again. He heard a groan.

The man on the roof stumbled. His gun clattered down from the eaves and hit the dirt in front of where Fiona was standing. She darted out from her hiding place and picked up the weapon.

"Give it up," Jesse called up to the man on the roof. "You haven't got a chance."

"I should have killed you the first time."

It was Richter, that son of a bitch. "Raise your hands."

He did exactly that. Jesse saw him clearly. He wore a mountaineering backpack. *The ransom.* In his right fist, Richter held a hand ax.

Time stood still.

Everything went into slow motion.

Jesse saw Richter draw back his arm. The ax hurled toward him, flipping end over end. The blade aimed at his chest, directly at his heart.

He heard Fiona scream.

Jesse hit the dirt.

The effort of flinging the ax threw Richter off balance. He slid down the roof, crashed to the ground.

Jesse leaped to his feet, but Fiona got there first. She stood over the man who had terrorized her with her weapon pointed in his face.

She growled, "Don't move or I'll shoot."

Jesse believed her. Gentle, sweet Fiona had changed a lot in three days.

LATER THAT NIGHT, Fiona stepped through the door to her bedroom. Her hair was brushed to a sheen and she wore her best peignoir of pale blue satin. Jesse was already in her bed. The light of a dozen candles cast enticing shadows on his bared chest.

Abby was spending the night with Andrea at the Carlisle Ranch. There were no bodyguards or ranch hands circling the perimeter of her property. Finally, she and Jesse were alone.

She walked slowly toward the bed. The satin swished around her hips. Almost everything had worked out perfectly. Nicole was exhausted but unhurt. Richter was in police custody. In his backpack was most of the ransom money. They'd found Zeke O'Toole, tied up and scared but still alive. Nate Miller, unfortunately, was still at large.

She sat on the bed and drew a line down the center of Jesse's chest. "When I saw that ax flying through the air toward you, I thought it was over."

"No way would I die before tonight." His grin was slow and sexy. "I had to outsmart death. To get to you."

"This is where you're meant to be."

He pulled her close. "With you, Fiona. Forever."

* * * * *

CAVANAUGH JUDGEMENT

BY
MARIE FERRARELLA

First published in Great Britain 2010
Harlequin Mills & Boon Limited,
Eton House, 18-24 Paradise Road, Richmond, Surrey TW9 1SR

© Marie Rydzynski-Ferrarella 2010

ISBN: 978 0 263 88271 1

46-1110

Harlequin Mills & Boon policy is to use papers that are natural, renewable
and recyclable products and made from wood grown in sustainable forests.
The logging and manufacturing processes conform to the legal environmental
regulations of the country of origin.

Printed and bound in Spain
by Litografia Rosés S.A., Barcelona

Dear Reader,

Welcome back to the Cavanaugh Justice series. This time around, we have Greer O'Brien's story. Greer and her two brothers are the illegitimate offspring of the late Mike Cavanaugh, Andrew and Brian's malcontented brother. Like her brothers, Greer thought that her father was a fallen hero, not a man who refused to live up to his responsibilities. Her mother's deathbed confession has actually hit her hard. It makes her resolve never to lose her heart to a male of the species, because men disappoint the women who love them.

But this is before she is given an assignment she would rather pass on: being the bodyguard for Judge Blake Kincannon, whose life is threatened by an escaped drug dealer. She and Blake have a history. Despite this, the two become aware of the strong attraction humming between them, an attraction neither one can continue to deny.

I hope you like this latest installment in the Cavanaugh saga and as always, I thank you for reading my book. From the bottom of my heart, I wish you someone to love who loves you back.

Marie Ferrarella

USA TODAY bestselling and RITA® Award-winning author **Marie Ferrarella** has written almost two hundred novels, some under the name Marie Nicole. Her romances are beloved by fans worldwide. Visit her website at www.marieferrarella.com.

To
Lily Sterkel.
Welcome to the world,
little one.

Chapter 1

Eddie Munro was the kind of man who reminded narcotics detective Greer O'Brien of the Aurora police department why she'd joined the force in the first place. To put low-life scum like him away.

The least acrimonious way to describe Munro was to say that he was a career criminal with a rap sheet that was longer than he was tall and, at five feet eleven inches, that was saying a great deal. There apparently was no hint of remorse in the man's heart, no well-buried twinge of guilt associated with any of the victims who he had harmed during his ambitious climb up the drug-dealing ladder. He was, and always had been, the most important person in his universe.

Greer could tell that simply by looking into the drug dealer's eyes. They were flat, cold and calculating, and could have just as easily belonged to a reptile as to a flesh and blood human being. She saw it now, in the courtroom, and she'd seen it then, when the sting she'd been part of had gone down, successfully snaring Munro in its net. They were dead eyes, silently telling her that this arrest was merely a temporary aberration, an obstacle to be surmounted.

He looked, she thought, as if he had some secret guarantee that he would be out again soon, pushing his people to hook naïve, thoughtless teenagers in search of diversion on drugs, eventually turning large numbers of them into wraithlike creatures willing to sell what was left of their souls for the next fix.

Greer could see that same look in Munro's eyes now, as she looked at him across the marginally populated courtroom. He was sitting at the defense table, dressed in a suit his attorney was hoping would transform him from a minor kingpin in the organization into a respectable-looking member of society.

But nothing could transform his eyes. They were looking at her and there was murderous contempt in the brown orbs.

Contempt and more than a small amount of anger that he was being inconvenienced this way.

It made Greer long—just for the tiniest of seconds—for the days of vigilante justice that had thrived in the Wild West before law and order had prevailed. Because vigilante justice would have disposed of worthless creeps like Munro without so much as a fleeting second thought.

There were no second chances with vigilante justice.

But even as she thought it, Greer knew in her heart that if such a thing as vigilante justice was alive and well, she would have been part of the first line of defense against it. It was inherently in her blood to uphold the law.

But that didn't mean she didn't find this whole tedious "due process" of crossing *t*'s and dotting *i*'s trying, she thought irritably.

Because it wasn't enough to catch vermin like Eddie Munro in the act and arrest him. He had to be convicted, as well—and that was always tricky. Despite the fact that the man was as guilty as sin, conviction was never a foregone conclusion, because there were lawyers involved. Lawyers who earned their fees—and possibly a rush, as well—by digging through technicalities, searching for that one little "something" that had been overlooked, some obscure loophole that would somehow serve to set the Eddie Munros of the world back on the street to prey on the defenseless.

The need to present the case against him and prosecute Munro to the full measure of the law was why she was here, sitting in a place she avoided like the plague whenever possible. More than half an hour ago she had solemnly sworn to "tell the truth, the whole truth and nothing but the truth so help me, God." She would have willingly sworn to almost anything if it meant locking away one more evil vulture for as long as legally possible.

It wasn't that courtrooms—or testifying—made her nervous. What they did was make her angry. Angry because, like it or not, all the hard work that she and the men and women she worked with in the narcotics division could be thrown out on one of those aforementioned technicalities. One overzealous movement by a wet-behind-the-ears rookie cop could jeopardize months of hard work.

But she knew that this was part of the game, part of the system, and she was determined to do everything she could to put that soulless pseudo Drug Czar of Magnolia Avenue, as Munro liked to refer to himself, away. She would have preferred putting him away for good, but ultimately, she would take what she could get. Every day Munro wasn't on the street was another day someone else potentially avoided becoming addicted.

Greer was well aware that every victory counted, no matter how small.

The sound of a door sighing closed registered and she glanced toward the back of the courtroom, just in time to see the chief of detectives, Brian Cavanaugh, make his way down the far aisle and slip into one of the near-empty middle rows.

What was up?

Greer couldn't help wondering if the well-respected chief was here because of the case in general, or because his daughter, Janelle Cavanaugh-Boone, was the assistant district attorney prosecuting this case.

Or if, by some remote chance, he was here to lend her his support. Brian Cavanaugh was, after all, her newfound uncle.

The thought would have coaxed an ironic smile to her lips if the overall situation hadn't been so grave. And if she wasn't currently on the stand, testifying and being relentlessly grilled by Munro's defense attorney, Hayden Wells, an oily little man who, despite his posturing, was not all that good at his job.

The latter discovery—that Brian Cavanaugh was her uncle, that she, Kyle and Ethan were actually related to the numerous Cavanaughs who populated the police force—still boggled her mind a bit, as she was fairly certain it did her brothers. Triplets, they tended to feel more or less the same about the bigger issues that affected their lives and learning that they had been lied to by their mother all their lives was about as big an issue as there was.

It was only on their mother's deathbed that the twenty-six-year-old triplets learned that the man they had believed was their late father, a war hero killed on foreign shores nobly defending freedom, never even existed. He had been created by Jane O'Brien in order to make her children feel wanted and normal. In truth, they were conceived during a brief liaison between Mike Cavanaugh, the sullen black sheep of an otherwise highly respected family, and their mother, a woman who had fallen hopelessly in love with the brooding policeman.

Angry, hurt, bewildered, the day after the funeral Kyle had marched up to Andrew Cavanaugh, the former chief of police and family patriarch, and dropped the bombshell that there were three more Cavanaughs than initially accounted for on the man's doorstep.

Rather than rejection and scorn, which was what she knew Kyle was expecting, she and her brothers had found acceptance. Not wholesale, at least, not at first, but rather swiftly down the line, all things considered.

Taken in by the family, that left Greer and her brothers to work out their own feelings regarding the tsunamic shift that their lives had suddenly experienced. To some extent, they were still wrestling. But at least the angst was gone.

Pacing before the witness stand as he addressed her, Munro's defense attorney paused. The slight involuntary twitch of his lips indicated that he wasn't satisfied with the way his round of questioning was going. At the outset, it seemed as if he was winning, but now that conclusion was no longer cast in stone. The balding attorney's voice rose as his confidence decreased.

The momentary lull allowed Greer to shift her eyes to the side row again. She was surprised to make eye contact with the chief of detectives. And even more surprised to see the smile of approval that rose to his lips.

He mouthed, "Good job," and at first, she assumed that Brian had intended the commendation for his daughter's efforts. But Janelle had her back to the rear of the courtroom—and her father.

The approval was intended for her.

Greer realized that a smile was slowly spreading across her own lips. She'd always told herself that, like her brothers, she was her own person and that approval didn't matter.

But it did.

She could feel the warmth that approval created spreading through her, taking hold. Ever so slightly, she nodded her head in acknowledgment of her superior. Of her uncle.

The next moment, she heard the judge's gavel come down on her right. Her attention returned to the immediate proceedings.

Alert, Greer waited to hear what the judge had to say, trying not to dwell on the fact that she was sitting far closer than was comfortable to Judge Blake Kincannon.

It wasn't that she had anything against Kincannon—she didn't. In her opinion, Aurora's youngest judge on the bench was everything that a model judge was supposed to be. Fair, impartial, compassionate—but not a bleeding heart—he was the kind of judge who actually made her believe that maybe, just maybe, the system could actually work. At least some of the time.

Added to that, Blake Kincannon even *looked* like the picture of a model judge. Tall, imposing, with chiseled features, piercing blue eyes and hair blacker than the inside of a harden criminal's heart, Kincannon was considered to be outstandingly handsome and quite a catch for those who were in the "catching" business.

No, Greer's discomfort arose for an entirely different reason.

She was certain that whenever Judge Blake Kincannon looked at her, he remembered. Remembered that she was the patrol officer who had been first on the scene of the car accident two years ago. Remembered that she was the one who had tried, unsuccessfully, to administer CPR to his wife as she lay dying. And remembered that she was the one who, when he regained consciousness at the hospital after the doctors had stabilized him, broke the news to him that his wife was dead.

Not exactly something a man readily put out of his mind, she'd thought when Detective Jeff Carson, her partner for the past year, had told her who the presiding judge on the case was going to be.

She'd been dreading walking into the courtroom for months. And now, hopefully, it was almost over.

The sound of the gavel focused attention on the judge. All eyes were on him. Kincannon waited until the courtroom was quiet again.

"I think that this might be a good place to call a recess for lunch." The judge's deep voice rumbled like thunder over the parched plains of late summer. And then he glanced in her direction, his eyes only fleetingly touching hers. "You are dismissed, Detective. The court thanks you for your testimony."

But I'm sure you would rather it had come from someone else, Greer couldn't help thinking even as she inclined her head in acknowledgment.

She rose to her feet at the same time that Kincannon did.

And then the commotion erupted so quickly, it took Greer a while to piece it all together later that day.

One moment, the courtroom was buzzing with the semi-subdued rustle of spectators gathering themselves and their things together in order to leave the premises, the next, terrified screams and cries pierced the air.

And then there was the sound of a gun being discharged.

But the tiny half heartbeat in between the two occurrences was what actually counted.

Greer had immediately glanced away from Kincannon the moment their eyes made contact when the judge dismissed her. Which as it turned out, she later reflected, was exceedingly fortunate for the judge. Because if she hadn't looked away, she wouldn't have seen Munro leap up to his feet and simultaneously push the defense table over, sending the table and everything on it crashing to the floor. That created a diversion just long enough for Munro, in his respectable suit, to lunge at the approaching bailiff, drive a fist to the man's gut and grab the doubled-over bailiff's weapon.

"Gun!" Greer yelled and, in what felt like one swift, unending motion, she leaped up onto the witness stand chair where she had just been sitting a second ago, propelled herself onto the judge's desk and hurled herself into the judge, sending the surprised Kincannon crashing down to the floor behind his desk.

Scrambling, she was quick to cover his body with her own.

The desk obstructing her view, Greer heard rather than saw what was going on next. There was the sound of terror, of people yelling and running and ducking for cover. And then there was the sound of a gun being discharged again—one round. Whether the gun belonged to the other bailiff or was the one that Munro had seized from the first bailiff she had no idea.

At this point, everything was registering somewhere on the outer perimeter of her consciousness.

What she was *acutely* aware of was that she was lying

spread-eagle over the judge, that he was on his back and she was on his front. And that all the parts that counted were up close and personal.

The infusion of adrenaline sailing in triple time through her body had her heart racing so hard she was certain that some kind of a record was being set. Greer felt hot and cold and light-headed all at the same time, a reaction definitely *not* typical of her. She struggled to regain control over herself and her surroundings.

Her eyes met Kincannon's. As if suddenly pulled into the belly of an industrial vacuum cleaner, all the noise and chaos surrounding them seemed to have faded into oblivion for just the slightest increment of a second.

And then she blinked.

"How long have you been under the illusion that you're bulletproof, Detective O'Brien?" Kincannon asked her gruffly.

The question instantly pulled her back into the eye of the courtroom hurricane. "I'm not," she heard herself answering.

"Then what are you doing on top of me?"

"Saving your life, Your Honor," she snapped.

Her heart slowed down to a mere double time. There was a criminal to subdue. The thought telegraphed itself through her brain. Greer scrambled up to her feet. As did the judge.

"Stay down!" she ordered sharply, circumventing his desk.

Kincannon clearly had no intention of being ordered around or of staying down, cowering behind his desk. His court had just been disrespected. The judge stood directly behind her, his robe billowing out on the sides like some fantasy superhero's cape.

"My courtroom," Kincannon informed her, raising his voice above the din, "my rules."

His courtroom, Greer noted as she swiftly scanned the area, taking everything in, was in utter chaos. It was also apparently missing one felon. The second gunshot that had rung out *had* come from the purloined weapon, and the bullet—whether intentionally or not—had hit the bailiff whose weapon had been stolen by Munro. The latter, on the job all of six months, was on the floor, clutching his shoulder. Blood was seeping out between his fingers.

Munro was nowhere to be seen.

Inside a secured courtroom with law enforcement officers throughout the building, Munro had done the impossible. The drug dealer had escaped.

A glance to the left told her the chief of detectives was missing, as well.

For one terrifying moment, an utterly unacceptable scenario suggested itself to her, but she dismissed it. Brian Cavanaugh was too much of a policeman to have ever allowed himself to be taken hostage. If Munro had even attempted it, she was certain the dealer would have been lying on the floor in several disjointed pieces.

The man would have instinctively known that avoiding the chief at all costs was the only way he was going to make it out of the courthouse alive.

Greer refused to believe that Munro had already gotten out of the building. Not enough time had gone by.

She ran through the double doors that led out of the

courtroom into the hallway. She didn't have to look over her shoulder to know Kincannon was right behind her. Did the man have a death wish? she wondered, annoyed.

There was more chaos beyond the leather padded doors. People, fleeing for their lives, were hiding in alcoves, pressed as far against the beige walls as humanly possible in an attempt to avoid the escaping criminal's attention.

Damn it, things like this just don't happen, Greer thought angrily.

Except that it just had.

She scanned the hallway again, hoping that she'd missed something. Hoping that Munro was trying to hide in plain sight. But he wasn't.

At first glance, it appeared that Eddie Munro had turned out to be far cleverer than she'd initially thought. The drug dealer had managed to disappear.

She saw the chief. He was standing a few feet away and had taken charge of the bailiffs who had come running in response to the gunshot. On the phone, he'd already put in a call for reinforcements.

"I want everything shut down," he ordered the uniformed men and women gathered around him. "Except for my people, nobody leaves, nobody comes in. Understand?"

Acquiescing murmurs responded to his words.

He looked at the bailiffs. "I want every courtroom, every office, every closet on every floor gone through." His penetrating look swept over the collective. "Do it in teams. I don't want anyone caught off guard. One damn surprise is enough for the day. You—" he singled out the closest bailiff "—call for an ambulance. I want that bailiff who got shot attended to."

The man rushed off to place the call. As the other men and women he'd just addressed scattered, Brian turned his attention to Greer. His eyes swept over her, taking full measure. Looking for a wound. Finding none, he still asked, "Are you all right, Greer?"

Self-conscious at being singled out this way—did he think she couldn't take care of herself?—Greer dismissed the concern she heard in her superior's voice. "I'm fine, Chief." And then she couldn't help herself. She had to know. "Why are you asking?"

He laughed shortly, shaking his head. "Well, for one thing," he began wryly, "I saw you take that half-gainer over the judge's desk—"

"She had a soft landing," Kincannon told him as he came up to the chief.

Greer shifted slightly. "Not so soft," she muttered under her breath. She'd been acutely aware of every single contour she'd come in contact with and *soft* was not the word that readily came to mind.

Calling out to Janelle, who he saw hurrying out of the courtroom and looking around, Brian didn't appear to have heard Greer's comment.

But the judge did.

Chapter 2

Greer turned around. The moment she did, her eyes met Kincannon's.

He'd heard her. She was certain of it.

What she didn't know was how he'd received the offhand comment that had just slipped out. Was that a hint of amusement she saw on his face, or was it something else? She'd never been around the man in one of his lighter moments—didn't even know if he *had* lighter moments—so she couldn't gauge what was going on in his head right now.

Talk about awkward, she thought. And it was of her own making. Someday, she was going to learn to think before she spoke, or at least that was what her brothers were always saying to her.

"Someday, that mouth of yours is going to get you

in a whole lot of trouble," Ethan had warned her more than once.

She could take that kind of a comment from Ethan far more easily than she could from Kyle. From Kyle, it sounded more like criticism. Besides, she was closer to Ethan than to Kyle, which was odd, given that the three of them had drawn their first breaths less than seven minutes apart. According to birth order, Kyle was technically the "oldest," then her, then Ethan. "The baby," their mother used to fondly call him.

Kyle had called him that, as well, until Ethan had given Kyle his first black eye. The word *baby* hadn't come up again in approximately sixteen years.

None of that changed the fact that her brothers were both right. She had a tendency to let her thoughts reach her lips, completely bypassing her brain. Most of the time, it didn't matter. But most of the time she didn't find herself on top of a judge who had a rock-solid body hidden beneath his imposing black robes.

Raising her chin, Greer stoically waited to be upbraided for her comment regarding the judge's body. Instead, without so much as uttering a word, Kincannon turned on his heel and made his way back into the courtroom.

Was she off the hook?

Or was he planning on denouncing her formally later on? Her experience with judges, as with lawyers, had not yielded a great deal of positive reinforcement.

"Greer." The chief's voice cut through the din in the hall. She turned around to face him, waiting to be dispatched where she could do the most good. Brian motioned toward the courtroom. "Stay with him," he instructed.

Greer opened her mouth to protest that she would be more useful looking for the prisoner, but then she shut it again, for once keeping her words to herself. She knew better than to argue with authority, even with someone as genial and affable as the chief. She wasn't about to abuse the fact that he was her uncle. Years ago in the school yard, she'd learned the wisdom of picking her battles judiciously.

"Yes, Chief." The sound of numerous feet running toward them told her that the officers Brian had sent for had arrived. She'd already turned away and was hurrying back into the courtroom. Behind her, she heard Brian continue to organize the search for Munro.

Greer wouldn't have wanted to be in the drug dealer's shoes when Brian found him for any amount of money in the world.

Entering the courtroom, she noted that it was mostly empty. She glanced toward Kincannon's desk.

He wasn't there.

Before her adrenaline had the opportunity to ramp up, she spotted the judge on the floor. He was kneeling beside the wounded bailiff.

Coming closer, Greer saw that the bottom of the judge's robe was torn and ragged. Though she hadn't thought it was possible, Kincannon had somehow managed to tear a long strip off his robe and was now using it to form a tourniquet for the wounded bailiff. Moreover, he was doing it himself rather than instructing the other bailiff to do it.

Admiration stirred within her. Too often judges thought themselves above the people they interacted with. Nice to know that wasn't a hard and fast rule.

"Lie flat, Tim," Kincannon told the bailiff when the injured man tried to sit up.

So he knew him, she thought. From the job or from somewhere else?

To underscore his words, the judge put the flat of his hand against the young bailiff's blood-soaked shirt and exerted just enough pressure to make the man remain down. In his weakened state, Tim could offer no real resistance.

Joining them, Greer squatted down beside the judge as she looked at the bailiff. "Better do as he says if you ever want to work in his courtroom again," she advised with an encouraging smile.

Tim looked like a kid, she thought. She did her best to sound upbeat for the bailiff's sake. He looked scared and he'd lost a lot of blood. She was rather surprised that Tim was still conscious, much less making an attempt to sit up.

"Nice work," she said to Kincannon, nodding at the tourniquet he'd fashioned. She slanted a glance in his direction, forcing herself not to look away too quickly. "Let me guess, you earned a merit badge in first aid when you were a kid."

Blake secured the ends of the strip as best he could. *That should hold until the paramedics get here,* he thought.

Sitting back on his heels, he continued to maintain eye contact with the frightened bailiff. He couldn't remember ever being that young. It seemed to Blake that somehow, through a trick of fate, he'd been born old.

"Nothing wrong with being an Eagle Scout," he responded.

"Wow, an Eagle Scout." Somehow, she had envisioned Kincannon being more of a rebel. Not too much call for rebels in the Boy Scouts. When he looked at her quizzically, she explained, "My brother Kyle only lasted a month in the Cub Scouts."

Kincannon continued looking at her. "Let me guess, he didn't think the rules applied to him."

Kyle *never* thought the rules applied to him. He made his own as he went along.

Of course, all that was going to change soon. Kyle had actually found his soul mate and was planning on getting married.

Who would have ever thought…?

Greer lifted a shoulder in a semi-shrug. "Something like that."

"Family trait?" Kincannon mused.

Greer looked at him. To ask that, the judge would have had to be familiar with her family. Granted, she and her brothers were all detectives with the Aurora police department, but she was not so self-centered as to think that the world revolved around her family. Besides, she usually kept a low profile.

She wanted to know his reasoning. "Why would you say that?"

"I'm a fairly good judge of character, no pun intended." He gave his handiwork a once-over to make sure it was secure. Satisfied, he nodded to himself. But rather than standing up, Kincannon looked at the woman beside him for a long moment. "Rather than duck out of range, the way everyone else in the courtroom did, you jumped on my desk, making yourself the most visible target in the room."

Her eyes narrowed just a little, even as she told herself not to take offense. She hadn't expected him to thank her profusely, but neither had she expected him to take her to task for it, either.

"With all due respect, Your Honor, I didn't exactly break into a tap dance, searching for my fifteen seconds of fame. I jumped on the desk because it was the fastest way to get you out of harm's way."

"It's fifteen minutes, not seconds," he corrected mildly, "and at thirty-four, I'm perfectly capable of getting out of harm's way on my own."

Greer squared her shoulders. *Infected with a little hubris, are we?* It looked as if she might just have to revise her opinion of Kincannon. Again.

"I'm assuming, Your Honor, that at thirty-four, your eyesight is still twenty-twenty."

Rather than answer in the affirmative, Kincannon's eyes held hers as he rose to his feet. "What are you getting at?"

She was in no hurry to blurt out her answer. "That Munro discharged the weapon twice. The second bullet went into the bailiff you just bandaged."

His eyes never left hers. Even so, there wasn't even the slightest hint as to what was going on in his head.

Was he taking offense, highly amused or just giving her enough rope in hopes that she'd hang herself?

Not today, Judge.

"You're going to tell me about the first bullet, aren't you?" he asked, his tone mild.

"Absolutely," she said cheerfully. Greer marched over to Kincannon's desk and rounded it, going directly to the wall behind it. He followed. She pointed to an area that was the exact same height as his throat was from the floor. Her meaning was clear. Had he been standing where he'd been a moment longer, he wouldn't have been with them now. "You were his first target."

Blake dismissed her conclusion with an indifferent shrug. "Coincidence."

Greer suppressed an annoyed sigh. So he was thickheaded. Maybe the bullet wouldn't have penetrated after all.

This wasn't the time to get into an argument, she told herself silently. There was nothing to be gained by butting heads with this man. Her energy could be better spent otherwise.

But that still didn't keep her from looking as if she was merely humoring him. She inclined her head like an acquiescing servant. "Have it your way."

Rather than taking her tone as confrontational, he murmured, "I usually do."

I just bet you do.

Greer pressed her lips together in a physical effort to keep a retort from making it out into the open. It wasn't easy.

But before she could give in to the urge to break

her silence, the doors to the courtroom were thrown open and two uniformed paramedics, pushing a gurney between them, hurried into the room.

"He's over here," Kincannon called out to the duo, beckoning the men over as he made his way over to the bailiff. They reached Tim at the same time. The wounded bailiff was no longer bleeding, thanks to the tourniquet, but he was exceedingly pale. "One shot to the chest," Blake told them. "The bullet's still inside. I just applied the tourniquet a couple of minutes ago."

The paramedic closest to him nodded at the information as he appeared to make a quick assessment of the makeshift bandage.

"Nice job, Judge," the man commented approvingly. His partner released the brakes that were holding the gurney upright. The mobile stretcher instantly collapsed like a fainting patient. "We're going to shift you onto the gurney, sir," the first paramedic told Tim. "It's going to hurt a bit," he warned.

Tim looked as if he was struggling to remain conscious. He moaned. His expression indicated that he had no idea where the sound was coming from.

"On three," the first paramedic instructed. The other paramedic fumbled slightly, bumping Tim's shoulders against the corner of the gurney. It earned him a black look from his partner. "Good help's hard to find these days," he commented, addressing his words to the judge.

Once Tim was on the gurney and strapped in, the two paramedics snapped the stretcher into its upright position again. "Let's get that wound looked at," the first paramedic said to Tim. With his partner, they began to maneuver the gurney back to the double doors.

"Judge," Tim suddenly called out, his voice weak and cracking.

Three quick strides had Kincannon catching up to the gurney. He trotted to keep up alongside Tim. The paramedics never stopped, never even slowed down.

The wound was undoubtedly more serious than first anticipated, Blake thought. Looking down at the bailiff's face, he asked, "What is it, Tim?"

Tim pressed his lips together. Were they trembling? Greer wondered as she followed beside Kincannon. And why was the bailiff looking at the paramedics as if he was terrified? Her next thought was that the young man was probably afraid. No one applied for the job thinking they'd get shot.

"I'm sorry," Tim was saying, then repeated, "I'm sorry."

Blake put his own interpretation to the apology. Tim was sorry that he hadn't been able to stop the prisoner from escaping. Blake squeezed the wounded bailiff's good hand reassuringly. "Don't worry, Tim, we'll get him. I promise."

There wasn't so much as a shred of doubt in the man's voice, Greer thought. Either Kincannon had a hell of a lot more confidence in the system and in the department's ability to track Munro down for a second time than she did, or he was just naïve.

Kincannon didn't look like a naïve man.

But then, she thought, smart people were fooled all the time. Look at her and her brothers. They'd been unwittingly duped for twenty-six years by the one person they had all loved unconditionally. That kind of thing shook up your faith in the world and made you reassess all your existing values and views.

Offering the wounded man an encouraging smile, Kincannon slipped his hand out of Tim's fingers. The judge dropped back as the two paramedics swiftly whisked the wounded bailiff through the double doors and out into the hall.

He walked like a man who owned his destiny and his surroundings, Greer thought, watching him cross back to her. Maybe he'd gotten over his wife's death and moved on. For his sake, she certainly hoped so. The man she remembered encountering in the hospital had been all but broken.

"You probably saved his life," Greer said as Kincannon came closer to her.

"You save some, you lose some." The remark appeared to be directed more to himself than to her.

Okay, maybe he *wasn't* over his wife. What else could his response mean? Did the judge blame her for not being able to save the woman? God knew she'd tried, doing compressions and breathing into the woman's mouth until she thought she'd pass out herself.

Greer could feel words of protest rising to her lips. Again she pressed them together. This definitely wasn't the time to get into that. Besides, the judge hadn't actually come out and *said* anything to accuse her. Maybe she was just being paranoid.

As she was trying to decide whether or not she was overreacting, she saw Kincannon make his way over to

Munro's attorney. The small, slight man looked very shaken. His hands trembled as he attempted to pack up his briefcase. Twice papers slipped out of his hands, falling to the table and onto the floor like giant, dirty snowflakes.

"Until I'm persuaded otherwise, I'm holding you responsible for Munro's escape, Mr. Wells," Kincannon said to the man.

In response, Hayden Wells abandoned his briefcase and began stuttering, unraveling right in front of them.

"I didn't— I wouldn't—" All but hyperventilating, Wells cleared his throat and tried again. "Your Honor, you can't be serious."

Greer saw the steely look that came into the judge's eyes. She certainly wouldn't have wanted to be on the receiving end of that, she thought.

"I can," Kincannon informed him, "and I am."

"But, Judge," Wells squeaked, his voice cracking out of sheer fear, "I had no way of knowing that this was going to happen. No way," he insisted. "I'm just as surprised as you are."

"I sincerely doubt that," Blake responded coldly.

Reining in his frustration, he set his jaw hard. This shouldn't have happened, he thought. There were supposed to be safeguards in place. Were all the security measures just a sham?

Taking a deep breath, ignoring the babbling lawyer, Blake slowly looked around the empty courtroom.

Frustration ate away at him. He sincerely regretted his own ruling which had specifically forbidden any videotaping of proceedings. At the time his thinking had been that he didn't want tapes to be leaked to the media, didn't want cases to be compromised because some reporter wanted to break a story.

But in this case, if there *had* been a video camera on, it would have caught the events preceding Munro's escape on tape and that would have been a godsend. Blake had a gut feeling that Munro hadn't acted alone. This wasn't a spur-of-the-moment thing. The man had to have had help. A *lot* of help. Blake was willing to bet a year's salary on it.

Wells was still sputtering that he was offended that someone of the judge's caliber would actually think that he would lower himself to aid a criminal.

"I could be disbarred!" he declared dramatically.

Greer had a feeling the man was just warming up. She was about to tell him to keep quiet when Kincannon beat her to it.

"Please spare me your self-righteous protests, Mr. Wells. I am well aware of your record. No one enters my courtroom without my knowing his background," he told the man. "Someone who loses as often as you do can't possibly support himself in this line of work without having something else going on on the side."

Wells's dark eyebrows rose all the way up his very large forehead, all but meeting the semicircle of fringe that surrounded the back of his head. "Your Honor, I give you my word—"

Greer didn't know how much more they could take. "That and two dollars will get you a ride on the bus," she observed.

Damn, she'd done it again, Greer thought. That wasn't supposed to have come out. Not because she didn't mean it, but because she had no idea how Kincannon would react to her flippant attitude.

But when her eyes met his, if anything, Kincannon appeared to be somewhat amused. Or, at the very least, in agreement.

"My sentiments exactly," he told her.

The din just beyond the double doors in the hallway suddenly increased, swelling to three times its original decibel level.

Hopefully, there was only one reason for that. "Maybe they found him," Greer guessed, looking at Kincannon. With that, she decided to see for herself. Moving quickly, Greer hurried out the double doors to find out. She'd intended to report back.

She should have known better. Apparently Kincannon didn't like to remain stationary.

"Maybe," she heard him agree, then add, "You stay here." Since she was all but out the door, he had to be addressing the order to Wells. "I want to have a few more words with you when I get back."

Greer stopped dead the second she was out the doors.

There were two paramedics in the hallway. Two paramedics pushing a gurney.

A feeling of déjà vu slid over her. That and a great deal of uneasy confusion.

She wasn't the only one experiencing it.

Even before Greer reached the paramedics, she had

a sinking feeling in the pit of her stomach. Something was terribly off.

The lead paramedic looked only slightly friendlier than a rattlesnake.

"Look, we got the call and got here as fast as we could. MacArthur Boulevard's a parking lot," he bit off, his words directed at the chief. "Now, is there a patient or isn't there? We're short-handed and we don't have any time for some damn game."

Instead of answering the man, Brian put in a call to dispatch.

"Yeah, Hallie, it's Chief Cavanaugh. How many ambulances did you send out?" He listened to the answer. "Okay, describe the paramedics." He frowned. "What do you mean you can't keep track?"

"Chief," Greer interrupted, pushing her way through the crowd. "Let me send her a picture so she can identify them," she suggested.

Brian paused. He looked at his cell phone uncertainly, then lifted his eyes to Greer's. "Does this—?"

She nodded, knowing what he was going to ask, sparing him the embarrassment of having to put it into words. "Yes, it does," she assured him. Taking his phone, she snapped a shot of the two disgruntled-looking paramedics. Done, she quickly forwarded it to the woman on the other end of the line, then handed the cell phone back to the chief.

Confirmation was almost immediate.

"You didn't send another team?" Brian knew the answer before he even asked the question. His mouth was grim as he muttered, "Thanks."

Flipping the phone closed, Brian regarded the officers gathered around him. The paramedics were all but forgotten. "Right under our noses," he declared, his voice low and steely.

He made Greer think of a volcano that was trying not to erupt.

Chapter 3

Confused, Blake looked from the chief of detectives to the animated narcotics detective at his side. It was now a foregone conclusion that the first set of paramedics who'd whisked Timothy Kelly away had been bogus. However, the rest of it didn't make sense to him.

"But why would they kidnap the bailiff? If they were in on the escape, wouldn't they have found a way to make off with Munro?" he asked.

Who said they didn't? Greer thought as she shook her head. "They didn't kidnap the bailiff, the bailiff was part of it."

Blake refused to believe it. He could remember Tim's first day on the job. So obviously wet behind the ears, the young bailiff had been so eager to please, so eager to do a good job, it had almost been painful to watch. "But they almost killed him," he protested.

Brian was clearly struggling to keep his temper under control. "*Almost* being the operative word," the chief pointed out.

"No, you're wrong," Kincannon insisted. "I know the man. He's shown me photographs of his wife, of his baby daughter. A man like that doesn't suddenly get up one morning and decide to help a career felon escape out of a courtroom."

He was having trouble with this, Greer realized. Rather than instantly become indignant because he'd been duped, Kincannon was searching for some elusive reason that would explain what happened and absolve the bailiff of any wrongdoing beyond being in the wrong place at the wrong time. She had to grudgingly admit she found that admirable. At the very least, that made the judge more of a human being than most who sat on the bench.

Reviewing the situation, she realized that there was possibly a plausible explanation that could be acceptable to both sides. The more she thought about it, the more it seemed to fit. She sincerely doubted that Kincannon could be easily deceived.

"Maybe he didn't just wake up one morning and decide to help a hardened felon escape," she suggested, her conviction growing stronger with each word. "Maybe Tim Kelly had no choice."

Janelle had been quiet this entire time, remaining out of her father's way as he took charge of the situation. But now she seemed compelled to point out the obvious flaw in her new cousin's theory. "They weren't holding a gun to his head, Greer," she said, her tone of voice barely masking the frustration she clearly felt over the drug dealer's escape.

Greer knew that Janelle had spent a great deal of time preparing this case and was almost certain she would have won. Now, it looked as if all that time she'd put in had been wasted.

"Maybe they were holding one to his family," she countered, standing her ground against her indignant cousin.

The moment she made the suggestion, Greer could see that the explanation was more than acceptable to Kincannon. But his opinion wasn't the one that counted here.

Greer shifted her eyes toward the chief, holding her breath. Waiting.

"Maybe," Brian allowed slowly. "Makes sense," he decided. The chief turned toward two of the officers he'd summoned. "Mahoney, Wong, find out the bailiff's address. See if there's anything going on at his house that shouldn't be."

"His name's Tim Kelly," Kincannon informed them to facilitate the search. "Human Resources can give you the rest of the information. Their office is located on the third floor. Three-seventeen," the judge added for good measure. He wanted to clear the young man, wanted it not to be Tim's fault. Otherwise, it would make him begin to doubt his own judgment, and that was a dark place he never wanted to revisit.

They had their instructions so the two officers took off.

Belatedly, Blake felt a surge of adrenaline kick in. He

needed to be doing something. Blake looked at Brian. "Is there anything I can do to help? To move things along?" he wanted to know.

"Unless you can pull a felon out of a hat, Judge, I'd say go home. You're free for the afternoon," Brian added. Kincannon looked at him in surprise, forcing Brian to state the obvious. "I'm afraid that court's adjourned for the day, Judge. Everyone's court," he clarified in case there was any question. "There're a lot of places Munro could hide and it's going to take a while to conduct a completely thorough search. The bastard's got to be here somewhere."

"Not necessarily." All eyes turned to Greer. "Think about it. The fake ambulance has clearance to be on the grounds—and to leave. What's to have stopped them from backing the vehicle up in front of one of the side exits? With all this commotion, even with all the backup you called in, the officers can't be everywhere at once." She spread her hands. "Munro ducks out where they're not."

It seemed like a very simple explanation—and very doable. Greer continued. "The fake paramedics come back, pushing a gurney with a wounded victim. They load it and the bailiff into the back of the vehicle." She snapped her fingers. "One, two, three, they're gone and we're still hunting for Munro."

Brian frowned. It made sense. And he didn't like it.

"Let's hope they're not as bright as you are." But even as he said it, it was obvious to those around him that the chief of detectives knew there was a good chance that Greer was right. He offered his niece a quick smile.

"Just glad you're on our side," he told her. Turning back to his men, he directed the new groups to fan out everywhere and double-check the locations, including the basement—just in case.

With everything being done that could be done, Blake decided that he might as well do as the chief advised and go home. But first, he needed to take care of a few things of his own.

Returning to the courtroom again, Blake went directly to his administrative assistant, an older woman who wore sensible shoes and nondescript suits that never called attention to her. To the casual observer, Edith Fields looked like the very prototype of what had once been referred to as a mere secretary. Edith was that and so much more.

The moment she saw him, the grandmother of six—two of whom she was raising herself—was on her feet. "Any news, Your Honor?" she wanted to know. Blake knew it had never pleased her that the wheels of justice ground slowly. She wanted every criminal to be thrown into jail quickly, and left there for the duration of a maximum sentence.

"We're being sent home, Edith."

The news was not received well. The woman looked down at the compact laptop that sat on her desk, opened and at the ready. She read one of the entries on the judge's heavy schedule. "I could reschedule the Brown case, Your Honor."

Left on his own, he would have said yes, but the day belonged to Chief Cavanaugh and the latter called the shots. Blake shook his head.

"No point. We need to clear out of the courthouse." He saw that Edith was far from jubilant about the turn of events. "Think of this as an enforced holiday. I'm sure Joe could use a hand with Emily and Ross," he said, mentioning the names of the two grandchildren who lived with Edith and her husband of forty-one years.

The woman had made it known more than once that she thought she was indispensable to his court. She sighed now, a child being sent to her room for no good reason. "If you say so, Your Honor."

"The chief of detectives says so, Edith," Blake corrected. He glanced over his shoulder. Just as he thought, the detective was still there, like a shadow he couldn't cast off without taking drastic measures. "If you feel uneasy about leaving the courthouse, Edith," he told the older woman, "I can have Detective O'Brien take you home."

Greer blinked. Had he just volunteered her services without consulting her? She wasn't part of his team, to be ordered about, she thought, irritated at his cavalier manner.

She was about to protest, but as it turned out, she didn't have to. His administrative assistant dismissed the offer with a haughty wave of her hand.

"I'm a big girl, Judge. I stopped being afraid of thugs like Munro when I was in grammar school. He doesn't scare me." Her things packed, Edith nodded at her employer. "See you in the morning, Judge."

Blake barely nodded. A moment earlier, he'd crossed to his desk and was about initiate the procedure that would power down his computer when the big, bold letters that were written across the monitor's screen caught his attention.

And then raised his ire.

When he made no answer in response to his assistant, a woman he obviously held in warm regard, Greer looked at the judge. She saw the angry look that had darkened his features.

Kincannon was a formidable-looking man, she couldn't help thinking. She definitely wouldn't have wanted to find herself on the receiving end of that look. But right now, she was more curious as to what had caused it. It couldn't be the ongoing situation because he seemed to have calmed down about that—unlike her.

Maybe, instead of throwing herself on top of Kincannon, the situation would have been better served if she'd had the wherewithal to tackle Munro and keep him from fleeing. Growing up with her brothers as playmates and partners in crime had taught her to be fearless, reckless and unafraid of pain if enduring pain resulted in achieving a desired outcome. In this case, it would have been preventing that poor excuse for a human being from making good his escape.

Greer took a second look at Kincannon's expression. Something was off.

"What's wrong?" she wanted to know. Not waiting for an answer, she rounded Kincannon's desk and came up next to him. Since he was staring at the computer screen, Greer looked at it, as well. For a second, the words seemed too absurd to be real.

And then they were all too real.

Back off or you and your father are going to die. Slowly and painfully.

She thought Kincannon was going to hurl the laptop across the room, but he restrained himself. She heard him mutter angrily, "Brazen son of a bitch."

There was no question that this had come from Munro. "Obviously, he believes in the family plan," she commented. The next moment, she was hurrying out of the courtroom again.

Turning away from the courtroom in an attempt to create a pocket of privacy, Blake quickly took out his cell phone and turned it on. One of his pet peeves was cell phones that rang during court, but right now he was glad he had forgotten to leave his cell phone in the top desk drawer in his chambers. It saved him precious seconds he didn't know if he could afford to waste. He was not about to continue underestimating Munro.

"C'mon, answer," he ordered, addressing a man who wasn't there. The message he'd left on the answering machine at home was just kicking in when he glanced toward the double doors in the rear and saw O'Brien coming back—and she had the chief with her. "Pick up, Dad," Blake instructed through clenched teeth. "Pick up!"

And then he heard the receiver being lifted on the other end.

Thank God.

"Bad day in court?" he heard his father ask. "The story's all over the TV," Alexander Kincannon, retired marine sergeant and practicing malcontent, grumbled. "It preempted my show. What the hell kind of security have you got down there? Can't even hang on to one skinny criminal?" he demanded.

Blake was not in the mood to get drawn into a lengthy discussion about how lax current law enforcement had gotten. He needed for his father to listen to him. "Dad, I don't want you answering the door."

He heard his father blow out an irritated breath. "What am I, twelve?"

For a second, Blake lost patience. "You're a hundred and seven, but I want you to make it to a hundred and eight, Dad. Don't answer the door, do I make myself clear?"

"Why?" the gravelly voice demanded, sounding significantly less combative than it had just a moment earlier.

Reaching the judge and able to make out what the person on the other end was asking, Brian raised his voice so that the judge could hear him over the loud voice on the cell phone. "Tell him I'm sending a patrol car over. It'll be there in a few minutes." He made eye contact with Kincannon. "We'll keep him safe."

Blake nodded his thanks toward the chief. "Dad, they're sending a—"

"I heard, I heard." Alexander cut him off. "I'm not deaf yet, you know." And then a degree of excitement entered his voice. "This have anything to do with that pusher who took a powder?"

"Maybe. I don't know yet." Although, he added silently, he was pretty certain that it was. Blake heard his father sigh dramatically and then abruptly terminate the connection. Closing his own phone, Blake slipped it back into the pocket of his robe. He looked at Brian, his gratitude rising to the foreground. "Thank you."

"Least I can do," Brian acknowledged, then he nodded toward his niece. "Greer alerted me to the message you received on your laptop." He lowered his eyes to the state-of-the-art computer on the judge's desk. "I'm going to have to take it, Your Honor. Maybe one of our people can trace where the e-mail originated." He knew for a fact that Brenda, his son Dax's wife, would all but make a computer sit up and beg. Maybe she could pull this miracle off, as well.

Ordinarily, Blake might have protested about protecting the privacy of his court cases, but in this case, there was no need. Brian Cavanaugh was a veritable pillar of ethics. So he nodded, turning the laptop around and handing it over to the chief.

"Whatever you need," he told the older man.

Brian closed the lid, securing it in place. "Right now, it's what you need that's important," he corrected. "It looks as if this Munro character feels he has a specific beef with you that goes beyond his own case. As I heard it, you sent several of his people away with the maximum sentence when they were convicted a couple of years ago."

Blake wanted no credit for serving justice. It was what it was. "Just doing my job, Chief."

"And now I'm doing mine," Brian countered. "You need protection, Judge."

Blake did not savor relinquishing his privacy, but there was his father to think of, so he nodded.

"A patrol car making the rounds every hour or so should do it," he speculated.

"What about the other fifty-nine minutes?" Brian asked mildly.

Blake's eyes narrowed as he tried to follow the chief's reasoning. "Excuse me?"

"The way I see it, Judge, until this drug dealer is caught, you're going to need twenty-four-hour protection, not just a patrol car passing by every now and then."

Blake didn't want to argue, but he definitely didn't want to acquiesce, either. "Isn't that a little extreme, Chief?"

"Death is extreme, Judge, everything else is a distant second," Greer pointed out, feeling that the chief could use a little verbal backup right about now. She could understand the desire to remain independent. In the judge's place, she'd feel the same way. But Munro would think nothing of putting a bullet right between the judge's eyes. It would seem like a crime to disfigure that noble profile with a bullet.

In return for her support, Greer saw the chief smile at her. She returned the smile, not recognizing the expression for what it was. Had she been part of the family longer, she might have known that the smile that was curving his mouth was the one Brian wore when he was about to deliver a very salient point, and triumphantly drive it home.

"I'm glad you feel that way, Greer."

She might not have been able to pick up on the chief's expressions, but there was something in his tone of voice that softly warned her she was in big trouble. Not the disciplinary kind, but the kind that meant she was on the verge of something she would regard as less than pleasant happening.

"Why, sir?" she asked her superior quietly, never taking her eyes off Brian's face.

Even as Greer asked for clarification, she had a sinking feeling in the pit of her stomach that she knew why Brian had just expressed his satisfaction at her agreement.

"Because I'm assigning you to be Judge Kincannon's bodyguard."

It was hard to say which of them was more averse to the news they'd just received, she or Kincannon.

"I'm not going into hiding," Blake protested with feeling.

"Nobody said anything about hiding," Brian told him. With enough effort, they could keep the judge safe and still presiding over his courtroom. But it would be tricky. Which was why he felt that Greer was the person for the job. She was a self-starter who thought outside the box.

"Look, Chief Cavanaugh," Blake began again, picking his words slowly, "I'm very grateful that you're sending a car to watch over my father, but I'm not a helpless old man—"

He could just hear his father's reaction to that description. At seventy-three, the former gunnery sergeant was still fit, still capable of pummeling someone to the ground with his fists as long as that someone didn't tower than six inches over him. There was nothing "ex" about this marine.

"A bullet is a great equalizer."

Had that come out of her mouth? Greer thought suddenly. Even suppressing annoyance at the confining assignment she'd just been handed, she found herself still performing like a good little soldier. Pressing her lips together, she caught herself longing for the days that she'd been a rebel. A rebel wasn't in danger of going comatose standing guard over someone. Being a bodyguard was only marginally better than being forced to sit in a car, maintaining surveillance on a suspect. She hated both assignments with a passion. Inactivity was not in her DNA.

But it looked like, judging by the chief's expression, she was stuck.

Maybe so, she thought the next moment, but she wasn't about to go down without a fight—or without going on record that she was less than thrilled with the assignment.

"That's right, it is," Brian agreed with Greer's succinct assessment. He smiled at his niece, clearly appreciating the backup. "Now," the chief continued, "until we finally catch this Munro character, you're assigned to the judge."

Finally. She didn't know if she had as much faith in the wheels of justice as he apparently did. Finally could mean days, or, more likely, it could mean weeks. She didn't want to spend weeks babysitting, even if the person she was watching over was an incredibly good-looking specimen of manhood.

She was a good detective. She belonged in the

field, damn it, not hovering over the judge like some misguided shadow.

"Chief, could I have a word with you?" she requested as he began to walk away.

Rather than answer verbally, Brian beckoned her to follow him as he walked out of the courtroom. With the judge's laptop tucked under his arm.

Chapter 4

Greer stared at the chief of detectives' back as she followed him into the hallway. Considering the stress and pressure he was always under, the man exuded strength and energy.

There was a lot to live up to being a Cavanaugh, she thought. People expected you to be at the top of your game, sharp and in good physical condition at the same time. It just went with the territory.

For the most part, the commotion in the hallway had died down. The area was relatively empty now. People had been taken aside for questioning and the rest of the police who'd been summoned were scattered throughout the building, conducting an intense room-to-room search.

But her mind wasn't on the hallway or what was happening beyond it. Greer's mind was on what she was going to say to the chief and how she was going to say it in order to hopefully get him to see things her way.

She *really* didn't want to take on this assignment and her primary reason didn't even have anything to do with her staunch dislike of inactivity. It went far deeper than that.

It was times like these that she really wished she had Ethan's golden tongue and his effortless ability to phrase things just right. But she didn't. All she could do was state her case as best as possible and cross her fingers that it was good enough. Cross her fingers that the chief would understand and see things from her point of view.

Putting her request in the form of a plea wouldn't carry any weight, she knew that. Even if it did, she didn't think she was capable of resorting to begging. Begging wasn't in her inherent makeup. She'd always taken her medicine and stoically faced up to her responsibilities, no matter what.

But in this case, it wasn't just that *she* didn't want to have to be the judge's bodyguard. She was more than fairly certain that Kincannon wouldn't want her hovering around him 24/7, or whatever ratio of time the chief decided that she had to put in. If the judge was forced to put up with a bodyguard—and from where she stood, she could see why it would be necessary—she was sure that she wouldn't be the man's first choice. Not by a long shot.

Brian abruptly stopped several feet beyond the courtroom's double doors. Preoccupied, searching for the proper wording, Greer almost walked right into him. Catching herself, she stopped approximately an inch shy of colliding with her superior.

Sucking in her breath, she quickly backed up so that there was a decent amount of space between them. Under no circumstances did she want to appear to be crowding the man.

"Now, what is it you want to talk to me about?" Brian asked her genially.

By his tone and expression, the topic of conversation could have involved something personal and inconsequential. But Greer kept her guard up. He might be her uncle, but here, on the job, he was the man who was ultimately in charge. Family ties didn't enter into it.

She reminded herself that, like the judge, Brian was tough, but fair. At best, she had a fifty-fifty chance. She'd had worse odds.

Greer forged ahead. "With all due respect, Chief, I'd rather you assigned someone else to be the judge's bodyguard."

"And why is that?" he asked her, his voice mild.

She cleared her throat, trying her best not to make this sound as if she was asking for preferential treatment, because she wasn't.

"The judge and I…" She stumbled, then tried again. "We have some history."

His expression never changed. "Were you lovers?"

Some of the air seemed to vanish from her lungs. Her eyes widened in disbelief. "No! No," she repeated, doing her best to sound calm this time. "I… That is, he…"

It was not in his nature to make his people uncomfortable. That went double for family. Brian raised his hand, interrupting the halting flow of words. "If you're about to refer to what I think you're going to refer to, I'm well aware of your 'history' with the judge, Greer," he told her.

She stared at him, stunned and at the same time, relieved that she wasn't going to have to relive the ordeal by rendering a blow-by-blow description for him. "You are?"

The nod was almost imperceptible. "I made it a point to familiarize myself with your files—yours and your brothers'," he clarified, not wanting her to think that he had singled her out for some reason. She was fairly new in this position and second-guessing was part of the process. He didn't want to add a strong case of paranoia. "I like to know things about my family—and the people who ultimately work under me," he explained, answering questions he knew she had to be thinking.

Greer took a breath. This had been easier than she thought. "So then you understand why I think it would be better if someone else was assigned to the judge?"

"No."

The one word answer came out of nowhere and hit her like a detonating bomb. "No?" she echoed, hoping she'd heard wrong.

"No," Brian repeated. His tone was mild, but there was no mistaking the firm undertone. "You are the most qualified to handle the job right now. You know the judge and, more importantly, you're familiar with Munro, with the way he thinks, the way he acts." That, he indicated, was of paramount importance. "That puts you several steps ahead of anyone else I'd assign to the detail," he told her. "It only makes sense that I put you in charge."

It might make sense to him, she thought, but that still didn't make her comfortable with it. "Chief." The single word packed all the appeal into it that she could muster.

The chief looked at her for a long moment, his gaze drying up whatever words she was planning to use. Drying up the words and her saliva, as well. It felt as if she had a mouthful of sand.

"You're not asking me to give you special consideration, are you, Greer?" he finally asked.

God, she didn't want him to think that. She shook her head with feeling. His tone had been low. Hers wasn't. "No, sir."

Brian's smile was easy, pleasant. "Good, I didn't think so." About to turn away, he realized that he hadn't finished yet. "How long will it take you to go home and pack some things?"

Somewhere distant in her head, she heard a door slamming. The door had bars on it. She was stuck. She was just going to have to make the best of it. "I've got a change of clothes in the car."

The information had Brian's smile widening. "You're a Cavanaugh, all right. Always prepared."

His compliment reminded her of something. Greer shifted slightly. "About that, sir?" she began, letting her voice trail off a little.

Brian waited.

There were seven of them, seven "new" members

of the family. There were the four who belonged to his bride of a little more than a year, and then there were the three who none of them had been prepared for. Triplets who comprised his late brother Mike's secret other family. Lila's children, all adults and all on the force, went by her first husband's surname while Greer and her brothers had her late mother's. All seven were told that they were welcomed to change their names to Cavanaugh if they wanted to.

Name change or not, that was what they were. Cavanaughs. But the decision strictly belonged to the seven individuals involved. He'd heard that it was going to be an "all-or-nothing" deal. The "jury" was still out on which way they would ultimately lean.

Or maybe the jury was ready to come in, he thought, looking down at the young woman who reminded him so much of Mike's daughter, Patience.

"Yes?" he prodded.

She pressed her lips together. "For my part, I've decided yes."

"Yes?" he echoed, unclear if it was "yes" she'd change her surname to Cavanaugh or "yes," she'd keep the one she already had.

"Yes," she repeated. "If it were only up to me, I'd like to change my last name to Cavanaugh. It'd be an honor."

"We'd all like that," he assured her. "Especially Andrew. And the honor goes both ways," he added. "Anything else?"

"No, sir, that's all." Finished, Greer began to back up, trying not to dread what lay ahead. She was fairly certain that the judge wouldn't bring up their first encounter, he seemed too self-contained for that, but she was fairly sure that the memory was probably never far from his mind. Which would make things very awkward and difficult between them.

Nobody said being a cop was going to be easy, she reminded herself.

"Good," Brian was saying. "Then go tell the judge that you're going to be his new houseguest for the foreseeable future."

Nodding, Greer drew in a deep, fortifying breath. There was no way around this.

Who knew, maybe they'd get lucky and one of the chief's men had already located Munro at the bailiff's house.

Greer had her doubts but she mentally crossed her fingers anyway as she turned around and pushed open the padded black leather doors. For what felt like the umpteenth time that day, she walked into the courtroom.

The judge wasn't there.

Adrenaline shot through her veins like a spring-propelled pinball. Greer quickly scanned the room. There was no sign of the man she was supposed to be guarding. The only one left in the room was the court stenographer, carefully packing up her steno machine.

Greer hurried over to the thin blonde. "Where's the judge?" she demanded.

Closing the case and snapping its locks into place, the woman picked up her equipment. She made no secret of the fact that she was eager to leave. The unexpected question made her frown thoughtfully.

"In his chambers, I guess," she replied.

"I hope you guessed right," Greer muttered under her breath as she hurried to the rear of the room. There was an exit to the right of the judge's desk. This had to be what he'd used to pull his disappearing act.

Damn it, she thought, finding herself in a narrow hallway, why couldn't the man stay put? Didn't he understand the gravity of the situation? Or did Kincannon understand it and just believed himself to be bulletproof?

Turning a corner, she found herself facing a closed door. She had her weapon out and ready to fire in one swift movement. There was no telling what she'd find on the other side of the door. For all she knew, Munro had been lying in wait for the judge in his own chambers. The drug dealer was just crazy enough to do it.

Biting off a few choice words, she kicked open the door, weapon aimed and poised to shoot at anything that made a wrong move.

Startled, the man inside the room swung around.

Kincannon.

Alone.

A hiss of air escaped through her clenched teeth and Greer lowered her weapon. Relief and anger converged within her.

Before she'd made her entrance, the judge had taken off his robe and hung it carefully on a hanger, apparently respectful of all the black cloth represented. He frowned now as she lowered her weapon.

"Most people knock before kicking down a door and bursting into someone's chambers." His voice was deceptively calm.

Greer's mouth dropped open. He was going to be high-handed and lecture her? Seriously? "First of all, I didn't kick down the door. It's still attached."

"The maintenance man will be grateful," he commented drolly.

"And second," she continued, pretending he hadn't said anything, "most people don't have an escaped felon threatening to kill them. Drastic times require drastic measures." Her look pinned him where he stood. "You shouldn't have wandered off like that."

"I'm a grown man and in possession of all my faculties," he told her tersely. "I didn't 'wander off,' I went to my chambers. For a reason," he added.

"To hang up your robe?" Greer guessed incredulously.

"Yes." He said the single word as if it was a challenge.

She was not about to back off. If this was going to work between them, he had to be aware of the rules. "You could have waited."

"I could have," he agreed. "But I didn't. Detective, I've been crossing the street by myself since I was six years old. Nothing's happened yet." He blew out a breath, as if he was trying to calm himself. "And in case you're interested, this isn't the first threat I've gotten," he assured her.

"It's the first on my watch," she informed him. And then she asked the question that was nagging at her.

"Since you were six? Seriously?" Who let their six-year-old cross the street by themselves?

"My father insisted. He wouldn't let my mother coddle me. Said it was important for me to become a man."

"At six?" she cried. "How many six-year-old men did he know?"

He'd never questioned his father's reasons or methods. That was just the way things were. "He was a marine, a gunnery sergeant in the corps."

The light began to seep in, shining on the situation. "That explains a lot."

He disregarded her comment. "What are you doing here, Detective? I assumed you weren't going to be 'watching over' me anymore. Isn't that what you wanted to tell the chief? That you'd rather pass on the assignment?"

They were back to awkward again, she thought. She didn't like him just "assuming" things about her—even if they were true. "The chief would rather that I didn't 'pass.'"

He looked at her, vindicated. Up until this moment, he'd just been guessing, but her admission had just proven him right. "Then you did protest."

She raised her chin. If she was going to have to do this, it was best if there were no hard feelings between them. "*Protest* is rather a strong word, Judge."

He laughed shortly. "Don't split hairs, Detective O'Brien. It's not your style."

Now he was assuming things about her? She didn't

care for being pigeonholed. "And how would you know what my 'style' was?"

The answer to that was far less complex than she might assume, Blake thought. "I'm the man you jumped on, remember?" He saw what he took to be a slight blush accent her cheeks and found himself momentarily intrigued. He hadn't thought that they made women who blushed anymore. "You're given to broad strokes," he continued with his analysis, "not tiny lines."

She had always been a big picture kind of person. It made taking care of details particularly difficult for her. There was always something that she missed, that she forgot. Right now, the fact that Kincannon had nailed her so accurately made her very uncomfortable. Made her feel as if he was poking around in her head, invading her space.

She resented it. This wasn't going to work. And while she wasn't about to go back to the chief with that—Kincannon could.

"If you'd rather have someone else assigned to you, Your Honor, please feel free to ask the chief," she told him. "I'm sure he'd listen to you."

"I'd rather that no one was assigned to me," he told her curtly, "but you saw where that went."

Tired of dancing around in circles, she shrugged off the whole situation. "Maybe you'll get lucky and the chief's men'll find Munro quickly."

Blake sincerely doubted that luck was on his side. Munro had probably gone underground. "Lots of places a man can disappear in this county." He looked at her pointedly. "Or out of it. If Munro had any brains at all, he's take this opportunity to flee the country—at least until things cool off for him."

"Oh, he has brains all right," Greer assured him. She'd dealt with people like Munro before, too often for her liking. In her opinion, they were the vermin of the earth. But Munro seemed to be a cut above the rest. Smarter. Sharper. And that worried her as far as the judge's safety went. "But he's also the type who relishes taking revenge."

Taking his jacket out of the small closet, Blake slipped it on over his light blue tapered shirt. "In that case, shouldn't you be the one with a bodyguard?" he asked. "After all, you were the one who pulled off that sting and brought Munro in."

"But you were the judge who sent away his buddies," she reminded him. And there was one more salient point. "And you were the one who got the e-mail."

To her surprise, just the barest hint of a smile curved the corners of a mouth that could have been called sensual under different circumstances. He shrugged at her words. "It was worth a shot."

Swiftly, she pieced things together. "You were trying to talk me out of guarding you?"

It was obvious that the man she was going to be protecting saw no reason to offer a denial. "I was."

Well, he'd wasted his time, she thought. "It's not up to me."

"And if it was up to you?" he wanted to know. "Would you guard me?"

She could smell the lather he'd used shaving. Or maybe that was the scent of his soap. In any case, he was standing too close, she thought. His space was commingling with hers and that was definitely interfering with her thought process.

Greer subtly moved over to where his robe was hanging and pretended to be interested in the texture of the weave. It was called survival.

The automatic response to his question would have been no. But this didn't require an automatic answer, it required one that had some thought behind it. The chief never said things just to hear himself talk. If he felt the judge needed a bodyguard, then he damn well needed a bodyguard. She'd already silently agreed with that judgment.

She worded her response carefully. "If there was no one else to do it, yes, I would."

His eyes held hers for a moment. She felt as if he was looking into her soul. "A truthful answer."

There was a reason for that. The judge wasn't the kind of man you lied to. Not without a great many consequences. "I've got a feeling you could see right through it if it wasn't."

Her answer amused him. Was she applying the catch-more-flies-with-honey-than-with-vinegar theory? "Flattery, Detective?"

Her answer was immediate. "Observation, Judge." She glanced at what he was doing. Briefcase packed, he was apparently ready to go. Striding, he got ahead of her by the time they reached the door.

"My car's parked downstairs," he told her, leading the way out. Devoid of people, the courtroom was as quiet as a tomb. Alert, she scanned the area as she took the lead, not letting him walk until she walked there first.

"We'll take mine," she informed him. There was no room for argument.

He did anyway. "I'm partial to my car." Reaching the elevators, he pressed the down button.

"And I'm partial to you breathing," she replied mildly.

The wording surprised him. "Really?"

"Okay," she admitted, "the chief is. And what the chief wants, the chief gets."

She was overreacting, he thought. He refused to be intimated by a cheap hood.

"And you really think that if I use my car, I won't be 'breathing' for much longer?" He didn't bother removing the note of mockery in his voice. "Just how much credit are you giving this two-bit criminal?"

The elevator arrived. She held her hand up, stopping the judge until she checked out the interior. There were two other people in the car, both wearing ID badges that connected them to Human Resources.

She motioned him forward with the barrel of her weapon. "The kind of credit that goes along with having a bogus paramedic team arrive on the scene well ahead of the real one. The kind of credit someone who could pull this all off should be awarded. Anything else?" she wanted to know.

"Yes. Are you always this annoying?"

The question caught her off guard, although she didn't show it.

"No," Greer finally replied. "If you believe my

brothers, sometimes I'm worse." The doors opened on the first floor. She waited for the two people to disembark, then motioned for the judge to follow her. "Let's go, Your Honor."

Rather than follow, he fell into step beside her even as he resigned himself to the inevitable. "I have no choice, I guess."

"Nope."

They made their way to the front doors. There were several police officers, all of whom she was familiar with, processing people out one by one. Recognizing them, one of the officers waved her and the judge by.

Greer stopped just before the doors and her eyes met Kincannon's. "Neither one of us do."

And, she had a strong feeling as they exited, neither one of them was very happy about this state of affairs, either.

Chapter 5

"So how is this going to work?" the judge asked her once they were in her car and she was pulling out of the parking structure. "Do I check with you before I take a breath?"

Greer kept her eyes on the road as she exited onto the street. She supposed she could understand his sarcasm. In Kincannon's place, she'd probably feel the same way.

No, she corrected herself, not probably, she would *definitely* feel the same way. She'd never liked restrictions and living with a bodyguard was the very definition of being restricted. But then, he'd chosen this career. No one had forced it on him.

"No," she replied mildly, acting as if he'd just asked her a legitimate question, "how many breaths you take or don't take is entirely up to you."

She heard him sigh. A glance in his direction told her he was staring out the windshield and frowning.

"You know this is completely unnecessary, don't you?" he said.

Anyone who could orchestrate a successful escape from a courtroom was a man to be reckoned with— and not underestimated. If Munro wanted to enact his revenge against the judge, then the judge needed serious protection.

"Sorry, Your Honor," she answered, "but I don't know anything of the kind."

"I know how to defend myself, Detective O'Brien," he informed her, his impatience barely contained.

She pretended she didn't hear the annoyance in his voice. "Good, then this shouldn't be a difficult assignment for me."

He tried again. He knew she was only doing her job, but there was no point in doing it with him. "My father was a marine."

At least you knew your father. Sparing him another glance, she forced a smile to her lips. "So you said. And I'm sure he was an excellent one."

It didn't end there. "The point of my reference," he told her caustically, "is that he insisted on teaching me self-defense."

She eased her vehicle into a right turn. She had a tendency to turn sharply and she didn't want him complaining that her driving was making him ill on top of everything else.

"Did he also teach you how to catch bullets with your bare hands?" she asked mildly.

"No."

She nodded at his reply. "Then I'm afraid you need me."

"Why?" he wanted to know. "Do you catch bullets with your bare hands?"

"No, but I have a gun—" Greer began. She no longer thought of him as the man whose wife she couldn't save. She was now beginning to regard him as a judge who was a pain in her anatomy.

"So do I," he cut in.

Greer was tempted to pull over, but the sooner she got him home, the sooner they would be out of this confining space.

She sighed. "Judge, this is going to go a whole lot easier for both of us if you stop fighting the inevitable." Stepping on the gas, she just made it through a yellow light. "I've been assigned to you and I'm not leaving until either Eddie Munro is caught or the chief decides to replace me, so you might as well make the best of it." She deliberately kept her eyes forward. "I promise I'll try to be as unobtrusive as possible. You'll hardly notice I'm there."

There was silence for a moment. Had she won? Greer slanted a look in Kincannon's direction and instantly became aware of Kincannon's eyes moving over her slowly, as if to take measure of every inch of her. More criticism was coming, she could feel it.

"Oh," the judge replied, "I sincerely doubt that."

The comment took her completely by surprise. As did the unexpected and sudden feeling of warmth that was spreading throughout her torso and limbs. The same kind of warmth that had zapped through her when she'd thrown herself on top of the judge to shield him earlier.

At the time she'd attributed the reaction to adrenaline and the sudden, gut-seizing fear that she might not get Kincannon out of the line of fire in time. This time there was no one pointing a gun, no visible threat at all.

There was just the judge, appraising her. And obviously seeing her as a woman.

Greer cleared her throat, searching for something to fill the uncomfortable silence. "I heard you mention that your father's living with you."

His living arrangements were no secret. After the accident that had claimed his wife, his father had come from Maryland to lend him moral support. Initially, he'd been in an emotional tailspin, one that, at the time, it didn't seem possible he would ever get out of. But eventually he did. His father stayed on. A month turned into two years. Enamored with the weather, his father showed no signs of wanting to leave. And although the man was rather difficult and cantankerous at times, Blake had to admit that he enjoyed having someone to come home to.

"He is," the judge replied, wondering where this was going.

From what she'd picked up, the senior Kincannon was not that keen on women in the services. She imagined that extended to having women on the police force. "Do you think he'll be upset?"

"What, that he didn't get his own bodyguard?" the judge guessed at her meaning and recalled his phone call to his father. "My father would be insulted if it was even suggested."

She shook her head as she took another slow right turn. "No, I mean with my having to remain on the premises for a while. If he's old school—"

That was the polite way to describe it. Chauvinistic could be another. "He is."

There was only one conclusion to be drawn from that. "Then this might not sit too well with him."

For the first time, Blake smiled and Greer caught herself noticing how his features instantly softened. He even looked somewhat boyish. That definitely wasn't the impression she had when Kincannon wasn't smiling. Then he looked strict and stern, like a man who was not to be crossed.

"No," he agreed. "You're right. It might not. I'd brace myself if I were you, Detective." But even as he said it, his smile widened. "It just might turn out to be one hell of a bumpy ride."

He probably thought that would make her ask to be taken off the assignment. *You don't know me, Judge.* "I've had bumpy rides before."

Kincannon didn't offer an argument, just a smile, a different kind this time. One that said he had some sort of inside knowledge that she wasn't privy to—yet. But she would. It was just a matter of time.

"We'll see, Detective," he said, an ominous promise in his voice. "We'll see."

"What are you doing home so early?" were Alexander Kincannon's first words to his son when Blake walked into his two-story house fifteen minutes later.

Before Blake could say anything in response, Greer walked in behind him. The senior Kincannon, who was nearly as tall as his son and seemed to have a good twenty, thirty pounds on him, grinned knowingly.

"Oh, I see. Looks like I got my answer." The words were directed at his son, but the ex-marine made absolutely no secret of the fact that he was staring at the woman beside Blake. The older man circled her as if to get the full effect. "Good to see you dating again, Blake. About time, too." And then his grin became positively wicked. "Did you bring one for me?"

Blake glanced at his watch. It had taken his father all of thirty seconds to embarrass him.

"I'm not 'dating again,' Dad," he answered, doing his best to remain patient with the man. He had no desire to lose his temper with his father in front of a stranger. For the most part, he was a private person. Far more private, apparently, than his father.

"Then who's this?" Alexander wanted to know.

"'This,'" Blake answered, using his father's exact phrasing, "is Detective Greer O'Brien." He paused for a moment before adding, "Our bodyguard."

Sky-blue eyes beneath bushy gray eyebrows that resembled miniature tumbleweeds widened incredulously. "Bodyguard?" the ex-marine hooted. His message was clear. The practical joke that his son was obviously attempting to play had just fallen flat. "Yeah, right." He turned toward the woman. His expression told her that he liked what he saw. "Who are you, really, honey?"

Honey. Greer knew she should have been offended to

be addressed that way, but she had a feeling that the older man didn't mean anything by it. In his generation, it was perfectly acceptable to address a young female that way. In a way, his manner was almost oddly endearing.

Maybe, she thought, because in a way, Kincannon's father reminded her of her grandfather. Her mother's father had been one of those grumpy old men with a heart of gold who existed in sitcoms and other people's family trees. He had been in hers and she'd loved him dearly—they all had—from the moment she'd known him until the day he died. She was ten at the time and completely devastated over the loss.

"Exactly who your son says I am," she told him. "Detective Greer O'Brien." Greer put her hand out to the senior Kincannon. "I've been assigned to keep you and your son safe and out of harm's way."

Alexander eyed her hand without taking it. "And who's going to keep you safe and out of harm's way?" he asked gruffly.

Greer never hesitated. "You, sir. We can watch each other's backs."

The answer couldn't have pleased Alexander more. He nodded his full head of silver-gray hair as he took the hand she was still offering. He shook it firmly and noted that she returned the handshake in kind. "I was a marine, you know."

The look in the man's eyes told Greer that she'd scored points. "I could tell by your bearing, sir. Once a marine, always a marine."

"You bet your a—backside," Alexander concluded,

stopping himself at the last minute from saying the word he ordinarily used.

Greer grinned, silently telegraphing that she appreciated the courtesy.

Releasing her hand, Alexander looked at his son. "So, aside from getting shot at, losing a prisoner and gaining a bodyguard with killer legs, how did the rest of your day go?" he asked.

"That about covers the highlights," Blake replied. Shedding his jacket and tie, the judge left them slung over the back of the first chair he came to on his way to the liquor cabinet.

When he took out a decanter of scotch, Greer tactfully suggested, "Shouldn't you have something to eat, first?"

Suppressing an irritated sigh, Blake glanced at her over his shoulder. "Detective, you were assigned to be my bodyguard, right?"

"Right."

He placed the decanter on the counter. "Unless I'm mistaken, that means you're supposed to guard the outside of my body, not the inside."

He was going to fight her all the way, wasn't he? No matter what she said. Well, she didn't join the force expecting it to be a piece of cake.

Greer crossed to him. "Having something in your stomach reduces the effects of the alcohol. I just wanted to make things easier on you."

His eyes met hers. His were a piercing blue, a shade darker than his father's, she noted. "What would accomplish that is if you folded your tent and disappeared into the night."

She refused to rise to the bait. Instead, she smiled brightly. She had a hunch that it drove him crazy. "Night doesn't come for several hours yet, Your Honor," she informed him.

"Is that when you leave?" Alexander asked, joining her.

"No." As far as she knew, there weren't going to be shifts. There was just going to be her. She had a feeling, though, as the assignment stretched out, adjustments would be made. "That's just when the judge would want me to leave."

Alexander snorted dismissively as he waved a hand in his son's direction. "Don't pay any attention to him. Outside the courtroom, Blake doesn't have the sense he was born with."

"I'm standing right here, Dad," Blake pointed out, raising his voice.

Alexander spared his son a withering glance. "You're six foot two, boy, and my vision's still good. I can see you."

"Then don't talk about me as if I'm not in the room," Blake suggested.

"Even when you are, half the time you're not." Alexander looked back at Greer and confided in a voice that had never quite dipped down to the level of a whisper, "His mind wanders worse than an old man's. Not that I'd know anything about that." He chuckled.

Greer nodded. "Didn't think you would. Mr.

Kincannon—" she began, only to have the senior Kincannon interrupt.

"Gunny," he told her. "Call me Gunny. I was a gunnery sergeant in the marines."

She inclined her head, wordlessly thanking the older man for the privilege of calling him by the common nickname awarded to all those who served as gunnery sergeants in the corps.

"Gunny," she echoed. "Could I ask you to show me around your house?"

The older man beamed, then cleared his throat as he went through the motions of summoning a sterner look. "I suppose I can find time for that."

The corners of her mouth curved. "I'd appreciate it, Gunny."

Squaring his shoulders, the still exceedingly robust retired marine began leading her to the next room. "Okay, that was the living room. Over here you've got your…"

As his father's voice faded away, taking his unwanted houseguest with him, Blake could only shake his head. He was far from happy about this unexpected turn of events. He hadn't lied to Detective O'Brien just to make her back off. He had been threatened before, threatened verbally with physical harm, he'd just never told anyone. And, because he'd never registered a complaint with the police, his life had remained his own.

Moreover, no one had come to shoot him dead. The threats had remained empty.

As empty as this one probably was. The only difference was that this time, the threat had been witnessed, so to speak, by the chief of detectives. That had made it official and there was no getting around the rules.

That didn't mean he had to like it. Or even think that the slip of a woman the chief had assigned to him would make a difference. If that despicable excuse for a human being, Munro, wanted to do away with him, Blake knew that, bodyguard or no bodyguard, the drug dealer was damn well going to try to kill him.

However, he liked to think that he was at least smarter than a hood like Munro no matter how much money the drug dealer had tucked away in a Cayman Islands bank account. And he didn't want the likes of Detective O'Brien getting in the way and possibly getting caught in the ensuing cross fire.

He didn't need her on his conscience. He already had Margaret.

Blake poured himself two fingers worth of scotch and brought the glass to his lips. He was about to take a hearty swallow when he stopped and then set the glass back down on the counter. With a sigh, he looked down and contemplated the contents he'd just poured.

Drinking wasn't going to make the situation *or* the detective go away and it just might have an unwanted effect his judgment. With another sigh, Blake took the glass and ever so slowly poured the amber liquid back onto the decanter.

He'd just put the stopper back into the mouth of the bottle when he heard his father's voice. It sounded as if the man was getting closer. The unnerving thing was that it was unusually jovial—for his father.

At least this detective had done one thing, he thought.

She'd managed to tame the savage beast that beat within his father's chest.

The woman, he mused, apparently had some hidden talents.

Walking into the family room, Greer glanced at the glass on top of the small bar and immediately noted that it was empty.

"Finished your drink so soon?" his father asked. There was a touch of admiration in his voice. "Didn't realize you could pack 'em away so fast, son."

"A lot of things you didn't realize," Blake replied mildly.

He was caught off guard when his so-called bodyguard not only came closer, she invaded his personal space. Glancing back at her guide, she said, "Your son didn't have a drink."

Blake said nothing, but their eyes met and held for a long moment, as if he expected her to follow up her theory with hard evidence.

His father picked up the glass from the counter. "Glass is coated."

"He poured it back into the decanter," Greer told him.

Okay, he wanted to know how she'd pulled off this parlor trick.

"And how would you know that?" Blake asked.

"Easy. You would have had to down the drink quickly and your breath would have reflected your consumption," she explained diplomatically. "There is no scotch on your breath. And the sides of the decanter have a little bit of an amber coating to them."

"Forensics 101?" Blake asked in a mocking tone.

Greer shook her head. "No, Agatha Christie. Miss Marple," she added, naming one of the famed mystery writer's more famous characters. "I forget which one of her books."

She heard Kincannon's father chuckling behind her. At least she'd won one of them over, Greer thought.

Chapter 6

Greer spent the next couple of hours going over every inch of the first floor of the house, inside and out, securing it wherever necessary so that the front door was the only way for anyone to enter or exit.

The judge had a security system which she re-programmed after advising him of the change and the new code. She did it just in case someone at the security company's home base had hacked into the system and acquired what was now the old code. Changing it, she'd told the judge, was going to be an ongoing daily proposition until the threat was over.

Kincannon hadn't looked overly happy about the idea of having to remember a new pass code every day, but at least he hadn't offered any resistance. He seemed far more interested in having her leave his office so he could get back to working on whatever it was that had claimed his attention.

She staked out the sofa, intending to spend the night on it. From there, she had a clear view of the door. Since she was an incredibly light sleeper to begin with, she had no doubt that any intruder attempting to enter the house would have her awake and on her feet in a matter of seconds.

Finished with her preparations for now, she walked back into the living room only to have Alexander ask her, "What'll you have, pizza or Chinese?"

Greer stared at the barrel-chested man, caught off guard by his question. "Excuse me?"

He raised the telephone receiver he was holding in the air as if to clarify that he was about to order in. "Food. So what'll it be?"

"You don't have to go to any special trouble for me," Greer protested.

"This isn't special," he informed her. "This is what we do every night."

Her eyes narrowed as the meaning of his words sank in. "You order in every night?"

"It's either that, or starve," the retired marine told her.

She shuddered to think what ingesting processed foods every night had to be doing to their digestive tracts. But then, maybe the old man was just exaggerating. "You don't have any food in your refrigerator?"

"Sure we've got food," he informed her matter-of-factly. "Leftovers."

"From the takeout," she guessed. Alexander nodded

his head. Didn't either of them have any idea about the value of proper nutrition?

"Well, yeah, sure," Gunny replied as if the answer was a no-brainer.

Very politely, she removed the receiver from his hand and replaced it in the cradle. "How long has it been since you had a home-cooked meal, Gunny?"

The senior Kincannon paused to think. And then he smiled as the memory obviously came back to him. "Well, there was that cute little Fraulein in Berlin... But that was about two years ago."

"You're kidding, right?" Greer said incredulously.

"Why would he kid about something like that?" Blake asked. Drawn by the voices, he walked into the room. Now what was this woman up to?

Greer shifted in order to look at both Kincannon men. "Let me get this straight, neither one of you has had a home-cooked meal in two years?" She stressed the last two words.

"You deaf, girl?" Alexander asked impatiently. He began to reach for the phone again, but she rested her hand on the receiver, immobilizing it.

"No, but I am stunned," Greer admitted.

"What's the big deal?" Alexander wanted to know. "It's all just fuel and it all turns into the same thing on its way out."

"Colorful," Greer commented. "Be that as it may," she continued, "you're not doing yourselves any favors with all that takeout food."

Curious and wanting to see for herself, Greer passed the judge's father and went into the kitchen. She opened the refrigerator. There were several bottles of beer, domestic and imported, a partial loaf of white bread, the wrapper only loosely tied and most likely harboring stale slices, and a lone stick of butter.

"You weren't kidding," she murmured under her breath as she shook her head.

"So, what'll it be?" Alexander repeated, on his way back to the landline. "Pizza or Chinese?"

"Hang on a minute," she called out. Crossing back to the living room, she took out her cell phone and went through the directory. She found the number she was looking for and pressed the buttons that would connect her. As the phone rang, she waited for someone to pick up on the other end.

Her wait wasn't long.

"Hello? Uncle Andrew?" The word *uncle* still felt foreign on her tongue, but she was getting more accustomed to it and she had to admit she liked the whole concept, liked the way it made her feel to be part of something bigger than just herself and her brothers. "This is Greer. I was wondering if you'd mind having three extra at the table for dinner tonight?"

"Mind? You obviously haven't been part of the family long enough," the man on the other end of the line told her with a pleased laugh. "C'mon over," he urged heartily. "The more the better."

"What time's dinner?" she wanted to know.

The answer was one that she would eventually learn to expect. "What time can you get here?"

Greer didn't bother trying to hold back the smile that rose to her lips. The man was every bit the legend he was made out to be. Warm and generous to a fault. The father figure every family patriarch *should* be.

"Just so you know," she told the former chief of police, "I'll be bringing Judge Blake Kincannon and his father."

"Thanks for telling me," he answered. "I'll make a point of calling Callie and telling her that Brent's presence is requested."

She was vaguely aware that Callie, Andrew's oldest daughter, was married to a judge. The two had met several years ago when Callie was assigned to find his kidnapped daughter.

"That's really not necessary," Greer assured the patriarch.

Andrew saw it differently. "Of course it is. Your judge gets to talk to another judge and Rose and I get a reason to make our daughter and her family drop by. It's a win-win situation."

They were right, Greer thought. There was no arguing with Andrew Cavanaugh. Not that she really wanted to. "We'll be there in forty minutes," Greer promised.

"Any time is fine," he answered as he broke the connection.

"We'll be where in forty minutes?" Blake wanted to know.

She would have had to have been deaf to miss the edge in his voice. "At Andrew Cavanaugh's house. We're invited to dinner."

"You invited yourself over," Blake pointed out. He was far from pleased with the turn of events. When not in court, he tended to prefer staying at home to going anywhere.

"Just beating Uncle Andrew to the punch," she told him cheerfully. "If I'd stayed on the phone long enough, he would have been the one doing the inviting. He really likes nothing better than to have a full house at every meal."

It was one of the first things she'd learned about the former chief of police. The only thing Andrew Cavanaugh loved more than cooking was having his family and friends over, eating his cooking. Any time, night or day, there was always something on the stove, always an extra chair to be pulled up at the custom-built, extra-long table.

No one who came over ever left hungry—or lonely.

"That's all well and good," Kincannon told her, a note of finality in his voice, "but I'm staying in tonight."

"You can stay in after we get back," she informed him cheerfully.

His eyes narrowed, darkening. "Detective, as I understand your assignment, you're supposed to guard me, not order me around."

"I have to do whatever it takes to keep you safe and well," she countered. "In case you're wondering, this comes under the 'well' heading."

He had no intentions of giving in. If he gave this woman an inch, he was certain that he was going to lose the proverbial mile.

"Look, Detective, my life's disrupted enough already. Much as I might appreciate the gesture, I don't feel like dropping everything and running over to the former chief's house."

To Greer's surprise, it was Alexander who came to her aid. "Oh, lighten up, Blake. You're not running anywhere, she's driving us. Right, O'Brien?"

"That's the deal," she answered with a broad smile. And then she turned to the judge. "I'll make you a bargain, Your Honor. You come with me tonight and tomorrow, I'll get someone on the squad to go shopping for me and I'll make dinner here."

"You cook?" Blake asked in surprise. A woman who looked as good as she did didn't have to know how to cook. He could see men falling all over themselves for the privilege of wining and dining her.

"Almost as good as Uncle Andrew," she said with just the right touch of modesty.

He did his best to remain steadfast, although he felt the ground beneath his feet turning to sand. And the vibrant detective who probably had no clue that she was getting to him at the speed of light was the sandstorm. Damn, under any other circumstances…but it was what it was and he had to remember that. This was a professional situation. He couldn't allow himself to let it get personal. Or intimate.

"That's not necessary."

"You let me be the judge of that—no disrespect intended," Greer added.

"None taken." This time, the judge fairly growled his response.

"Good, you came. We can get started," Andrew Cavanaugh declared heartily less than thirty minutes

later. Rubbing his hands together in anticipatory pleasure, Andrew had walked out to greet Greer and his
other two guests just as she pulled her vehicle up into
the driveway.

Andrew positioned himself on the passenger side of
the sedan so that Blake and his father had no choice but
to greet him and shake the hand that the former police
chief offered.

"Hello," he said warmly, "I'm Andrew Cavanaugh,
Greer's uncle, and this is my wife, Rose." He nodded at
the youthful-looking woman beside him.

The man was a hell of a lot more than that, Greer
couldn't help thinking. He ran a 24/7 kitchen and was a
saint to boot. Everyone in the family turned to him when
they needed emotional support. That was definitely far
and away more important than just being her uncle.

But hearing Andrew say it sent a warm, happy
feeling through her, as if, for the first time in her life,
she actually belonged somewhere.

"Alexander Kincannon," the older man said, taking
Andrew's offered hand first. "Gunny to my friends."

"I hope I'll number among those."

"Let me try your cooking and we'll see," Alexander
responded half seriously.

"I'm Blake Kincannon." Leaning forward, Blake
shook his host's hand. "You'll have to excuse my father,"
he apologized, slanting an irritated glance at Alexander.
"He doesn't get out much."

"Look who's talking," Alexander hooted. "If it wasn't
for going to court, I'd have to start referring to you as
The Shadow."

The reference was to an illusive comic book hero from the forties, but from the knowing look on Andrew's face it was clear he was familiar with it. Very neatly, the man got in between father and son, a human barrier to their escalating exchange of words.

"Judge," he said to Blake, "I took the liberty of inviting my son-in-law over. Brent's a sitting judge and I thought the two of you might have things in common to talk about."

He knew of only one Brent on the bench. "Brenton Montgomery?" Blake asked.

"Right here," a deep voice announced from the family room. The next moment, Brent had crossed over to his father-in-law's newest converts.

Greer caught Andrew's eye and mouthed, "Thank you," gratitude flowing from every pore. She knew the situation was tense for the two men she'd brought, but the last thing she wanted was a verbal confrontation between them.

She should have known she could count on Andrew not just to defuse the situation, but to generate a feeling of well-being, not only verbally, but also with the food he so deftly prepared.

Uttering a deep, satisfied sigh, Alexander Kincannon pushed himself away from the table after having consumed three generous helpings of the lamb stew that Andrew had prepared.

"You know, every time I've had a man cook for me, it's been less than a memorable experience," he confided, raising his eyes to look at his host. "Can't say that anymore. Well, I can," the man amended with a small grin. "But then I'd be lying. This has to be the best meal I've had, bar none, in more years than I can clearly remember. You do have a gift, Andy," he announced as if it were a new discovery, "you surely do."

"Thank you, Gunny. I take that as very high praise. Feel free to drop by anytime." Andrew turned toward the man Greer was guarding. "Same goes for you, Blake."

"Thank you, Chief." Blake glanced toward Greer. "But it looks like I'll have to get permission from my keeper, first."

Callie smiled as she looked quizzically at her newfound cousin. "Greer? Is there something you'd like to share with the group?" she deadpanned.

For some reason, the subject of the exact manner of the relationship between her and the judge and his father hadn't come up during dinner. To her relief, it turned out that Brent and Blake knew each other. The two men had gotten caught up in a conversation that revolved around a recent controversial court ruling. The others at the table added their own opinions and, for a while, it was just a typical Cavanaugh dinner where not only the food but the company was enjoyed.

As discretely as possible, Greer took a breath before answering. "I'm the judge's bodyguard," she told Callie, trying her best to sound matter-of-fact about the assignment.

A glance toward Andrew told her that the Cavanaugh patriarch already knew about the arranged relationship, as did his wife. But this was obviously news to his daughter and her husband.

For a second, Brent looked thunderstruck, and then he laughed at his own ignorance. "Of course. That was your courtroom on the news, wasn't it?"

Blake sighed. He was beginning to wonder, even at this early date, if he was ever going to hear the end of this.

"Yes, that was mine."

Callie was immediately sympathetic. "You were lucky you weren't hurt."

Blake looked at Greer, remembering. "Luck didn't have anything to do with it. I was tackled by Detective O'Brien in order to get me out of the line of fire," he told the others.

"I'd still call that luck," Andrew told him. "She could have been half a second slower to react and you could be lying in a drawer in the morgue right now, waiting to be cut open."

Alexander looked from his son to the woman he had taken almost an instant shine to.

"*She* tackled *you?*" he asked, clearly in awe of the information. He shook his head as if the information didn't compute. "But she's just a bit of a thing."

"I wouldn't underestimate her if I were you, Gunny," Andrew warned with a laugh. He slipped an arm around Rose to underscore his words. "The Cavanaugh women might look petite, but underneath all that softness, they're as hard as steel."

"Not completely," Brent corrected, exchanging a look with his wife that silently spoke volumes.

He could vouch for that, Blake caught himself thinking. The next moment, he banished the unexpected thought—and the memory it summoned—from his mind. It was time to get going—and to terminate this social gathering. Being around O'Brien this way was creating havoc with his thoughts.

Blake cleared his throat. "Chief Cavanaugh, as my father said, that was a really wonderful meal. But I'm afraid that I have to—"

Andrew was way ahead of him. He nodded understandingly. "You need to get back home. Of course. I won't keep you," he assured his guest, rising to his feet. Rising beside him, Rose began clearing away the dishes. Callie and Brent both joined her.

Feeling guilty, Greer began to follow suit only to have Andrew take the plates out of her hands and shift them over toward his son-in-law. "Tonight you're not just family, Greer," he told her. "Tonight you're a guest, as well."

The way she saw it, she'd imposed on his hospitality, bringing two more mouths for him to feed. The least she could do was help clean up.

"But I—" Greer got no further in her protest.

"No argument," he instructed with finality. "Next time I'll let you pick up twice as many plates," he promised with a wink. "But right now, you have to take the judge and his father home."

"Don't even try to argue," Rose told her. "The man still wears his badge pinned to his bare chest at night. He's used to being obeyed."

Andrew merely smiled. "Some habits are harder to break than others," he told his guests. "I'll walk you to the door," he volunteered, ushering Greer, the judge and his father to the foyer. He stopped just outside the threshold. "Now that you know the way, Judge, don't be a stranger. You, too, Gunny."

Blake looked at his host and realized that the man actually meant what he was saying. He *wanted* them to come by. Why? Despite the evening that they'd just shared, he and his father were all but strangers to Andrew Cavanaugh. Why would the former chief of police welcome them so warmly into his home?

He had no answer. Neither did he know where this quiet feeling of well-being that was softly whispering through him had come from. He decided, for the time being, to stop analyzing it and just enjoy the sensation for as long as it lasted.

Blake refrained from shaking his head, but he was still rather mystified.

Strange people, strange evening.

And, as he and his father walked to O'Brien's sedan, Blake had more than a fleeting suspicion that this wasn't going to be the last strange evening he was going to spend.

Chapter 7

Former gunnery sergeant Alexander Kincannon frowned as he watched the young woman in his living room remove the leather and suede decorative pillows that had been on the sofa.

"Don't seem right," he commented to Greer, "you spending the night on the couch. That's supposed to be strictly for husbands who've had cross words with their wives. Y'know, punishment. Not that I've had any experience with that."

"Didn't think you did." Greer hid her smile as she turned away, stacking the second pillow on top of the first. "Don't worry, Mr. Kincannon. I'll be fine."

His frown deepened just for a moment. "You got a learning disability, girl?" he asked. "I told you to call me Gunny."

She wasn't accustomed to being so familiar with a

man the senior Kincannon's age. It was hard enough for her to adjust to Andrew and his brother. "Sorry. 'Gunny,'" Greer acquiesced. "The sofa is more than adequate for my needs."

"It's not comfortable," he insisted. To prove his point, Alexander hit the cushion with the flat of his hand. It didn't give the way something that was a sofa would. "Fell asleep on that once, watching TV. It was like sleeping on a board."

Greer had a feeling that the man had fallen asleep watching TV more than once, but she kept that to herself. "That suits my purposes just fine. I don't want to be comfortable, I want to be on my guard," she reminded the judge's father.

Just then, the judge entered the room. His arms were filled with bedding. "So if this assignment runs a week—God forbid—you're planning to be awake the whole time? What are you, a zombie or one of the *undead* that seem to be so popular these days?"

Turning around to face him, Greer grinned. "Sorry to disappoint you, but I'm neither."

She was certainly acting as if she thought she was one of those creatures, he thought. "But you don't plan on sleeping."

"Catnaps," she interjected before he could continue. "I get by on catnaps."

Now there was a misnomer for an event if he ever heard one. "Every cat I ever knew spent most of the day 'napping.'"

The man was testy and argumentative. Was it just because she was here, or was there something more going on? They'd been here for only the past couple of hours and as far as she knew, nothing had changed. After dinner, she'd entertained the hope that he was coming around and that would make things easier on all of them.

Obviously not.

"Short catnaps," she emphasized.

Blake put down the bedding he'd gotten from the hall closet upstairs. There was a pillow, a blanket and two sheets. He nodded at the sagging stack. "Will you need anything else?"

"I don't think I'll even need this." Pulling the blanket out of the pile, she held it out to him. "It doesn't get cold this time of year," she explained tactfully.

He knew that. Did she think he lived in a bubble? "That was to put on top of the seat cushions and under the sheet to make it more comfortable for you—but I forgot, you don't want to be comfortable."

Ignoring the slight sarcastic tone, Greer continued to hold the blanket out to him. "I appreciate the thought, Judge."

Alexander seemed to realize the inequity of the situation. "Shouldn't there be two of you?" he wanted to know.

"Don't think the world is ready for that," Blake muttered under his breath.

Overhearing, Greer grinned before she could think better of it. "Once the dust settles, the arrangement will be reviewed," she assured the older man. "Most likely, my partner will be sharing the assignment."

Tufted eyebrows rose in hopeful query. "Another woman?"

Greer shook her head. "Sorry to disappoint you, Gunny. Not even on his best day." Taking the fitted sheet, she tucked it around the three seat cushions, swiftly preparing a makeshift bed for when she needed to use it. "You can go about your regular routine," she told the two men when neither of them moved but continued watching her. "Pretend I'm not even here. Think of me the way you think of your security system."

Blake took the opportunity to leave the room. He had work waiting for him in his den.

"Never thought of the security system as having killer legs," Alexander said, half to himself, half to her.

Greer laughed. "That's one of the nicest things anyone ever said to me," she told the older Kincannon. The man cleared his throat and grumbled under his breath in an attempt to disguise the fact that her response pleased him.

"You up to watching some TV?" Alexander wanted to know as he reached for the remote control.

"Sounds like a plan to me," she told him agreeably. Gunny sat down in the corner of the sofa he favored. After a beat, Greer joined him.

Fifteen seconds later, after the initial warm-up period, a commercial for a popular orange juice was literally splashed across the forty-six-inch flat screen. It was gone in an instant as Alexander, employing the remote, began channel surfing.

Suddenly, he seemed to realize that he wasn't alone. Grudgingly, Gunny held out the remote to her.

Rather than take it, Greer shook her head. "You're doing just fine without me."

"You don't mind my flying through the channels?" he asked, surprised.

"Your house, your prerogative," Greer told him, paraphrasing what his son had said to her when he refused to stay in the courtroom but joined her in trying to run down the escaping prisoner.

Fresh admiration entered the bright blue eyes as they crinkled. "You're all right, O'Brien." Alexander chuckled.

"Thank you." She inclined her head in acknowledgment of his words. "I take that as a very high compliment, Gunny."

He made a small, dismissive noise, uncomfortable with anything remotely resembling gratitude. "That's the way it was intended. Now watch the screen," he instructed gruffly, pointing toward the monitor with his remote.

Unable to concentrate because of the woman who was spending the night in his house, Blake gave up trying to work a little more than an hour into what had turned out to be a futile endeavor.

Biting off an oath, he closed the law book he'd been searching through—using books had always been far more satisfying to him than searching for information on the Internet. Try as he might, he still couldn't bring himself to trust something he couldn't hold in his hand.

Picking the fat tome up, he was about to place it back

on the shelf behind his desk when he stopped. He'd leave it on his desk until tomorrow, he decided. With any luck, he'd be able to get his thoughts together then.

With a little more luck than that, he'd be minus one houseguest.

Not that, under a completely different set of circumstances, he wouldn't have found her startlingly attractive. He would and, if he were being strictly honest with himself, he did. There were times when he felt that her incredibly light blue eyes saw right through him. She had the face of an angel, albeit a sexy angel, and a body made for sin.

Detective Greer O'Brien was definitely not a run-of-the-mill, ordinary woman who he could easily come across any day of the week.

He didn't know of any women who were willing to take a bullet for him.

But as noble as that might be, it also pointed to the fact that she was impulsive and impetuous. Which made her an unknown element in his life. He really didn't need that. And the sooner she was gone, the sooner he could get on with his life—such as it was.

Blake sighed. He found her presence in his house disturbing on so many levels. Until O'Brien had come crashing into him, landing on top as she brought him down, he'd thought that he'd completely shut down after Margaret's death. Shut down as a man. If he had needs, they were on such a deep, faraway level that he was not aware of them.

Or hadn't been until this morning.

Something else to hold against Detective O'Brien, he thought with another sigh.

Getting up, Blake crossed to the den's threshold and shut off the light. He could literally feel the tension. It was riding roughshod throughout his whole body, making his neck and shoulders ache as well as unsettling various other parts of him, physically and emotionally.

He really didn't need this.

What he did need was a good night's sleep. Maybe that would help him put some of this to rest. But as he started to go toward the stairs, he paused. He could hear the TV in the living room. It sounded like a Western.

Was his father still up?

Curiosity had Blake making his way into the living room. As he'd suspected, his father was still up. Or rather, propped up. The crusty old man had nodded off, as was his habit sometimes.

And he'd been right about the TV program. There was some old, classic Western playing on the set. His father favored Westerns, complaining that the current crop of filmmakers didn't have a clue how to make a decent one. For last Christmas, he'd gifted the old man with a complete DVD collection of John Wayne's more famous Westerns. Alexander Kincannon knew the dialogue to every one of them.

"You don't have to keep watching that," Blake told his unwanted houseguest as he walked up behind her. "My father's asleep."

She smiled, looking at her dozing companion. There was a note of affection in her voice as she told Blake,

"He lasted about fifteen minutes. It's probably the food. Eating as much as he did tonight makes a person sleepy."

"So does being in his early seventies," the judge pointed out. Right now, he mused, it was hard to believe that he was looking at a decorated war hero. His father seemed so docile. "I'll take him up to bed," he told her, stooping for a moment so that he could take one of his father's arms and slip it over his shoulders for leverage. He rose slowly, bringing the man up with him. The channel on the set remained the same. Still asleep, his father grunted as Blake brought him to his feet. "I said you didn't have to watch that," he told Greer again.

"I heard you, Judge." She made no effort to reach for the remote. "I happen to like Westerns."

One arm tucked around his father's midriff, the other holding the man's arm over his shoulders, Blake paused for a moment, studying her.

And then he shook his head. "You're a strange woman, Detective O'Brien."

Greer flashed a grin. "I've been told that. And if we're going to be housemates for a few days, you might as well call me Greer. It's less cumbersome on the tongue."

The word *tongue* set his imagination off before he could rein it in. Like slowly running his along the slope of her neck—and parts beyond. A warmth came over him. He wasn't having very pillar-of-the-community-like thoughts.

Had to be because he was tired, he thought defensively.

"Greer," he repeated. Not an ordinary name. Not an

ordinary woman, he thought as he began to slowly guide his father away from the sofa.

"Need help?" she offered.

"I've done this before," he answered. Then, after a beat, he added, "But thanks for offering."

The corners of her mouth curved. That cost him, she thought. The man was human, but it cost him. "Don't mention it."

Roused, his father opened one sleepy eye. "Movie over?" he wanted to know, mumbling his words. Releasing a huge sigh, he all but sank to his knees. Blake tightened his arm around the older man's waist.

"Yup," Blake lied.

Alexander's eyes drooped down again, shutting. "Who won?"

"The good guys, Dad," Blake answered. "Work with me here, Dad. We're coming to the first step."

"Step," Alexander repeated without any comprehension of the word. But he did raise his foot obligingly.

His back was to her and Blake couldn't see it, but he would have sworn that he *felt* the detective's smile widening.

After spending a generally restless, fitful night, Blake decided to get an early start on the day. As he came down the next morning, the aroma of fresh coffee greeted him. Fresh coffee and a scent he couldn't immediately place. All he knew was that it wasn't anything he'd smelled in the morning in his own house.

Not since before Margaret died.

Had to be his imagination, he told himself. That momentary sexual awakening he'd experienced yesterday had played havoc with his senses. That obviously included his sense of smell, he concluded.

His eyes shifted toward the sofa as he passed by the living room.

It was empty.

The bedding he'd given the detective was now neatly folded and stacked on a corner of the sofa.

Was she gone?

He doubted if he was going to be that lucky.

Making his way into the kitchen, he saw that he was right. She was in the kitchen, talking to his father. The aroma of freshly brewed coffee was her doing, he suspected.

How? As far as he knew, there was no coffee in the house.

As he walked in, his father turned and looked over his shoulder at him. "Pull up a chair, Blake. O'Brien's making us breakfast."

Confused, Blake looked down at the scrambled eggs with bits of ham that the detective had just put on a second plate—his, he assumed.

"Breakfast?" he echoed. "Out of what?" he wanted to know. "I'm fairly certain there's no recipe that turns beer into scrambled eggs and coffee." Nonetheless, he eased himself into the chair that was opposite the one his father was in. "Miracles a sideline of yours, Greer? Or did you sneak out to the grocery store early this morning?"

Leaving him and his father unattended would be

committing a dereliction of duty and they both knew it. *Trying to trip me up, Judge?* she wondered.

"Neither," she replied cheerfully. "Uncle Andrew had Aunt Rose slip some basic supplies into the trunk of my car when we weren't paying attention. He told me what he did just as we were leaving. I put them into the refrigerator when you were working in the den."

So that was what the chief had whispered to O'Brien last night. No doubt about it—the family was strange. "I earn a decent salary," he told her. "I don't need charity, however well intentioned."

She felt herself growing protective of the family patriarch—not that he needed her to defend him. She supposed that meant that she was really becoming a Cavanaugh.

"Uncle Andrew doesn't see it as charity. He calls it sharing. My new half sister, Patience, tells me that it's a habit of his. To refuse is an insult," she added.

Too busy eating and enjoying his breakfast, Alexander had remained silent during the exchange. Swallowing now, he put in his two cents.

"Try this, Blake," he urged, pushing the other plate closer to his son. "It's damn good." And then Alexander turned his attention to the woman who had so unexpectedly come into their lives, and, as far as he was concerned, brightened them. "You weren't kidding when you said you could cook."

"No point in lying about something like that," she answered, pleased that he seemed to be enjoying her efforts so much. She noticed that the judge left his plate untouched.

She got him a cup of coffee. Leaving it black, she moved it next to his plate and waited.

"You married, O'Brien?" Alexander asked her without warning.

"No." She'd come close once or twice, but then she'd come to her senses and broken it off. Relationships made her uneasy. They required too much commitment and yielded too much disappointment.

"Spoken for?" the senior Kincannon prodded.

"Dad," Blake said sharply. Alexander didn't appear to hear.

"No," Greer answered the older man's question.

Alexander pinned her with a look and asked, half seriously, "How do you feel about a retired marine?"

Unable to keep it back any longer, Greer allowed a smile to emerge. Humor danced in her eyes. "Respectful."

Greer answered the older man's question just as his son uttered another, far more exasperated, "Dad!"

What the hell had gotten into his father? Blake wondered. Yes, the woman was attractive, and yes, there was something about her that transcended the sum of her parts, something that could readily arouse a man if he wasn't careful, but he gave his father more credit than to behave like a smitten adolescent.

"Fella's got a right to know if he's got a chance," Alexander answered, clearly annoyed that his son felt he had to reprimand him like some errant kid. The retired marine shifted his attention back to Greer. "Do I?" The twinkle in his eye told her he was teasing her.

Greer shook her head. "I'm afraid you're just too young for me, Gunny."

Before either father or son could make a comment, Greer's cell phone began to ring. Putting down the spatula she was holding, she took the phone out of her pocket and flipped it open.

Turning her back to the two men she'd just served, Greer said, "This is Detective O'Brien."

Her partner didn't waste time with greetings or preambles. This wasn't a social call. "They found the stolen ambulance." His tone indicated that it wasn't a good find.

The bailiff's frightened face flashed through her mind. Greer tensed. "And?"

She heard Jeff take a breath before answering. "The bailiff was still inside."

She made the only logical guess she could. "Dead?"

"No, not then. The kid hung on long enough to reach the hospital. But he died on the operating table," Jeff told her.

What a waste. The second he'd agreed to help Munro escape, he'd been a dead man. It was all just a matter of when the bullet would find him. "Did he say anything before he died?"

"Yeah, as a matter of fact, he did. He said to tell the judge he was sorry, but he had to do it. They threatened to kill his family."

There was no comfort in knowing she'd guessed right. The man was still dead before he'd had a chance to live.

"And?" she prodded when Jeff didn't continue. "What about the family? Were they at the house?"

"Yeah." There was a long pause. "The wife was shot dead," Jeff told her grimly.

She felt her stomach tightening into a hard knot. "And the baby?" Greer forced herself to ask. Her voice came out in a whisper.

"Seems Munro—or one of his people at any rate—draws the line at killing babies," her partner answered. "The police found the baby wet and dirty and screaming…but alive. The chief's got your brother looking for the bailiff's next of kin."

A family man even in the worst of times, she thought. "Which one?" she asked.

There was momentary silence on the other end. And then Jeff answered, "Whichever one he can find."

"No, I mean which brother has he got out looking for the next of kin?"

She heard Jeff laugh shortly. "Oh, yeah, I forgot, you've got two of them. Ethan. And there's more news," he continued. "Someone tampered with the judge's car. It blew up when it was started. The officer never stood a chance." Greer closed her eyes. She'd had a feeling. Damn but there were days she hated being right. "By the way," Jeff was saying, "how's the babysitting detail going?"

"Better than it went for the bailiff and the officer," she commented darkly. And then, because she had to ask even though she had a feeling she already knew the answer, Greer asked, "No sign of Munro?"

"If there was, I would have told you that right off the bat," Jeff said.

"I was hoping you were saving the best was for last," Greer told him with a sigh. "Keep me posted."

"Will do." And with that, her partner broke the connection.

When she turned around again, slipping her phone back into her pocket, she found Blake staring at her.

"Tell me." The words came from Blake. It wasn't a request. It was an order.

Chapter 8

Blake's somber expression masked his thoughts as he listened to the sketchy details of what had happened to his bailiff, Tim Kelly, and the fact that his car had been wired to blow up the moment he started it. He made no comment during her swift narrative.

Kincannon looked almost preoccupied, but Greer knew better. The judge had heard and digested every word she'd said.

"And Tim's little girl?" he asked quietly. "Where is she?"

This, at least, she thought, was somewhat positive. "The chief of detectives is trying to locate the bailiff's next of kin before the social services system has a chance to swallow her up."

Blake nodded, taking the information in. They all knew that once a child was within the system, there were miles of red tape to untangle before that child could be extricated.

"Tim has—had," the judge corrected himself and she could see that the bailiff's death and the manner in which it happened had affected him far more deeply than the destruction of his vehicle, "an aunt who raised him. She lives in Santa Barbara." He paused, thinking. "Donna McClosky, I think he said her name was."

Greer had her phone out again. "This is really going to help, Judge," she told him. Two seconds later, her partner answered and she passed the information on. After terminating the call, she flipped the phone shut and tucked it away. "My partner's going to let the chief know what you said and get right on it." She paused for a second, debating asking the next question. Curiosity got the better of her. "You were close to the bailiff?" she asked, studying his expression.

Blake heard the note of sympathy in her voice. He didn't respond well to sympathy. It was too close to pity and that reminded him of other things.

Looking away, he shrugged carelessly. "He talked, I listened. Close?" he repeated the word, as if weighing it. "No. But he was young and enthusiastic and extremely likeable." He deliberately drew the focus away from himself by adding, "Everyone who knew him could tell you that."

Quietly sipping his black coffee, listening, his father looked at him. "Sounds like Scottie," Alexander commented.

"Scottie?" This was a new name, one she was unfamiliar with. Greer looked from one man to the other, waiting for one of them to enlighten her. By the look on his face, she had a feeling that her answer wasn't going to come from the judge.

"My younger son," Alexander told her stoically.

The older man, she noted, was staring at the remaining black liquid in his cup, avoiding her eyes. This was the first she'd heard of a sibling. "You have a brother?" she asked Blake.

"Had," Blake corrected tersely, grinding out the word almost against his will.

She waited for details, and, as she expected, it was the older Kincannon who ultimately filled her in. "Scottie was killed saving his platoon in Afghanistan. He was a marine," his father said with pride.

"He died a hero," Greer concluded.

Blake's face was stony. "Bottom line, he died," he said, his voice hollow.

A wave of compassion washed over her. Kincannon certainly had had his share of tragedies, she thought, her heart going out to him.

"A hero," Alexander repeated firmly, daring his remaining son to contradict him.

Blake had no desire to get into an argument this early in the morning. Scottie had wanted nothing more than their father's approval and had rushed off to enlist to fight for his country the minute he graduated college. It had been an utter waste of a decent human being.

Stifling a sigh, Blake echoed, "A hero," and let it go at that. He looked at Greer. "When you get Donna McClosky's address, let me know."

"So you can send her your condolences?" Greer

asked, thinking that Kincannon was a nicer man than he wanted people to believe.

Blake didn't answer at first, debating how much information to part with. But, given what he was learning about this woman's nature, he knew that she'd make it a point to find out. He might as well spare himself the interrogation.

"Costs a lot to raise a child these days. From what Tim told me, his aunt was just barely getting by. He was looking for a second job so he could send her a little money every month."

"You're gonna set up some kind of a trust fund for the kid?" It was a rhetorical question on his father's part. "Count me in."

Blake looked at his father. The only income the older man had was his pension. "You don't exactly have money to burn, Gunny."

His father's grin was a bit lopsided. "Yeah, I know, but I got this kid who lets me live at his place free. Been saving up for something special. This trust fund just might be it," he added with a nod of his head.

Generosity with a minimum of words. And a maximum of heart. For a moment, a surge of emotion threatened to close her throat. Yesterday, in court, when she sat in the witness chair, Kincannon had struck her as a somber, humorless man, a man who had evolved without a heart because of the loss he'd suffered. She would have never guessed that there was this caring side to him.

Just goes to show, you never really know about a person. "I'll get you that address," she promised.

"Good." Blake began to rise.

Greer was instantly alert. "Where are you going, Judge?"

"I have this flowing black robe." There was more than a touch of sarcasm in his voice. "It only seems to go with a courtroom as an accessory."

She ignored the sarcasm. "It's early, Judge," she pointed out, then indicated his plate. He'd barely touched it. "And you haven't eaten your breakfast yet."

"Won't go to waste," Alexander was quick to tell her, eyeing the plate. "I'll eat it if he's fool enough not to."

"No, he'll eat it," she told the other man, looking pointedly at Blake. "You wouldn't want to hurt my feelings, would you, Judge?"

Blake laughed shortly. "I don't think that's possible."

"You'd be surprised." That had slipped out unintentionally. She hurried to cover it up. There was no way she was going to let the judge think that she had a sensitive side. "At least try it," she urged. "I'll make you a deal. If you don't like it, you don't have to finish it."

With a sigh, Blake sat down again, resigned. "If I don't go along with this, you're probably going to try to force-feed me, saying something inane about a plane and an air hanger."

"Actually, I was considering a train and a tunnel, but a plane and an air hanger work just as well." Her straight face lasted only halfway through the sentence. The grin that took over threatened to split her face in half. "It won't hurt you to have something in your stomach,

Judge," she added seriously. "Think of it as a way to help you put up with the morning."

His eyes met hers as he raised the fork to his lips. "It's not the morning I have to put up with." There was no mistaking his meaning.

Rather than comment, Greer looked at Blake's father. He appeared amused by the exchange. "Is your son always this surly in the morning?" she wanted to know.

The shaggy gray head nodded sadly. "Afraid so, O'Brien. He's like this most mornings. Sometimes worse."

She took a breath and let it out, as if that somehow helped her fortify herself. "Something to look forward to."

"You realize that you don't have to," Blake pointed out. "No one's holding *you* prisoner."

She caught his meaning. "You're not a prisoner, Judge," she told him with all sincerity. "It just so happens that you and your father are two very special people that the Aurora police department would like to see continue living." She nodded at his plate. "So, how was it?"

He didn't follow her. "How was what?"

"Breakfast." When he didn't reply immediately, she realized that he'd consumed it all without even being aware of what he was doing. The man was definitely a challenge. "You finished it."

Blake looked down at his plate, a mild look of surprise momentarily slipping across his features. He didn't even remember chewing or swallowing, but he obviously must have. His plate was empty.

The woman was apparently still waiting for an evaluation of her culinary skills. "All right I guess. I'm still standing."

"High praise indeed," Greer said dryly. "But just for the record, Judge, you're sitting."

Pushing back his chair, Blake rose to his feet. "And now I'm standing."

Greer laughed, shaking her head. If she looked up *contrary* in the dictionary, she had a sneaking suspicion that she'd find Kincannon's handsome face staring back at her.

"Just no end to your talents, is there, Judge?"

He made no reply; instead, he asked a question. With nothing to lose, he thought he'd take a shot. "Any chance of my going to the courthouse alone?"

She flashed him a serene smile. "About as much chance as my growing two feet and playing on the Lakers by next season."

"What about my father?" He nodded at the elder Kincannon, fairly certain that he finally had her. "He doesn't go to court with me. How are you going to guard him *and* me? Even you can't be two places at the same time."

If he thought he was baiting her, he was going to be disappointed. "I am aware of that, Judge. I passed high-school physics with flying colors," she replied. "I have someone coming to stay with your father while we're at the courthouse."

She heard her former ally groan behind her. As she turned around, he said, "No offense, O'Brien, but I don't take kindly to being handed off."

Glancing at her watch, she noted the time. Taylor should be getting here at any moment. "I know, which is why I requested Taylor McIntyre for the job." She'd called the chief last night, right after the Kincannons had gone to bed. She had a feeling that Taylor would have more luck handling Gunny. The ex-marine might grumble about having women in charge, but he definitely responded to the female touch.

The doorbell suddenly rang. The cavalry had arrived. "And there she is."

"She?" Alexander echoed, instantly perking up.

She'd made the right decision, Greer thought. She glanced at the man over her shoulder, doing her best to suppress an amused grin. "Oh, didn't I mention that Taylor was a woman?" she asked innocently. "She's also the chief of detectives' stepdaughter."

"Anyone on the police force *not* related to Chief Cavanaugh?" Blake wanted to know. It seemed like the entire force was peppered with his relatives.

"There's got to be a couple of people," she deadpanned as she went to the door.

Greer opened it cautiously, acutely aware that even though she was expecting her step-cousin at this time, it still might be one of Munro's lackeys standing on the doorstep.

Fortunately, it was just Taylor.

The other woman did her best to summon a smile, or at least one that generally resembled one in passing. It took obvious effort.

"I'm not a morning person," Taylor warned by way of a greeting as she walked in.

Greer glanced at the judge. Taylor wasn't the only one, she thought. "There's a lot of that going around," she commented under her breath, then said with more feeling, "You should feel right at home."

Turning to the two men she'd spent the night with, Greer made introductions. "Taylor, this is Judge Blake Kincannon and his father, former gunnery sergeant Alexander Kincannon, retired marine," she added, knowing that the reference would put the older man in a good, hopefully cooperative mood. "Gentlemen, this is Detective Taylor McIntyre—" she looked deliberately at Alexander "—soon to be Detective Taylor Laredo."

"That's Cavanaugh-Laredo," Taylor corrected with a yawn. "I've decided to get my name legally changed." She saw the other woman looking at her in mild surprise. "Seems only right since Brian was more of a father to me, my brothers and sister than the guy who lent us his gene pool," she explained. Not waiting on ceremony, she purloined Greer's mug. There was still approximately four ounces of coffee in it.

Taylor drained it in less than five seconds. Putting the cup down, she asked Greer belatedly, "You didn't want that, did you?"

"Not half as much as you did," she assured the senior detective.

"You're getting married?" Alexander asked the new woman, interested.

Taylor beamed, her thoughts clearly straying to the man she was engaged to. Her devotion to her future husband was no secret. In fact, she'd once even confided that her fiancé could instantly raise her body temperature by five degrees with just a promising look. "As soon as we can set a date," she told the judge's father.

As if foiled, Alexander turned his attention back to Greer. "Looks like I'm just going to have to wear you down, O'Brien." He chuckled.

He wasn't going to stand here while his father all but made a fool of himself. "Time to go," Blake announced. "Nice meeting you, Detective." He nodded at the woman he was leaving with his father. She had his full sympathy, he thought.

"The pleasure was all mine," Taylor assured him. She stepped back beside her assignment for the day. "See you tonight," she told Greer. The glint in her blue eyes told Greer that she considered her new step-cousin's assignment the better one by at least a country mile.

Greer pretended she didn't notice.

With the Munro trial bumped indefinitely, Judge Kincannon's administrative assistant was forced to reschedule all the other cases and move them up on the calendar. Consequently, this morning, the judge found himself facing a child molester whose lawyer actually provided the defense that when his client indulged in recreational drugs, they turned the man into a completely different person. And it was *that* person who was the child molester. A stint in rehab, the lawyer declared, should clear everything all up.

It was all Blake could do to keep his ever increasing disdain for the defendant and his alleged crime from showing on his face. But at his core, Kincannon was a firm believer that everyone deserved their day in court and that they also deserved to be represented by competent counsel.

He was well aware of cases where the wrong man or woman was sent away for a crime they didn't commit. To his knowledge, his cases didn't number among them. He'd like to think that it was because he tried to keep proceedings as fair as possible, but he knew that there was also a good amount of luck involved.

He hoped to God that his luck never ran out.

It had been an extremely long day, broken up only by a quick recess for lunch, part of which was spent mediating a point of conflict for yet another set of counselors. When Blake finally got around to eating, he sent out for sandwiches from a local sandwich shop and had them brought to his chambers.

Ordinarily, he ate alone, usually at his desk. Most of the time, he would also be reviewing something that required his attention.

Today, though, he'd had to share his precious so-called free time with his bodyguard. It didn't sit that well with him. He valued the moments he was alone with his thoughts. With Greer, there was no such thing as being alone.

There was also no such thing as silence.

The woman seemed to actively have something against the latter because any time silence threatened to break out, she began talking again, filling the air with words to the point that Blake felt as if he was literally under attack. Occasionally, she came up for air, but that hardly seemed to last more than a couple of minutes at a time, and then she launched yet another verbal discourse.

Court was over for the day and they were now on their way home—and still she continued prattling on.

There was a headache behind his eyes that threatened to take over at any moment. He turned toward the woman in the driver's seat and asked, "Have you ever tried yoga, Detective?"

She wasn't into sitting quietly in a twisted position. Weight-lifting and cross-training were far more her style. "Once," she admitted, unaware that a slight frown slipped over her lips. "I didn't like it."

Blake sighed. It figured. "I had a feeling," he said, more to himself than to her.

"I'm not the type to sit around and mediate." She suspected he'd already guessed that, but she said it anyway. "I'm more of a doer." She extended it to her job. That was, after all, what she was doing here. Her job. "I like being out in the field, rounding up dealers—"

He had a feeling that this current assignment was going to drive her crazy if it extended beyond a couple of days. That made two of them.

"Then what are you doing here?" Blake asked her, slowly becoming aware that the scent of lavender and jasmine were subtly registering within the interior of the vehicle.

Greer chose her words slowly. The terrain before her could become uncomfortable territory at any moment. "The chief felt I was the best for the job because I was the one who'd studied Munro's habits and because…"

Her voice drifted off as she searched for the right way to say this. The least hurtful way to say this.

This time, the momentary silence made him uneasy. "Yes?"

Greer slanted a quick glance in his direction. Could it really be that Kincannon didn't remember her? He seemed far too sharp for that, but maybe he'd blocked it all out. Not all survival mechanisms kicked in on conscious levels.

She took a breath and then continued. "Because you and I have a history."

She'd said the last part softly as she drove away from the courthouse. Slowing down, she slanted another glance toward the judge to see if there was any sign that he knew what she was referring to. His expression remained identical to the one he'd worn a few moments ago.

"A history," Kincannon repeated. There was neither feeling nor a quizzical note evident in his voice. She had no clue if he did actually recognize her.

Okay, she supposed she had to ask, although, in asking, she was aware that she was bringing it all up for him again. Part of her really didn't want to do that. She hated seeing anyone in pain. But as long as she felt in the dark as to whether or not the judge remembered that she was the one who'd been first on the scene of his wife's fatal accident, she was going to constantly feel as if she was walking on eggshells, afraid of the information coming out at the wrong time.

It was a Band-Aid she had to pull off. Now.

"Is that what they call it these days?" Kincannon finally commented.

She took a breath. This time his voice said everything she needed to know. "Then you remember."

He looked at her for a long moment, the events of that dark day coming at him like a lethal assault on all fronts.

He could never think of that day without bitterly tasting the loss. He and Margaret were just coming back from dinner. It was their second anniversary and he couldn't wait to get her home. Couldn't wait to make love with her and count his blessings that he had found his soul mate so early in his life.

He never got to do either.

"That you were the one who cut my seat belt and dragged me out of the car wreck? That you worked over my wife for fifteen minutes, until the paramedics came? Yes, I remember."

Greer frowned to herself. How had Kincannon known how long she'd labored over his wife? When she'd finally sat back and silently admitted to herself that death had won, she'd seen that the man she later learned was a sitting judge in her area had slipped into merciful unconsciousness.

Looking at him now, she realized that she was sitting beside a man who made it a point to know as much as he could about everything. "You tracked down the responding paramedics and talked to them, didn't you?"

He nodded. It had cost him to do it. Had cost him even more to listen to the two men recount their own futile efforts to resuscitate his wife, but he'd hoped that if he did, if he knew everything that had been done, the very knowledge would somehow begin to usher in closure for him and he could start to heal.

He was still waiting.

Chapter 9

A movement at the back of the courtroom caught
Blake's attention despite the fact that the defense attorney
pacing before the bench was actively questioning a
witness.

For just a split second, his focus shifted away from the
proceedings and onto the man in the back of the room.
Blake felt his heart rate increase enough to be noticeable.
It was then that he admitted, if only to himself in the
privacy of his own mind, that the shooting incident had
actually spooked him.

He'd already been well aware of how tentative life
could be. One moment you were here, the next you were
gone. Just like that.

His brother had been larger than life with an aura of
tremendous energy about him. Scott had embraced life
and wanted to do great things. Margaret was the very

definition of sunshine, lighting up his life every moment she was in it. Everyone who knew her loved her. And in what amounted to a blink of an eye, they were both gone. Forever.

Even so, there was a part of him that still felt bulletproof. He felt as if he would go on forever, no matter what.

Probably because it no longer meant anything to him. Those who wanted nothing more than to go on living didn't. Those who didn't care one way or another, leaning toward not, went on interminably.

But being fired at the other day had made him jumpy, if only because he didn't like having the unexpected sprung on him. He liked things mapped out, liked knowing what was coming.

Court had been in session for the past three hours and the defense attorney had only begun to cross-examine the witness who was currently seated in the witness box. There was no reason for anyone to enter the courtroom at this point, no sequestered witness being summoned to give his or her testimony.

Yet someone had entered.

That someone was leaning over, saying something to O'Brien. Blake focused and noticed that the man in the gray sports jacket seemed, at least at this distance, to have the same coloring and features as his bodyguard. Except that he had dark hair and O'Brien was a blonde.

Whatever the man had said to her had O'Brien vacating her seat in the last row, where she'd been ever since court had begun today. The next moment, the man slid into the row, taking her place.

Before he could even form the question in his mind, O'Brien left the courtroom.

Had something happened?

Had Munro been caught? Or had whoever decided these things called off the bodyguard detail?

And who the hell was this new player in the back of his courtroom?

Curiosity he didn't think he possessed anymore rose to bedevil Blake. He wasn't going to get any answers now, not unless he called a halt to the proceedings and inconvenienced everyone but himself.

His curiosity would keep.

Blake forced himself to focus on what was going on in front of his bench. That was, after all, what they were paying him for.

The moment Blake brought his gavel down, declaring recess for lunch, he was on his feet. But rather than retreat to his chambers as was his habit, he stepped down from behind his desk and crossed to the back of the room. He had questions.

The man he wanted to question was coming right toward him. The closer the man came, the more Blake thought that he bore a striking resemblance to O'Brien. One of the Cavanaughs?

And then it hit him a split second before the man reached him.

"You're one of her brothers, aren't you?"

Humor quirked Ethan's mouth as he pretended to

look down at himself. "Does it show? I thought I hid the battle scars pretty well."

The other man was cracking jokes. Blake had his answer. "That would make you Ethan."

The amused smile widened. "That it would, Your Honor. What gave me away?" he asked, curious. A lot of people who knew them managed to confuse him with his brother and the judge was a complete stranger.

"You're smiling," Blake answered. "Detective O'Brien said that your brother Kyle was the more somber one."

"Not anymore," Ethan confided with genuine pleasure. "Kyle's been smiling a lot lately. Mostly due to Jaren," he added. "Jaren Rosetti is another detective on the force. Homicide."

This was far more information than he needed or wanted, Blake thought. What was it about the O'Briens—or the Cavanaughs for that matter—that seemed to compel them to feel that they were somehow responsible for maintaining the mental well-being of the world at large?

"Why are you here, Detective? And where's your sister?" For half a second, hope flashed through him. But then, oddly enough, it was followed by a strange hollowness. He instantly dismissed it, attributing the feeling to the fact that he was hungry. "Am I to assume by her absence that she's not required to hover around me any longer?"

"Sorry to be the one to tell you, but Greer'll be hovering for a while longer. I'm just here to spell her so that she can go home, pack a few changes of clothing and tie up a few loose ends. Specifically one important one."

He knew he shouldn't ask, knew he shouldn't care. Whatever the woman was up to didn't concern him. Except that he was curious.

Blake didn't have a clue where all this curiosity was suddenly coming from, but it prompted him to ask, "What sort of loose ends?"

All around them, people were emptying out the courtroom. Ethan stepped to one side to get out of the assistant district attorney's way. He offered the woman a quick smile. It was a purely ingrained reflexive action, brought on whenever he was in the proximity of an attractive woman.

"Greer needs to find someone to take care of Hussy for her." He chuckled softly. "Doesn't trust either me or Kyle to do it."

The name meant nothing to him. Did it refer to a car—he knew people who named their cars. A child? A cat? "What's a hussy?"

Ethan struggled not to laugh. "You're lucky you asked me and not Greer because that's a straight line she wouldn't be able to resist," he told the judge.

"Lucky," Blake repeated with absolutely no feeling. "So enlighten me."

The bailiff who had been sent in to fill the vacancy left by Tim Kelly's murder looked toward him, a silent question in his eyes. Blake nodded, giving the man permission to leave.

"Hussy is the dog my sister rescued," Ethan was saying.

"From a shelter?" Blake asked even as he told himself he really didn't care to be inundated with details about her life away from the job. What difference did it make to him where the animal had come from? Yet he was curious.

"From two coyotes that had decided Hussy would make an adequate breakfast. Skinniest thing you ever saw when Greer brought her home. She had to work really hard to get that dog to trust her."

Their eyes met and Blake couldn't shake the feeling that O'Brien's brother was telling him more than his words suggested.

"You should see Hussy now. Doesn't even *look* like the same animal. Don't tell her I said so, but Kyle and I think Greer's got a gift," Ethan said, lowering his voice. "She 'loves' things back to health."

What was that supposed to mean?

For that matter, Blake suspected he was having his leg pulled. The story didn't ring true. "Just what does a slip of a woman do to scare off two coyotes?" he wanted to know. The stories he'd heard made a point of the fact that of late, driven by hunger, coyotes were getting pretty brazen in the early morning light.

"Something'll get lost in the translation if I explain. You should ask her to show you sometime."

Not likely. Blake made a disparaging noise under his breath. He was in no need for an installment of show-and-tell. "I'll be going to my chambers to have lunch," he informed this newest Detective O'Brien he had to deal with.

Ethan nodded amiably, gesturing for him to go first. "Lead the way, Your Honor."

Blake remained where he was. Security had been doubled. A rat with a hip replacement couldn't sneak by the metal detector, much less a gun-wielding drug dealer. Just what did this O'Brien think was going to happen if he went to his chambers for some much-needed solitude?

"I'd prefer to have it alone," he informed the detective.

"I'm sure you would," Ethan responded cheerfully. "And I feel for you, Judge, I really do. But the chief'll have my head if I don't hang around you—and so would Greer." He inclined his head toward the other man just a little. "And to tell you the truth, she scares me a lot more than the chief does. Greer doesn't pull her punches," he confided.

There was just no winning, Blake thought with exasperation. Turning on his heel, he motioned for the other man to follow him to his chambers.

Greer didn't stop to catch her breath until she was in her car again, on her way back to the courtroom. She'd spent the past hour practically running from place to place, trying to get everything done in as short amount of time as possible.

There was a duffel bag in the trunk, stuffed with everything she'd need for a week's stay just in case this little detail she was shackled to dragged on and she didn't get a chance to get back to her place. She'd arranged for her next-door neighbor, Mrs. Rosenbloom, to pick up her mail. She knew the retired junior high school English teacher would like nothing better than to have an actual excuse to go through her mail.

The sprinklers were programmed on a timer set to go off every other day so that she wouldn't return to a dead lawn. Most important, she'd made arrangements for Hussy to stay with Patience. Her half sister was only one of two within the Cavanaugh clan who wasn't directly in law enforcement. Janelle was the other. The latter had thrown her lot in with the court system while Patience, bless her, was a veterinarian. More than that, she was a vet with just the right kind of touch.

Hussy, poor baby, tended to be a huge chicken when it came to being handled by anyone but her. Some in-depth investigative work on her part had uncovered that Hussy's former owner had abused her, using the small mongrel dog as a training tool for the pit bulls he was breeding. That was why the poor thing was missing part of her ear.

Skittish around people she didn't know, Hussy had nonetheless taken to Patience right from the start. Which was why she'd decided to leave Hussy with the woman instead of asking one of her brothers to swing by her house once a night to feed the dog and let her out in the yard.

Patience had been more than happy to look after the dog. And she wasn't housing Hussy in one of the runs at the animal hospital where other dogs whose masters were away were boarded. Instead, Patience told her that she was going to take the dog home with her.

Greer could have sworn that Hussy had smiled when she'd handed the leash over to Patience.

With her mind at ease, Greer felt she could give the proper amount of undivided attention to her assignment: making sure that Judge Blake Kincannon remained unharmed.

Her mouth curved slightly. She was sure that was going to just thrill the man. Not that she could really blame him. Being independent herself, she could certainly understand Kincannon's resistance to the situation. He was caught between a rock and a hard place. Refusing left him unprotected. No one liked feeling vulnerable, as if they had a target painted on their forehead. But men like Kincannon didn't like being forced to obey rules that were not of their own making, didn't like feeling hemmed in and trapped. Didn't like their every move being watched and shadowed.

The judge gave her the impression that he'd always shouldered his way through life. He was a protector, if she didn't miss her guess, not a protectee.

She felt for him. That didn't mean that she was going to let him have his way. She was here for however long the chief felt she should be.

Sorry, Judge. Sometimes we just have to play the hand we're dealt, she thought as she pulled into the courthouse parking lot. It was only half full, which meant that people were still out to lunch.

Her own lunch was sitting in a bag next to her on the passenger seat. Three different kinds of meat mated with two different cheeses and then drizzled with oil and vinegar before being stuffed into twelve inches of crusty French bread.

At the rate she ate, she figured it would be her lunch and possibly her dinner, as well. Dinner for Kincannon and his father was going to be something she'd put together once she brought the judge home. During her nonstop marathon hour she'd made a point of picking up some groceries. She'd deposited them at the judge's house just after she'd brought Hussy to stay with Patience.

For a few seconds, she debated eating her lunch in the car, then decided that she'd been gone long enough. Ethan was doing her a favor; she didn't want to abuse it. If she did, she knew she wouldn't hear the end of it for a very long time. Ethan had the kind of memory that elephants envied.

Besides, all things being equal, she'd rather be up in Kincannon's chambers than sitting in a hot car.

At the thought of the judge, Greer became aware of a strange feeling rifling through the pit of her stomach, unsettling it. Under different circumstances, she would have called what she felt butterflies, but there was no reason to *have* butterflies. This was just an assignment, no different from any other.

Okay, maybe a little different, but that didn't change the basics. She was a detective acting as a bodyguard. She was definitely not invested in this situation as a woman, only as an agent of the law. There was absolutely no reason for her to feel anything at all except responsible for keeping the man alive.

But there was a part of her that did wish Kincannon wasn't so damn sexy. It made things harder on her.

Doesn't matter if the man looks like Johnny Depp in one of his better roles, she upbraided herself. *Blake Kincannon is just an assignment, not a man.*

Right. And she was a turnip, Greer thought as she entered the courthouse lobby.

In order for her to get to any of the courtrooms—or even the bathroom for that matter—security required that she had to pass through a metal detector and then walk by the scrutinizing eye of a dour-faced policeman. The man made her think of a troll sitting beneath a bridge.

"What's in the bag?" the policeman fairly growled the question as he watched her place both of her weapons and her cell phone on the conveyer belt. He looked completely unimpressed when she flashed her shield at him. He was programmed to do a job and *nothing* was going to get in his way.

"A sandwich," she responded cheerfully. To prove it, she crossed to him and opened the bag so that he could verify the contents for himself.

The policeman, Officer DeVry, muttered something under his breath and waved her on. As she picked her weapons and cell phone up on the other side of the screening apparatus, Greer heard what sounded like his stomach rumbling audibly.

Greer raised her eyebrows as she looked in the officer's direction. "Hungry?" she asked.

"Yeah," he grumbled.

She'd always been good at small talk. It was a tool

to get people to relax around her. "When's your lunch break?"

"Not for a while," he complained. "They're short-handed because of the shooting and I can't go get anything for another ninety minutes."

Greer thought for a moment. Most likely, she was going to be dealing with this man for at least the next week if not longer. Having him view her in a friendly frame of mind might come in handy.

Taking the sandwich out of the bag, she separated the two halves. They'd already been cut by the boy behind the counter who'd built the sandwich for her.

Dropping one half back into the bag, Greer held the other half out to the officer like a peace offering. "Here."

DeVry eyed the offering suspiciously, making no move to take it from her.

"Here what?" he wanted to know.

The officer was sitting in a chair that had an arm extension on it. She placed the half she'd offered him on the extension.

"I'd take it as a personal favor if you had this half. I hate wasting food and there's just too much here for me to finish. Take it off my hands, Officer DeVry?"

With that, Greer turned on her heel and hurried over to the escalator before the bewildered officer could say anything.

She heard wrapping paper being quickly disposed of as the escalator took her up to the next floor. Greer smiled to herself.

Judge Kincannon's courtroom was empty when she

walked in. It looked as if court was still in recess, she thought.

Crossing the length of the room, Greer circumvented the judge's desk and went through the door on the left that led to the hall and to Kincannon's chambers. That door was closed, as well. She knocked on it once.

Not waiting for a response, Greer turned the doorknob and walked in.

Kincannon was at his desk, reviewing something that had him frowning to himself.

Nothing new there, she thought.

Her brother was on the leather sofa, reading a paperback book that he'd stuffed into his pocket earlier when she'd asked him to stay with the judge for an hour. Most likely he was reading a play, she guessed. Ethan had a weakness for theater productions. Being in them, not seeing them. Ethan was the family ham.

"Hi, I'm back," she announced just as Kincannon looked up. Tongue in cheek, she asked, "Did you miss me?"

"What I realized," Kincannon answered, "was that I'd missed the silence. In the past twenty-four hours, I haven't had any."

Rather than rise to the bait, she glossed right over it. "Ethan's not that much of a talker," she agreed, setting down the bag that now only contained half a sandwich.

Both Blake and Ethan laughed shortly, the sound merging. Just like when both her brothers used to gang up on her when they were growing up. She liked to point out that it took two of them to equal one of her.

"Compared to you, an auctioneer isn't much of a talker, either," Blake told her.

He wasn't fooling her, she thought. Her eyes crinkled as she drew her conclusion. The man *had* missed her. The fact that he would probably go to his grave rather than admit it didn't matter.

"Thanks for filling in," she told her brother. "You can go back to your homicide now."

Kincannon looked mildly interested. "She always boss everyone around?" he asked Ethan.

"For as long as I can remember, Judge. Good luck," he addressed the remark to Kincannon, not Greer. "And I mean that from the bottom of my heart."

"He means he would if he had one," Greer corrected.

Blake said nothing. He was too caught up in re-membering. Scottie and he used to engage in the same kind of banter. It reminded him how much he missed his younger brother.

"See you later, Greer." And then Ethan nodded at him. "Goodbye, Judge, nice meeting you."

"Goodbye," Blake murmured, already turning his attention back to what he was doing. And trying very hard not to notice that the woman had the crisp, fresh smell of the wind about her.

It seemed rather appropriate, he couldn't help thinking, seeing as how Detective Greer O'Brien had all but blown into his life.

Chapter 10

"So, what are we having tonight?" Alexander asked, seeming to materialize at the door the moment that Greer opened it.

Tired, Greer still grinned as she dropped her shoulder bag on the hall table and removed her weapon, still in its holster. She placed it next to her purse. Her secondary weapon she only removed when she was going to bed.

It was a little more than three weeks into her assignment and she and the senior Kincannon had hit a comfortable stride.

After what seemed like several initial false starts, she sensed that the former gunnery sergeant had begun to view her as the daughter he'd never had. His own wife had died years ago and, from what he'd told her, he'd never really gotten to know his late daughter-in-law. He, Margaret and his son would get together around the holidays, but only if he was stationed in the area, which wasn't very often.

Alexander now called her by her first name rather than by her last and things were now comfortable between them. Greer wished she could say the same for her and the judge. Though he didn't say it in so many words, Kincannon still looked as if he would rather she wasn't around, which made her job more difficult.

"In the interest of time," she said in answer to Alexander's question about dinner, "I was thinking of making shrimp alfredo."

Greer knew that she, like all the other Cavanaughs, had a standing invitation to drop by Andrew's anytime for a meal. She'd done it the first night because she needed something to break the ice, but left to her own devices, she liked cooking and there was something very intimate and bonding about cooking for these two bachelors.

Widowers, she silently corrected herself. Both men had loved and lost in the cruelest way nature could devise, long outliving the women they had vowed to love, honor and cherish to the end of their days.

At least they'd loved someone, she thought wistfully, which was more than she could say. Of course, it was hard to fall in love when you kept a tight rein on your heart the way she did. But she was determined not to be hurt the way her mother had been and the only way to prevent it was not to fall in love in the first place.

"Sounds good to me," the older Kincannon enthused. "I'm partial to seafood," he said, telling her something she'd already found out for herself. "Need any help?"

The offer, out of the blue, surprised her. Her eyes crinkled as she told the man, "I could use some company. You up for that, Gunny?"

"Sounds like something I can handle," Alexander told her amiably as he slid onto a stool by the counter. He watched her gather the ingredients that another detective had dropped off earlier. "You know, this isn't so bad, having a woman around."

She knew that as far as former gunnery sergeant Alexander Kincannon was concerned, he'd just given her a very high compliment. When she'd first arrived, Greer was well aware that the older man resented her intrusion into the home he shared with his son almost as much as his son did. Added to that was the fact that he didn't feel that women belonged in law enforcement doing anything other than sitting behind a desk. With all of that stacked up against her, things could have become a little dicey.

But they didn't.

"Wish your son felt that way," Greer said offhandedly as she separated the already cooked shrimp from their tails. She threw the shrimp, one by one, into a bowl and the shells surrounding their tails onto a paper towel.

"He minds less than he lets on," Alexander assured her. "Blake just has trouble letting his feelings show. He's used to keeping everything all bottled up."

She raised her eyes to the man sitting opposite her, barely able to suppress her smile. "Gee, I wonder where he got that from."

Alexander shook his head. "Beats me."

What really amused Greer was that Blake's father

was being serious. He didn't see the connection of his passing on his behavior to his son.

A noise behind him had Alexander swiveling his seat to the right to get a better look. Blake had just walked into the kitchen.

"Speak of the devil," Alexander marveled, chuckling under his breath. "Hey, Blake, we were just talking about you."

Blake stopped short of the refrigerator and the cold drink that had been his goal. Suspicion flittered across his features as he looked from his father to the woman who, unbeknownst to her, was increasingly getting under his skin.

"Why?"

Greer decided to answer before his father said anything to get her in trouble. There was no telling how the older man would deliver the truth.

"Your father seems comfortable having me around. I just commented that I wish you felt the same way."

Opening the refrigerator and taking out a can of soda, Blake popped the top. He took a drink, nudging the refrigerator door closed with his elbow. His eyes shifted toward her before he said anything.

"Hard to feel comfortable with someone shadowing my every step." He took another long sip and then laughed shortly. "I guess I should count myself lucky you let me use the bathroom by myself, without requiring me to share the experience."

Alexander's laugh was far less subdued or guarded. "Might prove interesting," he commented more to himself than to either one of them.

Blake sighed. He knew better than to take his father to task for making the comment. The odds were fifty percent against him that Gunny might say something even worse the next go-round.

So instead, Blake nodded at the pot that was growing crowded with shelled shrimp. "That dinner?"

"It will be," she answered.

Kincannon didn't usually come out of his office until dinner was ready. She'd learned in the first few days that the judge was a man of routines. That was good for her when it came to keeping tabs on him, but not so good when it came to the matter of the lowlife who was after him. A routine was something they could easily use to their advantage.

That's what you're here for, remember? she reminded herself. It was up to her—and the patrolmen who periodically drove by Kincannon's house—to keep the judge safe even within his routine.

"Something on your mind, Judge?" she asked mildly, filling a second pot with water and placing it on the front burner. A sealed box of angel hair pasta lay on the counter beside the stove burners.

He took a breath, as if silently saying *now or never.* "What are my chances of getting a furlong?"

She went on working, even as she raised her eyes to his face. She couldn't gauge what he was thinking. "From work or from me?"

He never hesitated. But he did, she thought, smile just the smallest bit. What was *that* all about? "The latter."

Dream on, Judge. It's just not *going to happen.*

"About a million to one." Greer raised her eyes to his

just for a fleeting moment. "Possibly even greater than that."

It was no more than he apparently expected. "That's what I thought," he replied with a nod. "I'll just tell them no."

Now he had her curious. Greer adjusted the temperature under the pot. "Tell who no?" she wanted to know.

Blake hesitated for a moment, debating just answering her question with a careless shrug as he left the room. But he knew her rather well by now. Greer wouldn't stop until she found out what he was referring to.

So he told her and saved them both a lot of needless interaction. "Aurora Memorial Hospital is having one of their fundraisers. They're trying to raise enough money to build a new leukemia wing."

"Worthy cause," she commented. Greer's voice was low, but there was no mistaking the genuineness of her feelings.

That surprised him. He thought the police force was only into pushing their own charities to the exclusion of all else. Apparently there were exceptions.

"Yes, it is," he agreed. "They asked me if I would say a few words to jump-start the donations, get them flowing."

She was still waiting for him to come to the heart of his dilemma. When he didn't, she prodded him. "So far, I don't see a problem."

Blake looked at her, his eyes meeting hers. "You, Detective, you're the problem."

In the middle of purloining a shrimp out of the bowl

to sneak a taste, Alexander sprang to her defense. "Hey, go easy on her, Blake."

Greer held up her hand for a moment, stilling her silver-haired protector. "That's okay, Gunny. My fault. I did ask."

The water began to boil and she slid out half the spaghetti in the box. The next moment, she'd removed the pot's lid, broke the spaghetti in half and rained it into the pot. She did the same with the second half.

Only then did she glance at Kincannon over her shoulder. "You're afraid I'll embarrass you?" she asked in a mild tone, as if they were merely discussing the weather.

It wasn't her but the situation that embarrassed him. "Most judges don't have bodyguards."

"Most judges didn't receive a threat on their lives and their family's lives via their personal laptop," she pointed out. Greer dusted her hands on the makeshift apron she'd tied on.

"If they do have bodyguards, those bodyguards *look* like bodyguards." And that, he concluded, made his argument for him.

Stirring the spaghetti, Greer turned her attention back to the shrimp. The judge's father had already disposed of four and was working on a fifth. Melting butter and garlic in the frying pan, she tossed in the shrimp that had escaped Alexander's questing fingers and began to stir.

"I could ask my brother to go with you," she speculated, "although he probably doesn't look burly enough to suit your purposes, either." Chewing on her lower lip, she considered the situation. "Or, I could just go disguised," she told him brightly.

"You mean as one of the hostesses serving drinks or appetizers?" He supposed that might work.

He was in no way prepared for what she was about to say next.

"No, as your date."

He looked at her, the words not registering. "Excuse me?"

Turning down the heat, Greer rested the stirring spoon on a plate since there apparently was no spoon rest. "I'm assuming that invitees are allowed to bring along a guest. Am I wrong?"

Hope had sprung eternal—for exactly three seconds before it had sunk to an ignoble death. "No, you're not wrong."

To her it was the perfect solution. "Okay, then it's all settled. You get to go to the fundraiser. Nobody has to know that I'm guarding you." The spaghetti was ready. She turned off the heat and began to look for a strainer.

"I'll know."

Instead of allowing herself to get deeper into a discussion where she apparently had the opposing view, Greer merely smiled.

"That, Judge, is the whole point. Knowing your back is covered so that you can relax."

A quick search through the cabinets told her that there was no colander. These people really *didn't* do any cooking at home, did they? she thought.

"Having you around has the exact opposite effect."

She put her seemingly futile search on hold and turned around to look at Kincannon. "Did you just give me a compliment, Judge?"

He had, but he hadn't meant to. "I'll be in my office," he told her abruptly, turning on his heel. "Tell me when dinner's ready."

Taking two towels—they didn't seem to have pot-holders, either—she picked up the pot with the spaghetti and slid the lid back only a fraction in order to drain out the water. Even so, she never missed a step and answered, "Will do, Your Honor."

The amusement in her voice followed him all the way down the hall.

Blake straightened his bowtie, looking at the reflection in his wardrobe mirror to get it right.

He had his doubts about this, about attending the fundraiser at all with Munro and his henchmen still on the loose out there. Fairly confident that nothing would happen to him in a ballroom full of people, there was still a very small part of him that worried. Not for himself, but for any innocent bystander who might get hurt if Munro did materialize to make an attempt on his life.

And as for having to go with a bodyguard, that still irritated him. He had no desire to have others think he was being coddled. It was bad enough that the people at the courthouse knew the details. Word had spread with incredible speed within the judicial community, both about Munro's escape and about the threat that the drug dealer had sent to his laptop. It didn't exactly take a genius to put two and two together and figure out what Detective O'Brien was doing, hanging around in his courtroom day after day.

Or what she was doing, going to this fundraiser as his "date."

Blake was really leaning toward calling the chairwoman of the gala, making his apologies and canceling his appearance when he came down the stairs.

Greer had gotten downstairs ahead of him. He could hear her talking to his father. His father had just said something to make her laugh and the sound seemed to almost undulate toward him like the movements of a seductive belly dancer.

He banished the image from his mind.

This was a bad idea, he decided, going with her under this pretext.

He was going to tell her that he wasn't feeling well. She couldn't try to argue him out of that, whereupon it was more than an even bet that if he told her he'd just decided not to go, she'd handcuff him to the interior of the sedan and drive to the hotel where they were holding the fundraiser.

Sick it was, he decided. He raised his voice as he approached the living room. "Detective, I've thought it over and—"

That was when it happened. That was the exact moment that he was hit by a Mack truck.

Or at least that was the way it felt to him. The sight of Greer completely knocked the wind out of him.

With her light blond hair curled and loose around her shoulders, she was wearing a strapless ice-blue gown, the hem just whispering along the floor as she turned away from his father and toward him. The top part—the bodice he thought he'd heard his wife once tell him it was called—seemed to be twinkling. He realized that there were hundreds of sequins responsible for that, for catching the light and flashing it back at him like so many tiny, flirtatious stars.

The rest of her gown, staying as close to her torso as he found himself wishing that he could, hugged her curves. It was only when she walked that he realized there was a slit in the front of her gown that went clear up to her thigh, exposing a near perfect expanse of leg. There was a sudden, almost uncontrollable itch in his fingers. He wanted to touch her.

He felt as if he was coming unglued.

The sensuous—it couldn't be called anything else and still be accurate—smile that greeted him made his insides spasm and tighten as if he'd suddenly received a powerful blow to his stomach.

Greer's eyes swept over him as if she was taking every inch of his six-foot-two-inch frame into consideration. "You clean up nicely, Judge."

"You, too," he heard someone with a deep voice murmuring. It was only after several moments that he realized that the words had come from him.

The smile she gave him in response stole his breath away. Again.

"Thank you," she said.

Alexander seemed amused by the exchange he was witnessing. Or maybe it was just the mesmerized look on his son's face that tickled him.

"You two just going to stand there, gawking at each other, or are you actually going to go to this begging fest?"

"Fundraiser, Dad," Blake corrected him, coming to. "It's a fundraiser."

The snort from Alexander told him that the former gunnery sergeant felt he knew better. "Hey, a rose by any other name...you know."

"Give it a rest, Dad," Blake said, trying to bank down the edge in his voice.

The doorbell rang before Alexander could fire back at his son.

Swinging around, Greer instantly tensed. Her hand flew to the pistol that was holstered high on her inner thigh.

The retrieval had attracted the undivided attention of both men.

"Damn, but you are a beautiful sight, Detective O'Brien," Alexander murmured under his breath, his eyes all but glued to the length of her exposed leg. "And I should be twenty years younger."

If she heard the senior Kincannon's declaration, she gave no indication. Her attention was completely focused on the front door and whoever was standing on the doorstep. Her partner was coming to stay with Blake's father while the judge and she attended the fundraiser, but that didn't mean that he was the one standing on the other side of the door right now. It could just as easily be one of Munro's people, ringing the bell to throw her off her guard and gain admittance.

Holding her weapon with both hands and aiming it

at the door, Greer approached it slowly. When she was less than five feet away, she called out, "Who is it?"

"The Big Bad Wolf," the deep male voice belonging to the man standing behind the door told her. "Now open up the damn door or I'll huff and I'll puff and I'll blow your door down."

"House," she said, relaxing. Lowering her weapon, Greer holstered it again. This time she was very aware that she had an audience. "Or else I'll blow your *house* down," she corrected her partner as she unlocked the door and opened it. "At least get it right if you're going to quote fairy tales to me."

"Sorry." The apology echoed with sarcasm as Jeff walked in. "I promise to do better next time." Getting his first glimpse of her, her partner stopped in his tracks. He made no attempt to hide the fact that he was staring at her and that he was impressed by what he saw. A low whistle of deep appreciation escaped his lips. "Especially if you promise to wear that dress to work when you finally came back to the office."

Greer laughed, shaking her head. "In your dreams, Carson."

That's where she'd be tonight, Blake thought, realizing that his self-imposed celibacy was disintegrating right before his eyes.

Detective Greer O'Brien was going to be in his dreams.

Looking just like that.

Chapter 11

Given the present circumstances, Blake hadn't expected to enjoy himself at the fundraiser.

But he did.

The evening actually went far better than he thought it would. Because of her.

After the first hour or so, he even felt himself beginning to relax. The initial tension he'd experienced when he'd arrived left his shoulders.

But even as that happened, a different sort of tension whispered through him, one he had a hard time defining. He had ceased to be concerned about someone pegging Greer for what she was, a law enforcement agent charged with keeping him out of harm's way—a fact that had originally threatened his manhood.

One look at the woman beside him in her present outfit and law enforcement was definitely the *last* description that came to anyone's mind. He was even less concerned that somehow one of the food servers that were mingling unobtrusively with the hospital foundation's invited guests would suddenly pull out a gun and either shoot him or take him prisoner. Those kinds of things took place in movies and in the procedurals that were currently littering the TV airwaves, not in real life. He was fairly certain that Munro had probably done the smart thing and fled the country.

What he was tense about, he realized as he accepted his second scotch on the rocks from the bartender, was the way he felt himself reacting to the woman who was, for all intents and purposes, hermetically sealed to his side as he interacted with various people who were in attendance tonight.

The only time he and Greer were separated, and not by all that much distance, was when he took the podium and gave his short address to the other guests. His speech was about the good work that the hospital did as it continued to maintain its high standard of excellence, year after year.

This was the hospital where, he recalled for the crowd's benefit, he'd woken up to discover that he could no longer check the box marked "married" on any form. Where he was told that his wife was dead. He knew, even before anyone said anything, that the E.R. team had done everything humanly in their power to bring his wife around. But Margaret had died on that stretch of road where the drunk driver had hit them and just kept going.

He asked the audience to dig deep into their pockets

so that Aurora Memorial could always keep their doors opened and could continue to be on the cutting edge of all the modern advancements that the medical world had to offer.

When he stepped away from the podium, applause ringing in his ears, he crossed back to the bar and ordered another scotch and soda.

Greer shadowed his every move.

"Easy, Judge," she whispered in his ear, keeping her voice low so that no one could overhear. The last thing in the world she wanted to do was embarrass him. "That's your third one."

Her breath along his neck created a piercing, seductive warmth that went right through him. It took iron will for Blake not to shiver in response.

Not to kiss her.

"Counting, Greer?" He'd almost slipped and called her "Detective." Not something one called their date unless they were locked in a bedroom, role playing, the judge mused.

"Just looking out for you," she said with a smile. "I surmise that you want to maintain the proper, dignified front in public."

Blake deliberately took a long sip from the drink the bartender had passed to him to show Greer that he was his own person and if he set the glass down—which he did—it was by his own choice, not because she'd subtly suggested that he do it.

Turning to face her, he was struck again by how beautiful she looked. And by how attracted to her he

was. Since they were in a crowded ballroom, he decided
he was safe.

"Do you like dancing, Greer?"

The smile that curved her lips looked incredibly
sensual and seductive. He felt himself responding to a
degree he had no longer thought possible. "In general
or specifically?"

Her question amused him. Maybe he *had* consumed
a bit much too quickly, he decided.

The next moment he dismissed the thought. What
he was feeling, Blake told himself, was the effect of
being here with all those traumatic memories. Not to
mention the effect of being here with this woman. The
combination was troubling and he'd resorted to what he
used to do in college: soak whatever was bothering him
in alcohol.

Unconsciously, he pushed the glass on the bar even
farther away. "Both," he told her.

"Yes—to both," Greer replied, her eyes meeting
his.

He felt something undulate in his stomach. Ignoring
it, Blake took her hand and wove his way to the space
within the ballroom that had been set aside as a dance
floor.

Reaching it, he turned around and took one of her
hands, tucking it in his and holding it against his chest
while he slipped his other hand around her waist. He
caught himself thinking that the woman felt smaller
than the image that she projected. Her waist bordered
on being tiny.

The tempo was soft, slow, a melodic old show tune

from the forties, and they swayed in time to the melody.
Her head was on his shoulder and Blake found himself
inhaling the scent that drifted to him from her hair.
Something sweet and yet arousing. He could feel his
gut tightening again along with a muted anticipation
awakening within his body. He tried to bank it down,
but he wasn't quite fast enough.

Greer tilted back her head to look at his face. "You
dance well."

"I'm a bit rusty," he allowed. "I haven't danced since—
I haven't danced," he repeated, abruptly terminating the
sentence.

She had a feeling he was going to say he hadn't
danced since the last time he'd done it with his wife.
Greer had no desire to dig up old wounds so she didn't
press for him to continue.

Instead, she nodded amiably. "Some things you don't
forget no matter how much time passes. Like riding a
bicycle, or dancing. Or making love."

And if she were tortured from now until the apoc-
alypse, she wouldn't have been able to say where that
last statement had come from or how it had found its
way to her lips. All she could do was pretend she wasn't
as stunned by it as he appeared to be.

In an effort to divert his attention, she just continued
talking. "Do you like Cole Porter?"

He stared at her as if he believed that she was a
collection of non sequitur statements. "Excuse me?"

"Cole Porter," she repeated. "They're playing 'When
They Begin The Beguine.' It's a song by Cole Porter. At
least I think it's Cole Porter. Or maybe it's by Jerome

Kern. He did the music for *Show Boat*. It's an old musical," she added when he looked at her quizzically. "I have trouble remembering which was which."

Blake laughed shortly. "I'm afraid I can't help you there. All I know about music is whether or not I like it."

"And do you?" she asked softly, turning her face up to his.

Blake felt a wave of heat that had nothing to do with the ballroom's air-conditioning system. It accompanied the sudden, unexpected dryness in his mouth. "Do I what?"

"Like it?" Her voice was husky, barely above a whisper.

"Very much," he replied. "Even if I have no idea what a 'Beguine,' is."

"It's a ballroom dance that was popular back then. I used to watch a lot of old movies on TV as a kid," she explained in case he wondered why she'd know an obscure fact like that.

Her breath was backing up in her lungs. Dancing had nothing to do with it. The man with her did. There were all sorts of feelings skittering through her that left her in a tailspin.

There it was again, she thought helplessly, that feeling that had popped up when she'd thrown herself on top of Blake in the courtroom.

Except that this time, it was bigger, more defined and definitely more forceful.

The applause around them registered abruptly and

he realized that couples were applauding because the music had stopped.

At least, the music that was coming from the band's instruments had stopped. The other music, the melody that seemed to have materialized in his head, was still playing. It took effort not to move to it. Effort not to respond to the raw, unguarded look in Greer's eyes when she slanted a look in his direction.

He had a feeling that she didn't know he'd seen her expression and he was relieved that they were out in public. Because in a moment like this, if they were alone, he might have been tempted to do something completely against his nature. Something completely outside the box.

Clearing his throat, he looked for something to say. "I've been meaning to ask you…your brother said you saved your dog by chasing away a couple of coyotes. He was kidding, right?"

"No, he wasn't," she murmured.

"How?" was all he could ask.

"Coyotes don't like loud, unexpected noises. I raised my hand over my head to seem bigger than I was and growled as loud as I could. They ran," she concluded with a smile that dared him to contradict her.

"And you did this because it just came to you?" he asked skeptically.

She laughed then and he caught himself thinking again how much that sounded like music to him. "Because I watch the Discovery Channel," she corrected. "You can pick up a lot of useful information there."

He wondered if they had a program devoted to surviving exposure to seductive bodyguards.

The fundraiser lasted a total of five and a half hours. After about four and a half, the crowd began to slowly diminish as people started making their excuses and slipping away, either to go home, or to grab a nightcap with a few intimate friends.

The judge, Greer noted, looked as if he was prepared to remain to the bitter end. Curious, she still didn't question him as to whether or not he was obligated to remain at the function, or if he merely wanted to. Hers wasn't to ask why, hers was just to protect unconditionally.

Remaining constantly alert, even as she absorbed the exceedingly positive vibrations coming from the man she was guarding, was taking a toll on her. But she couldn't put her guard down. Danger could come from any one of an endless number of directions.

There were a lot of people in here, people that someone on the fundraising committee could supposedly vouch for. However, the attending guests, not to mention the people catering the affair, were all scattered about like so many marbles. Rounding them all up to verify that they were exactly who they said they were and checking into their background would have taken far too much time. The fundraiser would long be over before she was even half finished.

She had to rely on her gut—and on luck.

When the judge finally shook his last hand and told her that they were going home, Greer could have cheered. Not that she minded being with him like this. Kincannon looked incredibly dynamic in his tuxedo. With hair the color of the inside of midnight and eyes a dark fathomless blue, he easily made her pulse accelerate. But keeping an eye out for anything out of the ordinary, any person who got too close to him, *was* exceedingly wearying.

Heading toward the door with the judge, she struggled to curb her enthusiasm. It took a great deal of effort not to just herd the man out of the building. As it was, she slipped her arm through his and walked faster. He had no choice but to keep up.

"I'll let you drive," Kincannon told her once the valet had brought up his new car and had hopped out of it. When she looked at him quizzically, he explained, "The last thing I want is to be pulled over by some overzealous motorcycle cop and wind up failing a breathalyzer test." Drinking was something he *always* kept under control. The specter of what had happened to his wife was forever with him and he was determined that no other family would *ever* be put through that sort of pain because of him.

She had no problem driving them home. The only beverage she'd consumed all evening was ginger ale. But the fact that he thought he'd consumed more than the acceptable amount of alcohol bothered her. It meant that she'd slipped up in watching him.

"Just how many scotch on the rocks did you have?" she asked as she slid in behind the steering wheel of the silver two-seater.

Getting in on the passenger side, Blake buckled up. "Three."

Three drinks over the space of the evening didn't seem like much and he didn't sound like a man who was even mildly inebriated. However she saw no reason to argue and she did like driving his vehicle. This was probably the closest she would ever come to driving a Mercedes sports car.

Still, she did want him to know that she thought he was perfectly fit. "You seem very sober to me."

Kincannon chuckled. "Hence the saying."

Greer glanced at him as she flew down the road. Traffic seemed to be nonexistent and the lights all seemed to be cooperating, turning green two beats before she reached the intersections.

"Saying?" she questioned.

"Sober as a judge," he replied, an amused smile flirting with his lips.

Okay, maybe Kincannon was a wee bit tipsy, she thought, revising her assessment. It was better to be safe than sorry.

"Good saying," she murmured, her mouth curving.

"I don't know," he countered slowly, as if he was rolling it over in his mind. "It brings an image of a dour-faced, stern individual to mind," he confessed. "Not the professional image I'm going for." He paused, thinking, then put the question to her. "What does fair and impartial look like?"

She slanted a glance at him. The moment he asked, the answer came to her. "Like you."

Silence slipped in and accompanied them the rest of

the short distance home. For once, she did nothing to break it. But she did notice that though he might have been embarrassed by her honesty, there still was the barest hint of a smile on his lips.

Detective Jeff Carson left the judge's house less than five minutes after they arrived. The older Kincannon, her partner told them as he struggled to suppress a yawn, had gone to bed over an hour ago. Beyond that, he had nothing to report, other than Gunny had taken him in poker, winning eight hands out of ten.

"I should have warned you about that," Blake confessed. "He's practically a card shark, a side effect of being posted in out-of-the-way places where they roll the sidewalks up at night." He reached for his wallet, obviously intending to make up for what her partner had lost.

Greer put her hand on his, stopping him from taking the wallet out. "Carson's a big boy, aren't you, Carson? No one forced him to play poker with your father."

"Big boy," Jeff echoed none-too-happily as he left. "G'night."

"Good night, Jeff." Greer closed the door, securing it. Crossing back to the sofa, she sank down with a huge sigh. "I'm going to change—as soon as I get the energy to get up again."

Blake looked at the sofa, shaking his head. He still didn't like the idea of Greer sleeping on it. "You know, you can use one of the guest rooms," he prompted.

She shrugged carelessly. Though she didn't use a guest room at night, she still had her clothes stashed in the one closest to the staircase. "I've gotten to like sleeping on the sofa."

He paused, scrutinizing her. "You lie as smoothly as you tell the truth."

Greer grinned, not bothering to dispute his assessment. "You pick things up along the way. Good night, Judge," she said, hoping that would send him on his way. It was late.

He needed to put distance between them. In his present state, she represented far too much temptation. Nodding, Blake murmured, "Good night." He was on his way out of the room, heading toward the staircase, when he stopped.

He had no idea why he stopped.

Maybe it was a need to unburden himself to this woman who seemed to coax words out of him so easily. Maybe the memory of their one intimate dance was still fresh on his mind, threatening to forever imbed itself into his memory. He couldn't be sure.

All he did know was that he remained standing where he was, staring at the staircase, telling Greer what he had never told anyone before.

"She wanted children, you know." He turned around to face Greer. "Margaret, she wanted children."

Greer stiffened ever so slightly, wondering if she should stop him right here before he wound up pouring out his heart. She instinctively knew he would regret that in the morning, regret telling her about his late wife's dreams.

But maybe the man *needed* to talk and she was, after all, a relative stranger as far as he was concerned.

Someone who would be out of his life soon enough. Until their paths crossed again.

Her heart ached for him as she looked at the pain in his eyes.

"No, I didn't," Greer finally replied in a low voice. "I didn't know that."

Blake nodded. Rounding the back of the sofa, he came and sat down beside her. "She did. I talked her into waiting."

She heard the guilt, the sorrow, and knew exactly what he was thinking. He blamed himself that his wife had died never experiencing the love of a child. "You couldn't have known that there was going to be an accident. Or that she would wind up dying. None of us gets to look into the future."

He shook his head. She didn't understand, he thought. Didn't understand because he wasn't clear, he was tripping over his own tongue.

"It wasn't the future, it was the present." Blake blew out a breath. He could see that he had managed to confuse her even more. "She was pregnant," he said with feeling. "The night she was killed, Margaret was pregnant."

Her eyes widened. No one had told her that. Granted she hadn't been involved in the inquiry, or in trying to find the hit-and-run driver who had ultimately wound up running them off the road. She'd just happened to be the off-duty officer who had tried to save two people whose paths she'd crossed.

"Are you sure?" Greer pressed.

He nodded, numb. "That was her big news. She told

me right in the middle of dinner, after I made some inane toast to our second anniversary. She almost burst, holding her secret in. It should have dawned on me when she refused to have a drink before dinner. Having a drink was always part of eating out for her," he explained, remembering.

The judge's face was drawn and Greer could literally see his pain. It was right there, in his eyes. He was struggling not to give in to it, not to let the tears that were shining in his eyes fall.

She was a firm believer in tears, in using them to cleanse away pain, to purge emotions. But men had their own set of codes. Greer had a hunch that shedding tears to relieve tension was just not part of it.

At least not for Blake Kincannon.

But code or no code, there couldn't be anything in his credo that said he was against receiving comfort from another human being. There couldn't be anything against having that other human being put her arms around him and offering him all the silent sympathy that she possibly could.

Which was exactly why Greer put her arms around the man she was supposed to be guarding. Why she held on to him even as Blake initially resisted the contact, trying to pull away. The sofa worked in her favor, foiling him because there was nothing he could do to make her physically back away.

"It takes a strong man to allow himself to be human," she told him in a quiet, firm whisper against his ear. "I'm sorry I couldn't do anything to save her that night," she added.

He'd passed out toward the end, but he'd been there to watch Greer's efforts in the first few minutes. He'd never seen anyone work so hard.

"It wasn't your fault," he told her. He raised his head to look at her. "I don't blame you," he added just in case Greer thought he did. If there was someone to blame, it would be the man driving the car that had hit them. Hit them and then disappeared into the fog that had spread out over the area like a huge cottony spider's web.

"If it wasn't for you, I would have died, too. I owe you my life," he reminded her. His eyes held hers. The attraction he'd felt and fought from the start was all but overwhelming him, pressing against him so hard, he could hardly draw a breath. "I owe you," he whispered, letting his voice faded away.

And then, the next moment, Blake wasn't talking at all.

And neither was she.

A fire had leaped into their veins simultaneously, ignited by feelings too strong to suppress, or to remain dormant and unacknowledged.

Maybe it was the three drinks that eroded his defenses, or maybe they merely made him more in tune to what was happening here. Whatever the reason, Blake sealed his mouth to her lips at the same time that he sealed his soul to hers.

Chapter 12

Greer prided herself on not being the kind of person who ordinarily lost control, the kind who got carried away if the situation was right.

Labeled by those in authority as a hellion when she was in high school, even then she'd been very much in control of herself, no matter what situation she found herself in. Because she liked to live life fast and hard didn't mean that she ever lost sight of end goals. Never before had she ever even entertained the idea and shouted, "The hell with consequences."

In her mind, she was forever the daughter of an unattached woman who dedicated herself to doing her very best to provide and care for the three children she'd given birth to.

Deep down, Greer was the girl who had been left by her father. Not willingly—she'd believed for more than the first two decades of her life—but the end result was that he was still absent. When she'd heard her mother's deathbed confession that she and her brothers were the product of an affair and that their biological father had deserted them, Greer had settled down and applied herself to becoming an upstanding member of society.

She became a rock.

And, within her heart of hearts, Greer trusted no man implicitly beyond her brothers. Because men left, men abandoned, and she saw the consequences of that. In the back of her mind, residing like an unwanted tenant, was the memory of her mother's socially isolated life. Oh, her mother had been a loving, warm woman who did the best she could but Greer sensed that there was a ragged hole in her mother's heart created by the man who wasn't there. Who'd refused to be there all those years ago.

That was never going to be her, Greer had vowed. And, in order for that to be true, she couldn't allow herself to fall in love with anyone, couldn't go so far into uncharted waters that she lost her way back.

It was a good, solid plan.

So what was she doing here, letting this man with his impossibly sensual mouth kiss her? What was she doing, kissing him back?

And wanting so much more.

Damn it, this wasn't the route to self-preservation. This was the way to self-destruction, the way to lose not just the battle, but the war.

And yet, even though her mind fairly shouted for her to abort her present behavior, to get out now before she slipped any further into the emotional quicksand she was standing in, Greer couldn't get herself to stop. Couldn't get herself to respond and obey. Or even move an inch away.

All she wanted to do was fan the flames that were blazing within her. Wanted more than she'd ever wanted anything before to experience lovemaking with this man.

Every inch of her body yearned for it, begged for it.

She was crazy, absolutely crazy, Greer thought. Maybe it was the flu, maybe she'd caught a strain that short-circuited the brain, making a person behave completely out of character.

Maybe—

She sucked in her breath, startled, as Blake drew back, creating a space between them that felt as big as a chasm.

Greer pressed her lips together, tasting him. She looked at Blake, trying to focus her thoughts, trying to focus her resolve as well as her line of vision. Most of all, she was trying to squelch this bereft feeling that threatened to swallow her up whole and break her down into little pieces.

Blake was talking to her. His mouth was moving but she wasn't absorbing what he was saying. She concentrated harder.

"We can't do this here," he was saying.

Well, thank God at least one of them had some common sense, she thought, breathing a sigh of both relief and huge, frustrated disappointment. The ache in her body felt almost unmanageable.

"You're right," she told him hoarsely.

Blake was rising to his feet. But rather than tell her good-night, he was taking her hand, coaxing her up off the sofa, as well.

Why?

"Come upstairs with me." It was both a question and a supplication.

Her pulse quickened again. The platform beneath her feet suddenly splintered and gave way, sending her free-falling through space. Greer stared at him. "But I thought you just said we can't do this."

"Here," Blake emphasized, underscoring the one word that counted. The one word she hadn't heard. "I said we can't do this *here*. We're out in the open on the sofa and my father sometimes comes down to get something to drink or eat. He has occasional insomnia," he explained.

There was no way that Blake wanted, at his age, to have his father stumble across him in a compromising situation.

"Oh." Greer took a breath. Her insides were actually trembling. What was up with that? She'd been in life-and-death situations and she'd never reacted like this. "Then you didn't want to stop kissing me."

He moved his head slowly from side to side, negating the mere suggestion.

"I'd sooner stop breathing," he told her honestly. And then her words hit him. Belatedly, he gave a different interpretation to them. "Unless you don't want me to kiss you."

He'd left it up to her, she thought, giving her the impression that he would go along with whatever her decision was.

Didn't it matter to him? Was it all just one and the same to the man? *Heads we make love, tails we don't?*

Greer refused to have this all on her shoulders. She lobbed the ball back into his court. "Do you want to kiss me?"

The sinfully sexy smile that rose to his lips out of nowhere made Greer want to throw her arms around him and seal her mouth to his—as well as several other parts of his anatomy. Even the mere promise of contact generated heat within her.

"I think I just answered that question, Greer." But instead of kissing her again the way she hoped he would, Blake moved his fingers through hers. "Come upstairs with me," he coaxed.

"Upstairs?" Did that sound as dumb as she thought it did?

"To my room," he added softly.

She let herself be drawn.

This, no doubt, was the way the mice felt, responding to the Pied Piper's irresistible music when he played it to lead them out of the town. Everyone knew what happened to them, she thought. They were led into the river to perish.

And yet, she couldn't stop herself, couldn't use the momentary break to regroup and refortify herself.

Couldn't offer up the slightest excuse as to why this shouldn't be happening. She could have cited, at the very least, that it was unprofessional of her to sleep with the very man she was supposed to be guarding.

Sleep.

Who was she kidding? She was praying that her time with Blake wouldn't have anything to do with sleep the entire night.

As if in a dream, Greer went up the stairs with Blake, her entire body heating in anticipation of things she had no business expecting or even hoping for.

She couldn't stop herself.

Blake opened the door to his bedroom, and then, rather than walk in, he abruptly stopped. He glanced down at the threshold. Once it was crossed, there was no turning back. Without a word, he raised his eyes to hers and waited.

Taking a breath, knowing that she should be calling a halt to this and yet felt powerless to do so, Greer stepped across the threshold and thus silently sealed her fate.

Following her, Blake closed the door.

And then they were alone. Alone and very much together.

She became aware of her heart pounding in double time as Blake began to kiss her again, his hands roaming along the curves of her body as if he was attempting to memorize every inch, as if he was familiarizing himself with a brand-new world.

The very thought made her heart pound even harder.

Desire and passion scrambled through him, vying

for possession, for some sort of fulfillment. He'd kept himself in check all this time, not just with Greer, but as far as all women, as well. He wasn't the kind of man who had needs to attend to on a regular basis, whose needs took control of him.

Going through the motions had never appealed to Blake, even before he'd ever met Margaret. To him, some sort of a relationship needed to precede becoming intimate with a woman. The act of lovemaking had to involve more than just body parts. The nebulous entity some people referred to as "the soul" had to be included.

If it wasn't, then everything else was just meaningless.

Right now, a sense of urgency filled him, as if he had to outrace his thoughts, because if they were still filled with images of Margaret and caught up to him, the feeling that he was betraying his late wife would hold him back. And he didn't want to hold back. Not now, not after he'd come so far so quickly. There was something about this woman—this woman out of hundreds of others—that set her apart. Something that spoke to him. That made him feel alive and made him long to remain that way.

Very gently, Blake slid the bodice of the blue gown down to her waist. For a moment, he just drank in the sight of her. And then he tugged on the clingy dress, bring it down to first her hips, then her legs, finally sending the shimmering cloth to the floor.

Greer stood there before him in high heels, wearing

a matching strapless light blue bra and a scrap of lacy blue nylon that doubled as underwear.

Her weapon was still holstered and strapped to her inner thigh.

Damn, he'd never seen anything sexier in his life. Blake brought his mouth down on hers.

He felt her lips curve in a smile against his. If there was something funny about all this, he was missing it.

Greer drew her head back just a fraction, her eyes smiling into his. "I think, in the interest of keeping the gun from going off and keeping you intact, I should take my weapon off."

Blake laughed shortly and nodded, releasing her. "Good idea," he agreed.

She made short work of carefully removing the gun and then placing the gun and holster on Blake's nightstand.

Blake lost no time in reclaiming her. The second she straightened up, he began to shower soft, openmouthed kisses on her shoulders, her collarbone, and then her breasts as he eliminated the lacy strapless bra.

By now, desire hummed through him like a freshly struck tuning fork. Though he wanted to rip it away, Blake was careful to slide the exceedingly thin thong down along her hips so that it joined the pool of shimmering blue material on the floor.

Blake couldn't catch his breath. The woman was incredibly beautiful. Just as beautiful as he knew she would be.

"Your turn," she murmured, her eyes holding his.

Blake looked at her, a puzzled expression on his

face. Rather than verbally answer, Greer immediately began to remove his jacket, his tie, his cummerbund, the brilliant white shirt he wore, as well as his trousers, socks and shoes.

She paused in the middle to admire and skim her hands along a rock-solid abdomen. She'd had a feeling that he had a good body, but she had no idea that it would be *this* bone-melting good. She'd seen professional trainers whose abs, chest and arms didn't look nearly as sculpted.

She had to ask. "When do you work out?" He hadn't gone to a gym on her watch and there was no exercise equipment in the house that she knew of.

He ended the mystery by saying, "Push-ups."

If that was the case, she thought, push-ups were highly underrated.

She separated him from the rest of his clothes in record time. And as she got rid of his shoes, Greer stepped out of her own, kicking them aside.

They were both nude, both vulnerable.

The moment she was finished undressing him, Blake pressed his lips to the hollow of her throat, sending the blood in her veins surging.

Needs began to slam into her. Pleading for attention, for release.

They fell onto the bed, their limbs tangling as the passion between them all but exploded.

Greer moaned, anticipation squeezing her in its grip. With each openmouthed kiss along her torso, she found herself coming closer and closer to a climax. She scrambled toward it, eager, yet afraid that once it found her, once she experienced it and the euphoria it generated began to fade, regret and remorse would swiftly follow.

But she had absolutely no choice in the matter. Her body had taken over and just like that, the sensation seized her, sending her flying over the edge. But rather than plummet to earth, the way she fully expected to, the climax flowered into another one and another after that. The rush was incredible even as it was exhausting.

For just a moment, she thought that she would be in its grip forever and ever.

She had no complaints.

Everywhere Blake's lips and tongue touched, she felt immediate fireworks, fireworks that went off in her very core. She wasn't sure just how long she could hold her own before she became too exhausted to breathe. Slick with sweat, she pulled him to her. Then, rolling her body into his, she managed to reverse their positions, putting herself on top.

Straddling him the way she would a motorcycle, she began to move, swaying her body against his. She saw the look in his eyes, the raw desire, and it excited her beyond all boundaries.

That was how he managed to catch her off guard. Blake surprised her by catching hold of her arms. In one swift, seamless motion, he reversed their positions again and he was the one looking down at her. Every breath he took undulated into her. She never took her eyes off him. This was a side to him she would have never guessed existed.

Didn't you? a small voice in her head whispered. She banked it down.

Blake threaded his fingers through hers, then raised her hands above her head as he positioned himself over her. Seductively, he began to move a little at a time, increasing his tempo. She gasped, arching. Inviting.

And then he was inside her and they were one entity, one being with only one desire vibrating between them.

Responding to an inner rhythm, Blake began to move his hips again, at first slowly, then with increasing more urgency. She shadowed his every movement, exciting him as much as he excited her.

And then it was a race, not to outdo but to come together.

When the pinnacle they were mutually striving for was reached, Greer bit down on her lip to keep from screaming out her pleasure.

She was breathless. And so, from the sound of it, was Blake.

It made the euphoria gripping her last longer.

She felt Blake hugging her, felt him tightening his arms around her and holding her closer. For one of the few times in her life, Greer felt protected, as if nothing could reach her, nothing could harm her.

Or her heart.

It was illusion, all illusion, and she knew it, but she clung to it nonetheless. Savored it. And pretended, just for a moment, that it was real. And that it would last for as long as she was alive.

Greer became aware that his ardor was cooling just

a bit. After a moment, he shifted his weight, moving off her and onto his back.

She was surprised that he continued holding her. Surprised and pleased, although she said neither. From her experience, men didn't like to feel crowded and any dialogue after the fact dealing with feelings was a signal for them to flee the scene as quickly as was humanly possible.

"You give this kind of service to everyone you're assigned to guard?" he asked, murmuring the question against her ear.

She was amazed, considering what she'd just experienced, that the feel of his breath along her neck was arousing her again. By all rights, she was more than half dead from exhaustion.

And yet...

He was still waiting for her to respond to what she assumed was a semi-serious question on his part. With a careless shrug, Greer gave him a non-answer. "This is my first bodyguard assignment. I'm playing it by ear and improvising as I go along."

"I see." He strummed his fingertips along her curves, enjoying her. "Very innovative of you."

She couldn't tell by his tone if he was serious or not. "Any complaints?" she asked.

"Can't think of one." He laughed shortly. "Actually, I can't think. You seem to have short-circuited my brain."

She raised herself into a semi-sitting position, resting her chin on his chest and looking up at him. "Maybe your brain's just resting since it wasn't needed."

"Oh, it was needed," he assured her. "Haven't you heard? The brain is the most sexual organ in the human body."

Tilting her head, she looked at him again, mischief playing on her lips. "I seem to recall hearing something like that, yes. So, you want to put it to the test?" she asked. Before he could answer, she continued, carrying on both sides of the conversation. "You want to *think*, Judge? Or do you want to *do*?" she asked, tilting her head as she waited for him to respond.

Rather than answer her the traditional way, Blake caught the back of her head, pulled her to him and brought her mouth down to his.

The kiss stretched down to the very edges of her soul.

She felt his desire for her resurfacing. Growing hard.

Greer grinned, doing her best to hide her own excitement. She had the answer to her question.

"I have my answer," she murmured against his mouth before she threw herself into round two. And lost herself in him completely.

Chapter 13

Sleep was an elusive element in Blake's life. Waking at least twice each night, he hadn't managed to come anywhere close to sleeping straight through the night since Margaret had died. He'd just accepted that this was the way things were, just as he'd accepted that he would never have feelings for another woman again.

He was wrong on both counts.

After making love with Greer a second time, he'd drifted off to sleep and slept through the entire night without waking up once.

Slept so soundly that apparently he hadn't heard Greer leave.

When, still semi-asleep, he'd reached for her, he'd found the other half of his bed empty. The sheets were cool to the touch on her side, which meant that she hadn't just left. She'd been gone a while.

Sitting up, Blake saw that she'd taken her clothes with her. And hung his up neatly, folding his socks and underwear and placing them on top of the bureau while his tuxedo and shirt had been returned to their hangers in his closet.

It was, he thought, as if last night had never happened.

Maybe that was the effect she was after, he thought. Maybe she wanted to physically deny what had transpired between them.

Blake scrubbed his hands over his face. He wasn't sure how he felt about that. He knew that a lot of men would have been relieved not to be held accountable. Not to feel that they were going to be tangled up in a bunch of strings and expectations.

But he wasn't like most men.

Still, if he pretended that nothing had happened, then he wouldn't have to feel as if he'd been unfaithful to the memory of his wife. That was something he'd expected to have weigh heavily on him once the passion and desire had cooled and faded and the lovemaking was in the past. But while he was, for the moment, emotionally on shaky ground, oddly enough, there was no guilt pressing down on him.

Maybe he was still in shock, he speculated, getting up. After all, he'd been fully prepared to face the rest of his life as a single man. Loving someone else wasn't even remotely on his agenda. Once was all he thought anyone could logically hope for.

But apparently, he could be wrong.

He *was* wrong, Blake amended, because last night wouldn't have happened if he hadn't felt something for the woman it was happening with.

Ever since he could remember, he'd always needed something more than just chemistry in order to want to be intimate with a woman, although, he mused with a faint smile as he headed off into the shower, there was definitely something to be said for chemistry. Last night had felt as if the whole damn lab had been set on fire and exploded.

As he turned on the water, he concentrated on that and not on the fact that he had let his guard down and allowed the notion of love to creep in.

Less than fifteen minutes later, Blake was dressed and making his way down the stairs. The scent of coffee greeted him when he was less than halfway down.

A man could get used to this, he thought. These past two years he'd forgotten what it was like, coming down to freshly brewed coffee, to the aroma of breakfast being made. Ever since Greer had been assigned to be his bodyguard, coffee and breakfast had suddenly become the norm again.

Careful, Blake, don't get used to this. She's not a permanent part of your life. Once they catch Munro, she'll be gone.

He found the thought more than mildly disturbing.

Taking the last step down, Blake could see that Greer was in the living room, folding up the bedding that she'd used. She'd spent the remainder of the night here, he realized.

Why?

"You came down last night?" he asked her, walking into the living room.

It hadn't been her imagination, she thought. She *had* sensed him.

Greer looked at him over her shoulder, doing her best not to flush. She'd left his bed sometime around 1:00 a.m. and come down, but bits and pieces of last night kept replaying themselves in her head until dawn. She'd gotten even less sleep last night than she ordinarily did.

Not knowing how he would react in the light of day after the night they'd shared, she kept her voice neutral. "I'm supposed to be your bodyguard, remember?"

"Couldn't have guarded it more closely than you did last night," he reminded her.

Was that amusement she heard in his voice? And if so, was that a good thing or a bad one?

Greer pressed her lips together. In either case, at least they were addressing the elephant in the living room right off the bat.

She cleared her throat. "About last night…"

He stood where he was, having no idea what to expect next. This was not a run-of-the-mill situation for him. "Yes?"

She forced herself to look into his eyes. "If you want to request another bodyguard, you are within your right to do so."

He stared at her, trying to extract the hidden meaning behind her words. "I don't understand. Why would I want another bodyguard?"

She lifted one shoulder in a shrug. "In case you don't feel comfortable, or…" Her voice trailed off as the words she needed to use deserted her.

He was silent for a moment, and then he smiled.

Slightly. "Looks to me like you're the one who feels uncomfortable."

He was right, Greer thought. She *was* uncomfortable. Uncomfortable with the emotions that he'd aroused within her last night, uncomfortable with how easily she'd capitulated to those emotions. She was usually stronger than that.

Damn it, she should have fought harder to resist him. He didn't strike her as the kind of man who would take advantage of the situation, or of her if she had said no. It had been up to her to stop things before they'd gotten out of hand. Instead, she'd wound up doing everything in her power to speed them along.

"I should have been more in control," she finally told him.

His eyes made her feel that he was looking into her soul, seeing all of her secrets. "There was no pillaging going on," he murmured wryly. "Seems to me that we were equally in control."

Greer read between the lines. Blake obviously thought she was talking about the actual lovemaking. But she wasn't. She was talking about the fact that she shouldn't have allowed last night to have happened in the first place.

The very thought of the night they'd spent together made her pulse begin to accelerate again. Damn it, what was *wrong* with her?

"You're blushing, Detective," Blake pointed out, amused.

She tossed her head, sending her hair flying over her shoulder like a blond shower.

"It's just hot in here." This time, she avoided his eyes. It was safer that way. "I've got to get back into the kitchen and finish making breakfast before the eggs burn," she said, breezing by him and heading toward the kitchen.

Turning on his heel, Blake followed her. "Isn't my father watching them for you?"

"No, I haven't seen your dad yet this morning. He told Jeff last night that he felt tired," she told him, repeating what her partner had said to her before he left. "Maybe he decided to sleep in this morning."

Blake frowned. His father was usually up with the roosters. "That's not like him," he commented. "But then, I wasn't myself either last night."

Entering the kitchen, she slanted a glance at the judge. "Regrets?" she asked, trying her damnedest to sound nonchalant.

"Maybe," he allowed. When she looked at him, he explained further. "That I didn't do it sooner."

She was doing her best to put emotional distance between them, but all the while, she caught herself yearning for an encore of last night. Damn it, was she losing her mind? She didn't behave this way. What had he done to her?

"It has been two years—"

He didn't let her finish. He realized that she didn't understand what he was saying. "That I didn't do it sooner with you," he clarified. He'd felt the sexual pull between them that first day in court, when she'd flown over his desk to shield him.

There went her heart, she thought, feeling it lodge

into her throat. Their eyes met and she caught herself holding her breath.

Don't buy into this, she cautioned herself. *It's going to hurt like hell when it's over if you do.*

She knew she was lying to herself. It was going to hurt like hell when it was over no matter what. She was already standing on the threshold of pain.

Greer changed the subject. "Maybe you should go upstairs and see what's keeping your father. Tell him breakfast is almost ready."

He nodded. "Maybe," he agreed, but instead of going upstairs, Blake remained where he was, trying to properly frame what he was about to say. Ordinarily, words were no problem for him, but he had no experience in this area. He wasn't someone given to exposing his feelings. But she obviously needed to be reassured, he thought. "I just want you to know that I enjoyed last night."

Greer took in a long breath, as if that would somehow help her maintain her outer calm. She'd indulged in a breech of protocol last night.

"Yeah, me, too. Doesn't change the fact that I behaved unprofessionally."

Did she think he was going to put her on report? "For the record," he told her, "you 'behaved' just perfectly."

With that, he turned away and walked back toward the stairs, leaving her to contemplate her own thoughts.

Why did life have to be so complicated? Greer wondered, swiftly stirring the eggs that threatened to harden in a clump.

If she'd met Blake under different circumstances, then maybe last night would have been the beginning of something special rather than just an anomaly.

An anomaly, she caught herself thinking as she went to the refrigerator, that she would have dearly loved to have happen again at least one more time before her assignment here ended.

But then—

Greer stopped looking for the butter and drew her head out of the interior of the refrigerator. She could have sworn she'd just heard her name being called.

Was Blake calling her? Or was that—?

No, she was right. She *did* hear Blake calling for her. Again. And there was an urgency in his voice. Oh, damn, what was wrong?

Turning the stove off and moving the large frying pan onto a cool burner, she hurried out of the kitchen. Passing the hall table, she grabbed her handgun, yanking it out of its holster—just in case.

She made it up the stairs in record time.

"Blake?"

Judge, she should have called him Judge, not something as familiar as his first name. She was on duty, for God's sake.

Once blurred, the lines were hard to restore.

"In here!" he called out to her.

Following his voice, not knowing what to expect, she burst into the doorway of the room he was calling from. She held her weapon out in front of her, braced in both hands.

It was his father's room. Blake had the senior

Kincannon on the floor, lying on his back. Blake was in the middle of counting off compressions, one hand pressed on top of the other and both pressing down on the older man's chest. His father was unconscious and Blake was performing CPR.

"Call 911," he cried. "I think he had a heart attack."

Stunned, Greer lost no time in putting in a call to her dispatch at the police station. Giving her badge number, she rattled off the circumstances and the patient's address.

Flipping her phone closed, she tucked it away again. "They'll be here right away," she guaranteed. "They like to keep Aurora's 'finest' in top running condition." She came closer to him. Blake hadn't missed a single beat, performing CPR for all he was worth.

"What happened?" she wanted to know as she looked at his unconscious father on the floor.

Blake shook his head. "I don't know. When he didn't answer my knock, I opened the door and found him like this." He knew that time was of the essence. The quicker his father got treatment, the better his chances for a full recovery would be. "I don't know how long he's been unconscious."

Greer bent down. Pressing two fingers against the other man's throat, she felt for a pulse. It was thin and reedy, but it was there. Relieved, she told Blake, "At least he's still alive."

"Yeah, but I don't know how long he'd been like this," Blake repeated, worried.

"It wasn't all night," she assured him. "When I was

getting my things together to go downstairs, I heard your father moving around in the next bedroom. That had to be some time between one and two."

Blake glanced at his watch as he continued working over his father. "It's six now. What if he's been like this for the past five hours?" he asked. "What if he—"

Greer laid a gentling hand on his shoulder. "Don't get ahead of yourself," she advised sympathetically. Looking at the man on the floor, she thought she saw a slight movement. Greer rallied around it. Slight was better than nothing.

"Look," she pointed out excitedly. "Your father's trying to open his eyes. His eyelashes just fluttered, I'm sure of it!"

Sitting back on his heels, Blake sighed with relief. He'd thought he'd only imagined it. Wishful thinking. But if Greer saw it, too, they couldn't both be hallucinating.

"Thank God," Blake ground out.

There was no masking his pleasure that his father appeared to be coming around and that, with a little bit of luck, was going to be okay. For one awful second, when he'd walked into the room after not receiving any answer to his knock, he'd thought the older man was dead.

The first thing that occurred to him was that Munro had somehow found out his address.

What if the drug dealer had somehow gained access into the house and had killed his father first? He would have never forgiven himself.

But to his relief, a quick check around his father's body showed no blood. There'd been no attack. Immediately something else suggested itself to him. And if that was true, it wasn't exactly a cause for celebration, either.

The words *heart attack* loomed over him with twelve-feet high letters.

Blake knew that his grandfather—his father's father—had died of a heart attack at a relatively young age. Gunny had bragged the other day about already outliving his father. Under normal circumstances, he gave no credence to superstitions, but he didn't believe in thumbing his nose at fate, either.

In the background, the sound of an approaching siren began to register, growing stronger by the second. They'd be here soon, he thought.

"Dad?" Blake cried. He leaned over his father's body, his lips close to the man's ear. "Dad, can you hear me?"

Lips that felt as dry as dust came together in an attempt to form words. When he finally managed, they came out in a whisper.

On her knees on the other side of Blake's father, Greer leaned in to hear what he was trying to tell them. His voice was too low.

"Could you repeat that, Gunny?" Greer asked, her voice deliberately loud.

"Not...deaf..." Gunny told her, his breath just barely sustaining him. He was obviously referring to the fact that his son was fairly shouting when he addressed him.

Shaking his head, Blake blew out a breath. "He's still an ornery old man," he observed. "That's a good sign."

"A very good sign," she agreed, patting his shoulder firmly. Getting up, she moved toward the doorway. "I'll go downstairs and let the paramedics in," she told Blake just before she left.

Blake wasn't sure if he said that was a good idea or if he'd only thought it without actually telling her that. His attention was completely focused on his father's ashen face. And on keeping him alive. "You hang in there, old man. Help's on its way."

"Don't…need…help…just…need…to…rest," Gunny gasped out the words as if each was being wrenched out of him with rusty pliers.

"If you don't want to be resting permanently, old man, you'll accept help," Blake all but ordered him tersely. "I'm not ready to lose you yet, understand?"

"Why? You…got…a…cute…replacement…waiting…in…the…wings," his father said, laboring over each word.

Oh, no, he wasn't about to admit to anything right now. And definitely not to his father. "You don't know what you're talking about, Dad."

He would have smirked if he could have. But he was almost too weak to even draw a single breath. Still, this might be the last conversation he was going to have with his son.

"Saw…her…coming…out…of…your…room…this…morning." Alexander began coughing.

"You *really* don't know what you're talking about, Dad. You're hallucinating," Blake told him. Now wasn't the time to get into this. Once his father was better— and once he knew if what was between the long-legged detective and him had a future, *then* there was time enough to talk about things. Right now, the only thing that mattered was that his father recovered. "Save your breath for something important—like breathing," he ordered.

The next minute, two paramedics came hurrying in. One of them was bringing a gurney. They collapsed it so that it was beside his father.

Rising, Blake moved out of their way, but not so far that he couldn't observe every move that the paramedics made.

"He's going to be all right," Greer told him, her voice confident and firm. For just a second, she rested her hand on his shoulder in mute reassurance.

Blake placed his own hand over hers, as if that could somehow transfuse some of her faith into him. As an unmanageable fear gripped his stomach, Blake only wished he could believe her. But he had always been, first and foremost, a realist and realists knew that everything could change in less than a heartbeat. It had already happened to him once.

Was it happening again?

Chapter 14

"See, I told you he'd be all right," Greer couldn't resist reminding Blake cheerfully.

It was a little more than twelve hours later and they were finally driving home again. Twelve hours earlier, Blake had ridden in the ambulance with his father and she had followed directly behind them in her car. Thinking ahead, she wanted to ensure that they would have a way home once things settled down.

Once she got a prognosis from the E.R. doctor, Greer contacted the precinct, placing calls to her captain, the chief and Jeff to bring them up to speed on this latest development and to assure all of them that, aside from being worried, the judge was just fine.

Once the danger had passed, they had left his father, alert and complaining, in the coronary care unit on the first floor of Aurora Memorial, the same hospital whose fundraiser they had just attended the night before.

It was a small world, Greer remembered thinking when she'd arrived there and parked her vehicle in the E.R. lot. The world got even smaller when one of the cardiologists who had been at that function and had engaged them in conversation during the evening turned out to be the doctor who was on call this morning. The physician wound up treating Blake's father.

Blake was not impressed with her prediction coming true. Mainly because it hadn't actually *been* a prediction. "You only said that because that's what people say to make other people feel better in dire times."

"No," she contradicted, easing down on the brake as she approached a red light, "I said that because I really felt your father was going to be all right. Gunny's strong as an ox and, for the most part, he eats rather healthy."

"For the past three weeks," he agreed, then told her, "That's all on you. Until you started cooking, takeout was all either one of us had had for the past couple of years. In my father's case, probably a lot longer."

She'd thought the takeout thing was just a temporary aberration. To think of two grown, capable men having nothing else but whatever food they could have brought to their door was mind-boggling.

"Seriously?"

Blake laughed shortly. "Seriously. You've made changes in his life. In our lives," he amended, then abruptly stopped. Maybe he'd said too much. He wasn't sure if he was ready to make these kinds of admissions yet.

"Nice to know," she murmured, more to herself than to him. Foot on the accelerator again, she switched lanes to move faster than the beige Cadillac in front of them. "Your father should be fine and back on his feet in a couple of days."

That was the projection the doctor had made, as well, but Blake wasn't buying into it wholeheartedly. "If that's the case, why wouldn't they let me take my father home again? Why are they keeping him in CCU?"

She knew the answer to that. "They're just following standard procedure. Everyone experiencing 'an epi-sode,'" she told him, referring to the heart attack his father'd had in the neutral terms that doctors used, "is kept in CCU for twenty-four hours because the doctors want to observe the patient, make sure nothing else is going on that could prove fatal."

It sounded to him as if Greer knew what she was talking about. "I take it you've been through this before?"

She nodded grimly. "One of the detectives in the squad, a guy by the name of Ray Walker." She always felt a story sounded more real and personal if the people in it had names. "The man should have retired long ago except that he had nothing to retire to except four walls and silence. So he managed to convince the chief to let him stay a little while longer. Well, one day he tried to chase down a perp over half his age and had one of those 'episodes.' Luckily, the ambulance attendants rushed him to this hospital."

She'd gotten him curious. "This Detective Walker, he still working at the precinct?"

Greer shook her head. "With such a recent history of heart trouble, the brass *made* him retire. They didn't want to hear any excuses."

He knew of former judges, devoid of any hobbies to hold their interest, who just seemed to fade away once they retired. Their lives seemingly without purpose, they died less than a year after they left the bench. In one case, it was more like two months.

"How did this detective handle his retirement?"

Greer smiled then. "Not too badly—I gave him one of Hussy's puppies so that he'd have something warm and loving licking his face each morning when he woke up." She'd visited Walker just before landing this assignment. Master and dog were doing just fine. Nothing could have pleased her more. "Seems to have worked out well for everyone."

Nodding, Blake put his own spin on the story. "So you moonlight as a terminal do-gooder?"

She'd never cared for the term "do-gooder" but she wasn't averse to the actual act. "Hey, life's hard enough as it is. No reason we can't make it a little more bearable for the people we interact with if we can."

Margaret would have liked this woman, he couldn't help thinking. They would have probably become good friends. The thought made him relax a little and allow his guard to slip again.

He thought of the past few weeks and said, "Well, you certainly made it more bearable for my father." And then, because that wasn't all, he lowered his voice and added, "And for me."

There it went again, she suddenly realized. Her pulse was accelerating just because the man had lowered his voice. Hearing it had made her imagination take off and she found herself thinking about last night. About every glorious second of lovemaking that had taken place between them.

She couldn't keep doing this to herself, Greer thought fiercely. She *knew* this wasn't the kind of thing that had a prayer of lasting. It was too overwhelming, too hot. And things that were too hot never remained that way. They cooled, returning to normal.

This was all happening because she and Blake were in an artificial setting which amounted to a highly volatile life-and-death situation. Once the threat, the urgency, was gone and life leveled off, so would his reaction to her. The level of passion and excitement that had exploded between them wasn't the kind of thing that had a long shelf life. It was evaluated in terms of days, not months or years. She *knew* that.

So why did she find herself praying that this could be the one exception?

For now, she had to stop torturing herself and put it out of her mind. She might be an optimist, but she'd stopped believing in Santa Claus a long time ago and believing that this relationship had a shot at outliving the dramatic set of circumstances they found themselves came under that heading.

They were here, at his development, and she wasn't a hundred percent sure how they'd gotten here. She needed to keep tighter control over her thoughts.

As they drove onto Kincannon's street, she saw that

there were parked cars all up and down both sides of the block, spilling out onto the next one. She heard the music and the noise of loud voices trying to talk over one another coming from the house next door to Blake's.

This can't be good.

Greer slowed her own vehicle down as she passed by the squad car where the two patrolmen charged with the task of watching the judge's house were parked.

"What's going on?" Blake asked them before Greer had a chance to.

"Someone in the house next to yours is having a birthday party, Your Honor," the officer behind the steering wheel told him. "There was a delivery truck here earlier. Never saw so many balloons in my life."

"The cake was huge, too," the second policeman put in with enthusiasm. "Made you hungry just looking at it."

The first man gave him an annoyed look for interrupting. "Everything makes you hungry." He turned back to face Blake. "People started arriving about the same time. Want one of us to talk to them about keeping the noise level down?" It was obvious that he was dying to do just that.

Greer glanced toward Blake, leaving the matter up to him. He shook his head.

"It's not so bad. Maybe they'll wear themselves out and wind down." Blake glanced at the clock in the dashboard. "Besides, it's only eight o'clock." Although disturbing the peace wasn't attached to any particular time, most people didn't register complaints about noise levels until after eleven. He saw no reason to do any differently.

The first patrolman looked slightly embarrassed. "When it's dark like this, I keep thinking it's later. How's your father, sir?"

"Doctor said he's going to be just fine. Thanks for asking," Blake replied.

Both officers smiled at the news. "Glad to hear that, sir," the more heavyset one said.

He wanted to get inside, to unwind and relax. With Greer. Blake nodded at the two patrolmen. "Well, good night, Officers."

Greer took her cue and drove on. Parking the car in Blake's driveway, she got out and waited for him to lead the way to the front door.

The noise coming from the house next door seemed to all but surround them now. Several people had spilled out of the house, clutching chunky glasses in their hands they would pause to sip from on a regular basis.

"Sure you don't want Officer Hogan to talk to your neighbors about the noise level?" she asked, leaning into him so he could hear her without having to raise her voice. What she did manage to raise, though, was her body temperature. That seemed to be the case every time she was closer than skin to him. And it was only getting more pronounced with each time.

But Blake shook his head and stood by his decision. "It's nice to hear some celebratory noise right about now," he told her. He looked over the lawn to the next house. "I've half a mind to join them."

As far as she could see, there was no reason not

to if that was what he really wanted. "We could," she told him.

"No," he contradicted with a smile, "we couldn't. I don't even know what my neighbor looks like." He'd been too busy, too caught up in trying to work as hard as he could to keep from thinking about Margaret, to meet any of his neighbors. "I wouldn't presume to crash his party. Until this threat came along, I'd even forgotten there were sunrises and sunsets."

Greer frowned, puzzled. In the background, one of the guests, a young teenage girl, shrieked with glee, then ran off, eluding the grasp of a teenage boy. "The threat did that for you?"

"No," he answered quietly, his eyes on hers. "You did."

"Oh, don't sweet-talk me, Judge." She was only half teasing. It was getting harder and harder to remind herself that this wasn't going to go anywhere. That their relationship had no hope of surviving once this assignment ended. "It makes my insides all melty. I'm not much good to you with a melty center."

Blake ran the back of his knuckles very slowly along her cheek, caressing her. "Oh, I don't know about that. There's something to be said for a woman who's tough on the outside, tender on the inside."

She grinned, doing her best to remain strong. "Funny, that same description could also be used to describe a steak."

Blake laughed softly under his breath as he disarmed his security system long enough for them to enter. "My favorite meat," he acknowledged.

Nothing she liked better than prime rib, nice and rare. "Mine, too."

His smile was swiftly decimating her. "Something else we have in common."

There was no point in tallying their similarities. It would only make the inevitable that much more difficult to bear when it happened. The only thing that mattered was that she continue doing her job, continue keeping Blake safe.

They were in the foyer and she needed to go through her routine, checking each room to make sure it was secure. Home security systems were all well and good, but even the finest system could be bypassed if the person attempting entry was clever enough.

"Stay right here," she told him, nodding to where he stood, "while I check out the house and make sure that it's secure."

"Don't you think that's a little over the top?" he asked her.

"Why?" She saw no reason to change her methods of operation this late in the game. "It's what I do every night when we come home from the courthouse. Things happen. Jeff said they were closing in on Munro and his people." Her partner had given her an update when she'd called him about Alexander's heart attack. "A man gets desperate at times like that. He must know that his number's up and that he's living on borrowed time. If he wants to hurt you, now would be the time to do it."

"But there's been a police patrol car across the street ever since we left for the hospital," he pointed out.

It was true, but none of that mattered. "Lots of ways

for a creative man to gain access. Don't you know that every time they build a better mouse trap, someone builds an even better mouse?"

"Strictly speaking," he corrected her with an indulgent smile, "mice aren't built, they're made."

"Same difference," she told him, undaunted. "Stay right here," she repeated. "This isn't going to take long."

He had no intention of standing here in the foyer like some hapless silent movie heroine, waiting for Greer to sweep through the area and declare it safe. "Haven't you learned yet that the fastest way to make me come with you is to tell me not to?"

The other times, he'd had his father to talk to when he'd come home. Now he had only his concerns to keep him company. "I'll move faster if you're not with me," she told him.

He sighed, giving in. "All right, but hurry this along," Blake urged her. "I have definite plans for tonight."

She drew her weapon. "Work?"

"Only in the broadest sense of the definition," he told her and she could hear the smile in his voice. "Actually, I'd say it was more along the lines of pleasure."

The living room was clear. She moved on to the kitchen, crossing the floor in short, measured steps as she remained on high alert.

"Oh?" She spared one glance over her shoulder in his direction. "Would you care to be a little more specific than that?"

His eyes were laughing at her. He was obviously enjoying himself. "Not really."

"Don't want to share with the class?" she asked, amused. "What happened to 'works well and plays well with others'?"

She heard him chuckle to himself. "Depends on who those 'others' are."

She stopped abruptly and for a moment, Greer lowered her weapon, as well as her guard. "Me, Blake. Me."

"I suppose I can arrange to give you a small, intimate preview," he allowed. Moving the hand that was holding the gun aside, he took Greer into his arms.

No, she couldn't allow herself to be sidetracked, Greer silently insisted. No matter how much she wanted to.

"Judge—"

"Blake," he corrected her, his voice low and seductive. Now that his father was out of danger, all he could think about was making love with Greer. All night long. "Don't backslide on me now, Greer. You were doing so well." His lips covered hers.

Her head was spinning and her pulse had already taken off. She could feel her body temperature rising. She struggled to hold desire back until she completed her check. With effort, she wedged her hands up against his chest and pushed him back.

"We shouldn't be doing this," she insisted.

"And yet, we are," he told her.

And then he kissed her again and her resolve all but went up in smoke. She wanted nothing more than to spend the night in his arms, completely lost.

But her training, her dedication to the job, all but screamed for her not to be derelict in her duties. She couldn't just throw caution to the wind, that wasn't her, that wasn't how she was wired. She was the one who had to put her life on the line for Blake. She was the one who very possibly stood between the man and a fatal bullet.

Damn it, she needed to stop thinking of herself, of the pleasure that he'd brought her in so many different ways. The only thing that was important was keeping him safe.

Time to start acting like the cop she was, she reminded herself.

For the second time, she put her hands on Blake's chest and pushed hard. She couldn't think, couldn't do her job, with his lips on hers. She needed to pull back while she still could.

"Blake, please, I need to make sure the locks are all secure on the windows and that if someone tries to come in, the alarm will go off."

The last thing on his mind were intruders. Blake shrugged away her suggestion. No one had tried to gain access to his house in the three-plus weeks she'd been here. There was no reason to think that tonight had been any different.

But he knew the futility of arguing with her. Sighing, he nodded, surrendering. "Do what you have to do."

She let out a shaky breath. God, but that man could scramble her brain faster than anyone she'd ever known. "Glad you see things my way."

He shrugged. As if there was a choice. "Is there any other way?"

"No," she agreed, "but it's nice to have you so agreeable."

The family room was next. Wide open, she cleared it in a moment.

Someone shrieked next door. Greer's head jerked in that direction, listening.

Was that good or bad? The noise, though muffled by concrete and wood, was swelling.

Again, she toyed with the idea of having the patrolmen ask the neighbors to keep it down to a friendly roar. All that noise was making her uneasy. Munro or anyone he sent in his place could easily use the party next door as cover. There were so many people there, it would be easy to just blend in and camouflage himself with the noise.

The thought made her more uneasy.

What if one of Munro's henchmen had already done that? Had already blended in with the party guests just long enough to gain access to the neighbors' backyard and then slipped inside Blake's house? It wouldn't be all that difficult do.

Her heart pounded as she examined the idea.

"Why don't you put some champagne on ice?" she suggested just before she went to check the second floor.

Making her way up the stairs, Greer took out her cell phone. She had no idea why, but her gut kept telling her that something was off. Maybe the party next door was making her nervous, she wasn't sure. But she knew she'd feel better if she had Carson around. Two sets of eyes were better than one.

Pressing the single key that connected her to her partner, she wound up listening to an answering machine. Damn, it was Saturday night. Why did she think Jeff was going to be home or somewhere where he could actually hear his phone when it rang?

Greer almost terminated the call, but then decided, since she'd called, she might as well leave a message. Otherwise, he'd quiz her about the aborted call and more likely than not, drive her crazy by putting his own less-than-upstanding spin on it.

"Jeff, this is Greer. Call me when you get this," she told the answering machine. "I think I might need backup here. I'm at the judge's house."

Finished, she put the phone back into her pocket. Closing the door to the bathroom after a quick peek, she opened Blake's bedroom door next.

And found herself staring down the barrel of a Glock.

"About time you got home, Cinderella."

Her heart froze.

Munro.

Chapter 15

"Drop your gun," Munro snarled as he raised his weapon, aiming it dead center at her heart.

Damn it, when was she going to learn to trust her gut? Greer admonished herself. She'd *sensed* that there was something wrong.

Adrenaline launched through her veins in double time. Rather than drop her gun, she mimicked his action and raised it so that, if fired, the bullet would create a hole in his chest.

"The way I see it," she said to Munro, her voice deadly calm, "our guns cancel each other out."

"Well, I don't see it that way," he snapped back. "Now drop your gun or my 'associate' in the next room drops your judge."

It was a five-dollar word coming out of a two-bit mouth. Munro's conceit was incredible. He actually thought he was going to get away with this, with killing a judge and a narcotic detective right under the noses of the Aurora police.

"You don't have an 'associate' in the next room, Munro," she said in the same calm voice, knowing it annoyed the hell out of the dealer. She knew he wanted her to cower, to show fear. "Nobody wants to 'associate' with a lowlife like you."

Steely, lifeless brown eyes locked onto hers. She could feel her blood run cold. This was a man who could kill without the slightest qualm.

"They don't, huh?" Munro taunted. "You confident enough to put that little theory of yours to the test, bitch?"

If this involved just her, she would have met what she felt was his bluff in a heartbeat. But it wasn't just about her. Even if she hadn't gotten so involved with Blake that he dominated her every waking thought, the man was first and foremost her responsibility and she couldn't take a chance that this cocky little bastard *wasn't* bluffing.

A malevolent smile curved his mouth. It was as if he was privy to her thought process. "Two seconds to make up your mind, bitch, and then that good judge of yours is history."

In her experience there were criminals who had a small amount of redeeming qualities about them. Munro didn't number among them.

"He's history anyway," she responded. The drug dealer had vowed to kill Kincannon. She had no reason to believe that Munro had changed his mind.

"Maybe. Maybe not," Munro allowed in a singsong voice, twisting his wrist and moving the plane of his gun—but not the barrel—as he spoke. "He cost me a lot of revenue when he cleaned up the streets, putting my regular customers behind bars. Maybe I'd be satisfied ransoming Kincannon back to the justice system that thinks so highly of him. We could call it 'reparations.'" His small mouth curved further in an evil smile that all but froze her blood. "What do you think of that?"

Greer continued to hold her weapon trained on his chest. "What do I think? I think that you're lying."

"Not as dumb as you look," he assessed, laughing to himself. It sounded a little like the sound a hyena made. "Still, I could use the money. Besides, the damn bastard's hard to kill. I know. I've tried. Got his wife, but not him. Lucky son of a bitch," he commented.

Her eyes widened. "You were the one who ran him off the road?"

He smirked at her naiveté. "Hey, I got people."

What he meant, she realized, was that he had someone do his dirty work for him. "I forgot, you're a big operator."

The smile faded as if he understood she was being sarcastic. "Yeah, I am. Now put that damn thing down," he ordered. A hint of the cold smile returned. "Or shoot me. The second you pull that trigger, there'll be another shot and the judge'll be dead. He doesn't have a gun like you do," he mocked her. "C'mon, Detective." He tapped the watch on the wrist of his gun hand. "Tick-tock."

Greer was torn. God help her, she couldn't take a chance.

"All right," she fairly shouted, raising her voice so that it would carry, either to Blake or the so-called other gunman in the house. "You win." Moving in slow motion, she lowered her weapon and placed it on the floor before her.

His unnerving smile widened at the word *win*. "Never saw it happening any other way. Kick the damn thing over here. Now!" he ordered when she made no move to do as he said.

"Greer, what's taking you so long?"

It was Blake. He sounded as if he was close by. There *was* no other gunman she realized, cursing herself.

The next moment, Blake walked into the bedroom. And stopped dead.

She'd been played, Greer thought, furious. The second she'd realized that, she knew exactly what Munro's next move was going to be. To kill Blake.

There were two ways to go. She could either dive for her weapon or throw herself over Blake and take the bullet she knew with certainty was coming. There was no time to dive for the gun and get Munro.

Greer did the only thing she could, she threw her body in front of Blake, at the same time crying, "My thigh," to him and praying he understood.

Everything happened in a blur.

By throwing herself on Blake, Greer managed to get him out of the line of fire.

But not without a price.

Munro's shot went into her shoulder, even as Blake, grabbing her, tried to twist her away and push her beneath him.

As she went down, Greer felt Blake's hands grope under her skirt and knew he'd understood. He'd secured her smaller, secondary weapon, pulling it free of its holster. From the floor, he shot straight up, getting off a shot that miraculously went straight into Munro's neck.

Blood spurted as the latter tried to shriek. The sound came out a guttural gurgle. Trying to stop the flow of blood with his hands, Munro sank down to his knees, then fell over.

Groggy, light-headed, Greer crawled over to the fallen drug dealer, putting her own hands over the hole in his neck. She needed to stem the flow before he bled out. Right now, it seemed next to impossible.

"911," she cried out to Blake, pressing the heel of her hand against the hole. "Call 911."

Blake was already on his cell phone, giving the pertinent information to the dispatcher on the other end of the line. Finished, he dropped his cell phone on the bed and focused his attention on Greer, not the man most likely dying in his bedroom.

That was when he saw the blood all along her shoulder and arm. "You're bleeding," he cried, horrified.

"I am?" She was still feeling numb, detached from her own body. Disoriented, Greer looked down at her torso. He was right, she thought. That had to be her blood, not Munro's. Taking a deep breath, she could now feel her insides beginning to shake. She didn't have time for this.

Her eyes swept over Blake. No blood. Good. "Are you all right?" she asked him.

"I'm fine," he snapped. Blake was angry at himself for not coming upstairs sooner. Angrier still when he thought that he might have lost her altogether. He wanted to hold Greer but he was afraid to touch her, afraid that he would only make things worse and hurt her. "Damn it, Greer, when are you going to learn you're not a human shield?"

"Easy. When you stop having people shoot at you." It took effort to talk. Her strength seemed to be deserting her at an alarming rate.

Was it her imagination, or was that the sound of sirens in the background?

"Do you think maybe you could take over?" she asked Blake, laboring over each word. "I'm not sure I can press down hard enough."

He looked down at the man who for almost the past four weeks had been such a threat to him. He didn't look so foreboding now. Eddie Munro's eyes were staring lifelessly at the ceiling. Blake bent down and felt for a pulse. There was none.

"I don't think any amount of pressure is going to help, Greer," he told her gently. "Munro's dead." Blake took another look at her shoulder. It appeared worse than he'd first thought. Blood was oozing down her arm. "You're the one who needs to have pressure applied to her wound."

As if in denial of his assessment, Greer rose shakily to her feet.

"No, I'm fine," she protested, but her voice sounded reedy and thin to her ear.

That was when the light-headedness really caught

up to her. She was vaguely aware of people coming into the room as the room began to spin. And then, abruptly, the people seemed to disappear, fading off into nothingness.

The fire in her shoulder overwhelmed her at the same time the rest of the room vanished.

When Greer regained consciousness, for a moment she had no recollection of what had happened, no idea what day it was or where she was. The scene around her came into focus by degrees.

She was aware of motion, of a faintly antiseptic smell and of someone holding her hand tightly. Greer had the faint sense that if whoever it was let go, she would wind up floating away.

Opening her eyes, she saw that Blake was sitting beside her. He was the one holding her hand so tightly.

Someone she didn't recognize was next to him. It took her another couple of seconds to realize that the man was a paramedic.

What had happened? How had she gotten here?

"Welcome back," Blake said, relief and emotion drenching every syllable.

She raised her head. The effort caused a herd of buffalo to pound their hooves across her forehead. She dropped her head back down. The swaying motion was making her nauseous. "Am I in an ambulance?"

"Yes," Blake answered.

She didn't belong in an ambulance. She had a report to write up. "Why?"

"Because the hospital is too far away for me to run there with you in my arms," Blake informed her simply.

"I don't need a hospital," Greer protested. She tried to get up again only to have him push her back down. It didn't require much effort on his part and that *really* upset her.

"You need a keeper," Blake told her, "but a hospital'll do for now."

"You're very lucky, Detective," the paramedic chimed in. "A little bit to the left and it would have gone through your heart. And you would have been on your way to the coroner instead."

"Lucky," Greer murmured. The buffalo herd was fading, but her head was beginning to spin big-time.

She was going to pass out again, she thought.

Greer tightened her grasp on Blake's hand, or at least tried to. She felt weaker than a day-old kitten. "Don't go anywhere," she whispered to Blake.

"Wasn't planning on it," he assured her with barely harnessed feeling.

She only heard the first word.

"They want you to stay overnight to be observed," Blake told her as she struggled to get dressed. He was torn between helping her and forcing her to remain. From where he stood, it would take very little strength for the latter.

It was several hours later. The E.R. physician had removed the bullet, cleaned out her wound and bandaged it. And while she was waiting for all that to happen, in between the tests they'd forced her to take, she'd told Blake about what Munro had said to her when they were alone. That he was the one behind the car accident that had killed his wife.

The news had stunned him into silence for a few moments. But then, to her amazement, Blake seemed to take it in stride and said the debt had been paid. Munro was dead.

"I really think you should listen and stay overnight," he pressed. He had come very close to losing her tonight. It brought home to him just how much he'd come to care for this woman fate had brought into his life for a second time.

"I don't want to be observed," Greer insisted. "I'm fine, except for the hole in my shoulder."

"And the blood loss," Blake patiently pointed out.

"Being manufactured and replaced even as we speak," she assured him cheerfully.

She looked down at the pantyhose in her hand. There was no way she was going to be able to get them on. With a half shrug, she stuffed them into the purse that was resting on the bed.

Blake pulled the purse away from her. "Damn it, woman, are you always going to be this stubborn?"

The answer required no thought. "Pretty much. But you don't have to worry about that." It was an effort to sound cheerful, but she'd already promised herself that when this moment came, she wasn't going to give in to emotion, wasn't going to wish that they had longer. It was what it was and now it was time to move on. For both of them. "With Munro dead, looks like you're about to get your life back."

"Yeah," Blake agreed, his voice flat. He blew out a breath. *Now or never.* "What if I told you I don't want it back?"

She stopped struggling with the buttons on her shirt. "I'm not following you. You liked being threatened?"

"I've discovered that I like the side effects of being threatened." She was still looking at him as if he was delivering a lecture in a foreign language. Frustrated, Blake blew out another breath. "Damn it, Greer, do I have to spell it out for you?"

"That might be nice," she responded. "My brain's a little fuzzy right now. I'm liable to think the wrong thing."

She was doing this on purpose, he thought. "This doesn't come easy for me."

"Someone once told me that nothing worthwhile is ever easy. Or maybe that was on the inside of a fortune cookie, I'm not sure." She ran a hand across her forehead. She was still a little light-headed, this time from the painkillers they'd give her while working on her shoulder. "It's all kind of muddled."

"Okay, I'll spell it out." If he had to, so be it. "But before I do, you have to promise me that you're going to stop throwing yourself on top of me."

Her grin was wicked. "I thought you liked that part."

That wasn't it and she knew it. "Not when there's gunfire involved."

He seemed to be missing a very salient point. "If

I hadn't thrown myself in front of you, Munro would have killed you—and you wouldn't have been able to get my backup weapon," she pointed out. "Nice shot, by the way." She stopped struggling with her clothes and paused to look at him. "You didn't tell me you knew your way around firearms."

He would have thought that was a given, considering his background. "Knowing my way around guns is part of having a father who spent his life as a marine. If you want your dad to pay attention to you, you pay attention to what *he* pays attention to." Not to mention that, for the first time in his life, he was grateful for the career his father had chosen.

"And you're changing the subject," Blake accused. If he was going to say this, he needed to say it now, before his courage flagged. "Don't take this the wrong way, but please just shut up and listen." His hand on her good arm, he forced her to sit down again. "I don't want my old life back," he repeated. "I want the new one, the one that I've been living with you."

She raised her eyes to his face but said nothing.

The silence got to be too much for him. Why wasn't she saying anything? Was he wrong? He'd felt sure that she felt about him the way he did about her, but now— "Say something."

"You told me to shut up and listen," she reminded him innocently.

"Now I'm telling you to talk."

She didn't want to get swept away, didn't want to risk her heart. "You want to keep on seeing me?"

"In a word, yes. But I want to do more than that."

"More than see me," she repeated. "You want to touch me?" she asked, humor curving her mouth.

"I want to marry you."

She wasn't prepared for that.

The air rushed out of her lungs. It took Greer more than a few seconds to recover and pull herself together. Her first reaction was to want to throw her arms around his neck and cry, "Yes," but she knew better. No matter how much she wanted to, she couldn't believe him. Couldn't let herself get carried away.

"You don't mean that," she told him quietly.

"Yes, I do," he insisted. He'd never meant anything more in his life. Especially now after what she'd told him about Margaret. Life changed in a heartbeat. He wanted his heart beating next to hers for as long as they both had.

Greer shook her head. "That's just the adrenaline talking," she insisted, hating every word she was uttering. "We've just gone through a life-and-death situation. Our whole relationship is based on a life-and-death scenario. You're not up to making any rational decisions right now."

The hell he wasn't. "I know what I feel, Greer," he told her firmly. "I'm in love with you."

But Greer refused to be swayed. "No, you know what you *think* you feel. In a week, when you're back in your courtroom, going about your daily routine, you won't feel the way you do right now."

Blake turned the tables on her. "And what is it that *you* feel?" He waited, knowing that her answer was the crucial one. That his whole fate hung in the balance.

If she told him she didn't love him, it would change everything. Not the way he felt about her, but it would change the scheme of the future he was envisioning.

That wasn't the point, Greer thought. "What I feel doesn't matter, Blake."

He took her hand, forcing her to look into his eyes. "It does to me."

She loved him. It had hit her like a ton of bricks when she thought Munro was going to kill him. She was willing to die in his place, not because it was her job, but because she loved him and wanted him to live no matter what.

He was still waiting, she thought. Waiting for her to tell him how she felt. "I can't tell you."

Blake didn't understand. "Why not?"

"Because you'll just use it against my argument." She watched as the smile unfurled on his lips a fraction at a time until it seemed to take over his entire face. "Don't grin at me like that."

"Why not?" He slipped his arm around her and drew her closer to him. "You all but admitted that you love me."

"We're not talking about how I feel about you, we're talking about you."

"We're talking about *us*," he corrected. "And you're wrong, this isn't adrenaline, or something that's just part of a temporary rush. I've been in love before, Greer. I know exactly what it feels like. It feels good. It feels right. The only rush I get is when you're in my arms, when I'm kissing you, when I'm making love with you.

No guns are involved then. Now, once and for all, do you or don't you love me?" he pressed.

He had her back to the wall. There was no way she could lie.

"I love you," she admitted. But as he moved to kiss her, she put her hand on his chest, holding him in place. "I'd still rather you took time to let the situation cool off."

"I can if you want me to," he agreed. "But the feeling will still be the same." He took her free hand in both of his. "None of us know how much time we have. Today is all there might be. I don't want to waste a single minute away from you. I don't want to put my life on hold anymore. I don't want to get myself lost in my work." The way he had when Margaret died. "The only 'getting lost' I want to do is with you. Now, we can wait if you want to—because I sure as hell don't—or you can give me your answer now and we can go home and start planning the rest of our life together. The choice is yours."

She wasn't that sure about that. "And if I say wait?"

He sighed. "Then I'll wait. Not patiently," he promised, kissing first her lips, then her forehead, then the hollow of her throat. "But I'll wait."

He knew it made her crazy when he littered her skin with small, tantalizing kisses like that, she thought. Despite everything she'd been through tonight, her pulse was racing again. The man had some kind of magic power over her, there was no other way to describe it.

"You don't play fair," she groaned, feeling herself begin to melt.

He laughed, kissing the side of her neck. "Playing fair wasn't part of the initial deal."

She was breathing hard and definitely not thinking clearly. But she was rejoicing. Every single inch of her was rejoicing.

"Yes," she breathed.

"How's that again?"

"Yes," she repeated with effort, "I'll marry you."

He laughed as triumph soared through him. "That's all I wanted to hear." He got off the bed, still holding her hand. "Let's go home."

"In a second." Standing up next to him, Greer wrapped her good arm around his neck, leaned against him and sealed the bargain with a heated kiss that promised to go on for a very long time.

Which was just fine with both of them.

* * * * *

INTRIGUE...

2-IN-1 ANTHOLOGY

FIRST NIGHT
by Debra Webb

Caught in a murder investigation, Brandon needs Merri to prove his innocence. And if they can survive their ordeal, their sizzling attraction may have a chance too!

CHRISTMAS GUARDIAN
by Delores Fossen

Millionaire Jordan instantly falls for the helpless baby left on his doorstep. But when the mother returns, with killers on her trail, he vows to protect them both.

•••

2-IN-1 ANTHOLOGY

A BODYGUARD FOR CHRISTMAS
by Donna Young

The clue to Jordan's hunt for his father's killers lies in the mind of beautiful Regina. With time running out, can he help her remember—*and set her heart on fire?*

THE MAN FROM NOWHERE
by Rachel Lee

Grant can't explain why he feels compelled to protect Trish. Especially as he struggles to convince her that his deathly promotions are based on dark truth...

On sale from 19th November 2010
Don't miss out!

INTRIGUE...

2-IN-1 ANTHOLOGY

SECLUDED WITH THE COWBOY
by Cassie Miles

After rescuing his wife from a kidnapper, Dylan is determined to seal the rift between them and remind her of their love...*one kiss at a time!*

THE CHRISTMAS STRANGER
by Beth Cornelison

When widow Holly hired sexy but secretive Matt to renovate her farmhouse for Christmas, she never expected him to heal her heart.

•••

SINGLE TITLE

BRAVO, TANGO, COWBOY
by Joanna Wayne

Alonsa caught Hawk's eye on the dance floor. But as the former navy SEAL searches for her kidnapped daughter, she may just steal his heart as well.

On sale from 3rd December 2010
Don't miss out!

2 FREE BOOKS
AND A SURPRISE GIFT

We would like to take this opportunity to thank you for reading this Mills & Boon® book by offering you the chance to take TWO more specially selected books from the Intrigue series absolutely FREE! We're also making this offer to introduce you to the benefits of the Mills & Boon® Book Club™—

- **FREE home delivery**
- **FREE gifts and competitions**
- **FREE monthly Newsletter**
- **Exclusive Mills & Boon Book Club offers**
- **Books available before they're in the shops**

Accepting these FREE books and gift places you under no obligation to buy, you may cancel at any time, even after receiving your free books. Simply complete your details below and return the entire page to the address below. You don't even need a stamp!

YES Please send me 2 free Intrigue books and a surprise gift. I understand that unless you hear from me, I will receive 5 superb new stories every month, including two 2-in-1 books priced at £5.30 each and a single book priced at £3.30, postage and packing free. I am under no obligation to purchase any books and may cancel my subscription at any time. The free books and gift will be mine to keep in any case.

Ms/Mrs/Miss/Mr _____ Initials _____

Surname _____
Address _____
_____
_____ Postcode _____
E-mail _____

Send this whole page to: Mills & Boon Book Club, Free Book Offer, FREEPOST NAT 10298, Richmond, TW9 1BR

Offer valid in UK only and is not available to current Mills & Boon Book Club subscribers to this series. Overseas and Eire please write for details.. We reserve the right to refuse an application and applicants must be aged 18 years or over. Only one application per household. Terms and prices subject to change without notice. Offer expires 31st January 2011. As a result of this application, you may receive offers from Harlequin Mills & Boon and other carefully selected companies. If you would prefer not to share in this opportunity please write to The Data Manager, PO Box 676, Richmond, TW9 1WU.

Mills & Boon® is a registered trademark owned by Harlequin Mills & Boon Limited.
The Mills & Boon® Book Club™ is being used as a trademark.